PRT

Benita Brown was born and brought up in Newcastle by her English mother, who was the youngest of thirteen children, and her Indian father, who came to Newcastle to study medicine and fell in love with the place and the people. Even at drama school in London, Benita felt the pull of the Northeast, as she married a man from Newcastle who worked at the BBC. Not long after, the couple returned to their home town and, after working as a teacher and lecturer and bringing up four children, Benita became a full-time writer. FORTUNE'S DAUGHTER was longlisted for the Romantic Novel of the Year Award 2007. Benita's other novels, A DREAM OF HER OWN, ALL OUR TOMORROWS, HER RIGHTFUL INHERITANCE, LOVE AND FRIENDSHIP, THE CAPTAIN'S DAUGHTERS and A SAFE HARBOUR, are also available from Headline.

For more fascinating information about Benita Brown, don't miss the exciting additional material in the back of this book.

Also by Benita Brown and available from Headline

A Dream of Her Own
All Our Tomorrows
Her Rightful Inheritance
In Love and Friendship
The Captain's Daughters
A Safe Harbour

Fortune's Daughter

Benita Brown

headline

First published in 2006 by
HEADLINE PUBLISHING GROUP

First published in paperback in 2007 by
HEADLINE PUBLISHING GROUP

I

Cataloguing in Publication Data is available from the British Library

978 0 7553 2328 9

Typeset in Sabon by Avon DataSet Ltd,
Bidford-on-Avon, Warwickshire

Printed and bound in Great Britain by Clays Ltd, St Ives plc

HEADLINE PUBLISHING GROUP
A division of Hachette Livre UK Ltd
338 Euston Road
London NW1 3BH

www.headline.co.uk
www.hodderheadline.com

To Norman, as ever

Chapter One

Newcastle, 1882

Daisy finished her song and the crowd went wild. They rose to their feet, clapping and cheering and waving their tankards until the ale sloshed over the plates of pies and peas, and dripped from the edges of the scarred wooden tables on to the sawdust-strewn floor.

Jack Fidler, small-time theatrical agent, had taken up a position at the back of the room so that he could watch the audience as well as Daisy's performance. He dragged on the cheap cigar clamped between his teeth and a column of ash fell down and scattered over his fancy waistcoat. He frowned slightly and flicked it off, but his smile soon returned. He was pleased with himself.

It had taken some persuasion to get Harry Carver to engage unknown Daisy for one night's trial, but judging by the reaction of the punters Harry would see that the gamble had paid off and he would no doubt want a repeat performance. Well, he would have to pay for it, Jack thought. He was not getting Daisy for a handful of small change. Oh, no. Harry Carver would have to reach deeper into his pocket if he wanted Daisy to sing here again.

And word will get round, Jack thought. And when it does we won't have to settle for a malodorous, lop-ridden drinking house down by the docks. It won't be long before Daisy will be performing on stage in more respectable theatres in Newcastle — and all over the North of England ... and even London. Why not? She's good enough. Top of the bill, she'll be. A true star. And I was the one who discovered her.

Jack's imagination took fire as he watched his protégée take another graceful bow. She looked so chaste and pure and so much younger than her eighteen years, dressed as she was like an innocent schoolgirl, clutching the doll that was the prop for her final song. She was so unlike the tawdry trollops who usually performed here, their ribaldries appealing to the lowest instincts in the vulgar rabble of undesirables who were Harry's customers.

But he hadn't blamed Harry for being doubtful. When the owner of Carver's Song and Supper Rooms had flipped through the sheet music Jack had brought along for the resident pianist, Harry had raised his eyebrows at the straightforward lyrics he found there. There was no smut, no innuendo and, to tell the truth, very little humour. Jack knew that he could have encouraged Daisy to go the other way to success — to develop an act based on catchy tunes laced with crude *double entendres*, especially as once he had cleaned her up the lass had proved to be so bonny. But it was the sheer power and beauty of her voice, not her physical appearance, that had prompted him to aim higher. And now he knew he had been right.

Sentiment, that's what he was looking for. The songs he'd chosen for Daisy appealed to the softer, kinder side of human nature. They were about love in all its guises — except the carnal. The song she had just sung about a little girl's love for a broken old doll had brought tears to the eyes of more than one raddled woman in tonight's audience.

True love, mother love, love of your family and household pets, and steadfast love of your childhood friends, not to mention love of your country. Those were the messages Daisy sang from her heart.

He watched her as she smiled at the audience and raised the old doll to her lips to bestow upon it one more kiss. The applause and the cheering rose to a climax. Harry saw the gleam in the eyes of some of the men and he admitted to himself with amusement that there might be a certain perversion in dressing a full-breasted and comely young woman in the clothes of a virginal schoolgirl. But as long as she had that sweet angel face of hers they could all pretend that her appeal – and therefore their response – was innocent.

Suddenly someone in the audience shouted, 'Encore!'

'Yes!' A fellow beer-sodden wastrel took up the call. 'Let's have another one!'

'More! More!' Soon everyone was shouting, and Jack caught Harry's eye as he watched from the other side of the room. Harry saw Jack's glance and grinned, giving him the thumbs-up.

'The doll song! The doll song! Sing the doll song again!' the crowd was shouting and then, to Jack's astonishment and rage, Daisy shook her head, smiled, gave a final curtsy and ran from the stage.

The audience, mostly men and some women of the rougher sort, groaned and began to sit down. Their disappointment was almost tangible as they took up their knives and forks again and supped their ale. Jack edged round the room towards the door that led to the backstage area. Harry got there a second later and grasped his shoulder, spinning

3

him round and forcing him to look up into his angry red face.

'What the hell's the brainless bitch playing at?' he thundered, drawing glances from some of his customers.

'Whisht, man, she's not brainless. Don't you see how clever the lass is?' Jack said. He was thinking quickly, calling on his wit and cunning to save the situation.

'Clever?' Harry's bushy black eyebrows met over his bulbous nose and his small eyes peered out menacingly. 'I don't call it clever to disappoint these customers.'

Jack risked a glance at the assembled ruffians and tried to control a growing sense of panic. 'Of course, it's clever. She's left them wanting more.'

He waited nervously while Harry looked around at his customers. His large dirty hand still gripped the shoulder of Jack's new coat and Jack hated to think of the greasy mark that would be left there.

'She's left them in a bad mood, that's all I can see,' Harry said eventually. 'And that could mean trouble.'

'Then you must avert that trouble.'

'And how am I supposed to do that?'

'Give them a free gill of ale . . .'

'What, all of them?' Harry was outraged.

'Well . . .' Jack thought frantically, 'hand out free tickets for tomorrow night.'

'What!'

'Tell them that entry to the show is free so long as they buy a full supper and at least one drink – you know very well they won't stop at one. Then tell them that Daisy Belle will be here again and that she'll sing for as long as they want her to.'

Harry's small eyes vanished even further into the folds of flesh as he thought about Jack's suggestions. 'Aye, I'll do that,' he said at last. 'As you say, a clever lass. She's made sure I'll take her on for another night. Are you sure you didn't put her up to this?'

'Would I play a trick like that?'

Harry scowled but a moment later Jack was relieved to see something approaching a smile lift the corners of the landlord's fleshy lips.

'So we'll see you tomorrow, then?' Harry said.

'Yes. At double the fee, of course.' Jack drew on his cigar, narrowing his eyes to watch through the smoke as Harry Carver's face purpled and the open pores on his nose seemed to dilate.

'Half as much again. That's as far as I'll go.' The words strained through clenched jaws.

Jack smiled. He knew he had won. 'No, double I said, and double I mean. You know she's worth it. I warrant you'll have queues along the quayside tomorrow.'

Harry wavered a moment longer and then he nodded. 'Right,' he said. 'Get her here on time and make sure she sings the doll song.'

The big man turned and began making his way around the room, stopping now and then to chat to his customers. Jack saw the disgruntled expressions change to smiles. He turned to continue the journey that had been interrupted. At the other side of the door he found himself in a dank and dimly lit alleyway that had once been the path between two equally grim tenement houses, but at some stage had been roofed over when the two buildings had become one. A flaring gas jet halfway along one of the walls provided the only light.

Before making his way to the door that led to the dressing room he paused to take one last drag of his cigar before dropping it and grinding it into the filthy floor. Daisy had

had the nerve to say that he couldn't smoke anywhere near her and he had agreed because he wanted to protect her voice. But what angered him was that it wasn't her voice she was thinking of. It was the child.

While he stood there he fought to control his anger with her. That rigmarole about Daisy being clever enough to leave the audience wanting more had all been pure invention in the face of Harry's furious indignation. Jack knew very well why she had left the stage when she had, and if she hadn't been so important to his plans for future riches he could have throttled her.

A damp wind blowing up from the river had found its way into the passage. It left clammy droplets of moisture on his face. He realized his skin had been burning; not just because of the heated fug inside the supper rooms but also because of his rage.

But he would have to be careful. He didn't want to frighten her away. Not at this early stage of their partnership and particularly not now that he had been allowed a glimpse of what was possible. Besides, he had a plan. The child was not going to be a problem for much longer. He grinned when he contemplated his own cunning and managed to turn it into what passed for a smile of pleasure and approval by the time he opened the door.

'Well, Daisy, that went well — very well, in fact,' he said. 'We're back here tomorrow and Harry will up the fee a little.' The half-truth came easily but Daisy didn't even look up at him.

His protégée was sitting before the makeshift dressing table with the child on her knee as she gazed down with tender concern into her daughter's troubled face. Harry looked beyond the two of them to their reflections in the mirror: two mothers, two children, the mirror images imitating every movement that Daisy and little Rose made. Even to the tears that were trickling down the cheeks of the dark-haired child. Rose was bonny, beautiful even, but her dark curls gave her a gypsy look that was so different from her mother with her pretty pink and white complexion and her angel-fair hair.

Oh, yes, Jack thought, Daisy looked virginal, and since he had found her, ragged and grubby as she sang for pennies on a street corner, she had never so much as looked at a man. Nor had she allowed Jack himself to touch her. Not that he had made any serious attempt to do so. He didn't believe in mixing business with pleasure, and his relationship with Daisy was strictly business.

But someone had got at her at some time. Some tinker lad, by the looks of the child, and as Rose was going on for three years old Daisy must have been barely fifteen when it happened. She had never talked about the child's father and Jack had not asked.

'Whisht, my bairn, my bonny darling,' she murmured softly. 'Divven't fret. Your ma's here now.' She pulled the child close and began to rock her to and fro. As the tears subsided and the dark-fringed eyes closed, Daisy shot a furious look at the other occupant of the room, Edna, the young nursemaid who looked after Rose when Daisy was working.

'Didn't you tell her that I wouldn't be long?' she whispered, her soft voice full of anger.

'I did,' Edna replied. She was still clutching the handle of the large new perambulator where Rose had been sleeping. 'I rocked her and sang to her and told her that her ma was coming, but once she was awake there was no comforting her. You know fine well that only you can do that.'

Jack was surprised at the girl's defiant tone. Normally she was in awe of Daisy who, for all her sweet looks, could be a termagant if the mood took her. Daisy could outscreech any other half-wild street urchin and yet she could be haughty with it. She was a natural for a life on the stage. And Jack was amused at how quickly the lass had adopted the airs that befitted what she considered her new station in life.

He would have to warn Edna to curb her tongue; to bite her lip when Daisy riled her. Daisy must not suspect anything, otherwise she would demand that Jack find another girl to look after Rose and he would have to lay his plan all over again.

Rose had fallen asleep and Jack watched as Daisy placed her tenderly in the perambulator, which looked like a miniature Bath chair but was large enough for the child to lie back in. She covered her daughter with the clean bedding she was so particular about.

He remembered what the pair of them had looked like when he had found them one cold winter's evening just a few months ago. Daisy's face had been streaked with dirt, her clothes ragged and her boots unlaced because they were too small for her. With one hand she held an old cap and with the other she grasped the handle of a low wooden pushcart, the sort that lads make with a box and old pram wheels.

But in this pushcart there was a small girl bundled up in a torn blanket. The child was clutching a doll. The very doll that had become Daisy's stage prop. Jack had seen straight away that the child was better nourished than the mother. It was obvious even then that Daisy did the best she could for her little girl.

Daisy, or Maggie as she had been then, had been singing in the streets and alleyways, catching the coins that were thrown to her in the cap. Jack had known at once that her voice was special and he was not surprised that the passing drunks, even the hard-bitten street women, had dug into their pockets for as much as they could spare.

He had watched their eyes light up for a moment as they listened; seen the anxiety and anger that had etched cruel lines on their faces fade as they listened to the girl's sweet voice. The voice of an angel, Jack had thought, and even he had been moved enough to think for a moment of his own long-suffering mother and how she used to sing to him and his sister, Maud, when they were small children.

Naturally enough the girl had refused to come home with him, even though he suspected that she was living rough, a street child, no doubt orphaned, and who had grown up fending for herself in the abandoned slums and back alleyways of Newcastle.

How fortunate that Maud was staying with him for her annual holiday. He had gone to get her and hurried back. His elder sister was always pathetically pleased to do anything she could for him. Unmarried and lonely, despite her comfort-able job in a great house, she sought his company whenever she could. Well, now it was time to repay him for putting up with her for all the years since their mother had died.

Maud, with her respectable manner and way of speaking learned from her mistress, Geraldine Leighton, had ignored Daisy and shrewdly gone straight to the child, stooping to exclaim over her and saying how cold the night was for such a little one to be out on the streets. Surely Daisy wasn't content to bed down in one of the crumbling slum buildings whose only inhabitants were other homeless folk and an army of rats. Surely she didn't want to go on feeding them from scraps and having to join the long queues of other unfortunates at the nightly soup kitchen. Not when something better was being offered to her.

'Poor child ... poor little girl ... how cruel ...' Maud had said, and more in this vein, directing her sympathetic gaze solely at the infant. Eventually Daisy had weakened and had agreed to go with her for at least one night's shelter.

One night in comfortable lodgings with good food on the table and a woman who seemed to be concerned for her precious daughter was all that it had taken to tempt Daisy to stay a little longer. And longer. Jack had marvelled at his sister's powers of persuasion and had to admit that without her help he would have struggled to clean the pair of them up and dress Daisy more suitably.

By the time Maud's holiday was over and she had left to go back to her job as companion to a rich gentlewoman, Jack had been able to persuade the girl that her best hope – and that of her child – was to remain with him and follow his advice. He'd begun to teach her how to perform properly and, as soon as he'd judged her ready, he had used his old contacts to get engagements for her – as Daisy Belle.

'What's wrong with me own name, Maggie Bell?' the waif had asked indignantly.

'How do you know your real name is Maggie Bell?' Jack had countered.

The girl had frowned and after a moment's thought she said, 'That's what I've always been called. It's the name me mother gave me.'

For a moment Jack panicked. He had never contemplated the possibility of a parent. 'And where is your mother?' he asked.

'In her grave – a pauper's grave. She died when I was a bairn.'

'And your father?' Jack asked tentatively.

'What's that? A father, do you say? What's a father when it's at home?' Suddenly she grinned and Jack had a glimpse of how she would be on the stage – how she would react with

10

an audience and how she would cast her spell. 'Well, if I ever had a father,' she continued, 'I've never set eyes on him.'

'So,' Jack said, 'about this name. Daisy sounds prettier than Maggie, don't you agree? More ladylike.'

She had scowled while she thought about it but eventually admitted that it did. 'But why Daisy? Why not Isabella or Victoria?'

'Because Daisy sounds young and innocent — and, in any case, people called Margaret are often called Daisy.'

The scowl returned. 'I divven't understand what you're on about.'

'You must try to say "don't", not "divven't",' he admonished. 'Margaret sounds like marguerite,' he saw the scowl deepen. 'A marguerite is a flower, a—'

'A daisy!' she had finished the sentence for him. 'I get it. And I like it. Daisy Belle it shall be.'

Jack had employed Edna to help with the child, and the engagements that followed were mostly respectable affairs in village halls and works' parties, also various celebrations in a few private houses. Daisy had been amazed when she discovered that these engagements paid quite well. Enough to buy new clothes for herself and for Rose and to put a little bit by. Jack had assured her that she could earn even more in future.

Tonight the engagement at Carver's Song and Supper Rooms had been a test. It would be her first appearance before an altogether tougher and more unforgiving audience, and she had carried them all before her. Jack's faith in her — and in his own judgement — had been verified. She would soon be ready for the big time.

Daisy was ready to go. She had taken the make-up from her face, gone behind the screen to change into her ordinary clothes and then put on her coat and hat. She placed the doll next to little Rose, tucking it in as tenderly as if it were another child, then took the handle of the perambulator herself, having given Edna the bag containing her stage costume and make-up.

'Wait a moment,' Jack said. 'I'll go and collect your pay.' And I'll make sure I get paid tomorrow's fee in advance, he thought. I don't want to give Harry Carver time to change his mind and maybe decide to cheat us after the performance.

A little later, and well past midnight, they were walking up one of the steep streets that led from the quayside to the respectable lodging house in Heaton where Jack had installed Daisy, Rose and Edna. Daisy insisted on pushing the perambulator herself and Jack could see that she was tired.

'If only you had agreed to leave the child in your rooms with Edna we could have taken a cab home,' he told Daisy.

'She stays with me,' Daisy replied tersely.

'I'm sure it would be better for Rose to be safely tucked up in bed than dragged along to the Song and Supper Rooms.'

He saw how she flinched at the words 'dragged along' but her reply was spirited. 'What? Leave her and have her wake up and wonder where I am like she did tonight?'

'Have you thought that she might not have woken up at all if she'd been tucked up in a nice quiet room rather than in a dirty, noisy drinking place?'

Daisy shook her head. 'It's no good, Mr Fidler. You'll never persuade me that a child should be anywhere else but with her mother.'

They'd had this argument before and it was obvious that she would never change her mind. She would have her own way. She always did as far as Rose was concerned. And sooner or later the child would obstruct Jack's ambitions. He was convinced that Daisy's voice could make him rich but it wouldn't do if it got known that the sweet, virginal girl who appeared on the stage was the mother of a little bastard. Other stars of the stage led rackety lives but purity was part of the image of Daisy he was selling. He would have to take steps to safeguard that image.

'I want you to rest tomorrow,' he told Daisy when they reached the lodging house. 'Let Edna help you as much as she can and in the afternoon you should go to bed and have a nap so that you'll wake up looking young and fresh and bonny.'

'I take Rose to the park in the afternoon.'

'Let Edna take her. That's what nursemaids are for, isn't it? You've seen them in their smart uniforms taking care of their little charges. You don't see their mothers with them, do you? Not those who can afford a nursemaid.'

He was appealing to her new image of herself as a woman who could afford to employ servants, but this delicious idea had to do battle with her fierce mother love and her desire to take care of her child herself.

'Well . . . I do need a rest.'

'Edna needn't keep the child out long,' Jack said. 'Just long enough for her to enjoy a bit of summer sunshine and bring roses to her dear little cheeks. It's just a short stroll along to Heaton Park. In fact, you can see part of it from your window. And, you know you owe it to Rose to be able to give the best performance you can if you're going to make a better future for her.'

'I suppose so . . .'

'You know I'm right.'

'We'd better buy Edna a smart uniform then, hadn't we? I don't want folk to think that Daisy Belle can't afford a proper establishment.'

Jack agreed and marvelled how Daisy, a poverty-stricken street urchin, had the power to surprise him. Where did she get her ideas from? *Proper establishment*, indeed.

'And now I'm famished,' Daisy said. 'I hope the wife has left a good supper out for us. A pork pie, a new loaf and some good strong cheese washed doon with a hot sweet potful of tea.'

Jack winced and not just at the idea of a supper that would have had him up all night with indigestion. '"Mrs Clarkson", Daisy, not "the wife". And "down" not "doon". You must attempt to speak properly.'

'Oh, aye,' Daisy said without rancour. 'I'll hev to remember that I'm a lady now, won't I?'

'*Have* to, Daisy, *have* to . . .' Jack began and stopped when he saw her broad smile.

'Don't worry, Mr Fidler,' she said. 'I know you're right. And I want to learn for Rose's sake. And I can learn quick, you know. Me mother taught me to read from bits of old books she'd found when I was just a toddler. She wanted a better life for me. So I'll do my best to set Rose an example and make sure that she grows up to be a proper lady.'

Always the child, Jack thought on his way back to his own lodgings. And for a moment he wondered if he was doing the right thing. Daisy had ambition all right, but a large part of it was prompted by her love for her daughter and her desire to make a good life for her. He wondered if he should allow things to go on as they were. But then he remembered tonight and how Daisy had left the stage when she ought to have stayed and sung at least once more. You couldn't afford to annoy an audience – even if you were a very big star – and Daisy was only starting out.

There had been other incidents. She worked hard in rehearsal but would stop immediately if Rose needed attention. And she insisted on taking the child with her everywhere. Jack had suggested in vain that once the engagements started coming in it would be better for Rose not to be brought up in theatre dressing rooms or dragged round from theatre to theatre.

'What should I do with her?' Daisy had asked.

'Leave her with her nursemaid. Other theatricals do.'

'Never.' And she would not be moved.

When Mr Fidler had gone Daisy lifted her daughter out of the pram and allowed Edna to manoeuvre it up the front steps and store it in the space under the stairs.

'Put the hood up and make sure you cover it completely with the waterproof,' she told the girl. 'I don't want any mangy cats to get in and make a bed for themselves and perhaps worse. Oh, and give me the doll. You can carry the bag up.'

While Edna secured the pram, Daisy carried Rose and the doll up to the top floor where they had a bathroom and three rooms – a sitting room and two bedrooms, Daisy's being the larger of the two. Rose's cot was in Daisy's room. She wouldn't be parted from her even when they were sleeping.

She was pleased to see that the landlady had left their supper out on the table in the sitting room and covered it with a clean cloth. Singing made her ravenous and now, for the first time in her life, there was always enough to eat – and more.

It didn't take long to settle Rose in her cot but Daisy left the door to the bedroom open while she and Edna did full justice to the late supper. Edna was tired, and retired to her tiny room and her narrow bed gratefully. She fell asleep almost immediately but Daisy stayed awake in her own more comfortable bed and lay thinking about how much her life had changed since Mr Fidler had found her singing in the streets.

Once in his comfortable diggings only a few streets away

from Daisy, Jack poured himself a glass of porter and lit another cigar. He sat by the fire and turned the problem over in his mind. Cynically he had convinced himself that what he planned would be better for the child too. But most of all it would safeguard Daisy Belle's reputation. Thank God she didn't show the least interest in the opposite sex. How on earth she had managed to get herself pregnant he would never know. He'd decided she must have been raped. That was the only feasible explanation.

He flicked ash into the fire and shook his head. It was pointless to speculate about her past. It was her future he was interested in and he was going to make her a very big star. Her greatest asset, apart from her voice, was the way she looked: young, virginal and pure. That was how he was going to build her up. A little white flower, a daisy, an untouched angel come to appeal to the audience's purest instincts. And that perception of her could so easily be ruined if Rose's existence was discovered.

No, he mustn't let things drift. Daisy would have hysterics but he'd already decided how to cope with that. He would put his plan into action as soon as possible.

Chapter Two

One afternoon a week later, Jack found Daisy standing at the window of her sitting room in the lodging house. Daisy had raised the bottom half of the window and was leaning out, resting her hands on the stone ledge as she looked along the road in the direction of the park.

The afternoon sun was strong and the street outside was busy as ever with delivery carts, carriages and horse-drawn trams. Street sellers shouted their wares, the loudest voices being those of the paperboys with the early edition of the *Evening News*. The noise from outside meant that she hadn't heard him enter. Jack had visions of her falling out so, not wanting to startle her, he coughed gently as he crossed the room.

She turned to face him. 'What are you doing here?'

He decided to ignore the barely concealed hostility. He knew that she thought him a hard taskmaster; if he was going to get the best out of her he would have to tread carefully. Jack grimaced. It wasn't just the noise of traffic; it was the ever-present stink of horse manure, inevitable on such a busy road, that he wished to shut out.

'Let me close the window,' he said, but before he could complete the action a great cry rang out from the street below, followed by the whinnying of a horse and the shouts of alarm of passers-by.

'What is it?' Daisy asked, and they both looked out in time to see a cab driver fighting to control his horse while a ragged boy dodged away from the flailing hoofs and fled across the road. On making the safety of the pavement he pushed startled and indignant pedestrians aside and climbed over the wall into the park.

'Young tomfool,' Jack muttered, but Daisy's face had drained of colour. 'The lad's all right,' Jack said. 'You saw him run away.'

'I know. But once when I was down by the Central Station I saw an old man go under the wheels of a tram. I think the horses had already knocked him senseless but the tram finished him off. One of the horses had come down as well. It was like a battlefield. There was blood running on the cobblestones.'

'Don't think about it,' Jack told her. 'Let me pour you a little brandy. Where do you keep your glasses?'

Daisy indicated a tray on the sideboard, which contained a wine glass and a bottle of port wine. 'I haven't any brandy,' she said. 'I don't like it.'

'Nevertheless.' He took his flask from his inside pocket and poured her a generous measure. 'Now sit down.'

Daisy sat by the table. She sipped the brandy cautiously. Jack drew back and looked at her. She was changing rapidly. No longer a suspicious, malodorous, half-starved street urchin but a comely young woman whose confidence was growing daily. And as for her appearance: the robe pulled on over her underclothes, her flushed complexion and the baby-fine strands of fair hair escaping from the pins – she looked and smelled quite delicious. She had taken to wearing rose cologne and its delicate aroma suited her. Daisy was all the more attractive, Jack thought, because she didn't seem to realize her own potent sexual allure. Long may she stay in ignorance, he prayed silently.

'You promised you would rest in the afternoons,' he said.

'I have been resting, but I thought Edna and Rose should be back by now. I'm watching out for them.'

'I'm sure they'll be here any minute.'

Daisy swallowed the rest of her brandy quickly and drew in her cheeks as if she had just taken some unpleasant medicine. She leaped to her feet and hurried back to the window.

'Look, here they come,' she said. Her whole mood had lightened at the sight of her child. Jack saw how the tension drained from her body.

She allowed herself to smile at him. 'You were right, I'll give you that,' she said. 'Since I have been performing every single night, I need the rest and I have to admit the bairn seems to enjoy herself in the park. She comes back smiling and happy, her little cheeks like roses.'

'I'm glad you feel that way. But if only you would try to relax a little more; take full advantage of the time to yourself . . .'

Daisy shrugged as if there was nothing she could do about that. 'But, anyway, why are you here?' she asked. 'You haven't told me. You don't usually visit in the afternoons.' She resumed her seat at the table, resting one hand on the green chenille cloth. She made a graceful gesture with the other hand, indicating that he should sit too. Quite the lady, Jack thought, and dropped his head to conceal his amused smile.

'I've brought good news,' he said. 'Carver wants you to sing at the Wine Croft, his place in the Bigg Market.'

'That's good news?'

'Very good. You'll be performing to a different class of customer.'

'Less drunken? Less foul-mouthed, you mean?'

'Well, I don't know about less drunken, but certainly less coarse in their cups.'

'Well, that's a blessing. I must say it's hard to keep a sweet face at times when I hear the language. It's worse than anything I ever heard on the streets. And they think some of the things they say are compliments! Sometimes I feel like stopping the show and shouting back.'

'Don't ever do that!'

'Divven't fret, I'll mind what you telt me. I shall try to be a lady and ignore them.' Daisy raised her chin and tilted her head at the same time, sitting up straight and holding a graceful pose with her hands.

'And remember you must talk like a lady too,' Jack reminded her.

She grinned. 'All right, then. But I'll be happy to see the back of that place, I can tell you.'

'Ah . . . well . . . we're not exactly leaving there yet.'

'What do you mean?'

'You'll give your performance at the quayside and then we'll dash up to the Wine Croft.'

'And then we'll *what*?'

'We'll hurry up to the Bigg Market and you'll start your act—'

'All over again? That's slave labour!'

'Well . . .' Jack shifted uncomfortably. Daisy was glaring at him.

'Whose idea was this? Yours? Carver's? Or did you cook it up between you?'

'The latter, I suppose. Harry Carver wanted you to start earlier at the Supper Rooms – to draw the crowds in sooner.'

'And no doubt sing for twice as long for the same money?'

'Yes, that was the idea but I wasn't having that.' Not unless Carver would pay double, Jack had thought to himself, and he had almost proposed that but then he'd had a better idea. A much better idea.

'Weren't you?' Daisy looked at him, her head slightly tilted, her eyes narrowed.

'No, I told him that you'd proved yourself a trouper and that if you could please that lot you could please any audience there was. So I suggested that you do your turn as usual at the Song and Supper Rooms and then go on to the Croft which, as I said, is a better sort of place.'

Daisy stared at him. He should have expected what she'd say next but she was often a jump ahead of him these days. 'And it will be a better sort of fee, no doubt?' she said.

'Of course.'

'It will be hard work, two turns in one night.'

'Granted. But no harder for you than it is for many, if not most of your fellow artistes.' Jack paused to observe her reaction to the way he had described her. He could tell that she was pleased to be referred to as an 'artiste'. 'The seaside troupes in particular,' he continued, 'they sometimes do three performances a day and there's no set payment – one of them goes round with a collection box and then the manager takes the lot and shares it out accordingly.'

'I hope they trust him.'

'I beg your pardon?'

'The manager.' She gave him an old-fashioned look and Jack realized that Daisy was learning fast. Once she started mixing with other performers and sharing their gossip and backstage wisdom he would have to be very careful how he handled things. He was relieved when she changed the subject.

'It'll be quite a dash up to the city with the pram, won't it?'

'The pram?' He saw the battle ahead.

'From the quayside to the Bigg Market. How long will we have?'

'I'm not sure yet. I'm waiting for Carver to tell me what time he wants you there. But we could always—'

'Take a cab? Forget it. I won't leave Rose behind and that's that.'

'Poor child.'

'Don't start that again!'

Jack was saved from the rest of Daisy's angry response by the sound of Edna coming up the stairs with Rose. The child was singing, her childish treble echoing sweetly in the stairwell. Her voice was unformed and the words weren't clear – in fact it was only childish babble – but there was no mistaking the tune; it was the doll song.

Daisy's opening night at the Wine Croft was a triumph. The audience, composed of young men with good jobs, a smattering of students and a handful of those from the better sort of families, loved her just as much as the riffraff who frequented Carver's Song and Supper Rooms on the quayside. And even though they considered themselves to be sophisticated young fellows about town they were just as moved by the sentimental nature of Daisy's repertoire. Jack had seen to it that at least one of the songs was all about a sainted mother's love.

Daisy complained at first about all the rushing around, but when she saw the amount of money she was earning she put up with it cheerfully. When she had sung on the streets she had been pleased to earn enough to pay for food and second-hand clothes from Paddy's Market for herself and Rose. And sometimes there had been enough left over to get them into a common lodging house for a night or two. But she only did this in the coldest of weather. She neither liked nor trusted the other lodgers she met there.

And as for going to one of the charitable organizations — that she could never do. Charitable folk were known to separate mother and child, sending one to the workhouse and the other to an orphanage. She had vowed never to be parted from Rose.

After leading the life of a street singer she had no idea of the sort of money she was really earning. She took what Jack gave her without question and spent it. Sometimes, instead of resting in the afternoon, as she had promised Jack, she would take a cab into town and dash around Fenwick's and Bainbridge's, buying any item of clothing for her or for Rose that took her fancy. Other times she would come back laden with toys and, when Rose and Edna returned from the park, Daisy would be waiting with a new doll, or wooden farm animals, or picture books, and once a miniature porcelain tea set.

She was a generous mistress and she also bought small gifts for Edna such as a brooch, a shawl or a pair of gloves. Jack had told her early on that she must pay her maid herself and Daisy hadn't questioned that. She paid Edna's wages and tipped her generously, having no idea that Jack was also giving Edna something from his own pocket.

This was not only because he would have to depend on her to carry out his plan but also to keep the girl sweet. Edna complained constantly about having to dodge along the back alleys on the way to and from the theatres with the perambulator so that folk wouldn't see Rose and connect her with Daisy. But right from the start Jack had passed Edna off as Daisy's younger sister and Rose as Daisy's niece. He'd spun Carver some tale about Daisy having promised her mother that she would always take care of Edna and the little one.

'You know what these poor families are like,' he'd said.

'Some of the womenfolk are too sentimental for their own good. Soft as clarts, as they say.'

Jack had spoken with a dismissive air as if it were all of no consequence but the landlord of the Song and Supper Rooms hadn't even cared enough to answer him.

One afternoon when it was time for her to take her rest, Daisy crossed to the window of her room in the lodging house and looked up at the sky. The rain seemed to be easing off, thank goodness, and as soon as it stopped altogether, Edna would be able to set off for the park with Rose. She hardly admitted it to herself and she certainly wouldn't admit it to Jack but she had come to look forward to her afternoon naps.

'I've made you a pot of tea,' Edna told her. 'Shall I take the tray through to your room now?'

Before Daisy could answer, Rose tugged at her robe. 'Doll, Mama, doll,' she said.

Daisy looked down at her daughter and smiled. Rose was ready to go to the park. Edna had dressed the child in her new emerald-green coat with the dark green trimmings and her bonnet with matching satin ribbons.

'Yes, you may take Dolly.' Daisy thought it strange that even though Rose had two of the loveliest, most expensively dressed dolls to be found in any toyshop, she still preferred the old broken doll they had found in a deserted house where they had been taking shelter. She gave Rose the doll and then turned to Edna. 'Don't let Rose walk through any puddles and splash her new white stockings.'

'We won't be doing much playing today. The ground will be wet for a while yet. We'll just have a nice long walk.'

'Do you think you should take the pram?' Daisy asked.

'Oh, no,' Edna replied quickly. 'Rose is getting a little too big for the pram and, besides, she doesn't like the other children to see her in it.'

'Doesn't she?' Daisy was astonished. Was Rose really so concerned about what other children thought? Perhaps she was and the sad fact was that Edna was in the position to notice things like this rather than the child's own mother.

'Well, I just thought it would be better to have the pram in case it rained again.'

'I'll take my umbrella and, anyway, once we're at the park we can shelter in the Pavilion Café.' Edna smiled. 'In fact I think we'll go there anyway and mebbes have an ice cream or a fancy cake.'

Daisy suppressed a pang of envy provoked by the thought that Edna was going to have this treat with Rose and not herself. She tried not to betray her feelings because if she looked sad Rose would not want to leave her and she did not want to spoil her daughter's fun. So she opened her purse and gave Edna more than enough to buy ice cream and buns for both of them. She crossed to the window and glanced once more at the sky where a watery sun was doing its best to disperse the lingering rain clouds.

'Off you go then,' she said. 'But if the rain starts again come straight back.'

'I will, Miss Belle.'

Daisy was struck by the usual feeling of surprise when Edna called her 'Miss Belle'. It sounded so respectful. Could this 'Miss Belle' person really be her, Maggie Bell, who had lived on the streets, sheltering in decaying buildings, and who had never been respected by anybody?

She concealed a small smile of pleasure and stooped to gather her daughter up in her arms. 'Here, pet, give your ma a kiss.' She was amused to see that as soon as she put her down again Rose raised a hand to straighten her bonnet, which had been knocked askew, and she pulled her ringlets into place. She's a neat little soul, Daisy thought. There's not an item of furniture or a tiny dish out of place in that dolls' house I bought her, and when she's done playing she puts her toys away without being asked.

She watched as her daughter pulled on her new white gloves without help from Edna. The child's face was solemn with concentration. Daisy had noticed that Rose liked to do things for herself and she worried that the unsettled life they were leading was making the child independent too soon. I love her so much, she thought, even though all the time I carried her I was wishing that it wasn't true – that such a thing could never have happened to me. But the minute I saw her – the minute the old woman put her in my arms . . .

'We're ready, miss,' Edna said. 'Now shall I pour your tea?'

'Don't worry, I'll pour it myself. I'll walk down to the front door with you.'

Edna frowned and for a moment Daisy thought the girl looked perplexed. 'What is it?' she asked. 'Is something the matter?'

'Well . . . no, but Mr Fidler said that it was part of my duties to look after you as well as the bairn. He said it was very important that you get your rest and that I was to see to it.'

'Very well. Pour my tea and leave it on the bedside table but I shall at least see you off from the top landing.'

Daisy took Rose's hand and walked out on to the landing with her, and a moment later Edna joined them. Reluctantly she relinquished her daughter's hand to Edna and then stood and watched as they went down the stairs. When she reached the bottom Rose turned and waved to her. Edna had already opened the front door and a shaft of sunlight fell across the child like a spotlight on the stage.

She looks so beautiful, Daisy thought. This is one of those moments that I shall always remember.

Once they had gone she realized how very tired she was and she retired to her bedroom gratefully. She removed her robe before slipping into bed and then sat up and reached for her tea. After the first sip she pursed her lips and looked at the cup disapprovingly. Drat, she thought, too much sugar. But she was too weary to get up, empty the cup and pour herself another one. She finished the tea and, half registering the slight aftertaste, she settled back in the mound of pillows that Edna had plumped up for her.

Paradoxically, when she was tired like this, she often found that she couldn't drop off to sleep straight away. No matter how weary her limbs, her mind was too active. So she would lie still and think about something pleasant; indulge herself with her favourite daydreams.

She conjured up pictures in her mind of herself and Rose living in comfort and a certain degree of splendour in a big house ... maybe a fashionable part of town or perhaps in the country where she could have a garden as big as a park ... maybe she would buy Rose a pony ...

But she knew that she would have to work hard if she were going to make these dreams come true. So she would switch her attentions to the means of obtaining such riches: her career on the stage. She would think about the new songs she had learned and the way Jack had taught her to move more gracefully as she performed them.

Sometimes she would go through her whole act in her imagination until she came to the bit she loved best — the moment when the audience would burst into wild applause; sometimes rising to a man and cheering wildly. At moments like this she knew that they not only approved of her but in a strange way they loved her. She could almost feel the waves of love and approval wafting up on to the stage and surrounding her. It made her feel warm and safe, and only then would she allow sleep to overtake her.

Today, however, she was ready to drift off quite quickly. In fact, there was an almost physical sensation of sinking down – no, being pressed down – into the feather mattress, which seemed to take on a life of its own as it rose to enfold her. But if her limbs felt like lead, her mind became somehow detached and acted independently of her body. She tried to conjure up the usual pleasant daydreams but they remained elusive, twisting like silvery ribbons and disappearing as some of her worse memories came back to torment her.

Daisy had lied to Jack. Or rather she had not told him the complete truth. Her mother was not dead, although she might as well have been, for Maggie had vowed never to see her again. But it was true that she did not know who her father was. There had been so many men in her mother's life that it was anybody's guess who had fathered her child.

Once she had opened the door in her mind to her past, the sights and sounds that came back to her assumed a dreadful reality. Daisy could no longer believe that she had escaped from that impoverished existence. This room, this comfortable bed – they were part of a dream, and if she could force her heavy eyelids open she would find that the reality was the festering slum where she had lived with her mother.

The squalor ... the stink of the open drains and the screaming of ... what was that screaming? It was her mother ... she was angry with her ... what was she saying? Yes ... Daisy's anguish returned as she remembered her mother's words ...

'You're lying!'

'No I'm not. Why don't you believe me?'

28

'Because I know him and he wouldn't do that!'

'How long have you known him? A couple of months? And how long have you known me? Fifteen years. I'm your daughter!'

'You're jealous — that's what it is. You don't want me to have a life of my own. A man of my own. Now you either take back what you said or you get out!'

She wouldn't take it back. How could she? And how could she stay after what the man her mother had taken into their home had done to her? So the life on the streets had begun. The begging ... the stealing ... she knew it was wrong but it was the only way to survive. And then the wonderful discovery that when she sang people would throw her money.

She had hardly noticed the changes in her body ... the sickness, the swollen breasts and the stopping of her monthly cycle — after all, it had hardly begun. And then the old woman she shared a ruined house with had told her what it meant.

'You'd best gan yem.'

'Never.'

'Then bide with me until the time comes and get yerself off to the workhouse. They'll tek the bairn from you and you can start again.'

But when the old woman had placed the newborn babe in her arms, Maggie had known that she could never part from her. The infant had looked up at her with unfocused eyes and yet Maggie had sensed the trust in them and her heart had been overwhelmed with love. So, no matter that the poor bairn had been conceived in pain and terror, Maggie knew that she could never part with her. Never hand her over to the cold charity of an orphanage where she would never know a mother's love.

Despite the ugliness of her life Maggie's child was as fresh and pink and white as an unfurled rosebud. After a day or two, when the babe had already learned to suckle, the old woman became uneasy.

'Are you going to give her a name before you take her to the workhouse?'

'Rose . . . her name is Rose. And she's not going to the workhouse, she's staying with me.'

And from then on life for Maggie Bell had become even harder. But she had vowed that her precious babe would never suffer the neglect that she had suffered at the hands of a feckless and uncaring mother. She would love her and cherish her and never allow any harm to come to her. They would never be parted.

I must have been more than usually tired, Daisy thought as she forced herself to open her eyes. Her limbs felt heavy and she didn't feel at all rested. She struggled to sit up and stared around the room with unfocused eyes. After blinking a few times the shadows dispersed but a sense of unease seemed to seep from the shadowy corners of the room and move stealthily towards her. The room was dark.

I've slept too long, she thought; it's time to get ready to go to Carver's.

Daisy pushed the bedclothes aside and lowered her feet to the floor. Finding her slippers, she padded over to her bedroom window and moved the curtains aside. The lamps were lit in the street outside but she saw at once that the reason for the dark sky was not the encroaching night but the heavy rain.

Rose will be soaking wet!

Daisy spun round and stumbled back to the bed where she snatched up her robe. There was a small fire burning in the hearth and she made her way to the fireplace and grabbed the mantel clock. Four o'clock. She had slept longer than usual but not as long as she had feared she had. But it was Rose's teatime and Edna should have brought her back by now. Perhaps she had, and Edna and Rose were sitting in the room beyond, already having their tea. Perhaps Edna, taking Jack's instructions to heart, had not wanted to awaken her.

Daisy stood still and listened. She could hear the rain beating on the window, the ticking of the clock and the crackle of coals in the hearth. But there was no sound at all from the other room. Edna must have told Rose to be quiet – to let her mother sleep longer.

Vaguely wondering why her head felt so heavy and why it was such an effort to put one foot in front of the other, Daisy walked to the door that led into her sitting room and opened it. She had convinced herself that Rose would be sitting at the table eating a boiled egg and toast soldiers with a cup of milk by her plate and a plate of bread and jam waiting for her. Perhaps her outdoor clothes would be drying on the fender and Edna would have wrapped the child warmly in her dressing gown. But the picture faded as the door opened and she gazed around the room. It was empty.

Daisy suffered a moment of panic before common sense returned and she realized that Edna must have decided to wait in the café in the park until the rain stopped. She hurried to the window and pushed aside the lace curtains as she scanned the street. She looked up at the sky. This has set in for hours, she thought. She turned decisively. She knew what she would do. She would get dressed and go down and hail a cab. She would instruct the driver to take her the short distance to the gates of the park and then hurry in with her umbrella and rescue her daughter.

She was just about to let the curtain fall when something in the street caught her eye. A cab had drawn up outside the house. Perhaps Edna had had the sense to hail one. Daisy watched as a figure descended. She frowned with puzzlement when she saw it was Jack Fidler. Perhaps some sixth sense told him he was being observed because he looked up at the window. The light from the nearest streetlamp fell across his face but, although he had undoubtedly seen her standing there, he did not smile.

He turned towards the cab and held up his hand to help someone else descend. Edna. Once she was standing on the pavement, Jack leaned down to say something to her. Their heads remained close together for a moment and then Edna too looked up at the window. She looked away quickly but not before Daisy had seen her expression. It was one of terror.

Jack paid the cabby and the man began to draw away.

'No! Wait for Rose!' Daisy spoke the words out loud. 'Edna — Jack — have you forgotten Rose is there? For God's sake stop the cab and get her out!'

But the cab pulled away into the heavy traffic and Jack and Edna started to walk towards the front steps.

I don't understand, Daisy thought. Where's the bairn? Why is Edna with Jack and why has she come back without the bairn? Has there been an accident? Can Rose have fallen from a swing in the park and is at this moment lying in hospital?

With a howl of anguish she turned and fled across the room and, tearing the door open, she made for the stairs.

Jack and Edna had barely climbed the steps when the front door was wrenched open to reveal Daisy standing wild-eyed, her features twisted in torment like a Fury in a classical play.

'Where is she?' she shrieked. 'Where's Rose? Why have you come back without her?'

Edna blanched and shrank back. For a moment Jack thought she was going to topple backwards down the steps to land on the pavement, and he put out an arm to steady her. To give her time to recover, Jack stepped forward and took hold of Daisy's arms, pushing her ahead of him into the cool tiled porch and on into the shadowy hall.

'Not here, Daisy, not in the street. Don't let people see you like this – think of your reputation.'

At first he thought she might strike him as she turned to glare at him, fierce with rage. 'Reputation? What the hell's that got to do with my bairn? And anyway,' she said, 'what are *you* doing here?'

'Upstairs,' he said. 'Let's go to your rooms.' He turned to Edna. 'Help me get her upstairs.'

No sooner were they in the room when Daisy shook them both off and turned to face them. 'It's bad news then?'

'Yes,' Jack said. 'Daisy, sit down.'

'No. Tell me. Has Rose been hurt?'

'You'll need to be strong.'

'Has there been an accident?'

Edna had crept behind Jack. Daisy saw her nod at the question. Daisy moved forward and reached round to seize Edna's arm. She pulled her forward. The girl was shaking.

'Right, miss,' she glared at the young nursemaid. 'Tell me what happened.'

She should be on the stage, Jack thought as he watched Edna going though the story they had prepared. Nobody would have guessed that she was speaking anything but the truth. The girl was word-perfect. She remembered to stumble over her words now and then and to wipe the tears from her eyes.

When the rain had started she and Rose had taken shelter in the tearooms, she said, but after a while the child got restive and kept asking to go home. She paused.

'Go on,' Daisy said. 'What happened next?'

'Well . . . I thought an ice cream would do the trick – would keep her happy – and I went to the counter. I told her to wait at the table but when I got back, she'd gone.'

'I don't believe you,' Daisy said. 'Rose always does as she's told.'

'Well . . . she . . . ' Edna hesitated.

'You're trying to say that she ran off. She's lost in the park. Is that it?'

'No. Oh, how I wish it was as simple as that. I ran out of the café. I dropped the ices—'

Good touch, Jack thought.

'And I was in time to see Rose making towards the gate. I – I couldn't catch her and, oh, Miss Belle, she ran straight across the road.'

'No!' Daisy howled. 'She's been knocked over, hasn't she? Is that what you're trying to say?'

Edna nodded and Daisy felt her world begin to change. 'She's in hospital, isn't she?'

'Yes, but—'

'I must go to her. Jack, go down and hail a cab. I'll get dressed.'

Daisy whirled round and headed towards the bedroom but Jack caught her at the door.

'No,' he said. 'You can't go and see her. She was trampled by a horse – her injuries were appalling.'

Daisy stared out from a face as white as parchment. Her voice was barely audible. 'All the more reason why I must go to her. She needs me.'

'She doesn't need you, Daisy, and I want you to remember her as you last saw her. Beautiful and – and whole.'

Daisy tried to block from her mind the meaning of his last words. 'Remember her?' she said.

'Yes, my dear. Remember.'

'Are you telling me that she's . . . ?'

'Yes, I'm afraid the dear child is dead.'

Daisy felt cruel fingers of ice reach into her body and squeeze her heart. She tried to speak but the muscles of her throat had frozen and no words came. The ice spread through her body and she gave herself up to a blessed numbness. Before Jack could catch her she fainted dead away.

Chapter Three

Daisy struggled up from the dark place she had inhabited ever since they had told her that Rose was dead. The room was warm, too warm, but the bed was snug and the eiderdown had settled around her to provide a cocoon of physical comfort. She didn't want to emerge from this place but she knew she must.

She tried to lift her head from the pillow and immediately felt as though unseen hands were pushing her down again. How long had she been sleeping? Hours? Days? Her mind struggled to work out why she should be here in bed when the sunlight was edging the curtains and spilling on to the brilliant colours of the carpet.

This was her afternoon rest. That was it. She had fallen asleep the moment Edna and Rose had left to go to the park. They would be back soon. Her eyes focused on the sunlit curtains hanging at the window. So it had stopped raining, then. Rose would come back happy and rosy-cheeked, and they would have a nursery tea together before she had to get ready to go to Carver's.

I'd better get up, she thought, and this time she made the effort to push back the bedclothes. The blankets and the eiderdown resisted her; she had to fight them and the effort made her feel dizzy. Finally she freed herself from their grasp and sat up. She closed her eyes, hoping that the room would stop spinning before she was sick.

Then she remembered that she *had* been sick and that Edna had brought a bowl and held it while she vomited until there was nothing left but bile. Edna had washed her and tended her as if she were an infant. How many days ago had that been? Two? Three?

She remembered Jack's voice saying, 'She's not fit to perform tonight. I don't know how long Carver will put up with this. He'll find someone else.' He had sounded vexed.

Another voice ... Edna's ... had replied, 'Well, it was your idea. And you told me to keep her under.' She'd sounded uncharacteristically argumentative. Surely Jack would reprimand her.

But no, instead he placated her. 'It's all right. You did the right thing. But after today we'll have to be more sparing with it. I want you to give her just enough to keep her biddable, dull her feelings, without making her useless.'

'You'll have to see to it. I won't be here, remember?'

Daisy dredged up that conversation. She knew they had been talking about her but her mind skittered away from the reason why she had been put to bed. She didn't want to think about that.

She opened her eyes and looked round the room. She was alone. Now that she was sitting up her wits cleared and her hearing, her sense of smell, her sight seemed to be sharper than normal. The ticking of the clock on the mantel echoed across the room and into her head. She winced with pain. The acrid smell of coals burning in the hearth caught at her throat. The room and all the furniture swam into focus. There was something hanging on the wardrobe. A darker shape and duller against the polished mahogany. A hanger had been hooked over the half-open door. And on the hanger there was something black. A dress.

She remembered, and with the memory came pain and distress. Edna had brought it into the room and hung it there during one of her lucid moments. Jack had told the girl that she shouldn't have bothered but Edna, with her new-found confidence, had said that Miss Belle would want to be properly attired for the funeral and that she'd bought a black hat and a veil as well. Jack could pay her for them.

The funeral.

Rose isn't coming back from the park. She will never come back. Today I will be burying my daughter.

It should be raining, Daisy thought. Doesn't it always rain at funerals, making the leaves drip and the smell of damp earth rise up and enfold the mourners huddled round the newly dug grave?

It had been raining when they had buried the old woman – the woman who had eased Rose's passage into the world. It had been autumn and the leaves were beginning to fall on the crumbling gravestones. Nameless and friendless, she had been placed in a cheap wooden coffin and buried in a pauper's grave. Daisy – or Maggie as she was then – had been her only mourner.

She had swaddled Rose tightly to her body in her shawl, not just because it was raining but because this was no place for a child. As the rain grew heavier she had paid her last respects to the only human being who had shown her kindness. She had hurried away through the dripping grasses when the gravediggers had begun to shovel in the clods of heavy earth. The sound of them landing on the coffin had followed her across the churchyard.

And now in bright sunshine, and with birdsong filling the air, they were lowering the tiny coffin of her beloved daughter into the ground. Edna and Jack were supporting her, each holding an arm to keep her upright. Jack had arranged everything in the three days since Rose had died. He had not allowed Daisy to say goodbye – to ask for the coffin to be opened – because he had told her that Rose's injuries were too awful for a loving mother to bear.

Remember her as she was when you saw her off to the park that day, he had told her, and Daisy recalled the moment when Rose had paused at the bottom of the stairs with the sunlight shining on her bonny hair, and she knew that Jack was right.

The gravediggers waited respectfully until Daisy threw the pale pink roses she had been carrying into the grave and then began the dreadful task of covering her darling child up for ever in the cold earth. Her senses numb, Daisy allowed Jack and Edna to lead her away.

'What are you doing?'

'It's no good. She won't answer you. She's been sitting like that all day,' Edna said.

It was the day after the funeral and Jack had just entered the room to find Daisy sitting at the table. Her robe was tied loosely over her nightdress and her glorious hair, unwashed and uncombed, hung loosely on to her shoulders. She stared into the mid-distance with unfocused eyes.

'You haven't given her . . . ?'

'No, not today. You told me not to.'

'Well, get her ready then.'

'She won't let me wash her.'

'Just tidy her up enough to make her presentable. It's almost time to go to Carver's.'

'I'm not going.' Daisy spoke at last but she looked at neither of them.

Jack controlled his irritation. 'Daisy, you must. You can't have any more time off. Your public will forget all about you.'

'I don't care. I'm not going back to Carver's – or anywhere, come to that. I don't want to sing again.'

Jack felt the panic rising. He hadn't bargained for this. It had not occurred to him for one moment that Daisy would not want to sing again. 'Daisy, you have no choice.'

'Yes I have. And I choose not to sing.'

'Do you want to end up in prison?'

'What are you talking about?' At last she looked at him.

'You owe a lot of money, Daisy. There's the rent for this place, for a start, and your accounts at Bainbridge's and Fenwick's – and not to mention Rose's funeral expenses.'

'Yes, but—'

'Well, all that has to be paid for.'

'I don't care if they put me in prison. Rose was my only reason for working so hard – to give her a better life.'

'Rose is in heaven, now. She's with the angels.'

'Don't!'

'Do you think she wants to look down and see you – the mother she adored – in some filthy prison cell?'

Daisy stared up at him, her face contorted by anguish.

'And how can you even think of not paying for Rose's funeral? You want a proper headstone for her, don't you? Didn't we agree that she should have a little marble cherub? Don't you feel you owe her that?'

Daisy rose from the table. Her face now expressionless, she walked across to the door that led to her bedroom. She paused in the doorway and without turning round she said, 'I'll get ready.'

Jack nodded to Edna and raised a hand to indicate that

she should follow her mistress. While he waited he thought without pleasure of the battle that lay ahead. He would have to keep the spectre of Daisy's debts over her head in order to make her work but he hoped and he trusted that her love of performing would eventually make her realize that she should go on – because without Rose she had nothing else.

When Daisy was ready to go she stopped and began to look around the room distractedly. In an instant Jack realized what she was looking for and cursed himself – and Edna – for not thinking of this before.

Before he could say anything, Daisy stopped looking, a hand flew to her mouth and, with tears in her eyes, she said, 'The doll . . . Rose took the doll.'

Edna looked flustered. 'You needn't sing that song tonight,' she said.

Jack was furious. Why on earth had the stupid girl allowed Rose to take the doll with her that day? 'Of course Miss Belle must sing the doll song,' he told Edna. 'Her followers love it.' He hurried over to Daisy and took her hand. 'The doll is with Rose. I placed it in her coffin myself. I knew that's what you would want.'

He was aware of Edna watching him and the look in her eyes made him glad that he'd decided to get rid of her.

'Did you, Jack?' Daisy's beautiful eyes were full of tears as she looked at him. 'I bless you for that.'

'And you must sing the song tonight – for Rose – especially for Rose.' He refrained from adding that Rose would be looking down from heaven, for he saw that Daisy's thoughts had already gone that way.

'But I can't sing it without the doll,' Daisy said.

'You shall have a doll. Go down with Edna. There's a cab waiting to take you to the quayside.'

Daisy went obediently with Edna, and Jack, waiting until

they had left the room, strode over to the toy chest in the corner of the room. Two of Rose's expensive dolls were sitting on top. He snatched one up and wrenched at one of the arms until it came loose from the body and hung down limply. He pulled at the hair until the golden curls became a wretched tangle and then, crossing to the hearth, he stooped down and rubbed the painted face on the coals in the coal scuttle. He looked at his work and smiled grimly. That would do. Daisy would have her broken doll.

There was a strange young woman waiting in the dressing room at Carver's. 'This is Nora,' Jack told Daisy. 'She is going to be your maid. Edna will show her what she must do tonight before she leaves.'

'Edna is leaving?' Daisy said. 'I didn't know.'

'I thought it best,' Jack said. 'I thought you might want that.'

'Oh, I see. You are right again, Jack.' Daisy smiled sadly and took Edna's hand. 'I want you to know I don't blame you. It was an accident. In fact, I blame myself. I should never have agreed to let you have the responsibility of taking Rose out in the afternoons. It was selfish of me to rest like that. I should have looked after my own child. What happened was a punishment.'

'No, Miss Belle! Please don't talk like that!'

Daisy saw that the girl's eyes had filled with tears and also that Jack appeared to be angry with Edna. He told her brusquely to start instructing Nora what to do and Daisy gave herself up to the preparations for her act. She sat listlessly while Edna applied her make-up, with Jack giving instructions to make her look as sweet and innocent as always when bathed in the light of the flaring gas jets that served as footlights.

She had agreed to come here tonight and yet she hadn't been sure if she would be able to sing. The place stank. Not just of hot greasy food and beer, but of old rank-smelling clothes and unwashed bodies. She had not eaten properly for days and she felt her strength failing. But the moment the curtain was raised and an expectant hush settled over the boisterous audience, Daisy knew that this — the stage, even if it was simply a raised wooden platform — was probably the only place where she would be able to come alive again. It was a place removed from real life. Away from worry, away from sorrow for the performer as much as for the audience.

When the music started the ice inside her loosened its grip on her heart. Warmed by the love she felt flowing towards her from the poor unfortunates in the audience, she was transported as much as they were to another world. She saved the doll song until the end, as she always did, and when she went to collect the doll from the wings she barely noticed that it was one of Rose's toys. She had to sing three encores before they would let her go. Jack came on stage and begged the audience to spare Daisy as she had another engagement at the Wine Croft.

'You were wonderful,' Jack said as he hurried her from the stage, across the dank connecting passage to the dressing room. 'Do you know you had some of those ruffians in tears?'

Daisy didn't answer him. As the applause died the ice surged through her veins once more. She held herself in reserve, already craving the moment when she would step on stage again and the ice would retreat for a while.

Edna had gone. It was the new maid, Nora, who helped her into her velvet cloak and carried her costumes and props. A faint smile touched Daisy's lips as she allowed Jack to help her up into the cab.

'I see you have had your way at last,' she said.

'What do you mean?'

She was puzzled by the sharpness of his tone.

'A cab,' she said. 'I am travelling to engagements in a cab.'

Edna put her travelling bag in the overhead rack and then settled herself in the corner of the Ladies Only railway carriage. Mr Fidler had reserved a seat for her and given her a generous payment. 'For the journey,' he had said. But they both knew that the money was more than she would ever need to buy a sandwich or a hot drink at one of the stations; it would also buy her silence.

It was Mr Fidler's sister, Miss Maud, who had found her the position as nursery maid in a big house in London. Edna could hardly believe her luck. A lady that Miss Maud had worked for some years ago had written to say that she needed a girl to look after her 'little late surprise'. A darling boy, apparently, who had come along and brought joy into their lives just when the lady had married off all her daughters and had thought her own childbearing years were over. Miss Maud had assured Edna that Mrs Blenkinsop was a good mistress who treated her staff well so long as they did their jobs properly.

Miss Maud had also told her that the family were prosperous. They had interests in a sugar plantation in the West Indies and, as well as the house in London, they also had a villa in the South of France. Obviously the nursery maid would have to go with them when they visited their villa, and Miss Maud had asked Edna if she would mind being so far away from home.

Well, of course Edna wondered if that hadn't been Mr Fidler's intention to have her as far away from Miss Belle as she could be, but as for mind! Edna had simply smiled and nodded. She had no intention of admitting that, given the sort of home she had come from, she was only too happy to leave Newcastle and never come back again.

As the train travelled further into the night, Edna settled back to try to sleep. There was only one other passenger in the carriage, a stout old woman who was already snoring. Edna was both tired and excited, but even though she kept her eyes tight shut, sleep evaded her. Perhaps it was the excitement about going to London and the new life that awaited her that was preventing her from sleeping; surely it couldn't be her conscience?

Apart from telling a cartload of lies about Rose running away and being knocked down she hadn't done anything really wrong, had she? Mind you, she thought it a bit cruel of Mr Fidler to lay it on so thick about the injuries, but he couldn't have Miss Belle looking into the coffin and discovering it was only filled with stones, could he? He'd had to bribe the undertaker well to get him to go along with the sham but Edna guessed that somehow he would make sure that Miss Belle ended up paying for that because she wouldn't question any bill that Mr Fidler put before her. Especially as the poor woman wanted the very best for her poor little girl.

However, Edna had persuaded herself that even though Miss Belle loved her daughter she wasn't much of a mother. It was shameful the way that poor little mite was kept out of a decent bed at night and taken to those dreadful places full of drunks and criminals, wasn't it? All in all, Edna thought that Miss Belle didn't deserve an angel child like that and that Mr Fidler had done the right thing to arrange things the way he had.

Tonight a lovely lady – a lovely rich lady – would have a dear little girl to love and care for. Rose would have a wonderful life and she, Edna, had helped to make that possible.

She turned her head so that she could look at the darkening countryside rushing by but only the occasional lights from a farm or a small village pierced the gloom. She closed her eyes again but she still couldn't sleep.

In another train, one heading north from Newcastle, Rose was sleeping fitfully. The child had been kept sedated ever since Edna had taken her to Jack's house and left her with Maud. Rose had been puzzled at first but willing to play with the toys that Jack had provided. But after a while she had cast them aside and, taking hold of the old doll, she had begun to cry for her mother. That was when Maud had given her the first dose of a draught she had ready and waiting.

After that she had kept dosing Rose until the little one was thoroughly confused, although she was careful to let her waken sufficiently to eat a dish or two of boily now and then; the soft bread soaked in warm milk and flavoured with sugar was the only thing the child could manage in her somnolent state.

Maud was sure the draught containing a little rum was harmless. Hadn't her former employer Mrs Blenkinsop told her that all the nursemaids in the West Indies used it constantly, and hadn't she encouraged Maud to use it with the Blenkinsop children? However, she was worried that she had forgotten the exact recipe. She hoped she hadn't made it too strong. She didn't want to addle Rose's wits permanently. She had promised Mrs Leighton that the child was not only pretty but as bright as a button. And Geraldine Leighton would be forever grateful to her for bringing her a much-wanted child. A comfortable future would be secured.

Of course, Jack had already paid her well for her part in

the matter, enough to put by with her savings and perhaps invest in a little house of her own one day. But Maud Fidler did not want a 'little' house. She had grown used to the easy life enjoyed by senior servants in a grand house. She did not eat or sit with the family but was considered superior to most of the other staff. She had her own sitting room and she was waited on by one of the younger maids. When the time came for her to retire she hoped to be pensioned off and given one of the small houses on the estate and looked after financially for the rest of her days by a mistress who considered herself to be in her debt.

Maud glanced at the pretty little bracelet watch Jack had bought her when he first asked for her help in stealing Rose from her mother. Now she admitted to a feeling of excitement as she contemplated the power bringing this child to Mrs Leighton would give her in the household at Ravenshill. She gathered her bags together and wrapped the blanket more securely around Rose, who was lying on the seat beside her. She noticed the trace of recent tears on the little girl's cheeks.

Well, that couldn't be helped, and Mrs Leighton would think it natural that a child would cry for its mother. No doubt it would tug at her heartstrings even more. And, thankfully, Rose was far too young to understand what was happening to her. As she grew she would no doubt forget the feckless creature who had thought it proper to bring up her daughter on the streets and in the drinking dens of Newcastle.

When the train pulled into the small country station the platform lights formed pools of warm light amongst the shadows. Maud peered out of the carriage window and saw that there was a faint mist. How dramatic, she thought; this is like a scene from a sensational novel or play and I am the heroine.

As soon as she opened the door, Angus, the Leightons' groom, hurried towards her and she handed him the sleeping child, then picked up her capacious handbag. Together, they left the station and walked through the clammy mist rolling in from the sea. The Leightons' carriage was waiting in the station yard and Maud could hear the jingle of harnesses as the horses pawed the cobbles.

'You have her!' Maud was startled to find Mrs Leighton leaning forward to look out of the open carriage door. She hadn't expected the mistress to come to the station herself.

'Yes, madam.' Maud waited while Angus handed Rose to Mrs Leighton and made sure that both woman and child were comfortable. Then he turned to Maud and helped her in.

Angus Gibson was a kindly man who, content to have his job at the big house and, furthermore, work with the horses that he loved, would never have questioned any order he was given. Maud wondered whether his wife Jane who worked in the kitchens, would question him about this night's business but, even if she did, she would learn no more than the information that had already been allowed to filter down to the servants' hall.

Mr Leighton, moved by his wife's distress at bearing yet another stillborn child, had allowed her to seek and adopt an orphan. He had stipulated that the child must be a girl and that left folk speculating that he still hoped for a son to inherit his land and his property.

Maud watched her mistress's anxious features soften as she gazed down at the child she held in her arms. Soon they had left the village behind and were travelling along the country roads towards Ravenshill and the mansion by the sea. They drew up at the main entrance and Mrs Leighton allowed Angus to carry the child up the grand entrance steps, but as soon as the door was opened she dismissed him and said she would manage.

'Allow me to carry the little mite up to the nursery, Mrs Leighton,' Maud said. 'We don't want you falling, do we?'

'You're right, Maud. I suppose I haven't quite recovered from my last confinement yet and, do you know, this child is heavier than I expected her to be.'

Maud was aware of a curious housemaid or two as they went upstairs. No doubt they had found some pretext to be about. Maud frowned at them and made a turning gesture with one hand, reminding them that they were supposed to face the wall when a member of the family appeared.

Once in the room that had been decorated so prettily as a nursery, Mrs Leighton removed her coat and hat and placed them on a chair. She sank gracefully on to a small sofa by the fireplace and leaned back to remove her gloves from her soft, delicate hands. It was obvious that she had not yet recovered from the birth of her latest child. Another stillborn baby.

Mrs Leighton had been out of her mind with grief. Convinced that she would never bear a living child, she had begged her husband to allow her to adopt and Mr Leighton agreed. Anything to keep her quiet, Maud thought.

'I'll stay and watch while you get her to bed,' Mrs Leighton said. 'But let me hold her while you take your coat off.'

Maud laid the still sleeping Rose in her mistress's arms and removed her coat and hat. She took one of the new nightdresses from the chest of drawers and laid it on the bed. She returned to the fireplace to find her mistress looking down at Rose wonderingly. 'She looks well cared for, in spite of the ragged clothes,' Mrs Leighton said. 'This is not at all what I was expecting.'

'And what was that, madam?'

'That she would be neglected.'

Maud had taken care to dress Rose in second-hand clothes she had bought at Paddy's Market on the quayside. Threadbare and patched, they probably had only one wash left in them. The child had to look as though she came from a poor family. But Maud had not realized that the look of the child herself might present a problem. Rose looked well fed and thriving.

'I suppose the woman did her best for her little one,' Maud said. 'I've heard how mothers starve themselves rather than see their children go hungry.'

'And that is why she was willing to part with her, I suppose. She wanted a better life for her daughter.'

'That's right, madam, especially as the father has run off and left them, and the poor woman believes that she might not be here much longer in order to care for her little angel.'

Mrs Leighton looked shocked. 'Are you telling that the woman is gravely ill? That she's going to die?'

'I'm afraid I am, madam. When I asked my – er – friend, Mr Givens, if he knew of any child that needed a good home he thought of little Rose immediately. His charitable works take him amongst the poorest families, as you know. I'm sure he thought this case the most worthy.'

'And I shall always be grateful to you for bringing me this wonderful gift. And grateful to Mr Givens, of course. I pray that his future work will prosper.'

'I'm sure it will, madam.' Mr Givens would prosper, all right, Maud thought, in whatever he chose to do. For in truth Mr Givens was no Samaritan. The man who had presented himself to Mrs Leighton with his tales of good works was in reality Maud's brother, Jack.

It was obvious that Mrs Leighton had accepted the rigmarole; why shouldn't she? And her delight in the child was quickly overcoming any dutiful regret for the mother. 'Rose! It's the first time you've told me her name,' she said.

Maud took the child from her arms and laid her on the bed. Mrs Leighton followed her and said musingly, 'Rose is a pretty name, isn't it?'

'I suppose so.'

'And yet, I confess, I want to change it.'

'Why's that?'

'Rose belongs to me now. She's my daughter and, like any parent, I feel I have a right to name her.' She paused. 'And yet I don't want to confuse the little angel.' She paused again while she thought about it and then she smiled. 'I know,' she said. 'I shall call her Rosina. It's not too different and yet I have chosen it. What do you think of that?'

'You must do as you please, madam. But there's one thing I can tell you. This is a very lucky child to find herself with such a loving mother.'

When the child was settled Mrs Leighton leaned over to smooth her brow and to kiss her. 'Good night, my little one,' she said. 'Tomorrow I shall get to know you.' She picked up her coat and hat and turned to face Maud before leaving. 'I must change for dinner now, but I have arranged for one of the chambermaids to help me dress. Tonight you must stay with Rosina. Tomorrow morning the new nursery maid will take up her duties and I expect you to train her.' She opened the door. 'I shall arrange for a tray to be sent up for you. Good night, Maud.' She closed the door.

Maud was left musing over the fact that Mrs Leighton, no matter how grateful she was, would never quite treat her as a friend. Once the child – the wonderful gift, as she had called her – had been accepted in her heart as her daughter, Maud had returned to being the servant, albeit a privileged servant. Mrs Leighton was a kind mistress and a good woman and it was as well that she would never know the truth about Rose.

Maud felt no guilt. She had agreed with her brother that Daisy Belle, as she called herself now, was hardly a fit mother for the little girl, dragging her from pillar to post the way she did. But Maud also knew that Daisy truly loved her daughter and she would never have thought of interfering if Jack, the younger brother on whom she doted, had not persuaded her that they could profit from the enterprise.

When Maud had told him that her wealthy mistress was considering adopting a child he had immediately come up with a plan. He had told her to introduce him to Mrs Leighton as Cedric Givens, a director of a children's charity, and after that it was easy. Of course, he had persuaded Mrs Leighton to part with an extremely generous 'donation' – and part of that was now nestling in Maud's own savings bank.

Maud had one moment of doubt. 'What if Mrs Leighton wants to get in touch with you in future?' she had asked her brother.

He had laughed. 'I told your mistress that her donation was going to help me set up a charitable foundation for the poor little homeless orphans in Australia. I may just forget to leave a forwarding address.'

Maud had not expected to have an easy night, for this was yet another strange bed the child must get used to. Rose – or Rosina, as she must be called in future – woke more than once and showed every sign of being heartbroken.

'Mama, where's Mama?' she asked over and over again, and she sobbed until her little voice sounded as broken as her heart must be. Maud, in her nightgown and curling rags, tried to pacify the child with toy after toy. The dolls and teddy bears were the best that money could buy and yet the child would have nothing to do with them.

In desperation Maud got the old broken doll out of her

bag and placed it in the child's arms. Thank goodness I hadn't already disposed of it, she thought as she watched the child settle, still sobbing, but clutching the doll to her as if she would never let it go.

Before closing her bag again she glanced down at the neatly folded clothes. The clothes Rose had been wearing when Edna had taken her to the park. Mrs Leighton must never see them. If she did she would never believe that Rose had come from a poverty-stricken family. Maud had planned to get rid of them as soon as possible. Maybe even sell them to a dealer.

But she had changed her mind. No, she thought, she couldn't do that. If they ever turned up, if Daisy ever saw them, the trail could lead to her. No, she'd better burn them. But then again, perhaps she wouldn't. She had the strangest feeling that she should keep them. You never knew what was going to happen in the future . . . maybe one day, though she didn't know how, she could profit from them.

And then, when the child was exhausted and settled into an uneasy sleep, Maud Fidler, weary though she was, found that sleep escaped her. She found her mind going over and over the events of the last few days. When Edna had first brought her to Jack's house Rose had been happy enough. Small as she was, she had seemed to remember Maud from when she and her mother had been living there.

She had accepted the drink Maud had prepared without protest and, as Maud and Edna drank their tea, the child had grown sleepier and sleepier. When her little eyes were closed Edna had slipped away. And then the most difficult time had begun when the bewildered child awoke and started asking for her mother. Nothing, it seemed, would stop her crying except drugged sleep. Jack had told Maud to keep Rose at his house until the worst of her protests were over.

Maud had wondered for a while if Rose would ever become calmer but, helped by the draught she was giving her, the child did begin to settle. Or rather to withdraw into some world of private misery. And now here she was. A new and better life was about to begin for Daisy's daughter. But better though it may be, Maud could not allow her gaze to linger on the face of the child she had betrayed.

Chapter Four

Dear Jack,

Mrs Leighton is delighted with the child and has taken her to her heart. I hope you are pleased with what I have done for you.

Your loving sister,
Maud

Dear Maud,

I am glad things are going well but there was no need to remind me of what you have done. You will find a regular cheque in the post as I have promised. In return you must play your part in making sure that Daisy never learns what we have done and that her daughter is still alive.

Daisy thinks that she is working to pay off her debts and also to provide a suitable memorial for Rose. However, I sense that she takes comfort from the way the public are beginning to take her to their hearts. And remember, the more she prospers, the better it will be for us.

Your brother,
Jack

Julian Leighton sat in solitary splendour at the head of the table in the dining room of his ancestral home. He had enjoyed a luncheon of oxtail soup, lamb cutlets and creamed potatoes followed by his favourite jam roly-poly pudding and custard.

'School food,' Geraldine laughingly called such a meal, but she admitted that ever since her days at an exclusive boarding establishment for young ladies in Oxfordshire, she had enjoyed such luncheons too. However, she had not deigned to join her husband at the table today.

When the young parlour maid brought him his coffee he instructed her to take the tray to the small table by the fireplace and leave him to pour it himself. 'And for heaven's sake leave that until later,' he said irritably when she began to clear the table. She hurried out of the room, looking surprised. Mr Leighton was usually the most genial of men. Something must have annoyed him – and she could guess what that was. His wife.

Julian sipped his coffee and stared moodily into the fire. The coals crackled as a spurt of rain made its way down the chimney, and he glanced round at the window as the wind hurled both rain and dead leaves against the panes. I got home just in time, he thought.

He had enjoyed his morning ride through the autumn countryside: the sky wide and greyish blue with only a hint of rain clouds; the wind stirring the browning fronds of bracken on the hillsides and the cries of the gulls driven inland by the gathering turbulence of the sea.

He had visited one of his tenant farmers while he was out. The man's family had farmed the land for generations. They had been there almost as long as the Leightons had lived at Ravenshill and they often behaved as if they owned the place. They were currently in dispute with a neighbour about the upkeep of certain dry-stone walls and it had taken all of Julian's diplomacy to resolve the matter. But the visit had been longer than he intended and he had been late for lunch.

In the past, if he was late for lunch, Geraldine, the most accommodating of wives, would have waited for him so that they could spend some time together discussing estate matters. Geraldine was entitled to do this as the money she had brought into the marriage had been not only necessary but almost a lifesaver. She also enjoyed the gossip he brought home for she had not been able to get out and about as much as she would have liked, owing to her difficult pregnancies and the effect they had had on her health.

But today, not only had she not waited, she had apparently not appeared in the dining room at all. Geraldine's companion, Maud Fidler, had met him as he arrived home and informed him that Mrs Leighton was taking her lunch in the nursery with their daughter, Rosina.

Daughter . . .

Julian lit a cigar and sat back. He watched the smoke curl upwards through half-closed eyes. In order to please Geraldine he had tried very hard to think of Rosina as his daughter and he had never allowed his wife to know how difficult that was. The child was pretty with dark brown curls and dark blue eyes and a wholesome complexion – despite the background she must have come from. Julian shuddered to think what that might be.

According to Maud Fidler this chap Givens had found the child in the festering slum dwellings that huddled around the Ouseburn in Newcastle. Apparently the mother was decent enough but Julian thought Givens would say that anyway. These soft-hearted do-gooders were so often blinkered, their love of humanity *en masse* blinding them to what individual human beings could be like and why some of them had ended up living in poverty in the first place. And what of the father? Apparently he had run off and left them to starve. What sort of man was that? An idle wastrel at the best, and at the worst a criminal of some kind. A thief or even a murderer.

What sort of blood ran through the veins of that innocent-looking child? It wasn't Leighton blood. It would be bad blood, in all probability, and no matter how lovingly Geraldine brought the child up, that inheritance could come out one day. And that would break Geraldine's heart. Julian worried about the way she had become obsessed with Rosina, refusing to acknowledge that the child was anything but her own flesh and blood.

She had instructed the entire household as well as their friends that Rosina must never be told that she was adopted. Good woman though Geraldine was, Julian knew she would have no hesitation in either dismissing or cutting dead anyone who broke that rule.

And he had gone along with this. Because he still loved Geraldine and he admired her pluck. She never complained but willingly became pregnant time after time in order to provide an heir for Ravenshill. Of course she was not just thinking of Julian. Like many women she craved a child of her own, and he sensed that she was growing almost demented when every one of her pregnancies ended badly. At first Julian had balked at the idea of adoption but Dr Lamb had actually encouraged it.

'If your wife is happy,' he had told Julian, 'if she has an infant to love and to hold close, it may work the miracle you are praying for. Many a time I have seen patients of mine adopt after years of trying for a child. The woman engages happily with the adopted infant and then manages to conceive and carry to full term a child of her own. I advise you to let Mrs Leighton have her way in this matter.'

'Very well,' Julian had replied. 'But it must be a girl.'

'Of course.'

Julian rose and went to pour himself a brandy. It was early in the day but he found himself thoroughly out of sorts. Despite Dr Lamb's confident prediction, Geraldine was not happy. Anyone could see that. She fussed over the child like a mother hen, bought the very best clothes and the most extravagant toys, but Rosina's continued despondency was driving her to distraction. As far as Julian was concerned, Rosina did not deserve such love and affection. She never smiled and spoke as little as possible. She was never outright rude or disobedient, in fact she was quiet and biddable, but in Julian's opinion her lack of response was a sign of either stupidity or a bad character.

Geraldine had assured him that this was not so. 'Rosina is unhappy,' she'd told him. 'She has been taken away from the world she knows and is grieving for her old life.'

'Then she is a very foolish child,' Julian had declared more than once, 'to grieve for a ragged, half-starved existence in a slum.'

For some reason this always made Geraldine uneasy. 'She wasn't half starved,' she would murmur. 'In fact she appeared to have been extremely well cared for.'

Julian would give up at this point. He had no wish to prolong an argument that would only serve to distress his wife even more. If the first passion had died, he was still very fond of her and genuinely wanted her to be happy. Besides, he still hoped fervently that she would conceive an heir, and if he had to indulge her in her foolishness in order to achieve that, then so be it.

When he had finished his brandy he wandered moodily

along to Geraldine's private sitting room where she saw to her correspondence, issued orders to the servants and went over menus with the cook. She wasn't there but he hadn't really expected her to be. It was Maud Fidler he wanted to talk to. Surprisingly, even though it was Fidler who had brought the child to Ravenshill, Geraldine did not encourage her to help with Rosina. After the first few weeks the task had fallen to Bridget, the nursery maid.

Maud looked up in surprise when Julian entered the room. She was sitting at Geraldine's desk, making lists. He strolled over and saw that she had the mail-order catalogues from Harrods, Gamages and the Army and Navy Stores spread out on the desk. They were all open at the pages of toys.

'Mrs Leighton has asked me to order Rosina's Christmas presents,' Maud said.

Julian leaned over to look more closely and saw that his wife had ticked certain items with a pencil. He raised his eyebrows. 'Rather a lot for one small girl,' he said.

'I know, but Mrs Leighton likes to indulge her.'

'And so she should,' Julian said, and he forced a smile. It would not do to let a servant think for one moment that he was in any way criticizing his wife.

'Did you want to see me, sir?' Maud asked. He thought she looked troubled but couldn't guess why.

'I was wondering how you thought Rosina is settling in.'

He watched as Maud wiped the nib of her pen and laid it down on the blotting pad. She appeared to give his question full consideration before looking up at him. 'Not as quickly as I'd hoped,' she said. And then she hurried on, 'But Mr Givens said that all children are different. They all develop a relationship with their new parents at different rates. We must,' she paused, 'we must persevere.'

'Expert is he, this chap Givens?'

'Oh, yes.' Julian thought that she looked flustered.

'I ask because you introduced him to us. But how well do you know him? I mean, is he a friend of yours?'

'No . . . not exactly a friend. I mean . . .'

'Look, don't be concerned. I'm not criticizing you,' he said. 'I just need to know. You see, I'm concerned that Mrs Leighton is making herself ill with worry whereas the whole purpose of this exercise was to make her happy and well.'

'Oh, I'm sure everything will be all right. The child just needs time to settle in, that's all.'

'I hope you're right, for if I come to believe that this business is making my wife ill I shall ask Mr Givens to find another home for Rosina.'

'Oh, don't do that!'

'I beg your pardon?'

'I'm sorry, sir. I didn't mean to speak out of turn. It's just that . . . she's such a lovely little thing . . . Rosina . . . and I believe it would break Mrs Leighton's heart to part with her now.'

Julian looked at his wife's maid-companion long and hard. He had never known her to be more than quietly respectful and yet here she was, looking flushed and upset because of a wretched slum child. Women were strange beings.

'You're a good sort, aren't you, Fidler?' he said. 'I know your intention in finding this child was to make my wife happy and now I believe you have come to care for the little creature yourself. Well, I will let things be, but I must ask you to help my wife in any way you can with the child.' Suddenly he smiled wryly. 'And perhaps you could persuade Mrs Leighton to spare some time now and then for her husband too.'

61

'I'll try my best, Mr Leighton.'

'Good. Now let me see those catalogues.'

Julian Leighton looked at the pages of toys. 'Well, I don't suppose that magnificent rocking horse would be suitable for a girl . . . pity . . . but maybe one day we will have such a thing in the nursery.'

'I truly hope you will, sir.'

'Now, I see Mrs Leighton has marked some picture books and a dolls' tea set as well as a baby doll with a cot. Well, you must order two of those pretty French dolls too. And what about that wardrobe full of dolls' dresses? And some more picture-books? But keep it a secret. It will surprise and please my wife to think that I have bought something for Rosina too.'

Julian flicked through the pages of Gamages' catalogue until he came to another section. 'And while you're about it I'd like you to order one of those fancy scent bottles with the perfume Mrs Leighton likes. Funny, she prefers that simple scent to any of the French perfumes she could have, and now I come to think of it I haven't bought her any since last Christmas. It must be a secret, mind.'

'Of course, sir.'

'Right, I'll leave you to get on with it. And when the goods are delivered I'll rely on you to field the extra things, wrap them and put them under the Christmas tree.'

He left the room, his mood restored for the moment.

Mr Leighton is pleased with himself, Maud thought. No doubt he thinks spending money on fine gifts can solve problems.

She took up her pen and began to write her list again but she made several mistakes and in a moment of irritation she screwed up the paper and threw it into the wastepaper basket. She started again but she was finding it very difficult to concentrate.

It wouldn't do at all if Mr Leighton became so frustrated with the situation that he decided to send Rosina back. Back where? There was no such person as Mr Givens. And in any case, hadn't Jack intended that this imaginary charity worker would be going to Australia? She, Maud, would have to find somewhere for Rosina. Well, she couldn't and she wouldn't. Her brother would have to think of something. But he wouldn't be pleased with her, and he might even demand that she hand back the money he had given her as well as stopping the regular payments.

No, she would have to do her very best to help Mrs Leighton overcome the wretched child's reluctance to respond. And that was going to be difficult considering that Mrs Leighton did not like Maud to have too much to do with Rosina these days. Mr Leighton didn't know this because his wife had not told him – or anyone – what had happened.

At first, with her mistress still weak from her latest failed confinement, Maud had spent as much time as possible in the nursery helping and instructing Bridget. Rosina had stopped whimpering and seemed to have withdrawn into a private world of utter misery. She would stare uncomprehendingly at Mrs Leighton and Bridget, but when she saw Maud, she actually brightened up a little. Maud thought she understood why. It was because she was a familiar face and a link with the world the child had known.

Sometimes she would hold her hands out pityingly and Maud would pick her up. 'Mama,' Rosina would whimper, and Maud knew very well that she was asking to be taken home. One day this happened just as Geraldine Leighton walked into the nursery.

'What did Rosina say?' she asked. 'Did she call you "Mama"?'

Maud thought she glimpsed anger in her mistress's eyes. 'No, madam.'

'She did. I heard it most distinctly. Have you been teaching her to call you "Mama"?'

'No, I swear I haven't. I think she was asking me to take her back to . . . back home.'

'This is her home!' Mrs Leighton's face flushed angrily. 'And I am her mother. If, for whatever reason, the child does not understand that, if there is the slightest possibility that she is confused, then I think it better that you should not spend so much time in the nursery.'

'But you are not well, madam. Not yet strong enough to do as much as you want to for the child. Please, let me help you.'

'No, I have made up my mind. You can help me in other ways — my correspondence, my household arrangements, shopping, whatever. But I do not want you in the nursery.'

Maud had thought her mistress had become unhinged and she did not dare oppose her. But she was far from happy. For although she did not really care that she would see less of the child, she had hoped to establish herself as the bringer of happiness. She had hoped that every time Mrs Leighton was grateful that she had a daughter, she would remember that it was Maud who had made that possible. But now Maud found herself banished from the nursery and destined for less important duties. Less important in Mrs Leighton's eyes, that was. That had not been part of the plan at all.

On Christmas Day Geraldine Leighton sat on the bed in the nursery and looked down at her daughter; she felt like weeping. Her daughter . . . that's how she thought of her. Already she loved Rosina so much that she could not imagine life without her. But although the child was quiet and biddable she had shown no sign of returning that love.

Maud Fidler was overseeing last-moment arrangements for the dinner party the Leightons were holding that evening, so Geraldine was free to come to the nursery and help Bridget as she bathed Rosina and brushed her dark curls. Now Rosina was sleeping and her eyelashes lay like dark crescents on her creamy cheeks. She was beautiful.

Geraldine had been so desperate for a child of her own that she had never thought to specify beauty or even whether the unfortunate babe should be whole of limb; she would have loved a cripple just as fiercely. But she could not help being thankful that the child that had been brought to her just a few months ago was outstandingly attractive as well as being robustly healthy.

The fact that Rosina was beautiful had made it a little easier for Julian to accept her, Geraldine believed. She knew how uneasy her husband had been about taking in the child of strangers. And she suspected that, kind though he was, he had still not been completely won over. But Julian, one of the most handsome men she had ever seen, liked to be surrounded by beauty of every kind. He had once told Geraldine that the first time he saw her at a ball in her father's house he had vowed she must be his. 'What fine children we will have,' he had said laughingly on their wedding night. 'What beautiful daughters and what handsome sons!'

'Shouldn't you be going down now, Mrs Leighton?' Maud Fidler had entered quietly and stood watching her from the doorway.

Geraldine looked up, her expression one of vexed surprise. 'I'll stay just a moment longer,' she said.

'I think your guests may be arriving,' Maud said.

'Has Mr Leighton sent you?'

'Yes, ma'am.' Maud came right into the room.

Oh dear, I suppose I should go, Geraldine thought. She knew Julian thought she spent too much time here and she didn't want to annoy him on Christmas Day. Not when everything had gone so well. She sighed. Well enough, she supposed, except that although she believed Rosina had lately begun to accept that this was her home, it was still difficult to win a smile from her.

Early that morning Geraldine had slipped out of bed quietly so as not to disturb her sleeping husband. She had pulled on her robe and gone to the nursery. She wanted to be there in Rosina's room when the child woke up and saw the stocking hanging from the mantelshelf. She was not sure whether Rosina had understood the significance of it when they had placed the stocking there together the night before.

When she had entered the room she was disappointed to find that Bridget was already there and must have given Rosina the stocking, for the child was sitting up in bed staring at the contents, which she had tipped out over the counterpane. As well as the traditional gifts of an apple, an orange and a few nuts, Geraldine had added a little net of chocolate coins and a tiny wooden Dutch doll with a removable pinafore and bonnet.

She didn't blame Bridget for she had not specifically told her to wait and, from the expression on the girl's face, the young maid was obviously as excited about Christmas as any child should be.

Rosina was staring at the doll wonderingly.

'Do you like it, sweetheart?' Geraldine had asked.

'Yes, thank you,' Rosina had said politely.

Geraldine suffered an agony of disappointment. She'd wanted so much to be there to watch Rosina's face when she first looked in the stocking. The moment had passed her by.

On the verge of tears, she had returned to her room but had consoled herself with the thought that there were still the presents around the tree to be opened.

Julian had said they should wait until Boxing Day to open the presents – that was the tradition – but Geraldine reminded him that on Boxing Day there was going to be a children's party and it would be better not to have too much excitement in one day. More than thirty children from farms and big houses in the surrounding countryside had been invited, as well as the children of the house servants and the people who worked on the estate. Her husband had given way as he usually did in matters concerning Rosina if he thought it would please her. And for that Geraldine was grateful.

After the disappointing start Christmas Day had gone well. Rosina had lunch in the nursery with Bridget. Julian had insisted that Geraldine should eat with him in the dining room and she had wanted to please him. But straight after lunch Bridget had brought Rosina down and they'd opened the presents together. Geraldine had been delighted to find that Julian had entered into the spirit of the occasion and when she discovered that he had actually ordered presents for Rosina himself she cried tears of happiness. He told the round-eyed child that these gifts under the tree came from Father Christmas.

Rosina had watched solemnly as the grown-ups opened their presents. Geraldine was touched to find that Julian had also bought a bottle of her favourite rose cologne and she gave him a box of white handkerchiefs with his initial embroidered in the corner. To Geraldine that bottle of cologne was more precious than anything Julian would give her the following day, even though she suspected it was going to be a pair of diamond drop earrings. She smiled as she thanked him and told him how clever he was to remember how much she liked it and that from now she would always wear it and it would be her favourite perfume.

Rosina took the dolls' tea set out of its box and regarded it solemnly but, rather than the beautifully dressed French dolls, it was the baby doll and the cot that she played with, putting the doll to bed and singing a funny little song to her. Geraldine had not been able to make out the words but she had heard Rosina sing this song before.

Now, at the end of a happy day, sitting in this beautifully decorated nursery and trying to imagine what squalor the little girl must have lived in before, Geraldine was forced to admit that no matter how much better off she was materially, Rosina was still grieving for her own mother. She thought of the judgement of Solomon and realized that she loved this little one so much that if there had been a way to return the child to her real mother and make both their lives comfortable she would do it even if it might break her heart.

But that was impossible. The poor woman was dead. Just before he sailed for Australia Mr Givens had written to her, thanking her for her generous donation and enclosing a letter from Rosina's mother. He said she had dictated it to him from her deathbed.

> Dear Lady,
> I am not long for this cruel world. I miss my little Rose but I know that what I did was for the best. The only thing which will make my passing easier is that I know my bairn will be well cared for.
>   God bless you.

There had been no name and Mr Givens had never mentioned one. He said it was just as well and that he hadn't told the child's mother who the benefactress was either. For some reason it was better that way. Sometimes the mother might change her mind, he said, and cause all sorts of distress; tearing the poor infant away from the happy new home.

Well, that was impossible now, Geraldine thought. The mother was dead and the father missing. Rosina's best chance of happiness was to settle here. One day she would, Geraldine told herself. She tried to forget the days, the weeks, that Rosina had sobbed herself to sleep every night and sat like a little ghost all day, silent and pale-faced. At least that didn't happen now. She looked confused more than unhappy, and sometimes frowned as if she were trying to remember something. Perhaps memories of her past life were fading. Geraldine hoped so.

'Mrs Leighton?'

Geraldine looked round to see that her companion was still standing there. 'Tell Mr Leighton that I am coming,' she told Maud. 'I'll just say good night to Rosina.'

Maud left the room and Bridget went on quietly tidying. Geraldine leaned over to kiss the child's brow and saw that despite all the pretty dolls Rosina now owned, she still preferred the broken doll she had brought with her. Geraldine had been horrified at the sight of it but had had the sense not to take it away from the child. She had not been able to resist cleaning its limbs and washing and mending the clothes but she was happy to let Rosina keep the doll if it brought her comfort. She smiled wanly as she tucked in the doll as well as the child.

'Good night, sweetheart,' she whispered.

Rosina stirred in her sleep and frowned. She didn't wake but became conscious enough to be aware that someone was bending over her, someone who smelled deliciously of roses.

Mama, she thought, and a wondering smile played on her lips. 'Good night, Mama . . .' she said softly before she turned and took hold of the doll, bringing it close to her body.

Deep in slumber she had no idea of the effect of the words she had spoken. Geraldine Leighton was crying with happiness instead of sorrow. The child – her daughter – had called her Mama.

Chapter Five

July 1888

Geraldine felt like King Canute. She sat in her chair on the beach and watched the waves coming ever nearer and, just like the king in the history books, she could not command the waters to turn back. Neither could she pick up her chair and retreat, not in her 'delicate' condition.

She turned her head in the direction of the children's happy laughter. The two nursemaids were hurrying northwards along the beach, following the helter-skelter progress of Rosina and her play fellow, Adam Loxley. Ben, the Loxleys' young stable lad, hardly more than a child himself, was running with the children, and from the whoops of laughter Geraldine thought he was having as much fun as they.

She hated to be a spoilsport but if they didn't notice her predicament soon she would have to call them back. It was time to move the chair away from the tide line to the dry sand at the foot of the dunes where they had left the hamper and the rugs. She could easily have done it herself, she thought, except that she had promised Julian and Dr Lamb that she would take every care. Nothing must be allowed to threaten this pregnancy.

The sun was bright and, bundled up in clothes designed to conform to modesty, she was uncomfortably warm. Geraldine was pleased when a light breeze sprang up. It was coming off the sea. Gratefully, she lifted her face towards the cooler air. She could feel tiny droplets of water but it wasn't rain, it was spray. She watched the breeze lift the spindrift from the frothy rim of a wave.

The next wave surged forward across the glistening sand and instinctively she lifted her feet although there was no need – yet. The movement caused an unpleasant pulling across her swollen abdomen and she tried to ease herself into a more comfortable position. The chair, a sturdy wicker affair from the garden room, could have done with more substantial cushions. She imagined that she could feel the ridged pattern of the wicker work even through her layers of clothing. 'The Princess and the Pea,' she thought. I'm like the princess in Hans Andersen's fairy story.

Geraldine loved reading stories to Rosina. Every night before her daughter slept she would come to the nursery and they would choose a book together. Geraldine still had some treasured books from her own childhood and she was redis-covering her delight in the old tales and fables. Rosina was everything she could have hoped for. She had changed so much from the unhappy bewildered child Maud Fidler had brought home. Geraldine still couldn't fathom what had brought about the first sign of a change on the evening of Christmas Day five years ago. But she would treasure for ever the moment when the sleepy child had smiled and called her 'Mama'.

After that the transformation of Rosina had been gradual. There had been days of happiness and genuine delight, but now and then there had been moments when her daughter had withdrawn, had entered some sort of brown study where she seemed to be trying to make sense of something that puzzled her. Geraldine had never had the courage to ask Rosina whether she remembered her previous life. Nothing must spoil things; selfish it may be but Geraldine wanted the little girl to believe that she alone was her mother.

Indeed, many of the local gentry and workers alike had no idea that she was not Geraldine Leighton's own child. Rosina had new clothes, a new name, and a new life. And, thank the Lord, she was both loving and cheerful.

The only part of the past that remained was the old doll. Geraldine would have liked to have thrown it away but she hadn't the heart to do so; Rosina was so attached to the poor broken thing. She took it to bed with her each night and could often be heard singing to it – a sad wordless little song, full of sentiment; perhaps the child's real mother had used to sing it as a lullaby.

Now the children's laughter grew louder. Urged on by Ben, they were racing back along the beach towards Geraldine. Bridget, who at last had noticed her mistress's predicament, raced even faster, calling over her shoulder as she ran for Adam's nursemaid, Sally, to hurry up. They all arrived together, the nursemaids, out of breath, pink of face and apologetic; and the two children, bless them, showing concern.

'There now, Mrs Leighton, let me help you up,' Bridget said.

'And Adam and I will carry the chair,' Rosina volunteered.

'I think it will prove too heavy, darling,' Geraldine said. 'Let Ben help you.'

Both maids hauled her to her feet. How undignified this is, Geraldine thought. How I hate being clumsy like this. But it won't be much longer and then, if God is willing, Rosina will have a little brother.

Or maybe a sister. An errant thought pounced from the place in her mind where it waited constantly to worry her. Please let this child I'm carrying be a boy, she sent up her usual prayer, and then Julian will be happy; he will have an heir to inherit the land and the estate, then maybe he will leave me in peace . . .

Geraldine knew how important it was to Julian that he have an heir. The land had been in his family for generations. She had come to believe that despite his ardent wooing, the only reason he had married her was that, thanks to her father, she had sufficient capital to restore and improve Julian's heritage. So be it, she had thought. He has been a good husband and he has indulged me over the matter of this beloved child . . . Rosina. Nevertheless, I will take care to leave her an inheritance of her own. For if I should die before Julian, as is likely, I'm not altogether sure that he would treat her in quite the same way as a child of his own blood.

Above her, the seabirds seemed to echo her melancholy thoughts with their haunting cries. It was July and the sun was shining, although here, on the Northumbrian coast, there was a breeze from the sea cool enough to temper the bright air. I must shake off this mood of despondency, Geraldine thought, and enjoy this day with Rosina. The time of my confinement draws nearer and there will not be so many more carefree outings like this.

Bridget and Sally supported her, one on each side, as they made slow progress up the gently sloping beach to the dunes. There was a sound of activity behind them.

'That's right, grab the curved bit and pull!' Geraldine heard Rosina say.

'Right oh!' That was Adam.

'Be careful, Master Adam, Miss Rosina.' That was Ben, and from the ensuing puffing and panting interspersed with giggles, Geraldine realized that the children, directed by the stable lad, were dragging the chair up the beach after them.

'Well done, boys!' her daughter exclaimed when the breathless little party and the chair arrived at the 'den', the place where the tall marram grass growing in the rising dune curved over to provide a sort of shelter for the hamper and the rugs they had left there when they'd first arrived. Rosina and Adam collapsed on to the sand and their nursemaids spread the rugs.

'Get up, Miss Rosina, and you too, Master Adam. Go and shake your clothes well away from here and then come and sit down. If your mother says it's all right we'll have our picnic now.'

Geraldine smiled and nodded. The short walk in the soft sand had tired her. She sat as comfortably as she could and watched as Bridget opened the hamper, gave everyone a napkin and a plate and their own packet of sandwiches. The nursemaid told the children, and Ben too, to sit still and behave themselves as a sandwich dropped in the sand would be a wasted sandwich, fit only for the scavenging gulls. Rosina and Adam tried their best to sit still, they really did, but they were happy and excited and one or two sandwiches did end up being 'hoyed' to the gulls, as Ben put it.

It's a good job Maud Fidler didn't come with us today, Geraldine thought. She would have scolded Bridget for not keeping better order and probably have hinted to Geraldine herself that such unalloyed happiness couldn't be right. Geraldine often wondered about Maud. She had always been the perfect servant, sometimes sensing in advance what Geraldine needed and taking care of every detail. And of course it was Maud who had brought her the gift of a daughter.

And yet . . .

She thought back to the early days before she had banished poor Maud from the nursery. Maud had never been completely at ease with the child. She was not exactly cold but she seemed to hold herself at a distance, preferring to leave most of the work to Bridget. Geraldine supposed that was fair enough. After all, Maud had been employed as Geraldine's own companion, not as a nanny. So it was even more strange that Rosina had clung to Maud the way she had, even causing Geraldine to believe Maud had encouraged her to call her Mama.

Now Geraldine felt guilty. She had come to believe Maud's explanation that the child had been asking to be taken back to her mother. Her earlier suspicion was surely an indication of the state she was in, Geraldine thought, loving Rosina so and yet worrying that she would never settle in her home.

So over the years Geraldine had relaxed the rules a little and she sometimes asked Maud to help with Rosina. The woman had seemed pleased to do so, and yet Geraldine had been surprised to see there were times when Maud seemed to be uneasy when she watched Rosina at play.

She had not imagined it. At first she wondered if her maid-companion found the child too boisterous but that was not the case. Rosina was no more exuberant than a normal child of her age; in fact there were often times when the little girl was quiet and thoughtful. Then one day she realized that it was when Rosina danced and sang that Maud was most unhappy.

Like many little girls of her class, Rosina had dancing lessons. As soon as she was old enough, Geraldine had arranged for a dancing teacher and her accompanist to come once a week to the house and take classes in the ballroom.

Then Geraldine invited mothers of other small girls in the surrounding countryside to bring their daughters along.

Some brought the girls' young brothers too – but only for the ballroom dancing. The classes were as enjoyable for the mothers as they were for the daughters. Geraldine made sure that generous refreshments were provided and the ensuing laughter and gossip cheered the lives of some of the bored young country wives.

To Geraldine's surprise and delight, Rosina soon proved herself to be the star of the little group. Not only was her coordination better than that of the other children, but she was genuinely lithe and graceful. And her singing voice was a joy. Even Julian was impressed if he strayed into the ballroom when the class was in progress.

But sometimes Geraldine saw his smile fade. When she asked him why, he told her that it was perhaps not entirely ladylike for the child to show off as she did. It was all right to be musical, it seemed, but not to be too – well – 'professional' was the way he put it. When Geraldine told him that she didn't quite understand what he meant he explained that the child sometimes looked like a performer – a stage performer – and that wasn't proper for a daughter of Julian Leighton. Geraldine began to wonder if this was what was upsetting Maud Fidler. Did she feel guilty perhaps that the child she had brought them was not always behaving like a proper 'lady'?

The children had finished eating their sandwiches but Geraldine had hardly touched her own.

Bridget, a kindly young woman, tut-tutted as she took the plate away. 'This won't do, Mrs Leighton,' she said. 'You know Mr Leighton wants you to look after yourself.'

'Did he tell you that?' Geraldine was surprised.

'He did indeed. In fact . . .' Suddenly Bridget looked

uneasy as if she had suddenly become aware that it might not be quite proper for a servant – and a lowly one at that – to be speaking to the mistress of the house like this.

'What is it, Bridget?' Geraldine asked, and she smiled encouragingly to ease the girl's obvious discomfort.

'Well, you see, Mrs Leighton, when the master discovered that you had invited Adam Loxley to a beach party with Miss Rosina today he was worried about you. That lad's such a lively little rip. Mr Leighton didn't want to spoil your enjoyment but he didn't want you to exert yourself and put – well, you know – put yourself in danger in your condition.' Bridget coloured furiously. 'I hope you don't mind me mentioning it, Mrs Leighton.'

'Of course I don't. The master told you to take care of me, which was very kind of him – and it's kind of you to take his request so seriously.'

Bridget smiled happily. 'It was my idea to bring the chair, ma'am.'

'Was it?'

'Yes, I didn't think it would be proper, if you don't mind me saying so, for you to be sitting on a rug, like the rest of us. Oh, I know you have done in the past, but now it's different and, besides, if you'd sat down like that I'm not sure if Sally and me could have got you up again. Oh!' Now Bridget's face was beetroot and she covered her mouth with her hand as if trying to gulp back the words she had just uttered.

Geraldine began to laugh, which disconcerted the poor girl even further. But Sally, Adam's nursery maid, couldn't help giggling and soon they were all almost helpless with laughter; the children too, although Geraldine was pretty sure they didn't understand the joke. And poor Ben, who did, was red with embarrassment.

Conscious that such abandoned merriment might not be good for her, Geraldine tried to stop by taking a few deep breaths. Bridget and Sally saw what she was doing and stopped laughing. Very slowly the laughter died in her throat, ending in a cross between a giggle and a burp, which set the two young nursery maids off again.

'You are lucky,' she heard Sally whisper to Bridget.

'Why lucky?'

'To work for a mistress like Mrs Leighton. Mrs Loxley doesn't even speak to the servants — apart from Mrs Benson, the housekeeper. Mrs Loxley would never have a bit laugh and joke with us like this.'

Geraldine tried her hardest to send a disapproving look. She was conscious that the children should not hear the grown-ups discussed like this. But she need not have worried. Rosina and Adam, encouraged by Ben, were gathering together their towels and their buckets and spades. Bridget and Sally, abashed but only slightly repentant, apologised and then began to pack up the hamper and prepare for the walk back to the house.

It was like an expedition, Geraldine thought, as their small party trekked along the narrow pathways that led through the dunes; some of the sand hills towering above them and the overhanging grasses creating shadows and adding a delicious sense of mystery. Adam Loxley insisted on leading the way. He had declared that he was Mr Stanley and he was looking for the source of the Nile. Rosina, Geraldine noticed, was only too pleased to follow where her friend led and even the stable lad, Ben, joined in the make-believe. He had upturned the chair and balanced it on his head with the folded rugs piled on top and was quite happy to declare himself a native bearer.

'What does that make us, then?' Bridget asked him.

She and Sally were carrying the hamper between them.

'Well, I'm the chief bearer and you're — you're my underlings.'

'Underlings, huh!' Sally declared, but she wasn't really offended.

By the time they reached the windswept country road that led to the house they were laughing and rosy-cheeked — all of them — and Bridget was happy to murmur to the other maid that in her opinion it did the mistress good to get out like this, though of course she must rest the moment she got home. It would be dreadful if anything happened to her or the baby she was expecting this time.

Nearly three hundred miles away in London Julian sat in the docklands office of his wife's family business. Geraldine's family had been shipping coal from Newcastle to London for generations.

Coal had brought them great wealth. Geraldine's father had not entirely approved of Julian as a son-in-law but he had brought up his only daughter to be a 'lady' and he had been swayed by the fact that marrying Julian would mean she would take her place among the landed gentry. Knowing full well that Julian needed an injection of cash to improve the family home, Thomas Bradshaw had been more than generous. If he suspected that it was Geraldine's money rather than her undoubted beauty that had been the main attraction, he overcame his misgivings, for Geraldine herself admitted to him that she loved the young man and that it would make her very happy to become Mrs Leighton. And if it was in a father's gift to use some of his wealth to ensure his daughter's happiness then so be it.

But Geraldine's young brother had died in a drowning accident at school and she alone had inherited the fleet of colliers. Julian found himself in the position of administering the business and had overcome his distaste for 'trade' when he realized he could turn things to his advantage. Instead of ploughing money back into the fleet he had extracted as much of the profit as he could. He had soon discovered a few tricks. For example, a lick of paint on a rusting ship could fool an insurance inspector into believing the necessary maintenance work had been carried out — especially if the inspector in question had been kept sweet. There were ways of doing that without resorting to outright bribery.

All had gone well for a number of years but now, as he sat at his desk and examined the most recent report his chief clerk had made for him he began to feel uneasy. The business was not exactly in trouble but he realized that he had been sailing close to the wind. He would have to take care. But it wasn't the thought that he might have squandered Geraldine's inheritance that bothered him, it was the fact that the work on his family home was still far from finished.

Ledgers and papers covered the old desk and Julian sat back and stared at them moodily. The room was warm, stiflingly so, and he couldn't open the window because if he did he would let in the stench from the quays below.

'Enough!' he muttered and he closed the nearest ledger with a thud. He would work something out but not today, he thought. He'd laboured long enough and now he deserved some relaxation. He left the desk for his clerk to tidy and sent the office boy to fetch a cab. Soon he was heading away from the river towards a leafy square in Kensington.

Once they arrived Julian paid the cab driver, tipping generously. Then as the cab drew away, Julian glanced up at the grand London mansion that his wife knew nothing about. She knew about the other house, just a short walk away, which was equally grand but not decorated quite so tastefully. In spite of her expensive education, Geraldine had no idea of taste and had been quite happy to go along with the latest mode in house furnishing although her innate reserve had saved the house from the more garish fashions or any hint of vulgarity.

Geraldine was good natured and easy to please; Julian almost wished she had been less so and perhaps more questioning on those evenings he had left her alone and had walked the short distance to the other house where he had established Blanche, his mistress. But Geraldine did not come up to London often – hardly ever since she had adopted Rosina – and, perversely, Julian missed the charge of guilty titillation supplied by knowing his wife and his mistress were dwelling within such a short distance of each other.

Blanche was not easy to please. She was often selfish and demanding, but Julian, well aware of her faults, was prepared to indulge her. Not that she possessed any great beauty. She kept her light brown hair clean and fashionably dressed, had taken care to regain her figure after the birth of her child, and she dressed in the best clothes that Julian could afford. But she was no more attractive than many women of her age and certainly could not be compared to his wife. It was her sexuality that had first attracted Julian and had kept him enslaved all these years. And had encouraged him to be more extravagant than he could afford.

During the cab ride from the office he had realized that selling one of the London properties would solve most of his money problems. Selling them both would provide more than he needed. Geraldine would agree readily to the sale of the London house. She enjoyed their trips to London but she preferred the country. He could find some reason why they should have a smaller establishment in town and she probably wouldn't even question him. But Blanche? Julian knew that she would object vociferously and probably sulk if he asked her to move to a smaller house that would inevitably be in a less fashionable area. She would sulk and deny him the pleasures of her bed until he changed his mind – which he would eventually.

Would it be fair to keep this house for Blanche and yet provide a smaller home for his legitimate family? He knew it would not be. He might be unfaithful but many husbands were, especially if their wives were incapacitated regularly with childbirth, but he was not a cad. He sighed, and then did his best to shake off the troublesome thoughts. Blanche would be waiting for him and for a while he would escape from his worries.

He stepped into the hall and entered his secret world. The house was filled with merry voices, children's voices. A small girl hurtled down the stairs towards him closely followed by other small girls.

'You've remembered,' Amy shrieked as she flung herself into his arms. 'Mama said you would!'

'How could I forget your birthday?' Julian asked. 'Did you receive my present?'

'Yes, yes, yes! It's wonderful. All my friends are very jealous, aren't you?' she disengaged herself from Julian and turned to ask her friends, a group of ten or twelve girls who were now standing and observing the scene somewhat shyly. Julian realized that they were not quite sure who he was.

'Amy, my dear, it isn't seemly of you to wish your friends to be jealous.' That was Blanche's voice as she came gracefully down the stairs. 'Now as you've thanked Mr Leighton for the magnificent dolls' house, why don't you take your friends into the dining room where the birthday feast is waiting?'

The little girls trooped obediently across the hall.

Blanche smiled as she came towards him in a rustle of silk; her expensive perfume preceding her. Julian was about to take her in his arms but she moved back swiftly. She coughed gently and turned her head, nodding towards the stairs. Julian followed the movement with his eyes and saw several young women descending. They were talking softly amongst themselves but Julian noticed that they glanced at him curiously.

'The girls' nursemaids,' Blanche explained *sotto voce*. Then, putting her arm through his, she drew him towards the dining room. She raised her voice again and said, 'Now, my dear Julian, I hope you will come through to watch your goddaughter blow out the candles on her birthday cake.'

Julian raised his eyebrows. He wondered whether the young women would believe that he was Amy's godfather. He knew it was impossible to avoid speculation about the elegant young widow that Blanche was supposed to be. The story they had put about was that he was an old friend of her late husband who had perished in far distant climes.

When Blanche had first moved into this house in Kensington with her infant daughter, she had been dressed in widow's black and had kept up the pretence of being in mourning. A widow was not permitted to accept social invitations for at least a year. Neighbours respected the proprieties of the situation and did not call.

When the mourning period was over, Julian was presented not only as her late husband's friend but also as Amy's godfather and the chief executor of the dead man's estate. However, none of Blanche's neighbours was ever invited to meet him. The household servants guessed at the truth, of course, but they were very well paid to be discreet.

'My goodness, Blanche, this is a little extravagant, isn't it?' Julian surveyed the dining table with dismay. There were silver salvers full of delicately cut sandwiches, others containing savoury pastries and towering cake stands overloaded with multicoloured sugary confections, as well as an enormous birthday cake with nine candles, each held by a beautifully crafted porcelain nursery rhyme figure. 'All this sophisticated fare for a handful of little girls?' Julian said. 'Has Cook lost her senses?'

'Cook didn't prepare this.' Blanche looked up at him and shook her head smilingly. She gestured gracefully with one arm. 'Just look at it.' She smiled her indulgent how-could-a-mere-man-understand smile. 'I had a caterer. Antonio.'

'An Italian?'

'Of course. He's very fashionable. Anybody who is anybody has him in for private parties and banquets.'

'Banquets? Amy is nine years old. Surely a little tea party with jelly and cake would have been more appropriate?'

'And have the nursemaids carry tales back about how penny-pinching I am? No, Amy is already at a disadvantage; I will not give the parents of her school friends any reason to criticize.'

Although she spoke softly, Blanche's cheeks were pink. Julian recognized the danger signal and knew he should back off, but he could not stop himself from saying, 'Criticize? Oh, I say, Blanche, I'm sure nobody criticizes you.'

For a moment her eyes blazed and then, no doubt remembering that they were not alone, she said softly, 'You have no idea, have you? No idea what these children's mothers might really think of me and of the strain this situation places me in.'

'Blanche — I'm sorry. You know that I would do anything — indeed, I do as much as I can — to make your life — and Amy's—'

'Your *daughter's*—'

'– life as agreeable as possible.'

'Everything except acknowledge us.'

'How can I?'

'You could div—'

Julian took her arm and, casting a swift glance at the happy scene at the table, he steered his mistress towards the large double doors that led into the magnificent conservatory. He opened one door and ushered her through. The air was humid and the scents of the exotic plants overpowering. Here and there, there were pools of water on the tiled floor from a recent watering. Julian positioned them behind a bank of lush foliage before he turned to speak.

'Divorce Geraldine? Never. My wife' he saw Blanche wince at the word, 'is completely blameless. And, besides, your position as the wife of a divorced man would be only a little better than that of—'

'Your mistress.'

Her mouth twisted unattractively and Julian looked away; however, he could still see their reflections in the large expanse of glass. The skies had clouded over sufficiently to turn the windows of the conservatory into large looking-glasses. Are they thunder clouds? he wondered. He concealed a smile; if they were then it was only fitting, for there was certainly going to be a storm of a more personal kind once Blanche and he were alone together. The thought did not dismay him; in fact he rather looked forward to the tumult – and what it would lead to.

Impulsively he seized her and pulled her into his arms. 'It's not such a bad life, is it? You have this lovely home – all the clothes and more than you and Amy could possibly need. Amy goes to a good school.'

'Yes, yes, all of that, but what galls me is that you can never acknowledge her.'

Julian sighed. 'I'm sorry, Blanche, but you knew I was a married man. You used to tell me that it didn't matter so long as we could be together.'

'Well, that was foolish of me. Now I realize that it does matter.'

'As I say, I'm sorry. But there's nothing to be done.' Julian turned away impatiently and Blanche caught at his arm.

'Don't let us quarrel,' she said. She was smiling. 'Not on our daughter's birthday.'

Julian raised his eyebrows. As quickly as it had gathered he saw that the storm had passed. Or had it? Julian had long ago come to suspect that Blanche knew just how far to push him. He, in turn, had learned to play on her insecurities. No matter how attracted he was to her sexually, he could cast her off if she ever became more tiresome. At least that's what he encouraged her to believe. In truth, he knew he would never do that. Not now. Not since Amy had been born.

Amy. The child was a small and equally imperious version of her mother. Perhaps even more so. And certainly she was already more beautiful. When she grew to womanhood she would be stunning. Julian had been captivated from the moment Blanche had first put the tiny bundle into his arms. No, he would never leave Blanche for that might mean he would lose Amy. His only child.

It was his joy at Amy's birth, a healthy, thriving child, and his guilty feelings towards his wife that had persuaded him to indulge poor Geraldine and allow her to adopt the little waif. And he did his best to be kind to Rosina. But all the time he was with her he was tormented by the feeling that it was Amy who should be enjoying the comforts of his ancestral home and Blanche who should be its chatelaine. She would adorn it so much better than poor worn-out Geraldine.

A burst of laughter from the room behind them and the sound of running feet drew them back towards the table. Matters between them were still unresolved but both knew that there could be no satisfactory solution.

The grand set pieces on the dining table were wrecked. It seemed the little girls had enjoyed the sophisticated savouries and dainty pastries after all – helped by the nursemaids, no doubt. Now the children were running round the table playing some nameless game.

'Perhaps you should put a stop to that,' Julian whispered. 'The little darlings will be sick and you don't want to send them home with spoiled party dresses.'

Blanche clapped her hands and the pandemonium stopped. 'It's time to light the candles on the birthday cake,' she said. 'Mr Leighton, would you do that for us?'

The children sang the birthday song obediently and held their breath when it was time for Amy to blow out the candles. Julian cut the cake but none of the children could manage more than a nibble or two of the dark, rich, fruity confection.

Blanche commanded the nursemaids to gather up the remaining children and lead them quietly and decorously upstairs again to the first-floor drawing room where the conjuror was waiting to perform his magic tricks. The children's eyes rounded with delight. This was obviously a surprise even to Amy. Julian thought that at least one little girl, a fat child in an emerald-green taffeta party dress, looked the worse for wear. Her complexion mirrored the colour of her dress, he thought, amused.

He was grateful once more when he looked at his own child and saw how beautiful she was compared to the other girls. When she was grown she would outshine her mother, he thought. He must find some way of making sure she married well. He could not bear it if she had to endure the second-hand existence that poor Blanche did.

'Are you coming up to see the magic show?' Blanche was halfway to the door.

'Of course.' Julian refrained from asking the cost. He knew very well that this sort of thing was expected at fashionable children's parties, but how different this occasion was from Rosina's birthday party a few weeks ago. Of course, they didn't know the date of the child's birthday. Maud Fidler had not been able to help them, so Geraldine had decided long ago that Rosina should have a birthday in June.

Early summer would be a good time to have birthday celebrations, she reasoned, for, depending on the weather, it might be possible to extend the festivities to the grounds with treasure trails and other garden games. Rosina had had such a party only three weeks ago and Julian couldn't deny that, with its simple foods such as bread and butter, cake and jelly, it had been a great success. But he had been worried about Geraldine. He had insisted that she refrain from joining in the games even though she loved to do so. She mustn't do anything to put herself or the child she was carrying in danger. Dr Lamb had confided in him that this pregnancy, whatever the outcome, would in all likelihood be the last Geraldine was capable of.

Geraldine, although disappointed, did as she was told. Despite her childlike gaiety she was a sensible woman. Long before the party, and in the weeks since, she'd followed the doctor's instructions: resting as much as she could and allowing herself to be cosseted and pampered.

But if only she wouldn't spend so much time with Rosina, Julian thought. Geraldine had assured him that it did no harm to read to the child or participate in a dolls' tea party. If she didn't do that she would be unhappy and bored, she'd said, and surely unhappiness and boredom would be bad for her and the child she was carrying. Julian gave in, persuaded by his wife's good sense but also by his own guilt – as usual.

And now, as he sat with Blanche and watched the conjuror, he had to restrain himself from reaching for her hand. He had no idea why he loved her so much, needed her so much, when he had a perfectly suitable and lovely wife waiting for him at home. Perhaps it was because, despite her imperious ways, Blanche needed him as Geraldine did not. Geraldine had come to him as an heiress, confident of her place in society, and of her beauty. Blanche had come to him as a supplicant. He had found her in the street – literally. She had been weeping outside the door of one of the office buildings in the docks. Her father had died and left her destitute, she explained, and his business partner in the small import company refused to speak to her.

What could Julian do but offer to help? He made investigations and what he discovered was a dismal tale. Blanche's father had gambled away his share of the business before dying of a heart attack. But Julian had managed to extract a small sum of money from his former partner as a gesture of goodwill. Then, somehow, Blanche had become his responsibility. And so it had begun.

Julian made a show of leaving the house before the nursemaids took their young charges home. It would not do for Amy's 'godfather' to look as if he were staying there. He promised Blanche that he would return, as he usually did after dark, and she whispered seductively that she would be waiting.

As he strolled through the pleasant streets towards his other house, the first large drops of rain began to fall. They made wide wet circles on the pavement. Julian quickened his pace in order to avoid a soaking. He started to run and began to laugh, exhilarated by the notion of braving the elements. It was not until he had closed the door behind him that he heard the first rumble of thunder. He had dodged the storm. He took this as an omen that his problems would soon be resolved.

Chapter Six

Blanche looked out of the drawing-room window of the house in the square. The room was on the first floor and she had a pleasant view of the central garden. The trees were drenched, the leaves still dripping. Steam rose from the wooden benches as the sun grew warmer. It was early; not even the rumble of wheels of a delivery cart broke the silence.

She had not been able to sleep and eventually she had risen from her bed, pulled on her robe and rung for her maid. She'd had no compunction about summoning the girl so early. After all, she was paid well.

She had breakfasted alone. Normally she would have waited for Amy to join her but she'd instructed the nurse-maid to let the child sleep. Amy had been exhausted when her party guests went home, exhausted enough, apparently, to sleep through the thunderstorm that had kept her mother awake. Blanche had lain miserably in her bed, diving under the bedclothes at every clap of thunder and wondering why she was having to suffer the frightening experience alone.

Why had Julian not returned?

She could understand his not wanting to get soaked to the skin and she had lain anxiously listening to the rain hurling itself against the windows and willing it to stop. Eventually the sound of the rain became less intense, but intermittent gusts that rattled the windowpanes told her that the weather was wild enough to keep anyone with sense indoors.

But when the wind died down and the rain almost ceased, she had been sure that Julian would brave the short distance and hurry to her bed — and to her arms. But she'd waited in vain, and now she was beginning to panic. Had she annoyed him yesterday with her extravagance and with her reminders of how unsatisfactory her position was? She knew that he would never divorce Geraldine, he had made that clear from the start, but she had never been able to accept the role of mistress, a kept woman. She yearned to take her place in respectable society. She would never be happy as a woman of the demimonde.

Nevertheless, her position would be even worse if she annoyed him so much that he decided to cast her off. She hoped earnestly that it was simply the storm that had kept Julian away and she vowed silently that she would try not to aggravate him in future.

Then, as if in answer to her prayer, she saw Julian's tall figure turn the corner into the square and hurry towards the house. She knew she must appear calm and she took several deep breaths before walking slowly to the escritoire. By the time Julian was shown in she was sitting with a pen in her hand, apparently writing a letter. She turned to him and smiled but the smile died on her lips when she saw his expression.

'Julian . . .' she began, and the pen fell from her hand as she rose to her feet.

He raised a hand to stop her and pointedly glanced towards the maidservant.

There were seconds of pure agony as Julian waited until

the door had closed and then he turned towards her, his expression grave. 'Geraldine . . . has . . .' he said, and his voice was ragged with emotion. 'There was a letter waiting for me at the house. I have a son.'

Blanche felt as though the world was collapsing around her. But if the room swayed she remained rooted to the spot. She couldn't have moved to save her life. An ache of disappointment and regret compressed her body so that she could hardly breathe. The light dimmed. She wondered if people could die of misery.

It's over, she thought. He is full of gratitude to his wife and riven with guilt because he was with me when his son was born. He will return to Northumberland and I will never see him again. She wondered how long she would be permitted to stay in this house. Now that Julian had a son to raise and educate, he would no longer tolerate his mistress's extravagant ways.

'I must go,' he said.

'Of course.' How could she send him on his way with pleasant memories? How could she make sure that he would remember their time together with tender longing? I must congratulate him, she thought, and I must wish him well. 'Julian . . .' she began before she realized that tears were streaming down his face. 'What is it?' she whispered, but already her heart had begun to beat faster.

'My wife . . . she didn't survive the birth.'

Blanche knew that she ought to offer sympathy but hope surged through her veins, bringing her to life again, and she could not force the proper words of condolence from her lips. In order to control her trembling limbs she clenched her fists, hiding them in the folds of her skirt. She must take great care not to reveal her joy. She knew the next words she uttered would be of vital importance.

'You must go to your son immediately,' she said. 'Poor motherless child. Have you made your travel arrangements?'

'My manservant is packing my clothes as we speak. I shall take the midday train.'

'It will be a long journey. Have you had breakfast?'

'No . . . I couldn't eat.'

'And no doubt you didn't sleep much either?'

He stared at her mutely.

'Then I hope you will take some breakfast here . . .' He began to shake his head and she went on hurriedly, 'Well, at least some coffee. You will need all your strength, my dear.'

Blanche crossed to the fireplace and pulled the bell rope. When the maid answered the call, quietly and efficiently Blanche ordered food and drink, and then she ushered Julian downstairs to the dining room. She sat with him at the table and talked softly of practical matters, even daring to mention that he must be very careful who he engaged to look after his newborn son.

She used the expression 'motherless' more than once, and as subtly as possible, she hoped, she began to put the idea in Julian's mind that he must marry again as soon as the mourning period was over. She also told him that he must not hesitate to ask for her help and advice. By the time he left he had recovered his spirits sufficiently to want to embrace her before leaving. But smiling sweetly and sadly she held herself aloof. She knew that her behaviour now must be beyond reproach.

When he had gone she ordered more coffee for herself and as soon as the maid left the room she went to the sideboard and poured herself a glass of brandy. She needed it to sustain her. She was weak with hope and yet filled with steely determination. She thanked the Lord that no one in Northumberland had ever heard of her, for now she had a purpose in life. She must begin the campaign to turn herself from mistress into wife.

Rosina had been told to wait in her room. Early that morning Bridget had helped her to dress in her new black clothes and then had hurried off to the nursery to see to baby George. He was crying. It seemed he had been crying ever since he was born barely a week ago.

'He's missing his mother,' Bridget had told her. 'The poor little mite is heartbroken.'

Rosina didn't see how this could be possible. George had never known his mother, who had died just after he was born, so how could he be missing her? It is I who am missing her, Rosina thought, and she wandered disconsolately over to the window and looked down on the garden.

A sparkling mist hung low above the ornamental pond and drifted in wraiths across the lawn but it was not a cold day. Rosina was uncomfortably warm. Her dress, which had been hurriedly made for her by the sewing woman who came in from the village to do the mending, was coarse and scratchy. Miss Fidler had produced the crepe material from the linen store, where it must have been mouldering for years, from the smell of it.

The bottom of the window had been raised a little, and when Rosina sat down on the window seat she could hear, very faintly, the church bells ringing in the village church. But this was different from the lively peals that summoned everyone to worship on Sunday. A solitary bell rang out slowly and mournfully. She had never heard anything that made her so sad – and at the same time struck terror into her heart. Quickly she used both hands to push the lower casement closed and she leaped off the window seat and ran across the room.

But now she could hear another sad sound – that of her

baby brother crying a thin hopeless wail that ended in gulping sobs. Instinctively she knew that he was hungry rather than heartbroken and she hoped that Bridget would soon have his feeding bottle ready.

I wonder if Bridget knows I am still waiting, she thought. She began to look around her room, seeking comfort in its familiarity. She loved this room, with its cheerful buttercup-yellow walls and the storybook friezes chosen by her mother. Rosina kept her room neat and tidy without being asked. There was not a toy or a picture-book out of place. She liked it like that. Every day before bedtime she began to put her toys away without being asked. To see the books arranged neatly on the shelves and the dolls sitting politely at their little tea table gave her a sense of pleasure that she was too young to understand.

Her mother had not been tidy. When she came to play with her she would pull books from the shelves until she found the one she wanted and leave those she didn't want scattered on the floor. Or if they had been dressing the dolls she would toss the unwanted dresses aside, sometimes letting them lie on the floor along with the books. When Geraldine Leighton had gone, Bridget would tut-tut and explain to Rosina that her mother had been brought up as a little rich girl should be and had maids to tidy her things for her right from the minute she was born.

But the dolls' house. Oh, how Rosina would despair when her mother rearranged the tiny pieces of furniture, placing them anywhere, seemingly having no idea which piece belonged in each room. Rosina would wait until her mother had gone before she began to tidy things properly. But they had such fun together, played such games, read such stories, that Rosina was prepared to forgive her mother anything. Except for leaving her alone like this.

Bridget said that her mother had gone to heaven to be with the angels. Well, why couldn't she have taken me with her? Rosina thought. And baby George too. Bridget had seen the expression on her face and had kneeled swiftly and taken her in her arms. 'Your mother didn't want to leave you, you know.'

'Then why did she?'

'Because God decided it was her time to go.'

'But that's cruel.'

'You mustn't let anyone hear you say that,' Bridget had told her.

'Why?'

'Because you must never question what God does. That would be wicked.'

'Then I must be wicked because I can't help questioning Him,' Rosina had said and then both she and Bridget had cried along with each other.

Eventually Bridget had wiped the tears from both their faces, and taken Rosina to sit on her knee in the comfortable chair by the hearth and cuddled her as if she were a baby. 'You'll have to be brave, Rosina. Nothing will bring your mother back, but you have George, your little brother and you can help me look after him. Your mother, God rest her soul, would like that.'

'Would she?'

'I'm sure of it.'

But Rosina had not been allowed to help with George, not allowed to hold him. Dr Lamb had told them it would be better if he was not handled too much because he was not thriving as he should be.

Where was everybody and why had she been told to wait here in her room? Rosina, usually obedient, felt thoroughly unsettled and she went to the door and opened it. How quiet the house was. George must have settled to his feeding bottle for he had stopped crying. Rosina could imagine him being held in Bridget's arms while she fed him. The only sound she could hear now was the ticking of the grandfather clock echoing up from the hall below.

Rosina went downstairs quietly and stood for a moment looking up at the face of the clock. The circle bearing the numbers and pointers was set in a square with a bouquet of flowers in each corner. Flowers of spring, summer, autumn and winter. And above the face there was a pretty painted arch where a moon with a painted face moved across a painted sky. Her mother had told her that this showed the phases of the moon.

Above the moon, curving round the arched sky, there were some words written. Rosina had learned to read long ago, taught by her mother from the storybooks they both loved so much. She had read the words on the clock face many times without thinking about them. Now she looked at them again.

'As the hours pass so passes the life of man.'

Suddenly she knew what they meant and she shivered. Every moment of her beloved mother's married life had been measured by this clock. And now it was over. Rosina would never again be able to pause here and look at the flowers, or the moon moving slowly across the heavens, without crying. With tears streaming down her face she turned and ran through the first open door. She found herself in the dining room, but immediately stopped and looked around in confusion.

The furniture had been rearranged. The big, old dining table had been moved against one of the walls and the chairs placed in little groups around the sides of the room. Other chairs must have been brought from other rooms because there were far more than usually fitted around the table.

Rosina went to look at the table. A great deal of food had been arranged on plates on the snowy white cloth. There were savoury pastries, small pies and tartlets, tiny sandwiches and fancy cakes, also jugs of water and bottles of wine. It looked as though the table had been set for a party. But how could Father think of having a party today, the very day when they were going to bury Mother in the cold ground?

Last night Bridget had come to Rosina's room and woken her up. She had put on her dressing gown and told her to hold her hand and come with her.

'Where are we going?' Rosina had asked.

'You're going to kiss your mammy,' Bridget replied.

'But I don't understand,' Rosina said. 'My mother has gone to heaven, you said so.'

'Hush, child. Just come with me. And you must be quiet as a mouse. No one knows I am doing this but I thought it only right.'

Rosina slipped her hand into Bridget's and went with her along the corridor and down the stairs. As they crept through the dark and silent house Rosina's heart was filled with joyous hope. Her mother had returned. She had been to heaven and decided that no matter that the angels welcomed her, she would rather be at home with her children.

'Where is she?' she whispered. 'In here?'

They had stopped at the door of the drawing room. It was a large, cold room that was hardly ever used. It was too big for everyday use. Her mother preferred her own cheerful sitting room and her father preferred the library, or they would sit together in the garden room.

Bridget took up an oil lamp from a table near the door of the drawing room. 'Now,' she said, 'let's go in.'

'Is my mother in there?'

'Yes.'

Bridget opened the door and paused. She gripped Rosina's hand more tightly and then they walked together into the room. The light from the single oil lamp hardly pierced the shadows ahead but as Rosina's eyes became accustomed to the gloom she saw that the curtains were closed and the furniture seemed to be shrouded in swathes and loops of black material. The large mirror that hung over the mantelshelf was completely covered by more black fabric and in between where they stood just inside the door and the hearth, Rosina could distinguish a shape that was completely unfamiliar.

It looked like a long low table, but it also was draped in black, and on the table there rested a wooden box. Standing on the floor, surrounding the table and the box, there were large vases and urns containing flowers; large white flowers that gave off a strange, sweet, waxy smell. Rosina found the smell overwhelming and she began to back away.

'No, it's all right, my bairn,' Bridget said. 'There's no need to be frightened.'

'I'm not frightened. But I don't like it here. And where's my mother?'

'She's in her coffin. Resting there as peaceful and gentle as the angel she always was. Now you must come and kiss her goodbye.'

'Goodbye? But I thought she had come back. Is she going away again?'

Rosina was utterly confused but she allowed Bridget to lead her towards the long box on the low table. Now Rosina saw that it was made of highly polished wood. The lamplight flickered and shone on its sides and on the shiny brass handles. Bridget let go of her hand for a moment and, slipping an arm round Rosina's waist, she hoisted her up, holding her precariously balanced on her hip while she tried to keep the lamp in her other hand steady. The shadows leaped and flickered across the walls and ceiling until Bridget regained her balance.

'There she is. She looks so peaceful. You can look down now.'

Rosina did as she was told. The box was lined with quilted white satin and there was a little pillow under her mother's head. Geraldine Leighton looked as though she was sleeping. She was dressed in a beautiful white gown; she looked like a princess – or a bride. Her hands were crossed, resting on her breast, and she lay still, so very still that Rosina wondered how she would ever wake her to say goodbye. And then she remembered that Bridget had told her to kiss her.

'If I kiss her will she wake up,' Rosina asked, 'like Sleeping Beauty?'

'No, my poor bairn, she won't wake up, never again. But in years to come you would never forgive yourself – nor me – if you didn't say a proper goodbye. Now lean over – gently does it. I don't want to drop the lamp. There you are – kiss her forehead.'

Rosina placed her lips on her mother's forehead. Her mother's skin was cold, so very cold. Bridget eased Rosina up again and, just as carefully, set her down on the floor.

'What are they going to do with Mama?' Rosina asked.

'The same as they do with all folk who depart this world. Tomorrow is her funeral.'

'Funeral?'

'They'll take her to the church and pray for her soul and then they will bury her.'

'Bury her? In the ground? But she'll be cold.'

'No, dear. Your mother won't be cold and she won't feel pain. Not ever again. Her spirit is in heaven with the angels. Didn't I tell you? Now, back to bed. And don't ever tell anyone about this. Your father didn't think it necessary for you to say goodbye but I didn't think that was right so I've risked my job to bring you here.'

Bridget had taken her back to bed and tucked her in. She had sat with her until they heard baby George begin to cry.

'I'll have to go, pet,' Bridget had told her. 'The new lass they've taken on to help me hasn't mastered the feeding bottles yet. Now go to sleep. I'll come in the morning to get you ready for the funeral.'

Rosina slept uneasily but then she had the most amazing dream. She was sitting with her mother in a beautiful garden that seemed to be floating on clouds. She didn't know why but she knew this was heaven. She looked up at her mother's face and saw that she was crying.

'Why are you crying, Mama?' she asked.

'Because you have to go now, Rosina.'

'No, I want to stay here with you.'

'You cannot stay, my darling.'

Her mother got up and took her hand. She led her to a gate made of golden bars and opened it. Before Rosina knew what was happening she found herself on the other side of the gate. She pushed at the bars but it wouldn't open.

'Goodbye, Rosina,' her mother said, and she walked away into the garden. She didn't look back.

And then the whole garden seemed to float away into the sky and Rosina was left in a cold dark place. She opened her eyes and found herself in bed. Her cheeks were wet with tears.

Bridget had come early for her and dressed her in her new black clothes as she'd promised, and then she had said that she must go and see to George but that Rosina must wait in her room until someone came for her. But she'd waited and waited and no one had come.

Rosina was hungry. She had not had any breakfast and she looked at the array of food on the table and thought she might take something. There was a plate piled high with little white iced fancies. She reached out to take one.

'Goodness gracious, what are you doing in here, child?'

Rosina spun round and saw Miss Fidler staring at her. Rosina dropped the cake in fright and then stumbled so that it was trodden into the carpet.

'Look what you've done!'

Miss Fidler swept over to the hearth and pulled the bell rope. Rosina knelt down and tried to pick up cake crumbs and pieces of icing.

'Leave that and get up.'

Rosina did as she was told and stared at Miss Fidler. Her mother's companion, dressed all in black, was a frightening figure. Rosina wondered what would happen next but Miss Fidler simply stared at her disapprovingly. When a parlour maid came into the room she turned and said, 'Fetch a brush and dustpan. Clear up that mess – and find Bridget. Tell her to come here.'

Until the maid returned there was absolute silence. Rosina, mortified, looked down at the mess she had made. Miss Fidler stood where she was, making no attempt to approach her. Rosina felt tears pricking at her eyes. Since her mother had died this house had become an unwelcoming and forbidding place. She had not seen her father since he had left for London some weeks ago, although she knew he had come home the day after her mother died. No one except

Bridget had spoken to her. Until now. And Miss Fidler was obviously very cross.

The maid came back and, getting to her knees, she began to brush the carpet vigorously with a hand brush.

'I'm sorry,' Rosina whispered, and the young woman looked up and smiled at her.

'Don't worry, pet. Just move back a little so that I can get all those crumbs. Oh, look, there's a bit of icing stuck to your shoe. Hold still, I'll get it. There you are. Now for this carpet. We'd better have everything shipshape before they get back from the church.'

'Get back?'

'Aye, they've gone to your ma's funeral. Didn't you know?'

'Be quiet, girl,' Miss Fidler snapped, and then turned to Bridget, who had just entered the room. 'Why is Rosina in here?' she asked. 'I told you to keep her in her room.'

'But I thought Miss Rosina was going to the funeral – I thought you would be taking her. I'm sure you said so last night.'

'Yes, well, plans were changed. But that does not excuse you. I came back early from the church to see if the funeral tea has been set out properly and I found Rosina in here eating cakes.'

'I only took one cake,' Rosina said. 'And I've had no breakfast.'

The parlour maid had finished sweeping up the crumbs and she stood up and smiled sympathetically at Rosina.

'And it's not Bridget's fault,' Rosina said.

'I beg your pardon!' Miss Fidler exclaimed.

The parlour maid hurried from the room.

'Bridget told me to stay in my room,' Rosina said. 'I didn't do as I was told.'

'I haven't time to discuss this now,' Miss Fidler said. 'I can hear the carriages arriving. Bridget, take the child back upstairs and make sure she stays there for the duration of the funeral tea.'

'I will, Miss Fidler, but may I ask you something?'

The older woman frowned impatiently. 'If you must.'

'Why were the plans changed? Why did you not take Miss Rosina to her mother's funeral? Did you forget all about her?'

'How dare you speak to me like that? Of course I didn't. It was not my decision to leave her behind. Mr Leighton did not want her at the church.'

Rosina looked from one to the other. Both women were angry but for different reasons. She sensed that Bridget was angry on her behalf and that Miss Fidler, usually so strict with all the maids, was somehow ill at ease.

Bridget shook her head as if she didn't believe what she had just heard. 'Didn't want her there,' she muttered. 'That's a fine thing.'

'The guests will be here any moment,' Miss Fidler said. 'You'd better go.'

'Very well.' Bridget took Rosina's hand. 'I shall take her upstairs but I'm not going to leave her alone in her room. Not today of all days. She shall come to the nursery with me.'

'But baby George——' Miss Fidler began.

'I know he's weakly but at the moment he is fast asleep in his crib. And I can see no reason why having his sister in the room with him should harm him.'

Bridget swept out of the room, taking Rosina with her. Miss Fidler followed them into the hall but she turned and walked towards the front door. She opened it. Rosina glanced down and saw her stand back respectfully as the funeral party began to descend from their carriages. They were all in black. Her father was one of the first to enter the house.

'There's Father,' Rosina said, and she paused. She wanted to run down again and go to him but Bridget held on to her tightly.

'Come away, pet. Don't bother him now. No doubt his grief has affected him terribly to make him behave so badly.'

'My father has behaved badly?' Rosina looked up questioningly.

'I shouldn't have said that. I'm sure he loves you, even if it's for the sake of your poor mama.'

Rosina was bewildered. She had never questioned the fact that her father loved her. It was true that he did not spend as much time with her as her mother did, but she thought all fathers were like that. Certainly Adam had told her that his father's business affairs often kept him from home for days on end. But whenever she did see her father he would smile and sometimes question her about what she had been doing that day.

But now it seemed that she had lost not only the mother she adored but, in a way she couldn't understand, she might have lost her father too. Suddenly she clung all the more tightly to Bridget's hand. Bridget, at least, did not seem to have changed.

'There, there, my little lass,' Bridget said, and she stooped to wipe the tears from Rosina's cheeks.

Later that day, after the mourners had gone home, Julian closeted himself in the library with Josiah Atkinson, his late wife's solicitor. The two men talked for at least an hour and when the old man took his leave Julian stayed where he was at his desk and stared moodily at the papers spread before him.

He acknowledged there was little to be dissatisfied with. In fact, Geraldine's death had left him better off financially then he had expected. Atkinson had explained that certain stocks and shares held in her name had doubled in value recently and, as Geraldine had no close relatives, she had willed everything to Julian. Everything, that is, save the bequest she had made to Rosina.

Julian had never really thought about it, so confident had he been that he would be his wife's sole heir. But it seemed that Geraldine must not have trusted him to provide for the child, for she had left her an inheritance in her own right. But at least Julian was to administer that inheritance until Rosina was twenty-one years old or married, whichever came first. It seemed Julian would have to assume ongoing responsibility for the child. There was no reason why he shouldn't; he had agreed to adopt her, after all.

He examined his feelings about Rosina and realized so long as Geraldine had been alive he had been happy enough to have the girl living here at Ravenshill. It had made Geraldine happy and for that he was grateful. Perhaps that happiness had led to the successful pregnancy and in that case he should be grateful to Rosina. But he couldn't force himself to love the child as much as Geraldine had done. Rosina was not his flesh and blood as George was.

George . . . his son. Poor, brave Geraldine had died giving birth to the heir he longed for. It would be betraying her trust if he did not care for Rosina as best he could. He would do his duty.

Just after Geraldine Leighton's death in childbirth, Maud Fidler and her brother, Jack, had exchanged anxious letters. Maud had expressed her fear that Julian, who had never loved Rosina in the way Geraldine had, would send the child away.

Jack had thought he would not do that but, if he did, it would probably be to some distant girls' boarding school. But whatever happened Maud must remain vigilant. Daisy Belle's fame was growing. She was about to set off to conquer London. It was more important than ever that Rosina's existence remained a secret.

Maud sometimes wondered if her brother, rather than arranging a kidnap, would have preferred the child to die.

Chapter Seven

December 1889

'It's very good of you to have Rosina here so much, Sybil.'

Sybil Loxley's elder sister, Muriel, stood at the window and watched her niece and nephew running round the garden with their friend Rosina Leighton. The lawn was frosted over and the children's footprints made tracks in the grass. As they laughed and called to each other, their breath left trails in the cold air. They were well wrapped in sturdy winter coats but Adam's mother had decided they had been out in the cold long enough and had sent a maidservant to bring them in. They would take tea in the nursery.

When the young maid appeared in the garden, her cheeks and her nose were bright pink and the sharp wind caught at her cap and would have blown it off had it not been secured with a hairpin. The children looked disappointed to have to abandon their game but they followed her back to the house obediently enough. Satisfied that her bidding had been done, Sybil turned to her sister and adopted an expression of someone who knew one's duty.

'*Noblesse oblige,*' she said.

'Oh – er – that's right.'

Muriel wasn't quite sure what *noblesse oblige* meant but she had a vague idea that it was to do with the better class of person having to do one's duty. Sybil moved in exalted circles since her marriage – and she never let an opportunity slip by when she could remind her older unmarried sister of this.

They had grown up together in a comfortable farmhouse. Their father worked hard and had prospered. Sybil, with her robust good looks, had done well to marry Hugh, a respectable solicitor and land agent, one who dealt with the property and business affairs of the gentry, whereas comfortable, homely Muriel had never married. She had stayed at home to help her parents. The fact that there were no sons and that one day she would inherit the farm did not really make up for the fact that her younger sister now moved in a different world. But at least Sybil invited Muriel to stay now and then.

'Will you have Rosina here for Christmas?'

With one last look at the garden, now silent as the shadows began to lengthen, Sybil turned from the window and made her way to the fireplace. 'Come and sit down,' she bade her sister. 'I told the girl to bring us tea by the fire.'

Muriel concealed a smile. Her sister never called her servants anything but 'the girl', even the older women. She never spoke to them unless she was giving an order and Muriel suspected that Sybil was heartily disliked by all who worked for her. The tray of tea and scones arrived and was placed on a small table. Sybil waved her hand dismissively and Muriel thanked the maidservant, who gave her a startled glance and a smile before she left the room.

'As for Rosina Leighton,' Sybil continued once they were settled with cups of tea and hot buttered scones, 'I offered to have her here as I did last Christmas but this year it's not necessary.'

'Not necessary?'

'Well, last year I simply don't know how Julian Leighton would have managed without the help of good friends and neighbours,' she allowed herself a brief self-satisfied smile, 'he was so distressed, poor man.'

'Naturally.'

'And it wouldn't have done to celebrate Christmas while he was in deep mourning.'

'Of course not.'

'He told me he couldn't bear the idea of Christmas at Ravenshill without Geraldine and he went off to London. He has a house there, you know.'

'I didn't. But why did he not take Rosina with him?'

'Oh, the London house wouldn't have been suitable for the child. That's what he said.'

'But he was prepared to leave her alone at Ravenshill?'

'Really, Muriel, don't look and sound so critical. The poor man was in a state of deep distress.'

'So you said. So you took pity on Rosina?'

'Well, it was Adam's idea, actually. He felt sorry for her. He asked me if she could come to stay over Christmas. When I considered the suggestion I decided it was a good idea.'

I'm sure you did, Muriel thought. She had noticed how her sister liked to keep in with the gentry and in this she was encouraged by her husband. Hugh was a clever man and he knew being thought well of brought in more business. Muriel had often speculated about her nephew's friendship with Rosina Leighton. Adam seemed much attached to the girl. She wondered if her sister encouraged the friendship simply because the Leightons were an important family, but decided to give her the benefit of the doubt and ascribe her good deeds to her nature, which could be kindly so long as it did not interfere with her own comfort.

'But you say that this year Rosina will not be spending Christmas with you?' Muriel took up the conversation.

'No.' Sybil gazed over her teacup. 'As I said, there's no need.'

Muriel was vexed. Sybil's expression, the pursed lips, the eyes wide with some sort of excitement, hinted that she was holding something back. 'Are you going to tell me why?' Muriel asked, barely concealing her impatience.

'Well...' Sybil replaced her cup and saucer on the little table and leaned towards her sister in a gesture that signified she didn't want anyone else to hear what she was about to say. This vexed sensible Muriel even further. There was no one else in the room – unless Sybil suspected there was someone hiding in that ridiculous suit of armour that Hugh had brought home from a house clearance.

'For goodness' sake, get on with it,' Muriel said.

'He's got married.'

'What? Who?' Muriel was perplexed.

'I thought that would surprise you,' Sybil said with a satisfied smirk.

'Maybe I would be surprised if I knew who you were talking about! Oh...I see...Mr Leighton has married again.'

'That's right. And nobody knows yet except Hugh and me.' Sybil put another scone on her plate and sat back with it. She took a bite and a dribble of butter ran down her chin. She looked like one of the fat farm cats who had managed to get at the cream. She dabbed at her chin with a napkin and then, through a mouthful of crumbs, she continued, 'He had to tell us because he wanted us to keep Rosina while he went to London.'

'London again.'

'Yes. The new Mrs Leighton is a young widow whom he met through some business acquaintances. That's where she lives – London – and that's where they were married just a day or so ago. He's bringing her and the child back to Northumberland tomorrow.'

'The child? Do you mean he took baby George to London with him?'

'Of course not. George is at home with the nursemaid, and there's that funny old stick Maud Fidler to oversee things. The child he is bringing home is the widow's daughter, Amy. I understand she is about the same age as Rosina.'

'That's nice.'

'What do you mean?'

'Well, she will be company for Rosina, won't she? I've often wondered about her rattling around alone in that great old house. And she will have a mother to take care of her instead of having to rely on the kindness of servants.'

'I suppose so.' Sybil looked thoughtful and Muriel wondered whether she was worried that Mr Leighton would not need her help in future; whether she would lose her little bit of influence.

'It's a bit soon, though, isn't it?' Muriel asked.

'Soon?'

'I mean for him to marry again. What is it – seventeen, eighteen months since his wife died?'

'Seventeen. And yes, I suppose it is soon, but it seems to be more acceptable these days for a man to marry during the mourning period. Especially if he has children to care for. He can even shed his mourning black for the wedding day although his new wife will have to take up half-mourning as soon as the wedding is over.'

'Poor thing.'

'Oh, don't feel sorry for her. She won't have to wear full mourning black and, besides, I'm sure that London fashions, being so far in advance of what can be bought in Newcastle, will have provided her with the most attractive silks in pansy or lilac. The annoying thing is that she won't be able to invite people home for a while – and likewise I won't be able to have her here.'

'You'll just have to be patient,' Muriel said.

Sybil sighed. 'I suppose so. Well, here's hoping that the new Mrs Leighton will recognize her obligations to those who have helped her husband in this most difficult of times.'

'When does Rosina go home?' Muriel asked.

'Not until Christmas Eve. Mr Leighton explained that he wants to allow his new wife and her child some time to settle in.'

'Poor little mite.'

'Yes, I suppose it will be bewildering for her to be uprooted and brought to a new home. After all, she has been brought up in London.'

Sybil said this as if London was the pinnacle of existence whereas Northumberland was the back of beyond. Muriel suppressed her irritation. 'I didn't mean Amy,' she said. 'I meant Rosina. Not only is she to have a stepmother and a stepsister, but she has been sent away while they move into her home. What does she feel about her father getting married again?'

'She doesn't know yet.'

'She doesn't know?'

'Don't look at me like that. It's not my job to tell her and, in any case, that's what Mr Leighton wants. He thought it best for it to be a lovely surprise.'

Muriel stared at Sybil in astonishment. It was obvious

that she thought there was nothing wrong with this arrangement. Fond of her though she was, Muriel had to admit that her younger sister was both shallow and a little stupid. For goodness' sake, she was a mother herself – could she not imagine what it would be like for Rosina, who had loved her mother dearly, to go home completely unprepared to find that someone had taken her place?

During her visits to Sybil and Hugh, Muriel had come to know Adam's playmate and she thought Rosina a thoroughly nice little girl. She was energetic and imaginative, and what's more, she was thoughtful and polite. No doubt she owed her good manners to the late Mrs Leighton, poor lady, who everyone knew had doted on her. And Adam, whom Muriel had a soft spot for, had certainly taken to Rosina. Even Adam's younger sister, Charlotte, who could be both difficult and sulky, was easier to handle when Rosina came to stay.

But what of this other child, Amy? Would she welcome having Rosina for a sister? And the new Mrs Leighton? She already had a daughter of her own so would she prove a loving mother to her stepdaughter? Muriel hoped so fervently, but to her way of thinking this was a bad beginning.

Bridget was sent to bring Rosina home. In the carriage on the way back to Ravenshill Rosina was full of chatter about the games she and Adam had played and the jolly times they'd had, but Bridget hardly spoke.

Then, when they were almost there, she said, 'Rosina, you must be prepared for a surprise.'

Rosina's smile almost broke the young maid's heart. 'A nice surprise?'

'Well, I suppose so.' In fact Bridget doubted very much

whether it was a nice surprise. Just a few days with the new Mrs Leighton as mistress of Ravenshill had made the household staff regret anew the passing of their kindly mistress.

'Has my father come home?' Rosina asked.

'Yes, that is why he sent for you.'

'And he has brought me something from London?'

'Yes . . . well . . . in a manner of speaking. Look, I'm not supposed to tell you so don't ask any more questions. But, remember, whatever happens, I loved your ma and I love you too.'

It was obvious that Bridget was troubled about something so Rosina kept quiet. When they reached home Bridget helped her down from the carriage, and Rosina, spurred by curiosity, ran up the front steps and arrived breathless at the door as it opened.

Miss Fidler stood there. She took one look at Rosina and said, 'I think you should go to your room and wash your face and comb your hair. Bridget, go with Miss Rosina and see that she is made presentable, then take her to the drawing room.'

Rosina supposed she was being tidied up to meet her father. On the way through the hall and up the stairs she noticed with pleasure that the house had been decorated with evergreen garlands for Christmas. There had been none last Christmas and, for a moment, she was saddened to remember why. She had been glad to go to Adam's house then, although nothing truly assuaged her misery. But Ravenshill was her home and the memories of Christmas with her mother were happy as well as sad, and she was glad that she and her father would be here together this year.

Bridget fussed over her more than she usually did, brushing her hair and tying her ribbons just so and, when she was pleased with the result, she stood back and examined Rosina critically.

'I want you to look your best,' she said, and then they went downstairs again.

Rosina wondered why they were going to the drawing room. It was formal and cold and hardly ever used. In fact, the last time she could remember going in there was the night she had seen her mother in her coffin and kissed her goodbye. But today Bridget knocked and, on hearing the command to enter, she opened the door and they went in together. Rosina gasped in surprise. A fire blazed in the hearth, the mantelshelf was decorated with holly and a large Christmas tree stood in one corner. It was covered with baubles that shone and sparkled as they caught the reflection of the firelight. The air, instead of being cold and musty, was warm and scented with pine.

'Ah, come in, Rosina,' her father said, and she ran towards him. 'Don't run!' he exclaimed and then, puzzlingly he added, 'I'm sorry about that.'

It was only then that Rosina noticed the other people in the room. A lady she had never seen before was sitting on the sofa near the hearth, and beside her was a blonde-haired girl of about Rosina's age.

'Don't scold the poor child,' the lady said as she rose with a rustle of silk and went to stand beside Rosina's father. 'You can't blame her for being eager to see you, Julian. And, don't worry, we will soon teach her proper manners. Life will be easier for you, my dear, now that I am here. Bridget, you may go.'

When the door had closed behind Bridget, Julian Leighton frowned. 'Rosina, close your mouth,' he said, and she realized that she had been staring at the lady in open-mouthed wonder.

'I'm sorry,' she mumbled, and she waited for enlightenment.

During the silence that followed the girl on the sofa laughed. 'What a little savage,' she said.

'Hush, Amy,' the lady said. 'You must not talk of your sister in those terms.'

'She's not my sister.'

'Your stepsister then. For I am married to her father and therefore I am Rosina's stepmother.' She glanced sideways at Rosina's father. 'But I hope the dear child will call me Mama.' She looked down at Rosina, who felt as though she were being judged and found wanting, for the lady's smile was thin. 'So you are Rosina,' she said.

'Yes, Mrs Leighton.'

'Oh, my dear, you must call me Mama.' She glanced at Julian as if appealing to him to intervene.

'Of course she must,' Rosina's father said, and then he cleared his throat. 'Rosina, this is your new mama.'

'I don't want a new one,' Rosina cried involuntarily, and immediately the atmosphere in the room chilled.

'Apologize at once,' her father said. He sounded angry.

'Why? Why must I say sorry?'

'Because you have been rude to Mrs Leighton – my wife – a lady who is prepared to love you like a mother loves her child.'

Rosina stared up at the lady. Her dress of lavender taffeta shone in the firelight. She was not pretty as her mother had been but, child though she was, Rosina could see the elegance of her poise and the elaborate way she wore her hair. She looked like a picture in one of her mother's magazines. She heard a gentle sigh and looked up to see that the lady looked distressed.

'We have made a bad beginning, dear child,' the lady said.

'But I forgive you. You would not be natural if you did not love your dear departed mother but, now, I am here and I want to fill that place in your heart. Come,' she held her hand out, 'shall we resolve to be friends?'

Though her voice was soft, Rosina sensed an underlying determination and, unwillingly, she took the lady's hand.

'Come and sit beside us here,' the lady said, and she drew Rosina towards the sofa. She sat down beside her daughter and indicated that Rosina should sit on her other side.

'There now, Julian,' she said, and she looked up towards Rosina's father. 'Your wife and both your daughters sitting together amicably. Don't we make a pretty picture?'

'You do. But I have not heard Rosina apologize.'

'Oh, let the child be, my dear. I don't mind.'

'But I do. Rosina – I am waiting.'

The lady who said she was her stepmother was holding her hand tightly. Rosina would have loved to pull away but she knew that would annoy her father even more. She felt herself take a shuddering breath and as she gulped in air she could smell her stepmother's perfume. It was heady and potent, not at all like her mother's light, refreshing rose perfume.

'I – I'm sorry,' Rosina said.

'That's right,' her father said. 'I want you to realize how lucky you are and not cause any trouble.'

'Yes, Papa.'

'I'm sure she won't,' her stepmother said. 'And now Rosina may go to her room. I think it better if she has her tea there today. She has a lot to reflect on.'

Rosina looked at her father. She wasn't sure whether she was being sent to her room as a punishment. His expression did not reassure her.

'Run along,' he said.

Rosina's hand was released and she slid off the sofa. But when she turned to go she caught her foot in her stepmother's skirt. To her horror she heard the material rip.

'Look what you've done!' the other girl exclaimed. 'Mama, the little beast had ruined your frock.'

Amy got off the sofa and kneeled down to examine a tear in the hem.

'Hush, Amy darling, the damage is slight. It will easily be mended.'

'I'm sorry,' Rosina whispered. She could feel hot tears pricking at the back of her eyes. Neither her stepmother nor her stepsister looked up at her.

'You'd better go,' her father said. His voice was cold.

At the door she turned back to look at the group near the fire. Her stepmother was looking up at her father. 'Julian,' she said. 'It's so lovely and warm here near the fire. Why don't we get a small table brought in and have our afternoon tea here together, just the three of us; like the family we are.'

Her father smiled. 'If you wish, my dear.'

And then Rosina could hold back her tears no longer. She was not wanted here. She turned and ran to the door. Before she left the room she looked back once more. Neither her father nor her stepmother was watching her. But Amy was. Her blue eyes stared at Rosina coldly and on her face there was a look of pure malice.

When she reached the sanctuary of her room Rosina flung herself on her bed and wept for her mother as she had never wept before.

That evening, as Blanche sat at her dressing table, she reflected that she had handled the situation well. She knew she must always give the impression of caring for Rosina, at least until she had discovered how much Julian cared for his adopted daughter. Even if he didn't love her the same way he loved Amy, his own flesh and blood, he would always have a lingering affection for the child Geraldine had adored.

And even if it became apparent that he did not care for the child at all, Blanche knew that to all outward appearance she must remain a loving mother for the sake of her reputation. She knew that the local gentry would regard her with suspicion and she must not give them any reason to criticize her or her behaviour.

But how aggravating it was to have the child in the house at all. Amy was Julian's daughter, and yet she could not be acknowledged as such. George was the heir, of course, and how grateful she was that Geraldine had managed to give birth to a living child, and that a boy too. She knew full well that if George had not survived the birth Julian would never have married her. He would have felt compelled to find a healthy much younger wife of good family, who would provide an heir for Ravenshill. Geraldine's death and George's survival had freed Julian to follow his heart. And I am the mistress here, she thought with satisfaction.

She turned her attention to her reflection in the mirror. She had dressed for dinner in grey silk and had put up her hair with the help of that plain-faced woman Maud Fidler. Fidler had been Geraldine's maid-companion, Julian had told her, and had been responsible for finding the unfortunate child Rosina. But it was strange, he said, that although Geraldine would be forever grateful to Maud Fidler, a coolness seemed to have grown between them. He thought it was something to do with Fidler becoming too close to the child but, having met the woman, Blanche doubted that.

Whatever the truth of it had been, she knew that Fidler would not do for her. She would find a younger, properly trained lady's maid. Perhaps she would persuade Julian to allow her to engage someone from one of the superior domestic agencies in London; she doubted if she would find a person of sufficient refinement in Newcastle. But she had to admit that Fidler had not done a bad job with her hair. It was only the reflection of the unsmiling face in her dressing-table mirror that had prompted Blanche to dismiss Fidler, saying she would manage to put on her jewellery herself.

She took a pair of cabochon garnet earrings set in gold from her jewellery box, put them on and then paused with her hand resting lightly on her throat before reaching for the matching necklace. After a moment's thought she returned the necklace and earrings to the box and leaned down to open one of the bottom drawers of the dressing table.

There they were, a tempting collection of leather jewellery rolls and cases that contained Geraldine's jewellery. Blanche had discovered them as soon as she had arrived. On learning with dismay that the room she and Julian were to share was the very room that he had shared with his first wife – and in which she had died – Blanche had opened every drawer and cupboard to make sure that all Geraldine's clothes and belongings had been removed.

'It's the best suite of rooms in the house,' Julian had told her. 'There's a bathroom, a small sitting room and a dressing room, as well as a small room for me if I should come in late and not wish to disturb you. There just isn't anywhere else suitable. But I've had everything of Geraldine's taken away.'

She had given a forbearing smile and not told him that something had been missed. Geraldine's jewellery. She wanted time to think what to do – or rather to go about what she had already decided. He might think it bad taste if she should bring the matter up too soon, but even a cursory look at the contents of the boxes had inspired her with the desire to own every last piece of it.

Some of it was old – heirlooms, perhaps? – and the stones would need resetting, especially the emeralds, but some was just perfect – better than anything Blanche had ever owned. Had Julian bought these pieces for his wife? Even at a time when she, Blanche, was already his mistress? He must have done. Bitter rage surged through her veins. Well, she was Julian's wife now. The jewels should belong to her.

Blanche wondered if she dared wear some of the pieces tonight. Perhaps those tiny rose diamond drops shaped like flowers and the matching necklace? They were wrapped in a velvet roll and she placed it on the dressing table and opened it up. The diamonds sparkled in the lamplight. She lifted up one of the earrings and let it dangle from her fingers, admiring the delicate workmanship. She held it against one of her ears. If Julian said anything – and he surely would – she could tell him that as she had found them in the dressing-table drawer she had assumed that he meant her to wear them.

But no sooner had she thought this than she realized it wouldn't do. He would never believe her to be so naïve and she did not wish him to think her greedy and acquisitive.

'What have you got there?'

Blanche started guiltily and turned to see that Julian had just entered the room.

'Oh . . . just . . . I found . . .'

'Geraldine's jewellery. Do you know, I had forgotten all about it.'

'Had you?'

'I suppose I'd better put it away. Pity really.'

Blanche had turned away from him and concentrated on putting the earrings and brooch back in the jewellery roll. Then glancing briefly in the looking-glass, she saw that Julian was smiling at her affectionately.

'Why a pity?' she asked as she picked up her garnet earrings and replaced them in her ears. She held her breath while she waited for his reply.

'Because I'd like to give them all to you.'

Avarice got the better of her and she knew that she sounded too eager when she asked, 'Then why can't you?' Julian sighed and shook his head. She endeavoured to soften her tone and inject it with sympathy. 'Oh, I see, it's too early, isn't it? We must wait a little longer before you can hand on Geraldine's possessions.'

'If only that were the problem,' he said. 'Blanche, my love, I'm afraid that the jewellery will never be yours. You see, Geraldine left it all to Rosina.'

'But Rosina is a mere child!'

'I know, and the jewellery will have to remain locked away for years for it was Geraldine's wish that it be handed to Rosina on her eighteenth birthday – before she receives her main inheritance at twenty-one – and I must respect that wish.'

'Of course.' Her smile was understanding and sympathetic. 'You are a good man, Julian. But now if you could leave me for a short while, I will finish getting ready for dinner.'

'Very well.'

Julian came up behind her and placed his hands on her shoulders. He bent his head to kiss the top of her head. She wanted to scream at him not to mess up her hair but he was looking fondly over her head towards the mirror so she returned his gaze and managed a tight-lipped smile.

When he had gone she hurled her hairbrush across the

room in fury. She felt that Geraldine's ghost was hovering over her, thwarting her every attempt to become the rightful mistress here. The jewellery would never be hers and so she would not be able to give any of it to her own daughter. Well, she must make it her business to see that Rosina, the little cuckoo in the nest, did not gain any more advantage over Amy. After all, Amy had much more right to be here at Ravenshill than Rosina did.

Chapter Eight

January 1890

'For goodness' sake, girl, didn't you hear me ring?'

The young parlour maid reddened and grew flustered under Blanche's haughty stare. 'Yes, Mrs Leighton, I heard you.'

'Well, you took your time in coming. You know, Elsie, this lackadaisical attitude really won't do.'

'Sorry, madam.' The girl sniffed audibly.

'Stop that,' Blanche commanded, 'and make up this fire.'

Elsie nodded and hurried to the fireplace. She took up the coal scuttle and was about to ease some coal on top of the fire when Blanche tutted with exasperation. 'Don't do that. You'll raise all kinds of dust. Use the fire tongs and place the coal on carefully.'

'Sorry, madam, yes, madam.'

Now the girl looked mutinous and Blanche thinned her lips in irritation. She really would have to have a word with Julian about the quality of the staff. It was all very well for him to say that his family had always employed girls from the village and the surrounding countryside, but they spoke with strange accents that she could barely understand and they just didn't have the same respect for their betters as the staff she had employed in London.

Blanche walked restlessly over to one of the windows. She gazed out across the formal gardens. Everything was rimed with frost and in the distance the leafless branches of the trees made stark patterns against the lowering sky. She shivered. Just to look at the world outside was enough to depress your spirits, and she thought she would never get used to the cold.

Ever since they had arrived in Northumberland and the Leighton family home at Ravenshill, the wind had come howling in across the German Ocean to bend the branches of even the sturdiest trees in the parkland and rattle the windowpanes of the old house Julian seemed so fond of. It was rather grand, she supposed. In fact, she had been surprised to discover the new wing was built in Palladian style and the furnishings, thanks to Julian rather than his late wife, were most elegant.

She had been half suspecting something that looked much older. The way Julian talked about his ancestors having been there since the year dot, she would not have been surprised to find a crumbling castle. But Julian had told her that the original building had been nothing much grander than a fortified farmhouse — whatever that was — and that over the centuries his family had prospered sufficiently to aggrandize themselves. Unfortunately some of them had got into the habit of living beyond their means and Blanche had worked out long ago that Julian had married Geraldine for her money.

Well, he has married me for love, she thought with a great deal of self-satisfaction, and if he is not quite as rich as I thought he was then so be it. Luckily he can sell one of the

London houses now, but not both of them. If I can't escape to the capital every now and then I shall die of boredom or the cold, one being as bad as the other.

But she had to admit that Christmas had been enjoyable. Julian was still in mourning and she had had to adopt half-mourning, so they were not expected to entertain the local gentry. However, the tree in the drawing room had been magnificent; even Amy had been impressed and she was usually so hard to please. The decorations in the main reception rooms had been holly and evergreen branches intertwined with sparkling gewgaws and were on a much grander scale than anything she'd had in the London house. Also handing the Christmas presents out to the assembled staff on Boxing Day had made her feel – well – rather feudal.

Yes, all in all, she believed that her life as a respectable married woman would be much better from now on; although there was a price to pay. And that was that she had inherited two stepchildren. The baby was no bother at all. Little George Leighton was a sickly child. That old harridan Maud Fidler kept an eye on the running of the nursery, with Bridget and an undernursery maid doing the physical work. Blanche had decided she would visit the nursery now and then in order to show a proper concern but she would try to do this when Julian was there to see how much she cared for his son. But Blanche found she was responsible for Rosina's care along with her own daughter, Amy.

She was considering engaging a governess. She was surprised that Julian had been content to send Rosina to the village school but, after all, the child was not really his daughter. Well, that wouldn't do for Amy. Obviously, whoever they employed would have to be responsible for both girls. Blanche didn't want any talk about favouritism or neglect. No, on the surface at least, Rosina must be treated equally.

Julian had told her that Rosina did not know she was adopted. Geraldine had wished the child to believe that she was her own daughter. Everyone down to the lowliest housemaid had conspired to keep the truth from Rosina because they had loved and respected Geraldine. But Julian's feelings about Rosina seemed to be mixed.

He had admitted to Blanche that, apprehensive about her true parentage, he had never really taken to the child. And yet, he'd said, since the very early days when Geraldine had assured him that it was natural for the little one to be fretful, Rosina had proved to be no trouble at all. Furthermore, she'd been a source of great joy to Geraldine and for that he'd been grateful. He certainly would do nothing to cause her hurt. So Amy must not be told. A child herself, she might let something slip. It was better if she believed Rosina to be Julian's real daughter.

This had not altogether pleased Blanche. For Amy *was* Julian's daughter and how aggravating it was that no one would ever know that. She must keep up this pretence of having been a respectable widow if she wished to take her place in society. How tiresome. But when she considered the matter, she realized that the charade was also better for Amy. She would not like her daughter to be looked on scornfully as an illegitimate child, even if her father had since married her mother. So she would have to make the best of the situation, and this would be made easier by the fact that Julian obviously doted on his pretty little daughter. Much more so than on the child who had grown up in his household.

What a strange little thing Rosina was. Nice-looking enough, but dark curls like a gypsy, and the way she moped!

Really, Blanche couldn't understand it. Surely she should have got over Geraldine's death by now. Unless all these long silences were a way of attracting attention. That could be it, Blanche supposed. Well, she wasn't going to succeed with her.

She looked at the two little girls now. One so dark and the other angel fair. They were sitting at a table with their scrapbooks. Each girl had an identical set of scraps. They had flowers, fruits, birds, animals, nursery rhyme characters and some special seasonal scraps featuring angels, Christmas trees and Santa Claus. The scraps were printed on sheets with each glossy little picture joined to its neighbours by paper tabs. Blanche saw how Rosina separated the picture she wanted most carefully while Amy, darling impetuous Amy, tore them off carelessly, sometimes spoiling one or more of the images.

She wandered over to the table to have a closer look and was piqued to see that, whereas Rosina had made a pleasing pattern on the page, Amy's scraps had been stuck on in a haphazard way with generous dabs of paste smearing the paper.

'That's nice, dear,' Blanche said unconvincingly, and her daughter, clutching the paste brush with sticky fingers, looked up and scowled.

'This is a silly pastime,' Amy said. 'I wish my friends could come and play with me but they're too far away.'

'You will make new friends, sweetheart. And we shall invite them here. You must be patient.'

All the time they were speaking Rosina simply got on with separating the scraps she wanted and carefully pasting them into her scrapbook. She never got too much paste on her brush and she was careful to use a bit of rag to keep everything clean. She knew perfectly well that Blanche was standing there but she didn't look up and she didn't say anything. She seemed to be utterly self-contained. Blanche felt like shaking her.

Elsie had finished seeing to the fire and she straightened up and coughed hesitantly.

'What is it?' Blanche asked.

'Is that all right, madam?'

Blanche walked back to the fireplace. 'It will do. Now, off you go but next time don't take so long to answer my summons.'

'Very well, madam.'

The girl hurried out of the room, seemingly relieved to go, and Blanche sat down on the small sofa for a moment before rising again and going to the bell pull.

'Bring me a tray of tea and biscuits,' she said when Elsie reappeared. 'And remember to wash your hands first.'

'Yes, madam.'

Blanche looked up into the mirror that hung above the fireplace and watched the girl as she made for the door. When she got there she looked back for a moment but, seeing that she was being observed, turned hastily away again. But not before Blanche had recognized what she interpreted as a look of pure insolence. She doesn't like me, Blanche thought, and was momentarily taken aback.

But by the time Elsie had returned with the tea and biscuits Blanche had quite recovered. She would find some excuse to have the girl dismissed. And because she had made up her mind to do so at the earliest possible opportunity, she allowed herself to smile sweetly and utter effusive thanks. As she sipped her tea she had the grace to wonder at herself. She didn't want to be the sort of woman who enjoyed doing battle with the servants.

This girl must go, she had already made up her mind, but

after that Blanche knew that she must set herself to win the heart of the Servants' Hall. She sensed that too many were comparing her unfavourably with the first Mrs Leighton. It seemed she had been a popular with them.

Geraldine Leighton had given Julian a son. A firstborn son, an heir. Blanche couldn't compete with that, and in any case she wasn't sure if she wanted to go through pregnancy again or even if she could. Amy's birth had been difficult and the doctor who had attended her had warned her that she might not be able to have any more children. Julian knew this. So she must make sure that her husband continued to be in thrall to her, and she was wise enough to know that would be difficult if he sensed there were underlying tensions in his household.

Men liked their daily lives to run smoothly. Poor Geraldine, good-natured though she was, had apparently not been the most efficient of mistresses. Hence Maud Fidler's powerful place in the hierarchy. Blanche frowned when she thought of Maud. So long as she was necessary in the nursery she would not be wise to cross her. But when George was a little older . . .

She glanced over at the table and saw that Rosina was still concentrating on her prettily arranged scrapbook whereas Amy was scowling mutinously at the mess she had made. For a moment Blanche's scowl mirrored that of her daughter. The wretched cuckoo, as Blanche now thought of Rosina, was making her own daughter seem inferior. She must take great care that, whatever they did, no one would have the opportunity to compare the two girls. Not even Julian.

Blanche sighed and lifted her slippered feet on to a little embroidered footstool before settling back on the sofa with her cup of tea.

* * *

It was a warm day in early summer and Muriel Graham paused as she tried to arrange her straw hat more tidily on top of her wayward grey curls. 'Are you sure it's all right for me to come with you?'

'Of course it is,' her sister Sybil replied. 'This is an informal occasion. Mrs Leighton asked me to take the children to play with Amy and Rosina, and while they are occupied I am going to advise her on who should be on her calling list.'

Muriel watched while Sybil sprayed herself with lavender water. She looks so pleased with herself, she thought. Invited to the big house to give advice. It's a wonder she can still get that bit of nonsense of a hat on her featherbrained noddle. Nevertheless, Muriel couldn't help being pleased. She had heard gossip about the new Mrs Leighton, about how although she was not exactly a beauty she had a metropolitan elegance and style that was most attractive to the local gentlemen – although their wives were as yet reserving judgement.

And that would probably be why Mrs Leighton had invited Sybil over, she supposed. No doubt she had recognized a fellow parvenue. Sybil's bonny face had secured her the life of a gentleman's wife and she took the greatest pains to cultivate county society. Muriel suspected that the new Mrs Leighton might have been from a more humble stratum of society than that in which her marriage had placed her, and that she was astute enough to cultivate someone who would not only feel honoured to be called her friend but who would be able to steer her through the treacherous waters of local manners and customs.

The 'girl' announced that the carriage was waiting and that the children were already ensconced. Sybil gathered up her handbag and parasol and swept out of the room like the grand lady she imagined herself to be. Muriel, smiling fondly, followed in her wake.

When they arrived at Ravenshill Manor the woman Muriel knew to be Maud Fidler met them at the door. They were not to be allowed in, apparently. Mrs Leighton and Amy were not quite ready so she had suggested that the Loxley party go straight to the summerhouse in the grounds where a maidservant was waiting to serve tea.

'The summerhouse?' Sybil enquired, her face betraying her sudden lack of confidence. 'I don't think I've ever been there.'

'It's not far.' Maud Fidler gave them instructions to walk around the house to the gardens at the back and take the path that led towards a wooded area where they would already be able to glimpse the summerhouse in a clearing.

'I know the way,' Adam said. 'Rosina and I have had picnics there.'

So they set off to the summerhouse. Sybil kept quiet. No doubt she's trying to work out whether this is a snub, Muriel thought. And was it? Muriel was not sure. Perhaps it made sense for them not to trail into the house if they were going to go straight out again. Or perhaps there is some other reason. In any case, Adam was happy.

She watched as her nephew ran ahead of them, turning now and then to call for Charlotte. He was obviously delighted to be here. After all, he had been friendly with Rosina since he had been brought along, a reluctant pupil, to join in the dancing classes that the former Mrs Leighton had arranged for the children. The lessons had been cancelled when the poor woman died. Muriel wondered whether they would start up again. It would be a good way for the new Mrs Leighton to get to know some of the 'best' families in the area. Although not all the children who attended had been born of 'gentlefolk'. Geraldine Leighton, God bless her, had not been at all discriminatory.

Sybil's ruffled feelings were soothed as soon as they walked into the clearing and saw the summerhouse. 'Why, it's more like a cottage!' she exclaimed. 'No, not a cottage, a Swiss Alpine chalet with its wooden veranda and the view down across the clearing and out to the sea.'

'Well, it would have to be a lake to be truly Swiss,' Muriel said.

'I beg your pardon?'

'As far as I know you can't see the sea from the Swiss Alps.'

Sybil shook her head in exasperation at her pedantic sister as she closed her parasol and walked up the central steps to the veranda. The wide veranda ran the whole width of the chalet and a fresh-faced young maidservant was waiting there to greet them. She performed a strange combination of a bob and a curtsy and went red in the face when she caught one foot in the hem of her skirt and nearly fell over.

Muriel heard suppressed laughter from one end of the veranda. She turned to see that Adam and Charlotte had made their way there and were talking to Rosina Leighton. Their cheerful young faces drew her towards them and she left her sister to the care of the young maid, who was ushering her along towards the other end of the veranda where a table and chairs had been set up.

'Would you like a cool drink, madam?' she heard the girl say.

'Why are you laughing, you young rogues?' Muriel asked the children.

'The parlour maid,' Adam explained. 'She nearly fell over.'

'It's not kind of you to laugh at another's misfortune,' Muriel admonished, but she could barely conceal her own amusement.

'Rosina says Molly is new to the house and Mrs Leighton has been telling her that she must respect people. Molly thinks that means she has to curtsy and she hasn't quite got the hang of it.'

'Poor young woman,' Muriel said. 'And is there no one to help her?'

'Rosina's trying to,' Adam told her.

'Really?' Muriel turned to look at Rosina, who had coloured slightly.

'Well, yes,' the child said. 'I mean, I'm not sure exactly what my stepmama means by respect but I know how to curtsy to your betters — we were taught in dancing class — and I give Molly lessons when she's looking after me.'

Muriel was intrigued. 'Molly looks after you?'

'Mm. Bridget has to spend more time with baby George. The undernursery maid can't manage on her own and Dr Lamb is not pleased with his progress, although he told my father that with proper care he should grow stronger.'

'I'm sure that he will,' Muriel said as reassuringly as she could, although without any real conviction. She had heard the rumours. She knew that it was more than likely that the poor little lad would not survive. 'So,' she said in an effort to be cheerful, 'so Molly helps with you and Amy?'

'Well, sort of. You see, Amy is mostly with her mother, whether at home or when they go visiting or into Newcastle to go shopping. Molly is left to take charge of me.'

'I see,' Muriel Graham said. And indeed she did. Those few words told her much about Rosina's new life with her stepmother. Poor child, she thought. First her beloved mother dies and now she must know that her baby brother is at death's door. And yet she seems to be coping with her rather lonely existence.

Thank goodness she has Adam. That thought popped

into her mind and cheered her. I must see to it, she decided, that she is invited to Sybil's more often. And I will have them both at the farm. That resolution made her smile and she continued, 'Well, I think that's very good of you, Rosina, to befriend Molly.' And she hoped fervently that the young maid would appreciate the help and be a friend to the forsaken child.

'Oh, look,' Charlotte said. It was the first time she'd spoken and now her bonny little face, so like her mother's, was alight with smiles. 'Amy and her mother are coming across the lawn.'

So they were. Muriel saw them when she turned round to peer through the trees. Two human confections of rose pink and white with matching parasols. She saw even from this distance that the child's frock was a copy of the mother's; exquisitely fashionable but surely too fussy for a child on a warm summer's day. Although the way the fabric flowed as they walked suggested it was the finest, coolest muslin.

She couldn't help glancing quickly at Rosina, dressed in a simple light blue dress with a smocked yoke. She wondered at the difference in style between the two little girls. Was Amy's mother trying to make a point? Was she trying to set her daughter far above Rosina? Well, if she was, some people – Sybil, for instance – might be impressed, but Muriel thought that at least in her simpler garb Rosina would be able to enjoy herself more and behave like a proper healthy child.

'Your stepsister's very pretty, isn't she?' Muriel heard Adam ask Rosina.

'Yes, she is,' Rosina answered, and there didn't seem to be any hint of jealousy. But then she added solemnly, 'I don't want to be pretty, though.'

'Why ever not?' Muriel couldn't help asking.

'Because it takes so long.'

'I don't understand,' Muriel said, but in fact she wasn't surprised at Rosina's answer.

'Well, you know, curling tongs and creams on your face and taking ages to decide what clothes you're going to wear.'

At that age, Muriel thought. Poor little Amy, then. But aloud she asked, 'Is that why Amy and her mother weren't ready when we arrived?'

'I suppose so. And they were quarrelling about what colour dress to wear.'

'Quarrelling? Amy was quarrelling with her mother?'

Muriel hadn't been able to disguise her disapproval and Rosina began to look uneasy. 'Well, you know, discussing the matter.'

'And who won?' asked Adam who, as a boy, had seen it straight away as a battle of wills.

'Amy, of course,' Rosina smiled with real amusement and her face was transformed.

Why, the dear little thing *is* pretty, Muriel thought. Not fashionably so with that dark hair, but her smile promises so much more than the simpering expression on that little china doll, her stepsister.

Muriel was comparing Rosina with Amy, who had just come up the steps on to the veranda ahead of her mother and was standing twirling her parasol like a true coquette. It was hard to believe she was only eleven years old, just like Rosina. Once more the good farmer's daughter wondered about the background of the widow Julian Leighton had made his second wife.

Charlotte was enchanted and ran towards Amy straight away. Adam stayed where he was but Muriel saw that her eleven-year-old nephew was staring at Julian Leighton's stepdaughter with a foolish moonstruck expression on his face. She felt like smacking him.

But instead she leaned over and whispered to Rosina, 'Well, whether you want to be or not, you are naturally pretty, my dear, and furthermore when you grow up I think you are going to be truly beautiful.'

Rosina's eyes widened with surprise. 'Do you mean I shall be like the ugly duckling?'

'Ugly duckling?'

'You know, in Mr Andersen's book of fairy tales. My mother used to read it to me and the ugly duckling turns into a swan.'

'No, dear, I didn't mean like the ugly duckling, for no one could call you ugly.'

'Oh, but—' Rosina stopped and looked embarrassed.

Muriel thought she knew why. 'Who has called you ugly?'

Rosina shook her head but the quick glance towards her stepsister betrayed her.

Muriel didn't feel like pressing the child. After all, it was none of her business and she knew that if she meddled she might make things worse for Rosina. She contented herself with saying, 'Well, whoever it was they were mistaken. But come along, we should go and join the others at the table.'

No one noticed or even looked up when Muriel shepherded Rosina and Adam towards the table and helped them find places. Mrs Leighton and Sybil were deep in conversation and so were Charlotte and Amy. The younger girl was gazing at the vision in pink with adoration and Amy was basking in the attention.

Muriel had to admit the tea that had been prepared for them was delicious. Cucumber sandwiches, cut in small triangles and seasoned with just the right amount of pepper and salt, ham sandwiches, cheese straws, honey cakes and raspberry biscuits. The chalet had a fully equipped kitchen so

Molly was able to serve tea and coffee and, of course, on a day like this, jugs of homemade lemonade.

Sybil and Blanche Leighton chattered throughout the meal and neither one of them bothered to include Muriel, but this left her free to observe those present; a favourite pastime of hers. The two women were well suited, she decided: both keen to impress, although Blanche Leighton was much more sophisticated. Muriel wished Sybil didn't make it so obvious that she considered it an honour to be here. She could never really forget that she had started life in a working farmhouse and sometimes her efforts to be a 'lady' were agonizing to behold. Not that she made a muddle of things; it was just that she was gradually turning into a different kind of woman altogether from the laughing, sweet-faced girl she had been when Hugh came courting.

After tea the children were allowed to 'play', although as far as Amy and Charlotte were concerned that meant sitting and gossiping just as their mothers were doing. Again, Muriel found herself in the role of spectator although she acknowledged this might be her own fault because she simply wasn't interested in joining in the conversation about the latest fashions and the decoration and furnishings in the nearby grand houses.

She was pleased to see that Adam, after his initial admiration for Amy, soon got bored with listening to her and his younger sister, and asked if he and Rosina could leave the veranda and explore the woods. They were granted permission on condition they didn't wander out of calling distance, and both looked grateful to be set free. In fact they didn't go far; they settled on a fallen tree trunk within sight of the chalet and Muriel could see them chatting happily like the old friends they were. She wondered what they were talking about.

And she saw how natural they looked together and then cursed herself for being a sentimental old maid and allowing her thoughts to take her into a rosy, romantic future in which her only nephew would find himself a good wife in Rosina. For if he had any sense he would choose Rosina rather than that shallow spoiled little madam Amy.

'Amy is such a sweet child, don't you think?' Sybil asked Muriel later when they had returned to Sybil's house and they were alone and enjoying a glass of Madeira together. 'Here, do have another ratafia biscuit.' She held out the plate.

'Thank you. Er ... Amy is sweet?' For once Muriel found herself at a loss for words.

'Oh, but of course she is. I mean she's so polite and refined.'

'I'm not sure if "refined" is what a child should be at that age.'

Sybil gave Muriel a disparaging look. 'Oh, well, the child has been brought up in London, you know. Things are so different there.'

'I'm sure you're right, dear,' Muriel said.

She didn't want to quarrel with her younger sister and spoil what had obviously been a wonderful day for her, but she wondered now, as she had often done in the past, whether Hugh ever despaired over what lay behind that pretty face and wished for a wife with whom he could have an intelligent conversation. Probably not, she thought. Hugh, like many men, was probably more concerned with what happened in the bedroom rather than face to face over the dining table. And there had been the matter of the substantial dowry – although it had been called an investment – provided by Sybil and Muriel's father, just as Hugh needed capital to expand his business. Muriel smiled thoughtfully.

Then, as she sipped her Madeira and nibbled at the oh-so-tempting ratafia biscuits, her smile faded and a dark cloud hovered over the rosy future she had been contemplating earlier. What if Adam took after his father?

Chapter Nine

Sybil Loxley was overjoyed when, towards the end of summer, an invitation arrived for her and Charlotte to go to Ravenshill.

'I hope you don't mind if I do not invite Adam,' Blanche Leighton wrote, 'but being a normal boy, he is refreshingly lively and surely would not enjoy being sent to play with the girls.'

Sybil wondered about that — after all, Adam and Rosina had played together happily for some years now — but she could hardly object and put her budding friendship with the chatelaine of Ravenshill in jeopardy. So Sybil decided that Adam would spend a day on the farm with his grandparents and Muriel.

The fact that it was raining when the day came sent Sybil into a frenzy of anxiety. She had half wondered whether she was going to be entertained in the summerhouse again and, if this were the plan, Blanche Leighton would surely cancel the invitation or, at best, postpone it until the next fine day. She was delighted therefore when the Leightons' carriage arrived as arranged to collect her and Charlotte. At last she was going to be allowed into the house. Surely from now on she could count herself as one of the Leightons' circle? Hugh would be delighted.

After a delightful lunch she stood in the doorway of the playroom at Ravenshill with Blanche Leighton and observed the three little girls. The skies were dark and rain beat on the windows. The lamps in the playroom were lit and a small fire burned in the hearth. Fires were necessary in this great old house all year round. Amy was showing Charlotte her dolls. But Rosina stood behind them, already left out of the conversation and looking ill at ease in the otherwise friendly and inviting setting.

'Don't they look sweet together? So pretty, two little angels,' Blanche said.

'And Rosina too,' Sybil added.

'Oh, of course. My stepdaughter. But she's different, isn't she? I mean, so dark, like a sweet little gypsy, whilst Amy and Charlotte are so fashionably fair with pretty pink and white complexions.' Blanche turned towards her guest and with a hint of concern, she added, 'I do hope Rosina isn't jealous.'

Sybil was startled. 'Why should she be?'

'Well, you know, I think sometimes the poor child imagines that I favour my own child whereas I make every effort to treat them both the same . . . for dear Julian's sake.'

'Oh, I'm sure you do. Rosina is most fortunate to have you to take care of her.'

Blanche smiled and lowered her head gracefully as if to acknowledge the compliment. 'But come,' she said. 'We shall go to my own little sitting room and take coffee and cakes, and you can tell me all the gossip of the countryside and who I should take the trouble to know, as well as those I should avoid.'

Sybil was almost ecstatic with pleasure. It seemed as though she was going to be Blanche Leighton's confidante and this in turn might gain her entry into elevated circles of county society that so far had been closed to her. She felt as though she was floating downstairs on a cloud of pleasure and then, at the bottom, Blanche laid a delicate white hand on her arm.

'Sybil, dear,' she said. 'I hope you are not offended that I didn't invite Adam today.'

'Oh, no, of course not.'

'You see, as I told you, I thought it would be tiresome for him to have to spend time with the girls and their dolls.'

'Oh, no, Adam would—' Sybil was about to say that Adam would have been quite happy to sit at the table and play jackstraws, or pachisi, or draughts with Rosina, and that they often enjoyed such games together, but she faltered when she saw that Blanche had adopted a serious expression.

'He might have wanted to play more boisterous games and I really couldn't risk any great disturbance in the house, not with baby George being so poorly,' her hostess continued.

Sybil was genuinely sorry. 'So there's no improvement, then?'

'I'm afraid not. I've had some sleepless nights, I can tell you. I am quite exhausted.' Blanche sighed and shook her head.

'Poor you. And how good of you to take care of the little one. Mr Leighton must be so grateful.'

Blanche gave a sad sweet smile and they continued on their way to her sitting room. She was satisfied that she had made a good impression on Sybil Loxley. No doubt the impressionable woman would carry tales of how truly good the new Mrs Leighton was; how she was being like a mother to Rosina and how she was making herself ill in tending to poor little George. And, of course, she did make a point of visiting the nursery at least once a day, taking great care to time her visits to coincide with the time that Julian came home. He always found her there.

She glanced at Sybil Loxley and could hardly refrain from laughing. The silly woman was looking round the house with goggle eyes, taking everything in, no doubt, to be reported to all and sundry. Blanche was pleased with what she had achieved just now. Also, she had managed to draw attention to Amy's beauty without saying anything too bad about Rosina.

She had known very well, of course, that Adam would have been no trouble and that he would have played any game that Rosina suggested. But it was not her intention to make Rosina happy. Grown woman though she was, she had to admit to a certain pleasurable satisfaction when she had seen the look of disappointment on the little cuckoo's face when the Loxleys arrived without her friend.

Upstairs in the playroom, Rosina found herself completely ignored. She decided to play on her own with her dolls' house and she sat before it happily enough as she took out the miniature people and laid them aside. Then she emptied the rooms one by one and cleaned the furniture with a soft duster. Soon she was lost in an imaginary world of comfort and happiness and loving families. So engaged was she that it took some while before the voices of Amy and Charlotte penetrated her imaginings.

Amy raised her voice slightly and said, 'Thank goodness I have met you, Charlotte. Now I will have someone to play with and I will not be so lonely.'

'But don't you play with Rosina?' Charlotte said.

'Well, yes, I do,' Amy answered, 'but she's not like the sort of friend I'm used to.'

'In London, you mean?'

'Yes. They are so ... so much more interesting. They know about all kinds of things, like the best shops and clothes and the latest fashions.'

'That must be nice.' Charlotte sounded both envious and impressed.

'I hated having to come here,' Amy said, 'but it won't be so awful if you will be my friend.'

'Of course I will!'

Charlotte sounded overjoyed but Rosina knew very well that Amy had favoured her because she would be easily impressed – not like Rosina herself, who found her stepsister empty-headed and boring. Although she was too kind to say so.

But Rosina's kind-heartedness had not registered with Amy, who not only ignored her whenever she could but sometimes seemed to go out of her way to cause trouble. Rosina had learned to be wary.

And then the other two girls began to whisper. 'Look at her now,' Amy said, 'sitting by herself tidying her dolls' house instead of playing with us.'

Rosina knew she had been meant to hear Amy's words but she pretended she hadn't.

'It's a very nice dolls' house,' Charlotte said.

'Not as nice as mine.' Amy sounded cross. 'Look, over there.'

Amy and Charlotte moved away and Rosina was left in peace for a while. She began to put the furniture back room by room and then had one of those moments when nothing seemed quite right. The room at the right side of the stairs on the top floor was decorated with nursery wallpaper. Rosina picked up the tiny cradle with the baby in it and was just about to place it in the room when she realized she had reached towards a room at the other side of the landing – a room that was decorated like a bathroom.

She had done this before: unthinkingly putting furniture into the wrong room while at the same time there had been a picture in her mind's eye of another room — a different dolls' house altogether. Once she had asked Bridget if she could remember if there had been another dolls' house when she, Rosina, had been younger.

'Bless you, I don't think so,' Bridget had told her, 'although I seem to remember a little cottage your mother had. Ever so sweet and small it was. There were dolls too. A countryman in a smock, his wife in her pinafore, and a baby — oh, and a cat and a dog. They're all in a chest in the boxroom. I think it was your ma's when she was a little girl.'

'It wasn't a cottage,' Rosina had said. 'I remember a house as big as this one.'

'No, pet, you must have dreamed it.'

Rosina hadn't mentioned the other dolls' house to Bridget again.

When she had arranged the furniture to her satisfaction she began an imaginary game with the dolls' house family. The cook was at the stove in the kitchen, the father was sitting in the library with a book on his knee — it had real pages and lines that looked like writing — and the mother was standing over the cradle in the nursery. Rosina imagined that she was singing to her tiny baby.

'Oh, do be quiet, Rosina, or if you must sing at least sing some proper words!'

She wasn't aware that she had been singing until Amy's imperious tone rang out.

'She's always humming that silly tune,' Rosina heard Amy tell Charlotte. 'Mama and I are really quite irritated by it. Oh, come along, I'm sick of this. Let's have a dolls' tea party.'

Rosina sat back on her heels and glanced round. The contents of Amy's dolls' house were scattered across the floor. Amy had gone to pull the little table and chairs out into the centre of the room and then she began to place the chairs around it.

'Get that box from the shelf,' Amy told Charlotte. 'The blue box; it's got the tea set in it.'

Charlotte glanced round hesitantly and then made her way to the shelves set against the wall near the window. Rosina heard a crunching sound and Charlotte stopped and looked down in dismay. She had trodden on one of the pieces of furniture from Amy's dolls' house; the dining table. Charlotte looked horrified. She glanced at Amy guiltily and, seeing that she hadn't noticed anything, she nudged the broken table aside with her foot. She found the box containing the porcelain tea set and soon she was setting the little table under Amy's directions.

When the delicate rose-patterned tableware and doll-sized cutlery had been arranged to Amy's satisfaction she directed her new slave to fetch another box, which contained plates of bread and butter and cakes made from modelling clay, painted realistically to resemble real food.

'There,' said Amy. 'Now go and get four dolls. You can choose,' Amy said as though she was doing Charlotte a great favour.

Charlotte began to gather up the dolls. Some lay scattered where they had left them earlier. Others were tidied neatly away on to the shelves. The latter were Rosina's dolls but Charlotte did not know that.

Before Rosina could say anything Charlotte had scooped up a doll that lay alone in a cot.

'What on earth did you bring that one for?' Amy demanded scornfully.

'I – I felt sorry for it,' Charlotte said.

'Sorry for it? For goodness' sake, it's a disgusting broken old thing not fit to be kept in a decent house. Give it to me.'

She snatched the doll from Charlotte and hurled it across the room. There was a cracking sound as its head hit the toy chest.

'No!' Rosina shouted, and ran to pick up her old doll. She examined its head and breathed a sigh of relief when she saw there were no new cracks in the glaze. 'You shouldn't have done that,' she told Amy.

But Amy wasn't looking at her. She was staring at the floor near Rosina's feet. 'And *you* shouldn't have done that!' she screamed. She stooped swiftly and gathered up some of the broken pieces of dolls' house furniture.

'What?'

'You've broken my dolls' house table.' She thrust the broken table under Rosina's nose. 'Look – the legs have come off and the little plates and the candelabra have been broken. There they are on the floor!'

Rosina clutched her doll. 'I didn't,' she said. 'I didn't break anything.'

From the corner of her eyes she saw Charlotte backing away. Her face had drained of colour and she looked truly frightened. Rosina shot her an appealing glance but she knew it was in vain. Adam's sister was not going to own up.

'Don't lie!' Amy shouted. Rosina thought how ugly her stepsister looked with her eyes popping and her face an angry red.

'I'm not lying. I didn't do it.'

'Then how did it get broken?' Amy demanded.

Rosina glanced at Charlotte again. The other girl looked away quickly. She could not meet Rosina's eyes. 'You left everything on the floor,' Rosina told Amy. 'Perhaps it got stood on.'

'Stood on by you.' She paused and gathered breath for a bellow. 'On purpose!'

Before Rosina could defend herself further the door opened and her father hurried into the room. 'What on earth is going on here? I could hear the racket in my study below.'

Amy immediately stopped screeching and her eyes filled with tears. 'We were just playing,' she said, and her voice broke into a sob.

Rosina's father frowned. 'Playing? First you were shouting and now you are crying. What sort of game makes you cry like that?'

'I . . . well . . . I'm sorry I disturbed you but it doesn't matter.'

His features softened and he came forward and took hold of Amy's shoulders. He looked down at her kindly. 'But it does matter because I don't like to see you upset like this. You must tell me what happened.'

Amy dropped her head and mumbled something; only the name 'Rosina' was clear.

'What's that? What about Rosina?'

'I don't like to say.'

'But I say you must.'

Doing a very good job of looking unwilling, Amy held out her hand to show him her broken dolls' house table.

'Did you do this, Rosina?' her father asked.

Mutely Rosina shook her head.

'Does that mean no? Well, in that case one of you is not telling the truth.'

'It's all right, Uncle Julian,' Amy said suddenly. 'I'm sure it was an accident.'

'That's not what I heard as I came into the room,' he replied. 'I distinctly heard you accusing Rosina of doing it on purpose.'

Amy hung her head and whispered, 'I know, but I shouldn't have done.'

'Then why did you say so?'

'Because I was so upset. It was wrong of me. But the dolls' house is special. You gave it to me, remember? Remember when you came to my birthday party in London? Well, I was so upset when I saw the furniture and the dolls all over the floor and the table broken, and I thought Rosina must have done it on purpose to hurt me. Especially as I sometimes think that she doesn't want me here. But I can see now that it was probably an accident.'

'Standing on the table might have been an accident,' Julian Leighton said, 'but pulling everything out of the house can not have been. Rosina, can you explain this?'

Amy had twisted everything to make it seem as if Rosina was guilty, not just of breaking the table but of emptying the dolls' house too. She was also pretending unconvincingly on purpose that she believed it was an accident. This would make Rosina's father admire Amy. It was all so complicated that Rosina had no idea what she could say.

'No, I can't explain it,' she said.

Her father looked at her sadly. 'I'll ask you again, did you pull the things out of the dolls' house?'

'No.'

'Oh, I'm sure they must have just fallen out,' Amy said.

'And did you stand on the little table and break it?'

'No.'

'As I said,' Amy interrupted, 'it must have been an accident. I see that now.'

Rosina's father smiled at Amy. 'It's very kind of you to want to shield Rosina,' he said, 'but it's no use pretending.' He turned to face Rosina once more. 'Rosina, go to your room and stay there for the rest of the day. I will have some bread and butter sent up for your tea although I'm not sure if you deserve anything at all.'

Rosina turned to go.

'Wait,' her father said. 'Do you have something to say?'

'No.'

'That's a pity. I had hoped you would have apologized for behaving this way.'

He looked at her expectantly but she remained mute as she tried not to cry.

'Very well, Rosina. I'm very disappointed in you. Off you go.'

Rosina waited until she got to her bedroom and then flung herself on her bed. She gave way to a storm of grief. Why had Amy been so mean to her? Even if she believed that Rosina had stood on the little table she knew very well that she had emptied the rest of the furniture on to the floor herself so why had she lied? And why had Charlotte Loxley not owned up straight away?

If she had done, Amy might have been cross with her but, even so, she shouldn't have let Rosina take the blame. And now her father believed that she was spiteful and a liar. She had been sent to her room and she had been expected to apologize for something she had not done. Rosina clutched the old doll to her heart and cried until her eyes were red-rimmed and her throat was sore.

When Bridget brought her tea she put the tray down and took Rosina in her arms. 'There, there, pet,' she said. 'Whatever it is you're supposed to have done, I don't believe it. That young madam your stepsister is the cause of it, I'll be bound. Now come and sit by the fire and see what I've brought you.'

Bridget removed the clean cloth that was covering the tray and Rosina saw that as well as the plain bread and butter there was a generous slice of cherry Madeira cake and a little dish of blancmange and jelly.

'Now eat that up and don't tell anyone, especially old Fiddlesticks.'

That less than respectful reference to Miss Fidler coaxed a smile from Rosina, and although she had not thought she was hungry she looked with interest at the contents of the tray.

'Now then,' Bridget said, 'take this plate and start with the bread and butter like a good girl. And I want everything on this tray eaten up, mind you. I had enough trouble smuggling the cake and the jelly out of the kitchen. I don't want to be carrying it back in again.'

'Thank you, Bridget,' Rosina said. 'You're kind to me.'

'Of course I am,' Bridget said, 'and remember, for the sake of your blessed mother, I'll always be your friend in this house, no matter what they do to you.'

Back at the desk in his study, Julian wondered whether he should have asked Blanche to go up to the playroom and deal with the problem. But if he had, Sybil Loxley would have been alerted to the fact that there was domestic discord at Ravenshill.

Julian was well aware that the wives of certain of his friends had felt sorry for Rosina when he had brought home a new wife and her daughter. Those who had loved and admired Geraldine had waited to see if Blanche would treat the girl properly.

Well, Julian could have told them that she had done her very best and had even tried to make excuses for Rosina when she behaved badly — just as Amy had done a moment ago. Julian sighed. Amy was still a child in many ways but at the age of eleven already showing promise of the beautiful woman she would be. Amy, his daughter whom he loved, his own flesh and blood. And yet he could not acknowledge her.

Whereas out of duty and gratitude to his late wife, Geraldine, he must go on treating Rosina, a stranger's spawn, as if she were his own daughter, which Rosina believed herself to be.

Amy does not know that I am her father. She cannot address me as such. Well, I can change that, at least, he thought. In the eyes of the world I am her stepfather and it would be quite in order for her to address me as Papa. I shall tell Blanche that as soon as that silly woman Mrs Loxley has gone home.

Julian stared at the papers spread out on the desk before him. He had made a new will after his marriage so that if anything happened to him, Blanche and Amy would be well provided for. He had even left a small legacy to Rosina, although he need not have done, as Geraldine had ensured that Rosina would have money of her own – as well as her jewels.

But his land and property here in Northumberland and the bulk of his fortune, he had left to George. And now it seemed as if his only son might not live long enough to inherit. Julian was almost worn out with anxiety. Blanche was doing all she could. Every time he came home from his ride he found her in the nursery. He was deeply grateful for the way she was devoting herself to George. But at the same time he felt guilty. For if he had known Geraldine's son would die in infancy, much as he loved Blanche, he would never have married her.

In Muriel's experience the seasons change in mid-September, but the last few days had been as warm as any summer day here in the hills, so she decided that while the weather held she would take the children up to the old Roman fort and they would have a picnic. When she went to Sybil's house to arrange it, Adam greeted the idea with enthusiasm but Charlotte raised objections.

'Does Rosina have to come with us?' she asked.

'Of course, that's the whole idea. You and Adam and Rosina and Amy. If your mother agrees to it I'll go and ask Mrs Leighton.'

'Amy won't want to come,' her niece said quickly.

'What makes you so sure?'

'She just won't. And I don't want to come either.'

Charlotte looked so uncomfortable that Muriel was sure there was more to this than her niece's usual contrary nature. Suddenly a possible explanation presented itself.

'What happened that day you went to play at Ravenshill?'

'Nothing.'

But the way Charlotte couldn't meet her eye told Muriel she was right.

'Don't you like Amy?'

'Of course I do. She's my friend.'

'I can't believe you have turned against Rosina.'

'No!' Charlotte sounded near to tears. 'I haven't.'

'Then why are you so reluctant to have her join the picnic?'

Charlotte dropped her head. 'Perhaps Rosina won't want to come if I'm going.'

'What nonsense.'

'No, it's not.'

'Explain.'

'I can't. I don't want to come on the picnic, that's all.'

The child looked so unhappy that Muriel let the matter drop. But she was convinced that something had happened, and from the way Charlotte was behaving she obviously felt guilty. Well, she would take Adam and Rosina to the fort and, if she was honest with herself, she knew she would enjoy the day more without Charlotte, who could be selfish and demanding, and Amy, who she suspected might be a bad influence on her niece. She didn't suppose she would ever find out what had happened when the three girls had played together.

When the day came she took the pony and trap and went to Ravenshill to collect Rosina. Mrs Leighton was still in bed – she ought to have expected that – and in any case she had not anticipated being received by her. A young maid, a friendly lass from the village, invited her to wait in the morning room. This was a mistake. In no time at all Maud Fidler appeared. Her countenance was as uninviting as ever.

'Miss Graham,' she said. 'You're up early.'

Muriel smiled. 'This isn't early for me.'

'Of course not. The farm.'

The woman made it sound as though Muriel's station in life was somehow inferior to her own. And yet Maud Fidler must have been no stranger to early mornings and hard work when she first went into domestic service, no doubt at the age of twelve or thirteen. But Muriel let any intended snub pass. She did not want to annoy this woman who seemed to wield a certain amount of power in the Leighton household and who might refuse to let Rosina spend the day with her just to spite her.

'Miss Rosina has not had breakfast yet,' Maud Fidler said.

'That's all right; she can have some at the farm.'

'Very well. I'll bring her to you at once.'

'But will Mrs Leighton mind?'

'Mind?'

'About the fact that Rosina is going out without breakfast.'

'If she does I will assure her that she will have a good

breakfast with you. Don't worry, Mrs Leighton will be only too pleased that Rosina will be out for the day.'

Miss Fidler hurried away and Muriel was left with the impression that Mrs Leighton wouldn't care one way or the other about the poor child's breakfast. In fact, she was pretty sure that the stern-faced woman wouldn't even mention it. She sat down, although she had not been invited to do so, but she hardly had time to wonder at the pictures in a fashion magazine before Miss Fidler returned with Rosina, who was smiling shyly.

'I shall bring her back this evening but perhaps I should give her her supper first?'

Miss Fidler agreed, only too hastily, Muriel thought, and saw them to the door.

'Oh,' Muriel turned just as the door was closing behind them.

'What is it?' Miss Fidler's tone betrayed her impatience.

'I forgot to ask, I feel ashamed, how is baby George?'

There was a pause. 'Not well, I'm afraid.'

'I'm sorry,' Muriel said, and when there was no reply she hurried Rosina to the trap and soon they were bowling away.

Maud didn't shut the door immediately. As she watched them go she pondered how convenient it was that Muriel Graham had offered to take Rosina for the day. Maud herself was finding it increasingly difficult to cope with the situation that had developed. Amy had taken a dislike to Rosina, goodness knew why, but she tried to cause trouble for the other child whenever she could. Rosina, miserable and bewildered though she was, did not give Amy the satisfaction of rising to the bait. This infuriated Amy, who would contrive to make it look as though the quarrel was Rosina's fault.

Blanche Leighton must have known the truth of it but she

always took her daughter's part and also she was clever enough to let her husband know there had been trouble between the girls without actually seeming to complain. The second Mrs Leighton had perfected a sweet, saintly, long-suffering expression, which seemed to have fooled her husband entirely. Only the domestic staff, particularly the younger maids, suffered from her vile outbursts of temper. She wanted to be rid of Rosina, Maud was sure of that, and she couldn't let that happen for she had come to suspect that Mrs Leighton also wanted to get rid of her.

For the moment she knew that Julian Leighton was influenced by a lingering gratitude towards her because she had brought Rosina to the house and made Geraldine happy. But if Rosina were not here, might he forget any obligations he might owe to his late wife's companion and send her packing too? And then what would she do?

She liked life in a grand house. The underservants waited on her just as if she were a lady. She had already set her heart on one of the cottages on the estate that would do very nicely for her retirement. No, she would have to keep the peace at all costs. How lucky that Muriel Graham had taken a liking to Rosina. Maud would encourage that friendship. If Rosina was out of the house Amy could not torment her and peace might reign.

Mr Leighton had decided against hiring a governess, thank goodness, for then Maud's own role would be diminished and perhaps that would be another reason for dispensing with her services. No, the girls, both Amy and Rosina, were to become weekly boarders at the Girls' High School in Newcastle after this school year and meanwhile, Rosina was to continue at the village school whereas Amy was to be tutored by the elder Miss Robson, a retired headmistress who lived in the village and would report to Ravenshill daily.

Once they started at the school in Newcastle, part of Maud's duties would be to accompany them to school every Monday morning and collect them every Friday. She would order their school uniforms and any books or musical instruments that were needed. In the holidays she would be in overall charge of them as before. And, as always, she would be responsible for the nursery. But the way things were going she doubted whether she would be needed in that role for much longer.

Rosina was delighted to find Adam waiting at the farm. They both sat down to porridge, toast and warm milk at the kitchen table. Adam's grandfather was already out and about, but his grandmother, a kindly woman, saw to it that the two children polished off every morsel she put before them while his Aunt Muriel made the sandwiches they were going to take with them.

When they had finished eating, Adam and Rosina helped to clear the table and then sat on a rug by the fire and played with the kittens.

'You're lucky to have somewhere like this to come to,' Rosina told Adam.

'Do you think so? Charlotte hates it.'

'*Hates* it? Whatever for?'

'Well, she doesn't like the muck in the farmyard – or the smell – and she doesn't think Grandmother talks quite properly.'

Rosina glanced over to where Adam's grandmother and Aunt Muriel were chatting as they wrapped the picnic food in clean tea towels. She knew what Adam meant but she didn't think it the least important that Grandma Graham talked like an old countrywoman. In fact her soft North Country accent was more musical and pleasing to the ear than the shrill tones of her stepmother.

'And as for my grandfather,' Adam continued, 'not only does he not talk properly but Charlotte says he has no table manners.'

'Well, what do you think?' Rosina asked.

Adam grinned. 'I can see her point. My mother says she could never invite him to our house for tea if any of her friends were going to be there.'

'But that's dreadful!' Rosina exclaimed.

'Yes, I know,' Adam agreed, but he looked embarrassed.

'I'm sorry, I shouldn't have said that,' Rosina said quickly.

'That's all right. I don't suppose he minds.'

Adam had his head lowered as he stroked the mother cat, who was purring loudly. Rosina could not see his expression and she did not know why, but she suddenly wondered if Adam was also ashamed of his grandfather.

'Right, you two,' Aunt Muriel said. 'I've packed everything into haversacks, one each, because we're going to walk there.' She handed them each a canvas bag and showed them how to slip them on to their backs.'

'Help!' Adam said. 'What have you got in here? Rocks?'

His aunt laughed at his expression. 'Only my homemade rock buns along with some of the sandwiches and a bottle of ginger beer. But you're the lad so it's only right you should have the most to carry. Now off we go!'

'Goodness,' Rosina said some time later, 'I didn't realize this was going to be quite such an expedition.'

Aunt Muriel smiled at her. 'Don't worry, we're not going much further; it's just that some of the old roads twist and turn around the countryside. Not like the Roman roads, eh, Adam?'

Adam grinned. 'No, the old Romans cut straight through hills and valleys as the crow flies. The Romans were famous for their roads. They had proper engineers and they built the roads as straight as possible so that the army could march from one place to another taking the shortest route.'

Rosina was impressed. Adam seemed to know so much, but she knew that his father often took him out with him when he made business calls around the county. Adam's father loved to spend time with his son and tell him things. Her mother had been like that; she had always found time to talk to her and to read to her. Since she had died there had been no one she could talk to about anything interesting. Except Adam.

Today she was happy to trail a little behind him along with his Aunt Muriel. The air was warm and sweet-smelling, but there was a cool breeze blowing in from the sea and rustling through the fields. The hedgerows were laden with berries, and falling leaves blew across their path. Occasionally they startled a rabbit, which would dart ahead of them and dive into a ditch or through a hedge. The only sounds were the bleating of sheep dotted about the surrounding hillsides and the beautiful trilling song of the skylarks.

The walkers stopped for a moment and watched the inconspicuous little brown birds fly up into the air, hover for a while, singing all the time, and then fold their wings and plummet back down to the ground.

Then hedgerows gave way to old stone walls marking ancient boundaries, and the path ahead began to rise more steeply. Soon Muriel left the road and led the children on to something that looked like a cart track, but the rutted sides and the centre were so overgrown with grasses and wild flowers that Rosina could easily imagine that no one had passed this way for centuries.

'There it is,' Aunt Muriel said, and she stopped and pointed. Rosina found herself squinting in the sunlight as she gazed ahead. At first she didn't know what Adam's aunt meant them to look at but then her eyes focused on what seemed to be a tumble of old stones.

'It's the remains of a Roman fort,' Adam said. 'I've been here before with my father but I don't think many people come here now. My father told me that in years gone by, the stones were plundered to build walls and cottages and even a bridge and a church.'

'That's right,' Aunt Muriel said, 'and our own family took some to build the farmhouse. I wonder if they ever thought about the people who first built these dwellings and lived in them.'

She reached into one of her voluminous pockets and brought out some papers. 'Look,' she said, 'here's a plan of how the fort was laid out – all the streets. And these other papers are drawings of what the buildings probably looked like. I copied them from a book when I was at school. I was a neat draughtsman, if I say so myself, and I could never bring myself to throw them away. Go on – take the plan and explore a little while I find the best place to sit and have our picnic.'

With the help of the plan and the drawings, Rosina and Adam followed the streets between the ruins of houses, workshops, granaries, a temple and something that looked like a trough for a fountain. At least that's what Aunt Muriel's extremely neat writing said it was.

'It's strange to think it must once have been crowded and busy, and now there's nothing left except these broken stones,' Rosina said.

Adam frowned as he looked at the plan. 'According to this, these steps lead down into a strong room,' he said. 'It's where the military commander kept the soldiers' wages.'

'Is that true?' Rosina asked.

'I have no idea,' Adam laughed. 'I made it up – about the wages, that is. But if it really was a strong room then some sort of treasure must have been kept here.'

'Let's see if there are any coins lying amongst the stones.' Rosina descended the steps cautiously.

'There won't be,' Adam said. 'If there ever were any coins left there they would have been taken years ago.'

Nevertheless, they had fun looking, but all they found were sheep and rabbit droppings, scurrying insects and a few hardy wild flowers pushing up through cracks in the old floor.

Rosina found it easy to imagine the lively clamour that must have rung through these streets, the laughter of children, the cries of their mothers calling them home. If she closed her eyes and concentrated hard enough she could even smell bread baking in the stone ovens and mutton broth cooking in the household stew pots.

'Come back, Rosina!'

'What?' She opened her eyes to find Adam grinning at her.

'You were miles away,' he said.

'No, not miles . . . years. I was years away.'

Adam shook his head. 'I don't know what you mean. But I do know I'm hungry. Come on, I'll race you back!'

Muriel had taken a tartan rug from her haversack and spread it on the ground. She had also laid out a clean tablecloth, and she had just finished setting out the sandwiches, the rock buns, the apples, and the ginger beer when she saw the two youngsters running towards her. Adam led as always and Rosina followed, her eyes not on the stony path but on Adam, trusting him to lead the way.

Muriel watched her nephew with pride. He was sturdy and bright and bonny. He would grow into a handsome, intelligent man. He's so confident, she thought, so secure in the love of his family and that's as it ought to be. But what of Rosina? She has had much to bear in her short life. Her mother dead and buried, her little brother barely clinging to life, and a father who ignores her most of the time because he is so taken with his new wife and her child.

No wonder she is drawn to Adam. I may be a sentimental old maid but it's plain that she adores him. And he likes her. But they are so young – who can know what fate has in store for them?

After they had had supper in the farmhouse kitchen Muriel took them home in the trap. Adam was delivered first and then they went on to Ravenshill. The breeze had died and the evening was warm and musky. It won't last, Muriel thought; soon the last fruits will have been harvested and the nights will be cold.

Rosina was half asleep as they jogged along the country roads; the clip-clop of the horses' hoofs ringing out, breaking the evening hush. Soon the massive outline of Ravenshill loomed on the horizon. Always dramatic, tonight it looked menacing. Muriel shivered. You read too many sensational novels, she scolded herself silently. Too many heroines wandering about at night, silly things, with nothing but a lighted candle to show the way and doom lurking in every shadow.

'What is it, Miss Graham?' Rosina asked.

'What do you mean?'

'I thought you said something.'

'No, at least I might have done but it isn't important. And by the way, I think you should call me Aunt Muriel. Would you like that?'

'Very much.'

They kept a companionable silence as they entered

through the main gates and followed the curve of the drive. It was then that Muriel noticed there were no lights in any of the windows. She drew up and the door opened immediately. The maid Bridget came hurrying down the steps towards them.

'I've been watching for you,' she said.

'What is it, Bridget?' Muriel Graham asked.

'I wanted to be here when Miss Rosina came home.'

'Why is that?' But Muriel glanced up at the shuttered windows and already knew the answer.

'Rosina,' Bridget said as she helped her down from the trap and then held her in her arms. 'You must be brave. Your little brother has gone to heaven.'

Chapter Ten

July 1891

Miss Winifred Robson wished her pupils a happy holiday, said goodbye to those who would not be coming back next term, and then turned to look around the single classroom of the village school. Always well ordered, the room with its rows of desks was now almost somnolent in the sunlight streaming in through the tall windows. Sparkling dust motes danced in the warm air.

One girl remained. Rosina Leighton moved gracefully from desk to desk collecting the inkwells on a tray and taking them over to the sink to be washed before they were stored in the cupboard until the autumn term.

'Thank you for staying to help me,' Miss Robson said.

Rosina, her abundant dark hair tied back neatly and dressed in her school smock, looked younger than her twelve years. She glanced up from her task and smiled. Miss Robson went to the blackboard and, taking up the rubber, began to wipe it clean. A neatly drawn map of Africa disappeared, as did a list of crops.

'I've finished the inkwells,' Rosina said.

Miss Robson turned to see her favourite pupil setting

them out to drain on the wooden bench. 'Thank you, Rosina. Do you want to go home now?'

'No, I'll stay and help you put everything away. I like it here. I'm sorry to be leaving.'

'I'll miss you,' Miss Robson said impulsively and then, fearing she had shown more emotion than was befitting for a village school mistress, she hurried on, 'You've been such a help with the younger children. Especially at reading time.'

'I enjoy reading. It isn't like lessons at all.'

'But I don't just mean when you helped them with their school primers, I mean story time. I was happy to let you take my place. You brought the stories to life; acting the parts and almost making them into little plays. Where did you learn to do that?'

'I think it must be because my mother enjoyed books and always read to me.'

'Very likely. But you show more than simply a talent for reading aloud; you almost become the characters you are reading about. You are as good an actress as any I have seen treading the boards in the theatres in Newcastle.'

'What boards?'

'It's an expression used in the theatre. It means the stage. Have you ever been to the theatre, Rosina?'

'No.'

'Oh, you must go some time. My sister and I love going to the theatre. We see all sorts of plays. Comedies, tragedies and good old-fashioned melodramas. The actors and actresses become the people in the drama – the stories. My sister, Euphemia, claims that she goes to the theatre to improve her mind, but as for me – well, it's just enjoyment pure and simple! And as far as I'm concerned the actors and actresses are magical people who transport you to a world of make-believe where, nevertheless, you will hear the truth.'

Rosina frowned. 'I think I understand.'

'And you know what I believe? I believe that one day you could become one of those magical people, Rosina.' Miss Robson smiled and shook her head. 'But I can see that would not be appropriate for a young lady in your position.'

'My position?'

'You are the daughter of the great house. I don't imagine that you will be expected to take up any sort of employment when you leave school. And, of course, you are not leaving yet. You are going on to a school more suited to your social background, as your stepmother wishes.'

'My stepmother wants Amy to go there so she agreed that I have to go too.'

Miss Robson was aware of Rosina's wry smile, the sort of smile that hinted at cynicism that a child should not feel. She suspected she knew the cause of it but thought it best not to talk critically about Rosina's stepmother. She spoke of her mother instead.

'I must admit I was surprised when your late mother sent you here to the village school,' she said, 'but she explained that she couldn't bear to part with you until she had to, and although you would go to the Girls' High School in Newcastle when you were old enough, it would be only as a weekly boarder. That way, she told me, she would have you home at weekends.'

'She told you that?'

'Yes. Oh, my dear, I've been thoughtless. You are crying.'

'I still miss her, you know,' Rosina said.

'Of course you do. Here, take this clean handkerchief. No need to return it – keep it as a memory of me. I embroidered the basket of flowers in the corner myself.'

'Thank you.'

Miss Robson had no idea what to say. She and her sister,

Euphemia, had decided long ago that Rosina Leighton was a neglected child. Not in any material sense, of course. She was clothed and fed adequately – better than most of the other pupils of the school, in fact – but maybe not treated quite as well as her stepsister, Amy.

Euphemia had been going to Ravenshill to teach Amy and she had often remarked that the child, quite disgracefully in her eyes, was dressed in the latest fashions chosen by her mother, whereas it was the dour Miss Fidler who was responsible for choosing Rosina's clothes.

No, the neglect suffered by Rosina was not material. It was emotional. When Miss Robson remembered what a warm loving mother Geraldine Leighton had been she almost wept. She had rarely seen the second Mrs Leighton herself but Euphemia, a keen judge of character, had described her as elegant, imperious, cold and ambitious.

Euphemia was the soul of discretion and was perfectly aware of the duty owed to the family who were employing her. She would never dream of carrying gossip to the village but, safely within the small house they shared, what was more natural than for one sister to confide in the other and discuss the minutiae of her day?

She had decided that Blanche Leighton was no lady. Or rather her origins were more humble that she liked to pretend. She had been lucky to catch the attention of Julian Leighton and, to give her her due, she seemed to realize this and made great efforts to please him. There was always an air of faintly disguised anxiety about her and the tension had increased since Rosina's baby brother had died.

Mrs Leighton spoiled Amy outrageously. The child got just about anything she wanted. Anything Rosina was given was almost an afterthought. And the strange thing was that Mr Leighton was just as guilty in this matter. He seemed to adore his stepdaughter and, although he wasn't exactly cruel to Rosina, his attitude could only be described as distant. Of late he had spent more and more time away from home. She understood he had to see to business concerns in London.

Mrs Leighton was always restless while he was away but consoled herself with shopping trips to Newcastle. She would often take Amy with her, even if it meant the child missed her lessons. They would come back with more clothes than a woman and a girl child could ever wear. But they never brought anything back for Rosina.

Euphemia had told her younger sister that she was glad the two girls were soon to go away to school. Not just because she found Amy a tiresome and lazy pupil, but because she hoped earnestly they would be treated on equal terms. There would be no favouritism at the High School.

But now the classroom was tidy, the books were locked away in the cupboard and the jars containing the wild flowers had been emptied and washed.

'I never like throwing flowers away while there's still some life in them,' Miss Robson told Rosina. 'I shall wrap these up in newspaper and take them home.'

'Let me do that for you,' Rosina said.

'Thank you, dear. Now,' the village schoolmistress looked round the tidy room with satisfaction, 'all done and dusted. I suppose we'd better go.'

They walked together along the sunny street as far as the neat little house where Miss Robson lived with her sister. Miss Robson gently removed a sleeping tabby cat from the top of the gate and opened it. The cat, indignant at first, began to purr when he saw who had disturbed him, and ran ahead of her up the path towards the front door.

But Miss Robson paused with one hand on the gate and said, 'Well, goodbye then, Rosina. I wish you success at the High School.'

'Thank you.'

The schoolmistress watched as Rosina Leighton walked away along the village street. She wished there had been more she could have done to make the girl happy. But at least she had done her best to make sure she'd had a good education, often lending her own books and giving her extra work to take home. Rosina was an intelligent child who would find it easy to adapt to the more academic work at the school in Newcastle; unlike Amy, of whom Euphemia had despaired. It was hard to understand why Mr Leighton seemed to prefer the vain and shallow Amy over his own sweet Rosina. Winifred Robson could only hope that one day the child's fine qualities would be appreciated.

At the same time as the younger Miss Robson had been saying goodbye to her pupils at the village school, her elder sister, Euphemia, was tidying the schoolroom at Ravenshill. She gathered up her books and put them into her bag. She picked up Amy's exercise books and glanced at them briefly. She shook her head over the scrawling writing and the many blots. She didn't suppose Mrs Leighton would examine them but perhaps Mr Leighton might want to see how Amy had been progressing. He would be disappointed. She had done her best but the child simply wasn't interested.

Her reluctant pupil had already fled the school room, leaving books and pencils in an untidy muddle. Miss Robson tidied the table top and, picking up her bag, she turned towards the door just as Mrs Leighton entered the room.

'Well, then, we must say goodbye, Miss Robson,' Blanche

Leighton said. 'And I must thank you for everything you have done for Amy.'

Euphemia thought the woman looked troubled but didn't imagine it would be about anything to do with her daughter's lack of academic ability. There was something else worrying her. But she was doing her best to be gracious. The schoolmistress suppressed a smile. She's playing the part of a great lady, she thought. She is conscious of the place she believes she holds in society and is treating me like someone of a lower order. Well, I'm not having that.

'I'm afraid I have done very little for your daughter,' Euphemia said with a wry smile.

'Oh . . .' Mrs Leighton was startled. 'I'm not sure what you mean.'

'It isn't that I haven't tried my very best but I'm sad to say that I have found Amy a most reluctant pupil. In spite of my efforts she still does not know all the multiplication tables, her spelling is haphazard and the only way I could get her to read was to borrow your fashion magazines.'

Mrs Leighton actually smiled. 'I know. And don't feel you have to apologize.'

'Doesn't what I have told you give you cause for concern?'

'Well, I suppose I would have liked her to enjoy her schoolwork more but it's not important.'

'*Not important?*' Miss Robson was aware that her voice had risen with indignation.

'No. I mean, considering Amy's station in life she does not need to be academic, does she?'

'Her station in life?'

'As the daughter – I mean stepdaughter – of Julian Leighton she can expect to marry well and be kept in comfort for the rest of her life.'

'And that is important to you?'

Blanche Leighton looked astonished. 'Well, of course it is.' She attempted a light laugh. 'But I can see that you don't agree with me.'

'No, I'm afraid I don't. Especially as Rosina has an entirely different attitude. Despite the fact that she has been a pupil in a simple village school she is a scholar that her father should be proud of. And yet I imagine she holds the same station in life as Amy.'

Mrs Leighton gave no answer. She simply shrugged and bade Miss Robson goodbye, sweeping from the room slightly less graciously than she had entered it.

She had angered her, Euphemia Robson thought. She didn't like her daughter to be compared unfavourably with her stepdaughter, and Miss Robson supposed that was natural enough. But she wished she hadn't said anything. She had the feeling she had just prompted more ill feeling towards Rosina.

Amy came into Blanche's elegant small sitting room and found her mother standing by the window and watching as Miss Robson walked down the drive carrying her bag. It would be a two-mile walk back to the village.

'Has the old fusspot gone for good?' Amy asked.

'Don't talk like that,' her mother snapped. 'It's ill mannered and ignorant. Now go to your room and stay there until I send for you.'

Amy stared at her mother; she was too shocked to say anything. She had never been spoken to in this manner. She tried a tentative smile, making sure that her lips trembled.

'Mama . . .' she began, expecting her mother to say sorry. But the angry expression did not change. Colour flooded Amy's pale face. How dare her mother speak to her like that? She wouldn't have done so if Papa had been home. She turned and ran from the room, shaken and tearful. She pulled the door after her so that it slammed.

'Amy!' Her mother turned and hurried to the door. She wrenched it open but it was too late: Amy was already more than halfway up the stairs. A curious housemaid stood at the bottom and watched her progress.

Blanche went back into her sitting room quickly. She did not want the maid to see her distress. She would have to try to make amends with her daughter later; perhaps promise her that she could choose any outfit that she liked from Harrods' mail-order catalogue. She sighed and resumed her position at the window. Julian should have been home by now.

He was supposed to have returned from London on the early morning train. Blanche had sent Angus with the carriage to the station but it had returned empty.

'Mr Leighton was not on the train,' the groom had told her, 'and there was no message.' By that he meant that Julian had not sent a telegram to the stationmaster to tell him why he was delayed and what train he would be taking.

So Blanche had sent Angus back to the station with the instructions to wait there all day if necessary until the master arrived. Angus hadn't questioned her order but no doubt his wife, who worked in the kitchen, would have seen to it that he took some provisions with him although Blanche had not ordered her to do so.

As the time of each train arrival came and went, Blanche grew more and more restive. There had been a time, in the early days of their marriage, when Julian would catch the very earliest train from London in order to be with her as soon as possible. Back at Ravenshill, he would leap from the carriage and hurry into the house, sweeping her up in his arms without regard for any servants who may have been watching. But ever since his baby son's death the previous year he had become withdrawn and moody. George had been the heir he had longed for. There had been Leightons at Ravenshill for centuries. Though never a truly grand family – indeed, they had probably started out as outlaws and sheep stealers – once they were respectable the land and the property they had acquired had been handed down directly from father to son without a break in the line. Until now.

Blanche shivered. Despite the warmth of the day she felt cold. She crossed to the fireplace and warmed her hands at the small fire. Then she forced herself to look up at the gilt-framed mirror that hung over the mantel. She studied her face anxiously, searching for the first signs of ageing. There were none. Her skin was smooth and wrinkle free. She knew she looked much better than the wives of most of their country neighbours, who had no idea how to take care of themselves.

Julian still desired her, she was sure of that. He proved it every time they went to bed together. But she was beginning to suspect that he had never loved her in the romantic sense. Furthermore, if Geraldine had lived, he would have been more than happy to carry on as before with a wife in Northumberland and a mistress in London.

And now he regretted marrying her. She had realized that the only way to make him happy would be to provide him with a son and so she had thrown caution to the winds and tried desperately to conceive. But nothing had happened. It looked as if Amy was going to be their only child. Blanche raised her chin and looked into the mirror as a steely resolve took possession of her. If I can't bear Julian a son, she thought, then Amy must be the heir to Ravenshill.

Reassured by her still youthful appearance but worried by the possibility that lines might begin to appear on her smooth forehead, she determined not to frown. And then she heard the sound of the coach coming up the gravelled drive and her anxious expression eased into a smile.

Heedless of what the servants might think, she rushed out of the room and crossed the hall to the front door. Pulling it open, she hurried down the steps just as the coach swept past with a scatter of loose stones, then rounded the east wing of the house to turn into the stable yard. She had got there in time to see that the coach was empty. Angus had returned to Ravenshill without his master.

The afternoon sun was still high in the sky. Bees drowsed in the cottage gardens. Rosina crossed the village green, starred with daisies, and made her way up a gently rising path towards the church. She stopped now and then to pick flowers growing at the sides of the track. Butterflies, meadow brown and marbled white, hovered above the clover and the buttercups.

The paths in the churchyard were cooler, winding as they did below the sheltering elms and the ancient yew trees. The church had stood there for centuries, the oldest headstones now so weathered that it was no longer possible to read the names of those who lay there in the cool, dark earth. But on those headstones that had stood the test of time, the same few names were repeated time and time again. These were the names of families who had peopled the village and the surrounding farms for as long as it was possible to remember.

The Leightons were no different except that over the centuries their graves became grander; the stone urns larger, the wings of the angels spreading wider, the carved epitaphs more elaborate. The marble angel guarding the most recent Leighton grave shone creamy white in the dappled shade of a beech tree. A glass jar that had once held marmalade looked incongruous at the base of such a magnificent memorial. It held a bunch of faded wild flowers.

Rosina laid down the flowers she had picked on the way up the lane and lifted up the jar. Like Miss Robson, she hated throwing flowers away so, as she always did, she walked the length of the path and laid them on a neglected small grave that no one ever visited. It looked like the grave of a child.

Then she took the glass jar to a water butt that stood behind the church and, using the metal cup, she filled the jar with fresh water. She made her way back to the grave that held her mother and her baby brother.

At the village station Julian Leighton told Angus to load his luggage into the carriage and to go back to Ravenshill without him.

'It's a fine day,' he'd said. 'I'd like to walk back and stretch my legs after the journey.'

The country roads were quiet and while he walked he would have time to think. He knew there was no solution to his problem. He had married Blanche because he'd thought he had an heir to Ravenshill. But George had died. He still desired Blanche and was resigned to lying in the bed he had made for himself. But that did not mean he could be happy about it. He supposed Blanche might yet conceive again and, knowing what pain she had suffered when Amy was born, he respected her for being willing to try. But he had very little hope that they would succeed.

So who would inherit Ravenshill? Rosina, who did not know she was adopted, or Amy, who did not know she was his daughter? The estate was not entailed; he was at liberty to leave it to whom he pleased. Did he care what people might say if he chose Amy over Rosina? No, why should he? He would be dead and gone and would not have to suffer censure. But his reputation would suffer. Was that important?

His instinct was to make Amy his heir. She was his only child and he loved her with all his heart. Rosina would be provided for — in fact, she was already provided for in Geraldine's will, so there was no reason for him to feel guilty. Nevertheless, he felt that he ought to make his peace with his late wife's shade so, after walking through the village he turned and made his way up the track to the churchyard.

After Geraldine's funeral he had felt too guilty to visit her grave. Guilty because he had not been at home when she had died in childbirth, and guilty because as well as grief he had felt joy that he could marry Blanche at last. But then his baby son had died and had been laid to rest with his mother. Julian had thought he might faint when the tiny coffin was lowered into the dark cavity. The thud of the first sod on the lid of the coffin had been so final that he had returned to Ravenshill in a daze of grief from which he had still to recover.

A drowsy silence lay over the graveyard like a shroud, but Julian became aware of the drone of insects and the occasional rustle of birds in the leaves of the old trees. Once his senses had been alerted he could hear his own footsteps and feel the beating of his heart.

When he neared his wife's last resting place he stopped and stared. A small figure was kneeling by the grave. It was a dark-haired girl in a school smock. A child from the village? She was arranging flowers in a glass jar. Wild flowers. He recognized buttercups, white clover and red campion. But why was she putting them on Geraldine's grave?

He started forward and his shadow fell across the kneeling child. She looked round, startled. It was Rosina.

'Father!' Rosina looked surprised but then she smiled. 'You're home!'

'What are you doing here?'

Rosina looked puzzled. 'Flowers ... I've brought some flowers.'

'And you think those flowers are fitting for my wife's grave?'

'Your wife ...' She frowned. 'My mother ... and my brother. Yes, I do.'

'Wild flowers growing in the hedgerow like weeds?'

'My mother liked wild flowers. We used to pick them together. She showed me how to press them.'

'And do you come here often with flowers for her?'

'As often as I can.'

Rosina looked crestfallen and Julian felt guilty. Always guilty, he thought. Guilty because he had betrayed Geraldine with Blanche, and now guilty because while he had never visited my wife's grave, this child – the child he did not want to adopt – had been tending the grave when it should have been him.

'Are you angry with me?' Rosina asked.

'No.'

'You sounded angry.'

'I was shocked. I didn't expect to find anyone here.'

'I miss her,' Rosina said. 'When I come here I feel close to her.'

Julian thought it was probably unhealthy for the child to talk like that but he acknowledged that she might be lonely. More guilt.

'Will you come here again, Papa?' she asked him.

'Why do you ask?'

'We could come together.'

'Perhaps.'

She looked disappointed.

'But I'll tell you what I'll do,' he said. 'When you go to

school in September I'll make sure that there are fresh flowers here every week.'

'Will you bring them yourself ?'

'Maybe.' He knew he wouldn't. He could just imagine Blanche's reaction if he started visiting his first wife's grave regularly. 'Well, sometimes I will.'

'I'll be home at weekends,' Rosina said. 'Then we could come together, couldn't we?'

'Rosina, I don't think I want you to come here again – at least not so often.'

'Why?'

'Your . . . your mother wouldn't like it.'

'I don't understand.'

'You are still a child. You must not dwell on the past so much.'

'But I was happy then.'

More guilt. 'And you will be happy again.'

She didn't respond but to his consternation he saw tears well up in her eyes. 'You'll make friends at school,' he told her. 'You will have other girls to talk to, to play with.'

He did not mention that she already had Amy for he had realized almost as soon as Blanche and Amy arrived at Ravenshill that the two little girls would never be friends. He could not bring himself to blame his own daughter for this; instead he convinced himself that Blanche was right and that Rosina was jealous of her stepsister.

'Shall we walk home together?' he asked.

Rosina nodded.

'Here.' He offered her his handkerchief but she shook her head.

'I have one,' she said, and took a pretty embroidered handkerchief from her pocket. 'Miss Robson gave it to me.'

'Miss Robson?'

'At school.'

'Oh, of course.'

Julian wondered why the schoolmistress had had to offer Rosina a handkerchief and concluded that she must have been crying earlier. He suppressed a groan. If Geraldine was looking down from heaven she would have every right to reproach him.

'Come along, then,' he said, affecting a lighter tone. 'We shall walk home and you will tell me what you would like to do as a treat before you go to the High School.'

'A treat?'

'Yes, you know, something out of the ordinary. Something we don't do very often.'

Rosina thought for a moment and then she remembered her conversation with Miss Robson. 'I would like to go to the theatre,' she said.

'The theatre?' Julian was surprised.

'Yes, Miss Robson goes to the theatre with her sister. She said it was magical.'

Her father smiled. 'In that case we must go. If the good Misses Robson approve of a trip to the theatre, how can I object? We'll all go to the theatre, shall we? A family party. I shall make it my business to find something suitable.'

He saw the shadow that crossed Rosina's face and knew it was because he had mentioned that they all would go. But he couldn't help that. Rosina would have to accept that she was part of a family. She couldn't expect to have him to herself.

But whatever she might have been thinking she didn't complain. Suddenly, and he didn't know why, he offered her his hand. Perhaps Geraldine's spirit had prompted him. They walked along in harmony and soon reached the approach to Ravenshill.

Blanche had not left her post at the window since Angus

had reported to her that the master was walking home. She was determined to greet him cheerfully, but it took every ounce of self-control to maintain her smile when she saw him coming up the drive holding Rosina's hand. She crossed to the fireplace and rang the bell to summon a maid. When the girl arrived Blanche asked her to go and bring Miss Amy to her.

When Julian walked into the room he found his wife and daughter rising smilingly from the sofa where there lay a scatter of magazines.

'Julian, my dear,' Blanche said. 'I'm so glad you have found the little miscreant. Where on earth have you been, Rosina? You really should come straight home from school, you know. I've been so worried about you.'

Chapter Eleven

Early September, and a sudden shower drenched the city streets and sent people scurrying for cover in the shops and arcades. Sun shining through the rain made rainbow patterns on the wet cobbles and pungent steam rose from the ever-present heaps of horse manure. Maud Fidler held a lavender-scented handkerchief to her nose. She had not thought to bring an umbrella so she was relieved that the hansom cabs were allowed to enter the grand portico of the Central Station.

Once there, she descended from the cab amidst the usual bustle of travellers and, after paying the cabbie, she hurried into the station and made for one of the cafés that opened on to the main concourse.

There was nearly an hour to wait for the train and she was in need of refreshment. She had risen early to supervise the loading of the girls' boxes on to the carrier's cart and then, feeling affronted but not daring to oppose Mrs Leighton's command, she had gone with the cart to the station. Certain that Mrs Leighton had intended to demean her by making her travel like some village woman or lesser servant, she had sat in angry silence next to the driver, seething with resentment all the way to the station.

With the luggage safely stowed in the guard's van she had

been able to relax until the train reached Newcastle. But she would have enjoyed the journey more if she had not been sitting all alone in a second-class carriage while the family travelled first class. Maud had always travelled first class when she accompanied the first Mrs Leighton.

Mr and Mrs Leighton were taking the girls to school themselves that morning, although this would be Maud's job every subsequent Monday. After school each day, Amy and Rosina would go with the other boarders back to one of the school boarding houses – that owned by Mrs Forsyth, and the better establishment of the two, Mrs Leighton had been assured. It was certainly the more expensive, with some of the pupils having rooms of their own. Blanche Leighton had decided that Amy should have one of these single rooms, whereas she thought Rosina would be happier in the dormitory.

The next time Maud would see the girls would be on Friday when she would meet them at the school gates and take them home for the weekend. Mrs Forsyth would be responsible for their laundry.

During the preceding months Maud had taken them into town to Isaac Walton's for their school uniforms, had ordered the name tapes and had sewn them on herself instead of leaving it to Bridget. She wanted to establish how dependable and useful she was. Now that the cot in the nursery was empty and the undernursery maid dismissed, Maud had worried that Mrs Leighton might decide that Bridget could very well look after the girls.

Ironically the one thing that had saved her, she thought, was Mrs Leighton's snobbery. She affected to disdain the way that local people spoke and Bridget still talked like the village lass she was, whereas Maud had no discernible accent. Therefore Mrs Leighton considered her more suitable to be in charge of arrangements for her precious Amy.

And Maud still had her housekeeping duties, although she supposed there were many well-trained women younger than she capable of taking her place. Fortunately Mr Leighton didn't like too much change and he considered that Maud was used to the running of the place, whereas someone else might upset the established order.

When Geraldine Leighton was the mistress of Ravenshill Maud was more companion than servant, but the second Mrs Leighton did not treat her as such. The very fact that she thought Maud was close to her predecessor made her dislike her. She knew Maud was responsible for bringing Rosina to the house. Mr Leighton, despite his dislike of the notion of adoption, was grateful that she had made his wife happy; Mrs Leighton saw her as the person who was responsible for providing a rival for her own daughter.

Just before Maud reached the door of the café the shouts of a newsboy caught her attention. She could just about make sense of the garbled call and she hurried across to buy the first edition of the evening paper. The placard at the lad's feet spelled out what he was saying and Maud's hand trembled as she proffered the required penny. She folded the paper and put it in her capacious handbag, then hurried back to the tearoom. She would have a cup of tea, and perhaps something stronger, before she opened the paper to read the story.

She ordered a pot of tea and a toasted teacake and also a glass of brandy. Delaying the moment, it was only after she had finished eating that she opened out the newspaper. She ignored the advertisements that covered the first page and found the item she was looking for. The headline was almost the same as the bold words on the newsboy's placard:

DAISY BELLE THE TOAST OF PARIS!

Raise a glass to Newcastle's very own songbird. Local lass Daisy Belle has captured the heart of every red-blooded Frenchman. Even the sophisticated Parisians have been won over by her sweet songs of true sentiment.

Each evening, after the final curtain, scores of enthusiasts follow her down the Champs-Élysées, throwing flowers into her open carriage and calling out, *La poupée! La poupée!* By this they mean that they want her to sing the song about the broken doll, the very song that carried her to the pinnacle of fame in the British Isles and may soon make her celebrated throughout the world.

One balmy night last week Miss Belle did indeed indulge her many admirers. She instructed the carriage to stop and there, in the heart of that most romantic city, she rose to her feet and sang for them. Illumined by the streetlamps, dressed all in white and cradling the doll to her bosom, she was the picture of lovely womanhood. This reporter has been told by a reliable source that many of the audience at that impromptu performance went home with tears in their eyes.

It has also been conveyed to me that Miss Belle returns the affection of her Gallic public and she has decided to buy a house 'somewhere in France'. But she does not intend to make this her permanent home. She has sent a message to you that her heart remains in Newcastle and that she will return to this grand old city as often as she is able.

Maud folded the paper and put it in her bag. She signalled to the waitress to come to her table and ordered a second glass of brandy. Then as she sipped it, she thought about what she had just read. She detected her brother's hand in this story. He had told her long ago that most newspaper reporters, especially in the provincial press, are lazy and they would welcome a nicely written piece that could be published without too many corrections.

She suspected that every word of this news item had been written by Jack. Even though Daisy was famous now, he never missed an opportunity to thrust her name into the public eye. When he had discovered her singing in the streets he had been prepared to take a gamble on her and it had paid off. By managing her career he had been able not only to get the most lucrative contracts for Daisy but he had always made sure that he did very well out of it himself. Daisy had become fabulously wealthy and so had Jack.

And he couldn't have done it without me, Maud thought. At the beginning my brother relied on me to win the girl's confidence and persuade her to leave the streets and take shelter in his house with her child. Rose . . .

Maud shifted uneasily in her seat as she remembered the next time Jack had asked her to help him. Rose had recognized her, trusted her, and that had made it easier to spirit her away. She suppressed, as always, the feeling that she had betrayed the little girl's trust. Jack had told her that it would be better for the young singer not to be encumbered with an illegitimate child. And, although Maud heartily agreed with that, there was no denying that Daisy's heart had been broken.

But Rose had been taken to a good home; a settled existence. Geraldine Leighton had loved and cherished her. No child could have had a better life. Rose had accepted her new name – Rosina – and had come to believe that Geraldine was her mother. All would have been well if only Geraldine had lived. Maud tried not to think of Rosina's life now with her stepmother, Blanche, and that spiteful little miss, Amy, as her stepsister.

There had been a time when she sensed that Mr Leighton had wanted to send Rosina away, perhaps find a foster home for her. But if he had done that he surely would have had to tell the child she was adopted. And Mr Givens – Jack – had insisted that that must never happen. As Rosina grew, like many adopted children, she would wonder who her real mother was, and why she had been given up, and perhaps try to trace her.

That blessed doll! Maud thought. Why hadn't she followed her instinct and destroyed it when she took Rosina to Ravenshill? But at the time it was the only thing that would pacify her. And she still treasured it much more than any of the expensive dolls Mrs Leighton had bought her. And that song ... the song Daisy Belle was famous for ... Rosina remembered the tune and maybe even some of the words. If she knew she was adopted it was not too far-fetched to imagine that she might think she had some connection to Daisy.

Jack had paid her well over the years to make sure that Rosina stayed safely at Ravenshill. Once Maud had thought she herself would stay there for the rest of her life and, when her working days were over, retire to a nice little cottage on the estate. But the new Mrs Leighton disliked her – that was obvious. And Maud no longer had the same authority in the household.

If it were not for Jack and Rosina she would look for another position – but what sort of work would she find at her age? And did she really want to start again as a servant? Her savings were not quite enough to buy a little house to retire to – at least not in a respectable part of town. Maybe she could persuade Jack to increase the payments he sent her. Perhaps it was time to remind him again of what he owed her . . .

Maud looked at her watch and realized it was time for the train. She left the café and hurried towards her platform. On the way she took the newspaper from her bag and stuffed it into a waste bin.

That evening Rosina lay in bed in the dormitory and thought about her first day at the High School, which was so very different from the village school. The large red-brick building, new and imposing, was twice, even perhaps three times the size of the old village school built from mellow local stone. The village school had one large high-ceilinged classroom into which all the pupils crammed, no matter what age they were. Here at the High School there were separate classrooms with no more than twenty desks in each. And these were individual desks with a chair rather than the linked rows with one long bench. Each desk had a lid that opened to reveal a storage space for books and writing tools.

Not much work had been done that day. New textbooks for the autumn term syllabus and clean exercise books were handed out, and each girl was given a timetable to fill in, supervised by one of the school prefects, Julia Grey, a tall, graceful girl with a no-nonsense expression. The timetable had to be copied from the blackboard as plainly and as neatly as possible. Amy got into a muddle almost straight away and was in a state of tearful rebellion by the time her second untidy smudged attempt was rejected by Julia.

'Rosina,' the lofty creature said as she tore up Amy's third attempt, 'I think you had better copy the timetable out for your sister before the school runs out of paper.'

'She's my *step*sister,' Amy muttered, but nevertheless she

was pleased to let Rosina complete the task for her. And later she allowed Rosina to tidy the inside of her desk before Julia came round to inspect it.

'Goodness,' the girl in the desk behind Rosina murmured, 'how on earth has the little muddlehead got it into such a mess already? We've only just put our new books in there.'

After the inspection, as they lined up to go to the dining room for lunch, the same girl whispered, 'Poor you, having to sit next to your sister.'

'My *step*sister,' Rosina said with a grin.

'Yes, I heard that, and I couldn't help noticing that you are not close or I wouldn't have said anything.' She hesitated. 'But perhaps I shouldn't have. My mother tells me that I am sometimes too forthright; that I am not always tactful and that I disconcert people.'

Rosina had never met another child who talked in such a manner but she realized that no offence was meant. 'No, it's all right. Amy and I . . . Amy and I are very different. I don't suppose she would have chosen me for a sister if she had had any choice.'

'Well, they've sat you next to each other in class but you don't have to sit with her at lunch, you know. Each form has a table and we're allowed to choose where to sit at that table as long as we do it in an orderly fashion. I hope you'll sit with me.'

Rosina found herself looking up at the girl, who was a head taller than herself. She had light red hair, greenish-grey eyes, and a pleasant smile.

'I'd love to,' Rosina said.

'Good. My name's Joanne. Joanne Bartlett.'

They went down to the dining room together.

Rosina knew from the start that she and Joanne were going to be friends. They had fallen into conversation as if they had known each other all their lives. Joanne Bartlett was not one of the weekly boarders. She lived in Heaton and had to catch two trams each day to get to school in Jesmond. The first tram took her to the Haymarket in the city centre, and the next a little over half a mile to the school in Jesmond. On fine days she walked this last part of the journey – that is, if she was not late, as she frequently was, being a harum-scarum sort of person, she told Rosina.

At the end of the school day they parted like old friends, each happy that they would meet up again tomorrow. And now here Rosina was, sharing this large room they called a dormitory with five other girls from the school. All of them were good company and Rosina even felt a little sorry for Amy in her single room, no matter how many extra comforts were provided. She couldn't join in the laughter, or the gossip, or the whispered conversations; strictly forbidden after lights out. As Rosina settled down to sleep she knew she was going to be happy here.

When the week ended she was sorry she had to go home to Ravenshill, but only those girls whose parents lived too far away from the school – such as Grace Williams, whose father was a missionary in China – stayed on at school during the weekends and often for the holidays too. Grace went to stay with an aunt in Dorset during the long summer holidays.

Amy couldn't wait to get home and lost no time in complaining of how miserable she was at school. She told her mother it was because she missed her so much but Rosina knew the real reason was that she was not indulged as she was at home. But she had made a friend too: Susan Gutteridge, the equally spoiled daughter of a minor aristocrat. Her mother was delighted when Amy was first asked to spend the weekend at Susan's home.

Rosina was pleased too, because she was allowed to go

home with Joanne and this became the first of many weekends with the Bartletts, where she spent some of the happiest days since her mother had died. The atmosphere in the Bartlett house was warm and friendly; the comfortable but slightly overfurnished rooms so different from the formal elegance of Ravenshill.

She remembered that in her mother's day the family home had not been so stylish; in fact, it had been slightly shabby but with a lived-in look. But her stepmother had transformed the place so that every room looked like an illustration in one of the magazines she had delivered monthly.

Every time Rosina went home with Joanne she thought how lucky she was to have found such a friend, but Joanne insisted that she was lucky too.

'Who else would put up with my disconcerting manner and be happy to dress up and act out the plays I write?' she'd said.

'But I like it. It's fun,' Rosina had assured her. 'I like pretending to be other people.'

As the term drew on, Rosina realized that she was not looking forward to the holidays. Her stepmother wanted them to go to London for Christmas. She wanted to stay in the Leightons' London house, do some shopping, give dinner parties and attend the more fashionable entertainments. Amy wanted to have a party for her old friends. Rosina was dismayed by the prospect. Amy would hate having her there and she didn't think she would have much in common with her stepsister's friends.

One break-time, when she and Joanne had been set the task of watering the classroom plants, she told her friend how much she was dreading it.

'Surely you don't have to go to London if you don't want to,' Joanne said.

'I don't imagine they'll let me stay at home on my own.'

'You'll hardly be on your own with a house full of servants, but I know what you mean. Your stepmother would be worried in case she was accused of neglecting you.'

'You know I'd like to be there by myself. It would be like the days before they came there.'

'They? Don't worry, I know who you mean. But if you don't think your parents will allow you to stay—'

'They won't.'

'Then tell them you can come and spend Christmas with me. I'll get my mother to write to your stepmother straight away.' Joanne had a moment of doubt. 'She will agree, won't she?'

Rosina smiled. 'I'm sure of it. She would be free of me for the entire holiday and no one will be able to say she's neglecting me if I'm to stay with my best friend. She can tell people that she didn't want to disappoint me.'

'Is that what I am? Your best friend?'

'Of course. Why do you ask?'

'Because of what you've told me about Adam.'

'Oh, Adam ... Well, it's not the same, is it?'

'I don't know.'

The two girls looked at each other; Joanne's gaze was searching and Rosina's embarrassed. Then both seemed to shrug it off at the same time.

'So you'll come to the *maison* Bartlett for Christmas?'

'Yes, please. I'd love to.'

And Rosina meant it, but she had to suppress a certain feeling of regret. If she had been at Ravenshill, Adam's Aunt Muriel might have invited them both to the farm and they could have resumed their friendship as if neither of them had been away to school. But as she was sure that her stepmother would not have agreed to leave her there it was pointless to think of it. She could only hope there would be time to see her old friend, however briefly, before the others set off for London and she went to stay with Joanne.

When she and Adam did manage to spend a day together at his grandparents' farm, Rosina was gratified to find that he was disappointed that she wouldn't be at home much longer. But he hadn't come home from his boarding school alone. He had brought a friend, a boy from school, whose parents lived in India where his father was a civil servant. Rosina sensed that this boy would not have been pleased to have a mere girl tagging along so perhaps it was for the best that she was going to Joanne's.

On Christmas Eve Rosina and Joanne stood at the window of the first-floor drawing room in the Bartletts' large house on Heaton Road. Joanne was staring up at the gathering clouds.

'Do you think it will snow?' she asked. 'Those clouds look so dark and heavy.'

'I'm not sure,' Rosina said. 'They could just be dark because night is approaching.'

'I do so want it to snow while you're here,' Joanne said. 'The snow makes every garden in the street look as good as the next one and the dusty old town appears to be quite beautiful – like that poem we read at school, you know.'

Rosina looked out across the busy road with its tramlines and constant flow of traffic. The streetlamps dropped pools of light on to the frosty pavements. It was so different from the view of parkland and forest and distant hills at Ravenshill, but nevertheless she found it fascinating. She stared out at the roofs and the chimney pots and began to recite:

'When men were all asleep the snow came flying,
   In large white flakes falling on the city brown,
Stealthily and perpetually settling and loosely lying,
   Hushing the latest traffic of the drowsy town . . .'

'That's right,' Joanne said, 'and even though the poem is about London it could be about any city, don't you think?' Without giving Rosina time to answer she hurried on, 'And you recited that so beautifully you almost made me see the snow floating down. You have a gift, you know.'

'Stop that,' Rosina said. 'You're being disconcerting again.'

They smiled at each other's reflections in the darkening windowpane as they remembered their first conversation at school. As well as each other, they could see the reflection of the fire burning in the hearth and the sparkling tinsel and baubles on the tall Christmas tree in the far corner. The large comfortable room looked warm and safe and welcoming.

'And now,' Joanne said, 'we'd better have a last rehearsal.'

Joanne had written one of her plays especially for this occasion. It was a sort of pantomime with a prince and a princess, a villainous uncle, a mysterious old woman and a trusty servant. She had informed Rosina that there would never be more than two characters 'on stage' at the same time and that they would be able to play all the parts between them with the aid of cloaks, hats and a false beard or two. Rosina was doubtful about the whole enterprise but she entered into the spirit of the thing good-naturedly and had even suggested one or two changes to the script.

They had just got to the happy ending in the final scene when the door opened and Joanne's mother came into the room. 'Time to close the curtains,' she said.

Mrs Bartlett, tall and sandy-haired like her daughter, drew the heavy plum-coloured velvet curtains across the wide expanse of the bay and then crossed to the hearth to build up the fire. 'They're all busy helping in the kitchen for the party tonight,' she said. 'I don't want to burden them with little jobs like this.'

Rosina knew that by 'they' Mrs Bartlett meant the household staff. The Bartletts were comfortably off. Joanne's father owned a chain of tobacconists. But the family did not behave in a grand manner. She reflected that not even her own mother, who had been a considerate mistress, would have made up the fire herself or even drawn the curtains, and as for her stepmother, Blanche Leighton would ring the bell and send some poor maid upstairs if she had forgotten a handkerchief.

'I've asked Cook to send you up a tray of warm milk and bread and jam,' Mrs Bartlett told Joanne and Rosina. 'Nothing fancy because I don't want you to gorge yourselves. There'll be quite enough to eat this evening when the family arrive for dinner.'

Looking a little distracted, Mrs Bartlett hurried out again as a maid appeared with the promised tray. She set it down on a small table.

'Thank you, Mildred,' Joanne said and again Rosina reflected that she had never heard either her stepmother or her stepsister say thank you to any of the servants.

'Now where are you going to sit?' Mildred asked Joanne and she looked around the room frowning. Most of the chairs had already been set around the sides of the room in readiness for the guests. Joanne had explained there would be parlour games after the meal.

'We'll put some of those big cushions on the floor,' Joanne told the maid, 'and have a sort of picnic by the fire.'

Mildred smiled at them and shook her head. 'Well, I suppose that's all right, seeing your mother asked me to bring the tray into this room, but mind you don't make a mess. I've enough to do this evening without coming in here with a dustpan and brush.'

If any of the maids at Ravenshill spoke to Amy like that she would have a tantrum, Rosina thought.

While they ate their bread and jam and drank the warm milk, Joanne, who had no brothers or sisters, tried to tell Rosina about the uncles, aunts and cousins who were coming to join them for the meal that night.

'It must be wonderful to have a big family like that, especially if you are close,' Rosina said. 'Do you know, I haven't thought about it until now, but I do not know a single aunt or uncle or cousin, or any kind of blood relation.'

'You have your father.'

Rosina gazed thoughtfully into the fire. 'Yes, but I don't feel close to him. We don't talk to each other much or laugh and joke like you and your father do.'

'But he's kind to you, isn't he?'

Rosina considered the question. 'He's not unkind. It's just he doesn't seem to notice whether or not I'm there most of the time.'

'I expect he's busy.'

'Yes, that will be it.'

There was an awkward silence. Rosina could have said that Joanne's father was also a busy man and yet he had time for her. And from the look of her Joanne was making a great effort not to say something disconcerting.

After visibly biting her lip Joanne spoke first. 'Come along,' she said. 'It's time to make ourselves beautiful – although you will have an easier job of it than I will.'

A little later, as they sat around the generously laden table in the ground-floor dining room, Joanne told Rosina the names of the uncles and aunts and cousins, but said not to worry if she couldn't remember them all. 'Sometimes I get them mixed up myself,' she said. 'Especially as at least three of my boy cousins are called Albert.'

After dinner everyone went up to the drawing room for the promised parlour games. They started with blind man's buff, went on to hunt the slipper and then, when the older aunts and uncles were out of breath and ready to sit down, Joanne announced that they were going to be treated to an entertainment. She had already hidden the cloaks, hats and other props behind the curtains in the bay, and she and Rosina retreated there to get ready for the performance.

The first character to appear would be the mysterious old woman, played by Rosina and, standing behind the velvet curtains dressed in a long cloak with a hood, she suddenly felt nervous. Although she had acted in many of her friend's plays by now, there had never been anyone to watch them other than Mrs Bartlett and occasionally Mr Bartlett too. Now she was going to go out there and perform before people she didn't even know. She found herself backing towards the window and came up with a shock against the cold glass.

'What are you doing?' Joanne hissed. 'It's time to begin.'

Rosina stared at Joanne with wide eyes. 'I think I'm frightened,' she whispered.

'Oh, that's all right,' her friend said. 'It's only stage fright. All actors get it. You've got to learn to overcome it, that's all, and now's the time to start. Now get out there and read the prologue.'

Joanne came towards her and dragged her away from the window. Then with one hand she pulled back one of the curtains just wide enough to allow Rosina through, and with the other hand she gave her an almighty shove. The play had begun.

Long before the entertainment was over Rosina had forgotten all about her nerves and was thoroughly enjoying herself. If the younger children gasped in surprise and delight, she was happy; if the older members of the audience clapped spontaneously she was absolutely elated. What a wonderful thing to do, she thought, to be able to entertain people like this.

At the end of the performance she and Joanne took their bows. At her friend's insistence they kept vanishing behind the curtains and popping out again as long as the applause lasted until Mrs Bartlett stood up and thanked everyone and said that was enough or her curtains would be ruined.

'Now you two had better just sit quietly for a moment and come back down to earth while our guests take their leave,' Joanne's mother told them. 'As it is I don't know if you will be able to sleep tonight.'

Come back to earth, Rosina thought. That's a good way of putting it for I certainly have been somewhere else while I was acting, although I don't know where exactly.

Later, when the guests had gone, Mrs Bartlett came up to Joanne's bedroom to say good night. 'You are a natural actress,' she told Rosina. 'Do you like the theatre?'

'I think so, but I've only been the once, just before I started at the High School. My father took us to see that children's entertainment at the Theatre Royal, *The Naughty Fairies*.'

Mrs Bartlett smiled. 'That piece of nonsense about a stolen child? A bit young for you but I imagine it was fun. If Joanne and I hadn't been away on holiday we would have gone to see it. But now I'd better say good night,' Mrs Bartlett said. 'And don't talk for too long, will you? Is it any use my telling you that Father Christmas will not pay a visit if you are both wide awake at midnight?'

'No use at all, Mother,' Joanne said. 'We're far too grown up not to know that it's only my father dressed up in a red robe and false white whiskers. And, actually, he expects me to be awake and peeping out in wonder from under the bedclothes. But please don't tell him that I know; I shouldn't like to spoil his fun.'

Although both girls were tired they couldn't sleep. There had been too much excitement. Mrs Bartlett had put the light out so Joanne opened the curtains a little to let the moonlight stream in. They talked softly. Joanne told Rosina of her mother and father's love of the theatre. They would take Joanne to see dramatic plays, comedies, operettas and even grand opera.

'You can imagine how excited my mother was when she discovered that a famous singer used to live in this very same street.' Joanne suddenly sat up and pushed her bedclothes aside. 'Come here and I'll show you.' She got out of bed and went to the window. She pushed up the lower half. 'Hurry up, Rosina.'

Rosina joined her reluctantly, shivering in the cold. They both leaned out.

'There,' Joanne said, and she pointed along the road to where the houses looked out on to the park. The roofs sparkled with frost. 'That house at the end, can you see it? That's where the singer lived, although she wasn't famous then.'

'Is she an opera singer? And please would you shut the window? It's freezing!'

Joanne laughed and closed the window as requested. Rosina scuttled back into her own bed and her feet sought the stone hot-water bottle.

'No, she isn't an opera singer,' Joanne said. 'She's a star of the music halls – variety, you know. She's called Daisy Belle. Have you heard of her?'

'No, I don't think so.'

'What — not even the song that made her famous? Well, the gossip round here is that she and her sister had rooms in that house along there. And Daisy was very kind to her sister who had a small child — a little girl. And one day the little girl was run over. Some say it happened on this very road as she ran out of the park gates, but others say they can't remember the incident and it must have happened somewhere else — probably in town. Anyway, Daisy Belle's sister was so grief-stricken that she went away. She just packed her bags and went. And Mrs Clarkson — she used to own that house before she retired to the seaside — well, she said she'd never forget what a terrible state the poor woman was in, even if the poor little girl was her niece and not her own daughter.'

Rosina remained silent.

'What is it? Have I upset you by telling you such a sad story?' Joanne asked.

'No. It's distressing, of course, but I suppose it happened a long time ago.' But Rosina was more disturbed than she liked to admit. And she couldn't really say why.

'Well, I suppose we'd better get to sleep,' Joanne said. 'I wouldn't want to upset my father, who thinks I still believe it's Father Christmas who will be coming to fill those stockings at the end of our beds.'

Once Joanne had made her mind up she could fall asleep quickly. Rosina had learned that during the weekends she had stayed with her. But Rosina lay awake for a long time. She had meant to ask her friend about the song Daisy Belle was famous for. She didn't know why but she thought it might be important.

When she did fall asleep she had the strangest dream. She was back in the theatre watching the play that her father had taken them to see. The play about the stolen child. The stage was like fairyland, with giant flowers and young girls dressed as fairies with pastel-coloured, sequin-strewn dresses and gauze wings. They danced gracefully as they led on the beautiful child they had stolen from her mother. The dream was true to the play in every detail except one. Instead of the orchestra playing ballet music, one of the fairies, the one with golden hair, was singing. Her voice seemed to come from far away and although Rosina recognized the melody she could not make out the words.

Rosina stirred in her sleep uneasily. She knew that if she tried very hard the words would come back to her. But the dream faded before the fairy had finished singing. Rosina, sinking deeper into sleep, did not know that her cheeks were wet with tears.

Chapter Twelve

June 1897

Adam Loxley was on his way home from his school in Berkshire for the last time. His trunk and his boxes were in the guard's van of the train. He stood in the corridor of a first-class carriage and leaned on the brass rail that ran along the windows as he smoked the cigar that Geoffrey had given him.

His friend Geoffrey Sanderson, whose father had an import and export business in the London docks, had handed round the Havana cigars solemnly to the favoured group and told them to think of him, so far away from England's pleasant clime, when they smoked them. Geoffrey was to be sent to the Far East to 'learn the trade', just as his father had done before him.

Adam didn't really enjoy the cigar but he persevered for the sake of friendship, and also because it seemed a grown-up thing to do. Half closing his eyes as the cigar smoke curled around him, he thought back over his schooldays. He had made good friends at school, some of whom might even prove to be friends for life, but now he was glad to be going home to Northumberland. He was relieved that his father had decided to take him into the family business straight away rather than insisting that he go to university, as some of his friends' fathers had.

He didn't need to go to university. He knew he was bright enough to work with and learn from his land agent father, and he had enough confidence in himself to believe that he would be good at the job and expand the already successful business even further. And apart from that, he loved the North Country. He just couldn't imagine being away from it for another three years or more. He had been proud to bring his friends home in the holidays — lads whose parents were abroad in the service of their country, for example, and who did not have any convenient relatives so would have had to stay on at school throughout the vacation.

He had felt a territorial pride when he had taken his school friends out into the wild countryside, or to ramble on the stretches of pale golden beach with the sand to run along and the sea to swim in when it was calm enough. And there were the ruined castles to explore. But he had never felt able to take his friends to his grandparents' farm. He knew he wouldn't have been able to pass his grandfather off as the 'gentleman farmer' he had let them assume his mother's father to be.

Adam's mother had welcomed them and fussed over them, her mother-hen feelings quite genuine, although Adam knew that she was secretly pleased to be hostess to some of the sons of families she considered to be higher up the social scale than the Loxleys.

As they all grew older, Adam sometimes caught a speculative look in his mother's eye and he suspected her of viewing one of the lads as a suitable husband for his young sister Charlotte. God help the man who ends up with Charlotte, Adam thought on these occasions. Oh, she was pretty enough, but so mealy-mouthed and such a little slave to Rosina's stepsister, Amy.

Charlotte would harass their poor mother until she had a dress, or a coat, or a pair of shoes just the same as Amy's latest purchase. And Adam knew for a fact that their mother had sometimes had to argue with their father to justify some item that he had considered an unnecessary expense. Hugh Loxley, whose land agency was prospering, nevertheless had realized some time ago that he had better curb his much-loved wife's extravagant tendencies.

If only Charlotte could have taken Rosina for a model. Rosina, so clever and steadfast, and – he felt a little uncomfortable to admit this – who obviously adored him. It was only after Adam had been sent away to school that he fully realized what a good friend Rosina had been. Almost as good as a boy in their earlier days, Rosina had been ready for any adventure on the seashore or on the hillside. Sometimes they had walked for miles together with a few sandwiches and a bottle of lemonade for sustenance.

Adam could never remember exactly what they had talked about, only that they had been perfectly natural together. The only thing that vexed him about Rosina was that sometimes she fell silent for no apparent reason and he would catch her, sitting on a slope beside him perhaps, with her arms wrapped round her drawn-up knees, gazing into the mid-distance with a faint frown as if she were trying to solve some conundrum – some puzzle whose solution always eluded her.

'What do you think about?' he had asked her only the last time he had been home from school.

'When?' she asked.

Adam, who had trouble dealing with any concept that couldn't be described in practical terms, found it difficult to explain but he tried.

'Sometimes you look so far away. Even when we're in the middle of talking about something it's as if you suddenly stop listening – or rather that you're trying to listen to something – to someone else.'

'Do I?'

'You must know you do.' Adam was irritated. She looked hurt by his tone. 'I'm sorry,' he said. But in truth he didn't know why he was apologizing.

She was silent for a while but then she smiled at him ruefully as she tried to answer. 'You'll think I'm silly,' she said.

'No, I won't think you're silly. Please go on.'

'Sometimes,' she said, 'sometimes I feel as if I shouldn't be here.'

Adam was flummoxed. 'What on earth do you mean? Not be here? Not be here with *me*, you mean?'

He looked faintly offended and she smiled. 'No, there's no one I'd rather be *here* with,' she emphasized the word 'here' and spread her arms to take in the veranda of the chalet, 'than you.'

'But?' he prompted.

'I mean I have the feeling that I don't belong at Ravenshill.'

'You don't like living in the country?'

'No, I love the country.'

Adam was relieved to hear it. For so did he. He could not imagine life in a city, although it was fun to visit now and then, and for some time now, without actually forming the idea into words, he had been envisaging a future with Rosina by his side.

'So what exactly do you mean?' He was beginning to get exasperated.

'The house . . . it feels so strange . . . my father . . .'

'Is your father not kind to you?'

'Oh, yes. He's kind. Or rather he is not unkind.'

Adam frowned. Rosina was talking in riddles. Suddenly he thought he knew the answer. 'Are you jealous?' he asked.

She opened her eyes wide in genuine surprise. 'Jealous?'

'Of your stepsister?'

'No, of course not.' But she had flushed and she looked away from him quickly.

'Don't be ashamed to admit to it, Rosina. No one would blame you. My Aunt Muriel says it's quite shameful sometimes the different ways in which you are treated, you and Amy. I mean, you are still a weekly boarder at the girls' school in Newcastle whereas the minute Amy was sixteen she was sent off to a finishing school in Paris.'

To his surprise Rosina smiled. 'Poor Amy.'

'Poor Amy? What do you mean?'

'She hated school – and I think the school was pleased to let her go. It was my stepmother's idea to send Amy off to Paris. She told my father that she thought we needed to be educated separately for a while because Amy was not flourishing. She hinted that it was my fault.'

'So they sent only Amy to Paris? I say, that's not fair!'

'Yes it is. Quite fair. I didn't want to go and I said so. I have made friends at school, one in particular, and I'm quite happy to stay right here in England until I'm eighteen, whereas Amy was bored. And when Amy is bored she is impossible to live with. I'm glad she went to Paris without me. Oh dear.'

'What's the matter?'

'Does that make me sound spiteful? I didn't mean to be. You see, Amy is happy at her finishing school learning etiquette and table manners and a smattering of French. And I am much more contented at the good old High School. And I'm not a bit jealous. Although I must admit I envy her the dancing lessons. The only time we have dancing at the High School is if it's too wet to play hockey or netball. And then it's only Miss Crump thumping out a tune on the piano while she passes on her out-of-date knowledge of ballroom dancing.'

Adam could see the wistful expression on her face but her words had brought back a childhood memory and he spoke without regard for her feelings. 'Do you remember those dreadful dancing lessons we had when we were children?'

'You mean the lessons my mother arranged? Of course I remember. I loved them.'

'Really? All those little girls prancing about and showing off, and their reluctant brothers dragged along by the scruff of their necks to partner them in the polka?'

'But if you hadn't been dragged along, as you put it, you and I wouldn't have become friends, would we?'

'You're right.' He grinned. 'Thank goodness for those *wonderful* dancing lessons. Your mother was an angel to invite us all!'

Rosina laughed at him and they smiled fondly at each other. The talk turned naturally after that to a dance that was to be held in the village hall before they both went back to school and they agreed to go along, taking Adam's Aunt Muriel, who loved such occasions, especially if they were going to have the old country dances.

To Adam's relief Rosina had not said any more that day about the feeling she had of not belonging. He was annoyed with himself for asking the question. She had assured him that she wasn't jealous of her stepsister so it was probably some unfathomable female stage she would grow out of. He hoped so.

As for going dancing, well, girls liked that sort of thing and Adam supposed it wouldn't harm to indulge them now and then. The theatre too. Adam frowned; he remembered how much Rosina would chatter on about plays and ballet and even the opera, for heaven's sake. There again, an occasional visit to the theatre where you might meet the right sort of people wouldn't harm. In fact, it might be good for business to have a wife who was knowledgeable about such things. A wife with an education suitable for the modern woman and from a good old-established family. Adam had been considering for some time that Rosina might be just the girl to fill that position.

And now he was on his way home for good and he had the most wonderful surprise planned for Rosina's birthday. He had ordered, from the Army and Navy Stores, the latest Rover lady's bicycle, the Imperial, which was the most expensive model, and had it delivered to his grandfather's farm. Aunt Muriel was looking after it. He'd also ordered the gentleman's model for himself, so that he and Rosina could bicycle through the countryside together, taking picnics with them and enjoying the scenery and the fresh air under the wide Northumbrian skies. He was convinced that that would drive away those silly ideas Rosina had of not belonging.

'It is so sad that you will not be here for your birthday, *chérie!*'

Beryl Earnshaw, her French accent execrable but enthusiastic, clasped her hands in a dramatic gesture as she and Amy took their walk together around the shady gardens of their finishing school in a fashionable suburb of Paris. The school, favoured by the aspiring English middle class, was run by Miss Elkington, an English woman who had first come to France as a governess to a French family. She had stayed with the family until her charges had grown and married. Her employer, grateful for everything she had done for his daughters, had bought the school for her.

There were those who said that she had done more for the girls' father than for the girls themselves and that was why he was so excessively grateful. Miss Elkington could certainly be considered a beauty, although her charms were fading now.

'But of course I shall have to go home. My birthday is not until next month. The school will be closed. We will all be going home. And never coming back here,' she added cruelly, and glanced sideways at her companion to see the effect of her words. She concealed a smile when she saw Beryl's face take on the expression of a puppy who has been scolded. Amy began to walk more quickly.

Beryl, short and plump, panted a little as she strove to keep up with the object of her adoration. 'I know,' she said, 'why don't you come home with me?'

Amy stopped walking but she didn't immediately face the other girl. When she did she managed to look as though this idea had never occurred to her. 'Home with you? To Leeds?'

'Yes. I mean, we don't live in Leeds — that's where the family mills are. We live in Harrogate. Honestly, Amy, you'd love it.'

'Mm . . .' Amy looked as though she was considering the idea. She continued her promenade, at the same time slipping her arm though Beryl's. Beryl flushed with pleasure.

'Harrogate is a fashionable town and there's lots to do, you know,' Beryl said. 'My mother has so many friends; we're always being invited somewhere or other. And my brother will be home. Maurice. You like Maurice, don't you?'

'Your brother? What has he got to do with anything?'

'But I thought . . .' Poor Beryl flushed brighter than ever, this time with embarrassment.

Amy took pity on her. 'You're right. I did enjoy your brother's company. He was most amusing. But I hope you don't think I would come to visit you in Harrogate just because Maurice is going to be there.'

'No — no, of course not.'

Beryl didn't know what to say. She had adored Amy ever since they had both arrived at the school on the same day, but Amy had made friends with other girls far prettier and more confident than Beryl was — although she did consent to talk to her and even go for walks with her during one of her periodic spats with someone as spoiled as Amy herself was. Amy would pour her heart out to Beryl and Beryl would agree with every word Amy said, even though this meant she lost friends because of it. For the strange thing was that Amy would be forgiven and would become the centre of the group again, whereas Beryl became more and more isolated.

Then, just a few weeks ago, Beryl's older brother, Maurice, had been in Paris on business for their father, visiting a celebrated dress designer who had made enquiries about some cloth the Earnshaws could supply. While he was there, naturally he had come to the school to visit his sister, who happened to be sitting with a group of her classmates in the garden when he arrived.

The other girls had been astounded. Beryl was short, Maurice was tall; Beryl was plump, and that was putting it kindly, and Maurice was lean and muscular. But the most striking difference of all was that Beryl was plainer than plain whereas her brother was as handsome as a hero in one of the romantic novels the girls kept under their pillows and read in secret when they should have been learning French vocabulary.

Maurice had been allowed to take Beryl out for walks and for little treats to approved cafés, although Miss Elkington had instructed him not to allow his sister to overindulge in pastries. One day he had surprised her by asking her if she would like to bring a friend with her on one of these expeditions. She had not known what to say. She knew very well that the other girls were jealous and she wanted to keep her brother to herself.

'A friend?' she'd asked at last. 'I'm not sure if Miss Elkington would allow it.'

'Leave Miss Elkington to me,' he'd said with a smile, and Beryl had been left in no doubt that Maurice would be able to charm the principal of the school into agreeing to the plan.

'All right. But who shall I—'

'Amy,' Maurice said decisively. 'Ask pretty little Amy.'

So she had and then had spent the most miserable day she could remember.

At first Amy had been surprised – or at least she had pretended to be surprised. '*Me?*' she had said. 'Your brother wants to go for a walk with *me?*'

'With *both* of us,' Beryl said quickly, for once very nearly annoyed with the girl she admired so much.

'Well, I'm sure I don't know why,' Amy said as she preened in front of the looking-glass in her room, 'but I suppose I had better put on my new hat.'

The walk started off well, with Maurice talking to both the girls about nothing in particular. 'Pleasant day . . . lucky in the weather . . . what pretty parasols you both have . . . do you visit the art galleries at all . . . ?'

After a while they stopped at a café that had tables set out on the pavement under an awning. He found a table and ordered coffee and pastries. He also ordered a brandy for himself and asked the girls if they would mind if he had a cigar. Beryl didn't know that Maurice smoked cigars but he was two years older than she was, twenty to be precise, so she supposed he was grown up enough to smoke if he wished.

The pastries were delicious. Maurice seemed to have

forgotten his promise to Miss Elkington not to let Beryl overindulge. Either that or he just didn't notice, because by now he was addressing his remarks solely to Amy, who had nibbled at one pastry and then left most of it. Beryl saw it on Amy's plate and wondered if her friend would mind if she finished it off for her. She was just about to ask when the waiter appeared with more coffee and another plate of pastries.

'Indulge yourself, little sister,' Maurice said with a smile. 'Neither Amy nor I will tell Miss Elkington.'

'Oh, but aren't you going to have any more?'

'No. Amy and I have decided to go for a walk. Not far, but we want to explore the little cobbled street that winds its way uphill over there. Wait here for us.'

'No, I'd like to come with you. I mean—'

'You would hate the walk uphill, you know you would,' Amy said crossly.

'I wouldn't. I, oh dear . . .'

Beryl half rose from her chair. She was flustered and her napkin fell across her coffee cup. She watched in horror as the snow-white linen stained a milky brown.

'Here, have my napkin,' Amy said, 'and do sit down again, Beryl, before you knock the table over.'

Maurice removed the stained napkin and laid it carefully on his own empty plate. 'Don't worry about that,' he said. And he and Amy had gone before she could protest further.

Even now, when Beryl thought about that day she burned with shame. Try as she might she could not remember the moment when Maurice had asked Amy to go for a walk with him and when Amy had agreed. Had she, Beryl, been too busy eating forbidden pastries to pay attention? That must be it. And so she was left on her own with nothing to do but eat up all the pastries that remained.

She had lost sight of her brother and her friend almost immediately and she had no idea why they would want to explore the little cobbled street that looked so dark and dingy, overhung as it was by the tall buildings on either side. It was more of an alleyway than a proper thoroughfare and Beryl was pretty sure that there wouldn't even be a shop front to stop and stare at.

She had been acutely aware that people were looking at her. And she could imagine what they saw: a fat, clumsy English girl who had been left on her own because she simply wasn't interesting enough to bother about. By the time Maurice and Amy returned, subdued but with an air of suppressed excitement, Beryl was near to tears. There was no conversation on the way back to school.

After that day Maurice had called at the school one more time and taken them out again; to the same café. Beryl had resigned herself to being left on her own and this time felt no guilt about devouring as many pastries as Maurice cared to order.

And then he had gone back to England. He had not written to Beryl but then he rarely did. The pupils of the school were allowed to receive letters only from their families, so Beryl had half suspected that Maurice would write if only to enclose a note for Amy. But he hadn't. Whether Amy was bothered by this or not, Beryl could not tell, but she had been perfectly sweet to Beryl ever since. So much so that Beryl had almost believed she had a real best friend at last and was dreading the day when they all departed for home and she would never see Amy again. That was why she had written to her mother and asked if she might bring Amy home with her for a visit.

'So would you like to come home with me?' Beryl asked now. 'You could stay until your birthday and we'll have a party. My mother loves arranging birthday parties.'

'Well . . .' Amy said, 'I would have to ask my mother, of course.'

'Oh, my mother will write to her.'

'Very well, if my mother agrees, I would love to come home with you.'

Beryl knew very well that Amy would probably not have agreed if she hadn't told her that Maurice would be there, but she felt no shame. She was wise enough to see all Amy's faults and to know that she did not always behave admirably. But Beryl couldn't help it. She knew that as long as fate permitted she would be Amy's slave.

'Are you sad to be leaving school?' Joanne Bartlett asked.

The two girls stood at the window of the sitting room in Mrs Forsyth's school boarding house. Rosina had been a weekly boarder there all the time she had been at the Girls' High School. They watched as Rosina's bags were carried out and loaded into the carriage that Joanne's father had sent to convey his daughter's school friend from the boarding house in Jesmond to the Bartlett household in Heaton. Joanne had remained a day girl throughout her school days.

'Glad to be leaving? Yes . . . no . . . I don't know,' Rosina said, and the two girls smiled at each other.

'What am I to make of that answer?' Joanne asked.

'I've been happy at school,' Rosina said, 'but as I'm nearly eighteen years old. It's time I ventured out into the world.'

'Of course, me too. I'm ready to do some venturing!'

Joanne struck a pose with one hand on her hip and the other held out as if she was grasping a sword. Being taller than average, Joanne had usually had to take the part of a male character in the plays she and Rosina had enjoyed acting in; both in the little bits of nonsense that Joanne wrote for fun and the school plays that were performed for an audience of parents.

'Pray let me go a-venturing by your side, kind sir,' Rosina said in a mock-dramatic voice as she dropped a graceful curtsy and, regardless of the fact that they were nearly eighteen years old, both girls burst out giggling.

Eventually Rosina sighed and looked perplexed. 'But what am I going to do with myself now?' she said. 'You have no brothers so your enlightened father wants you to join him in his business, but as far as I am able to gather, my father has no plans for me at all.'

'Surely he will expect you to find a husband?'

'And devote myself to domesticity? But what if I don't? I suppose I could train to teach and try to make some sort of independent life for myself.'

'What about Adam?' Joanne asked.

Rosina looked at her sharply. 'What do you mean?'

'Adam Loxley. From the way you talk about him I have always believed that he is special to you.'

Rosina smiled. 'Yes, we're good friends.'

'Just friends? Have you never hoped for more than friendship?'

'Perhaps I have. I'm not sure. I know he means a great deal to me.'

'And you to him, no doubt.'

'I . . . I hope so.' Rosina paused. 'But that still does not solve my problem. Am I to just sit around at home until the day he — until the day someone asks me to marry him?'

'Many young women do, you know. It would be nothing to be ashamed of. But look, your boxes are all stowed safely; I think it's time to go.'

As she spoke, Mrs Forsyth hurried into the room. 'Well,

Rosina, it's time to say goodbye. I shall miss you. And you, Joanne, you have always been a welcome visitor.'

Mrs Forsyth walked out with the girls to the carriage and stayed to wave them goodbye. Just a few streets away they had to pass the school and perhaps it was only at that moment that they realized they would never be entering its portals again. Both girls fell silent until the carriage turned the corner. They didn't speak again until they reached Joanne's home, the big old house near Heaton Park where Rosina had spent so many happy times over the last few years.

Perhaps as a newly married couple Mr and Mrs Bartlett had hoped to fill the many rooms with a happy brood of children, but Joanne had proved to be their only child, and she had come late at that. Nevertheless, if some of their dreams had come to naught, it was still a happy household.

Mr Bartlett had started out with one little tobacconist's, hardly more than a kiosk, on Shields Road, the long main thoroughfare that lay on the boundary of Byker and Heaton. His wife, with no children to occupy her, had helped him in the business and had soon opened her own little confectionery shop next door. Now they were the owners of a chain of both confectioner's and tobacconist's shops across Tyneside, the shops always being next door to each other if possible.

Mr and Mrs Bartlett adored their only daughter, and her father planned to take her into the business as soon as she left school. One day, in the far future, it was to be hoped, Joanne would be the owner of both business concerns and her father wanted her to know the trade as well as her parents did. No future son-in-law must be able to either ruin the business or swindle Joanne out of her inheritance.

Mrs Bartlett, perhaps feeling guilty that Joanne had no

siblings, had encouraged Joanne to bring her school friends home and she had become particularly fond of Rosina. During the school term Rosina travelled home to Ravenshill on Friday afternoons and returned to school on Monday morning. During the winter months the journey was tiresome, and sometimes Rosina didn't go back to Ravenshill for weeks on end. Once Amy had gone to finishing school in Paris, Rosina found that she could stay with her friend Joanne whenever she liked. Her stepmother seemed relieved not to have her come home.

Mrs Bartlett, as tall as her daughter and almost as slim, was pleased to greet Rosina. 'Well, my dear,' she said, 'we plan to make the most of the week you will be staying with us, especially as you will be here for your birthday.'

'Mother!' Joanne exclaimed, and shot her mother a meaningful glance.

'Oh, don't worry, Joanne,' her mother replied. 'I won't say another word.'

The two women looked at each other and burst out laughing. Joanne smiled and she hugged her mother in front of their guest quite unselfconsciously. Mother and daughter were not only completely easy with each other but there was no hiding the love they felt for each other. Rosina suffered a pang of loss and longing.

She had loved her mother just as fervently, and she was confident that her mother had loved her. Life had never been the same for Rosina since Geraldine Leighton had died giving birth to George. And then her baby brother had died too, and Rosina had felt like a piece of driftwood washed up on an alien shore. She had never been truly close to her father, and once he had remarried he became wholly occupied with his new wife and her daughter.

Blanche Leighton was not like a cruel stepmother in a

fairytale but at best she was distant and cool, and at worst she could be spiteful. Not to Amy, of course. Rosina had often watched the warmth and physical closeness between her stepmother and stepsister and wept alone for what she had lost. How she longed over the years to be gathered into motherly arms if she was ill or had suffered some childish accident. How she had longed to be told stories . . . read to . . . or sung to.

Sometimes she would take her old doll, the doll that had been part of her life for as long as she could remember, and go to the chalet in the woodland clearing. There she would sit with the doll in her arms and croon an old song. A song without words. Had she ever known the words? She thought she must have done, for she believed her mother had sung it to her when she was a baby. But if that was so, why couldn't she remember the words as she could remember all the nursery rhymes that Geraldine had taught her?

As she grew older she began to realize how memories could be inconsistent. How cruel of time to steal away what had once been a comfort. And even worse, there was something she hardly dared admit to herself: the face of her beloved mother was fading from her memory as the years passed. At least, not fading exactly – somehow it merged with another face, the face of someone she didn't know at all. Or perhaps she did . . .

Mrs Bartlett told the girls that a light tea was waiting for them in the dining room. 'Just bread and butter and a few currant scones because – oh dear, you had better know, Rosina – we are going to eat at a restaurant tonight.' She glanced at her daughter. 'It's only fair to tell her, dear, because she will want to look her best for the occasion.'

'You're right, Mother.'

So that is the meaning of the looks Joanne and her

mother exchanged before, Rosina thought. They are taking me to a restaurant. How kind they are.

When they entered the dining room Rosina was surprised to see Mr Bartlett sitting at the table. Joanne's father did not usually come home from business as early as this. Mr Bartlett was tall and a little portly, with dark hair quickly going to grey. He was dressed in his business suit and he looked up guiltily.

'Ah, Joanne,' he said. 'I needed a cup of tea.'

'And a large slice of Madeira cake too, I see.' Joanne smiled at her father. 'I don't know how you persuaded Cook to give you any but, don't worry, I won't tell Mother. Not this time, at any rate.'

Mr Bartlett smiled at Rosina. 'They do nag me,' he said. 'My wife has taken it into her head that I ought to lose weight. And I don't get any support from this daughter of mine. They're positively cruel.'

'It's only because we worry about your health, Father.'

'I know, dear. And now you've made me feel guilty.'

He looked so doleful that Joanne hurried over to him and, placing her hands on his shoulders, she kissed his forehead. 'Oh, for goodness' sake enjoy your piece of cake, Father. A little treat now and then won't hurt. And now we'll sit down and join you.'

Joanne poured the tea and while they tucked in to bread and butter she asked, 'Does Mother know you're home?'

'She does. It was at her express order that I came home early so that she would have plenty time to smarten me up for the theatre.'

At his words Joanne spluttered and nearly choked over her cup of tea. She placed the cup carefully in the saucer and dabbed at her lips with her napkin.

'Father!' she exclaimed.

'What have I said?'

'You've let the cat out of the bag. First Mother let slip that we're taking Rosina to a restaurant and now you've let her know we're going to the theatre. Honestly, my parents,' she said, turning to Rosina, 'they're like children. Simply can't keep a secret. I don't know what to do with them.'

But the love and pride in her voice belied her words. Mr Bartlett, after looking abashed for a moment, began to laugh.

Joanne turned to Rosina. 'I'm sorry,' she said.

'Don't be. Now I can begin to get excited and enjoy the anticipation.'

After the light meal, they went up to Joanne's room.

'What a wonderful family you are,' Rosina said.

Joanne looked round, startled. 'Wonderful? Why do you say that?'

'I suppose it's because you are so full of life – and love and, oh, everything.'

'Goodness, Rosina, I thought I was the one who had permission to disconcert people. Please don't talk like that or you will embarrass me.'

'I'm sorry. I didn't intend to make you feel uncomfortable. But I do want you to know how much it means to me to be able to come here and to have a friend like you.'

'Rosina Leighton, stop this at once and allow me to change the subject.' Joanne crossed over to the window and took a small flat silver case from her pocket. 'Now before we begin to bathe and change our clothes I suggest we relax a little.'

Joanne opened the case to reveal two neat rows of white tubes, one in each half. They were kept in place by elastic bands.

'Cigarettes!' Rosina exclaimed.

'Not just any old cigarette,' her friend replied. 'These are

223

a special brand, Hibiscus. They're deliciously mild and fragrant, possessing that delicate aroma so much appreciated by smokers of cultured taste! Or so it says on the box. Would you like to try one?'

'No thank you.'

'Are you sure?'

'I've heard it's a bad habit.'

'Maybe. But it's also a quite delightful habit.'

Rosina watched while Joanne took out one of the cigarettes and put it in her mouth. Then she lit it using a match from a small box that she also took from her pocket. A moment later she coughed and tried to disperse the cloud of smoke she produced by waving her hand about. As two fingers of that hand were still clutching the cigarette she only succeeded in creating more swirls of smoke. Rosina began to cough. She backed away.

'Sorry!' Joanne turned to the window and, releasing the catch, raised the bottom half. 'I'll stand here,' she said. 'That's what I usually do in case Ma comes in and finds out what I've been doing.'

'Your mother doesn't approve?'

'She thinks it isn't ladylike.'

'And your father?'

'Actually he doesn't mind. He brings them home for me from stock. He and I sometimes escape into the conservatory after our evening meal and I have a cigarette while he has a cigar.'

Rosina sat on Joanne's bed and watched as her friend held the lace curtain up with one hand and leaned forward to exhale the smoke out of the window. A memory stirred somewhere at the back of her mind. Her mother had not approved of anyone smoking in her presence. No that wasn't right; her mother hadn't minded at all when her father had a cigar. So it wasn't her mother then. But who had it been? She frowned in concentration but the memory remained elusive.

It vanished altogether when Joanne turned and said, 'I can sense your disapproval.'

'No . . . really.'

'Yes, really. But don't worry,' she smiled, 'because we really must get ready.'

She stubbed the cigarette out on the outer windowsill, then closed the window. She placed the stub in an empty packet. 'To be disposed of later,' she said. 'Now, what are you going to wear?'

The question startled Rosina. As she hadn't known until a short while ago that they were going out for the evening, she knew she would not have anything suitable in the collection of clothes she had brought with her, which consisted of school uniform skirts and blouses and some less formal dresses to change into in the evenings.

'Oh dear,' she said, 'but I didn't know . . . I haven't got . . .'

She heard Joanne give a soft chuckle and she looked at her in surprise to find her friend smiling at her delightedly. 'What is it? Why are you smiling?' She couldn't believe Joanne would be amused by her discomfort.

'I was teasing; it's all taken care of. Not for nothing was I the star of old Briggsy's needlework class!'

Joanne hurried to the large mahogany wardrobe that took up almost all one side of the room. She opened one of the doors and, reaching in, lifted down not one but two gowns shrouded in dust wraps. She laid them on the bed and then unwrapped one of the gowns and held it up for Rosina to admire.

Rosina could not hide an initial reaction of disappointment as she looked at the creamy white folds of silk taffeta. 'But it's your school party dress!' she exclaimed.

'Yes, it's the one I wore to the school Christmas dance. And this one,' she took up the other gown and removed the dust cover as she spoke, 'is the dress I wore to the previous Christmas dance. I only wore it to the one dance and one choir festival and then I outgrew it. And as I am quite a lot taller than you are I used my exceptional needlework skills to alter it to your size. Go on, try it on. There'll be just about enough time to make a few quick adjustments if need be before we bathe and get ready.'

Joanne helped Rosina out of her skirt and blouse and into the gown. And it was only when she led her over to the cheval glass and told her to look at herself that Rosina realised that clever Joanne had done much more than alter the dress to fit. To the high, demure neckline she had added row upon row of seed pearls interspersed with tiny green beads in a choker effect. She had repeated the pattern on the cuffs of the tapering sleeves and those sleeves had now acquired graceful points that came down over the backs of her hands. She looked wonderingly at the 'mutton-leg' puffs at the shoulders and also at the five tiny puffs that had been raised along each forearm.

'It's beautiful. This must have taken you hours of work,' Rosina said.

'It did. But you know I like that sort of thing. And a future successful business woman must have a relaxing hobby, don't you think?'

'Thank you so much. I wish I was as capable as you are,' Rosina said with a smile of affection.

'Hmm.'

'What is it?'

'Well, it's all very well being capable but I sometimes wish I could be beautiful like you.'

'Me? Beautiful?'

Joanne frowned. 'You really don't know, do you? Those dark gypsy curls and that creamy complexion, eyes so dark blue that some folk think they are brown. You are absolutely stunning, my friend.'

Rosina looked at herself in the mirror and tried to see the wondrous creature that Joanne had described.

Her friend laughed and asked, 'Why don't you believe me?'

'But my "gypsy curls", as you describe them, aren't really fashionable, are they?'

'Tosh to fashion! That's what I say.'

But Rosina persisted. 'I have always thought that to be really beautiful you should be pale and blonde and dainty like – well, like my stepsister, Amy.'

'Amy's pretty enough, I suppose, but dainty? You've been reading your stepmother's fashion magazines. I never did understand what "dainty" is supposed to mean.'

'Small and slim and yet with a womanly figure.'

'Not like me then?' Joanne said ruefully.

'Nor me.'

'Oh, but there's a world of difference between you and me. As I said, you are truly beautiful, whereas I am a tall, ungainly, freckle-faced, sandy-haired girl. That's what our beloved headmistress informed me as politely as she could when she advised me to acquire some womanly skills if I wished to find a husband. She dragooned me into the advanced needlework and cookery classes.'

Rosina laughed. 'And I remember how you protested!'

'Yes, well, I didn't shine in the kitchen but she did me a favour making me become a needlewoman. And if she doesn't think I'm going to find a husband, well she should know that several of the young confectionery and tobacco representatives who call on my mother and father have paused to pass the time of day with me. They actually seem to prefer a woman who has a head for business.' Joanne paused and grinned. 'And one who will take no nonsense from them!'

The two friends smiled at each other affectionately and Joanne took the two dresses and laid them carefully across her bed. 'Come along,' she said, 'we must take our baths. The sooner we have washed off all traces of school for ever the sooner we will take our proper places in this world as grown-up women!'

An hour later they stood in Joanne's bedroom again and took turns to admire themselves in the cheval glass. Rosina saw how clever her friend had been with the alterations of the evening gowns. The gowns were still white and virginal but they had been taken in skilfully to outline the figure. The bodice was slightly pointed and the skirt hugged the hips and then gradually flowed outwards in graceful folds.

'I was tempted to alter the neckline more drastically, you know,' Joanna said. 'Scoop it out entirely and go décolleté, but I decided Ma would have a fit if we revealed our necks and shoulders to public view.'

'I'm glad you reached the decision you did,' Rosina said.

'Oh, you would have been all right with your creamy skin – no, really, don't protest – but all I would be revealing would be thousands of freckles. Ma despairs of them. I can't tell you the number of lemons that have been squeezed in an effort to bathe them away.'

'But lemon juice—'

'I know, I know. All that the lemon juice does is dry my skin, and the freckles are as bad as ever.'

Rosina sensed that Joanne, normally so cheerful and optimistic, was really bothered by her freckles and was just about to say how cheerful and sunny-tempered the freckles on her face made her appear and that, in her opinion, Joanne was indeed attractive, but at that moment there was a knock at the door. Joanne called out for the person to enter, and when the door opened the girls were surprised to see Joanne's father.

Mr Bartlett looked very smart. He had changed from his business suit into evening clothes. With his hair perfectly combed and his beard trimmed, Rosina thought he looked distinguished.

He pretended to be amazed. 'I came to collect two schoolgirls,' he joshed, 'and instead I find two beauteous young women!'

'Stop it, Pa,' Joanne said. 'Rosina might not appreciate your teasing ways.'

'But I'm not teasing, my dear,' her father replied. 'I am indeed gratified that I shall be the lucky man to escort you and your friend to the theatre tonight. Are you ready?' His tone had changed slightly when he asked the question. Rosina thought his eyes were sad as he looked at his daughter.

'What's the matter, Pa? Is it our hair? Do you think we shouldn't have put it up?'

'Not at all. You are no longer a schoolgirl, Joanne, no matter what your mother thinks. And that's the problem. You are growing up, my dear. I must face the fact that one day you will leave us.' He smiled at his daughter affectionately. 'But now there is a more immediate problem.'

'What is it?'

Joanne's father raised his hand and they saw for the first time that he was holding not one spray of white flowers but two. Each corsage was made with two creamy white gardenias and dark green waxy leaves. He gave Joanne and Rosina one each.

'Where will you pin these flowers? At your neck, at your wrist or in the abundance of curls you both have?'

'Thank you, Pa, they're lovely,' Joanne said. She made a decision immediately. 'In our hair, I think. Now that we are old enough to pin it up.' She hurried to her dressing table to find some hairpins. In no time at all she pronounced that they were ready to go.

'Is Mother ready?' she asked.

'Almost. But she wondered if you would help her pin up her hair. She says you have more idea of the latest style than she has.'

'Bless her,' Joanne said. 'Don't worry.' She was already walking towards the door. 'It won't take long. I know exactly what will suit her best.'

When Joanne had gone Mr Bartlett smiled at Rosina. 'Has my daughter provided you with an evening cape?' he asked.

Rosina assured him that she had, and picked up one of the two capes from the bed where Joanne had laid them. Mr Bartlett helped her into it and then he picked up the other one.

'I'll take this for Joanne and we'll wait downstairs,' he said.

Rosina and Joanne's father went down to the entrance hall. Once more Rosina found herself comparing life at the Bartlett home with her life at Ravenshill. Over the years she had got to know Joanne's family well and she liked them so very much.

Mr Bartlett was hard-working, but he was also very much a family man. He loved to spend time with his wife and daughter and, as far back as Rosina could remember, he had always attended events at school such as concerts and plays. Rosina's own father had never come unless Amy had a small part in the play or concert. Her stepmother probably insisted, Rosina thought, and yet her father seemed genuinely interested in his stepdaughter's achievements, no matter how small. The fact that Rosina was playing a leading part didn't seem to impress him.

She heard a noise behind her and turned to see Joanne and her mother coming down the stairs. 'At last!' Mr Bartlett said with mock impatience. 'The cab has been waiting a good twenty minutes!'

He smiled up at his approaching wife and daughter, and Rosina knew that whatever happened in the future she had been truly fortunate to have met these good people and to have been made welcome in their home.

Chapter Thirteen

Rosina learned they were going to the second house at the Grand, a theatre near Byker Bridge. In order to be in their seats at eight o'clock when the curtain would rise, Mr Bartlett had ordered the meal in advance. When they arrived at the Gondola restaurant on the upper floor of a building on Shields Road, they found the owner, Mario, waiting for them. He bowed flamboyantly, then showed them to their table himself. Mario looked very grand, Rosina thought, and, with his dark hair and side whiskers, very Italian. His speech and his gestures were extravagant.

'Don't be fooled by that phoney accent,' Joanne whispered. 'I heard him lose his temper with one of the waiters once and what came forth was pure Tyneside.'

For some reason Rosina and Joanne found this very funny and they began to giggle like the schoolgirls they had been so recently. Mrs Bartlett smiled at them enquiringly as if she wanted to be let in on the joke and Mr Bartlett, guessing what had caused the merriment, shot them a reproving look. But Rosina saw that his whiskers were twitching as though he were suppressing a smile.

Italian in style the restaurant might have been, and Rosina was sure there would be exotic Mediterranean dishes on the grand-looking menu, but her friend's father had stuck to what he knew and liked. The meal began with mock-turtle soup, continued with grilled lamb cutlets with green peas and new potatoes, and finished with raspberry and redcurrant tart and custard. Only the wine was Italian. Or at least Mario said it was. Mario brought it to the table himself and made a great show of wrapping the bottle in a napkin then pouring a little for Mr Bartlett to taste.

'It's all right,' Joanne whispered to Rosina. 'The wine must be the real thing. Pa knows his wines.'

Rosina saw that Mr Bartlett was nodding his assent as Mario began to fill their glasses. Well, half fill in the case of Rosina and Joanne; after all, they had only just entered the grown-up world. As Rosina enjoyed her dinner and sipped her wine, she noticed how the Bartletts behaved as a family. They actually seemed interested in what each other had to say and, although sometimes the discussion touched on serious matters, good humour and laughter were never far away.

After the meal Mario escorted them to the waiting cab. The journey down Shields Road to the theatre near the Ouseburn did not take long and soon they could see crowds hurrying in the same direction. The summer evening was balmy, the sky still light, with only a hint of lilac-coloured shadows hovering over the grey slated rooftops. The prospective theatre audience was a motley crew of young and old, poor and comfortably off.

Some of the young women wore attractive summer dresses in pale coloured muslins. Some had flowers in their hair like Joanne and Rosina, but some wore hats with abundant floral decorations. This set Rosina and Joanne giggling again as they imagined what it would be like to sit behind one of these creations. They would not have this problem themselves as Mr Bartlett had reserved a box.

The foyer was crowded, and Rosina noticed an air of heightened excitement, which surely must have been caused by more than the anticipation of the evening's entertainment. Heads dipped together, were raised again, and the person talking would join another group where the process was repeated. She didn't have time to puzzle over this, however, as Mr Bartlett was already escorting his wife up the grand red-carpeted staircase, and Joanne grabbed Rosina's hand to pull her along after them.

The box was large enough for them all to have a 'front row' seat, and after removing their evening capes and hanging them on a row of hooks on the back wall Rosina and Joanne occupied themselves by observing the audience. Rosina had never been to the Grand before. In fact, her only trips to the theatre since her father had taken her to see *The Naughty Fairies* had been organized by the school, who had taken parties of senior girls to the Theatre Royal to see respectable classical plays such as those of William Shakespeare. The Grand in Byker had a different atmosphere entirely.

Here were gathered representatives of many different sections of society, although Rosina didn't think the upper classes would venture to this part of the city. Looking down into the front stalls, Rosina could see respectably dressed couples, some with their children. One indignant young woman was complaining to a lady with a large feathered hat sitting in the row in front of her. The young woman complained that her little girl would not be able to see the stage even if they tipped the seat up for her to sit on – and that would be uncomfortable for the poor mite.

The gentleman with the behatted lady gestured as if to suggest that all the mother and daughter had to do was change places. They did so. And then it became obvious that the young mother would not be able to see through the feathered plumes either. Suddenly the lady with the hat shrugged and laughed and took it off.

'Thank goodness for that,' Joanne whispered. 'I thought it might be hat pins at dawn!'

Rosina noticed that there was the same excited undercurrent here in the auditorium as there had been in the foyer. She raised her eyes to look along at the seats in the dress circle and saw people nodding and smiling as before. It was harder to see what was happening in the upper circle where the seats were less expensive and the audience therefore less well dressed. And as for the gods, the precipitous layer of seats above even the upper circle, they seemed to soar up into some dim and distant region far above the earthly plane.

I should be terrified to sit there, Rosina thought. The seats in the gods were very cheap and tonight they were filled with a noisy and restless crowd. From what she could see of them they were poorly dressed and their rough voices echoed down over the auditorium. Joanne saw Rosina's expression of doubt and she said, 'Don't worry; they'll behave themselves once the performance starts.'

'You've been here before?' Rosina asked.

'Many times. Pa brings us whenever there's a suitable programme. I think he would even if he didn't get free tickets.'

'Free tickets?'

'Whenever a new show is about to begin someone goes round and asks shopkeepers and the like to place a poster in their window. In return they are given a couple of free tickets for the opening night – or the Wednesday matinée sometimes if the show is popular and the tickets for the evening show are at a premium.'

'How lucky you are to have this opportunity,' Rosina said. 'Do you like the theatre?'

'Yes. I mean, I think so.'

'Aren't you sure?'

'Oh, yes, I'm sure. I believe it's more than like. I think tonight I have fallen in love.'

'In love?' Joanne looked startled. 'Have you spotted some handsome young man in the stalls?' She leaned forward and scanned the audience. 'You'd better point him out to me.'

'No!' Rosina laughed. 'No, you goose, it's nothing like that. I didn't mean I had fallen in love with a person.'

'For goodness' sake explain yourself.'

'I have fallen in love with this.' Rosina gestured towards the stage and the heavy crimson gold-braided curtains. Then her outstretched arm circled high above and took in the circle and the upper circle and the gods. 'And all these people too,' she added.

Joanne raised her eyebrows. 'What, all of them?'

'Yes, all of them. But only in a manner of speaking. People who have come to be cheered, to be lifted, to escape from everyday life for a while.'

There was a movement below, and Rosina looked down to see that the musicians were entering the orchestra pit. They carried their instruments and their sheet music, and they began to settle themselves, getting ready for the performance ahead.

'And I think I am about to fall in love with those gentlemen too,' Rosina said. 'Oh, don't you see, Joanne, it's the theatre I have fallen in love with. Not just the building, not just the people, but the whole atmosphere.'

Joanne stared at her and for a moment she looked perplexed as if she didn't know how to respond to such unexpected passion. 'For once I don't know what to say — except that you have disconcerted me considerably.'

'I'm sorry,' Rosina said. 'I shall try to behave myself once the performance begins.'

She smiled at her friend but she knew her smile was wobbly. She was aware that the programme in her hand was shaking. She had no idea what had made her say such things and she was embarrassed. Joanne reached for the programme and opened it up, resting it on the velvet padded ledge in front of them.

'Let's see,' she said. 'We must prepare ourselves for the entertainment ahead of us. We had better be forewarned as to whether we are supposed to laugh or cry.'

Rosina was grateful to her friend for bringing her back to a state of near normality. She leaned forward and the two girls perused the programme together. They discovered that the evening's entertainment was to consist of two one-act plays and a programme of recitations. The first play, *The Lost Heiress*, would be 'a dramatic and heart-rending story of virtue rewarded'.

'For that read melodrama,' Joanne whispered.

And the second play, *Who Will Tell Father?*, promised 'an engaging look at one day in the life of an elderly widower left to raise three high-spirited daughters'.

Joanne laughed. 'Pure knockabout comedy, I should imagine.'

'But what about the recitations?' Rosina asked. 'They're placed between the two plays.'

'To give more time for the set to be changed, I should think,' her friend said. 'And also give the principal actors more time to change costumes and make-up. They'll probably wheel out the very old members of the cast to recite ancient poems and dramatic speeches they learned absolute aeons ago. I've seen this sort of thing before – the gestures and the declamatory style will have you bursting with the effort not to laugh out loud. Oh, and by the way, there will be two intervals and Pa has decided to spoil us. He has ordered ices for the first interval, and coffee and cream buns for the second. He says the cream buns are a treat for us but, in reality, it's Father who loves them.'

The orchestra were still tuning up, the strange noises mingling with the chatter of the audience. Rosina looked around the auditorium once more. She had noticed that the box opposite to them had remained empty. Joanne had told her that this was called the royal box and was where honoured guests or important people sat. Now she saw that some of the audience seated in the stalls kept looking up at this box expectantly.

'What do you think is going on?' she asked Joanne without turning to look at her.

Her friend leaned forward. 'What do you mean?'

'Look. The box – the royal box – is still empty and many of the audience keep glancing towards it and talking about it.'

'Obviously someone special is coming to the performance tonight,' Joanne said. 'Probably someone famous and word has got round.'

'Why haven't they arrived yet? It must be getting very near time for the curtains to rise.'

'Good manners,' Joanne explained. 'We've been here before when an ancient but famous comic actor came to see the show. He didn't want to disrupt the proceedings before the show began.'

'Disrupt?'

'Well, you know, everyone would clap and cheer and curtain-up would be delayed. So he slipped in quietly just as the house lights dimmed and retreated to the back of the box during the intervals. Then at the end he stood up and made a little speech and the audience nearly lifted the roof off with their cheers and shouts and stamping.'

'How exciting! I wonder who the famous guest will be tonight.'

'I haven't a clue, I'm afraid, and it's too late to mingle with the crowd and ask questions – look, the conductor is tapping his music stand.'

The musicians sat up and looked at the conductor. A moment later the music, a lively arrangement of tunes from light opera, filled the auditorium, and the audience stopped chattering and settled in their seats. The house lights dimmed, there was a quick burst of applause for the orchestra and the curtains opened to reveal a depiction of a room in a gloomy-looking mansion. There was no one on the stage except a pretty young maidservant who was making a great show of how hard she was working as she swept and cleaned.

The play was all about finding the 'lost' heiress to the country estate and it was pretty much like Cinderella, really, Rosina thought, as the house filled up with false claimants, two of whom were decidedly like the ugly sisters. It was nonsense and yet it was gripping. Especially when the hero appeared.

'My goodness,' Joanne whispered, 'isn't he handsome?'

'Mm,' Rosina said, and both girls immediately peered at their programme in the dim light of the box.

'Tom Carey,' Joanne murmured. 'He's a fellow to look out for.'

Tom Carey played the part of a rich young landowner whose job it was to settle the affairs of his deceased friend and neighbour. No matter how nonsensical the play, Rosina thought, he was very convincing and she whispered her opinion to Joanne.

'You're right,' her friend whispered in return. 'He makes it all somehow believable. And apart from his most delicious voice he has what they call stage presence.'

'Er — yes, he does.'

Rosina wasn't quite sure what stage presence meant but, given her friend's experience of theatregoing, she thought she must be right.

'And doesn't he suit those tights and knee britches!' Joanne added.

'Be quiet, you two,' Mrs Bartlett leaned towards them and remonstrated. But she tempered her words with a smile.

Rosina tried to follow the play but found her gaze continually straying back to the young actor. When he took his bow at the end of the performance she noticed that it was the ladies in the audience who clapped the most enthusiastically, their white evening gloves fluttering like doves in the semidarkness.

A tray of ices was brought to their box in the first interval and, with the house lights up again, Rosina did not forget to look across at the opposing box. How annoying, she thought, I did not notice the moment the occupants arrived and now they are sitting back in the shadows as Joanne said they would. She noticed that other members of the audience were also peering towards the royal box in vain.

The orchestra was playing music that could only be described as dramatic. Rosina supposed that was to ready the audience for the serious nature of the dramatic recitations to come.

When it began it was as funny as Joanne had said it would be, except that Rosina found it sad, for the elderly performers who stood there before the curtain acting their hearts out did not intend the poems and the speeches they recited to invoke humour.

'They are the relics of a previous style of acting,' Joanne whispered to her. At the end of this part of the programme Joanne and Rosina decided to applaud enthusiastically. They even started a chorus of 'Bravo', and were delighted to see how easy it was to lead the audience to follow their example. Although no doubt one or two wags in the crowd were not sincere in their compliments. But the aged thespians were delighted and one of them led the way offstage dabbing at his eyes with a large white handkerchief.

During the second interval, while the Bartletts and Rosina enjoyed their coffee and cream buns, Rosina noticed that the volume of chatter in the auditorium was rising in a crescendo of laughter and enjoyment. The musicians were playing an arrangement of comic tunes, probably hinting at what was to come, and by the time the curtain rose again, everyone seemed to be on the edge of their seats, ready to enjoy every last minute of their night at the theatre.

The curtains parted to reveal a cheery set showing a comfortably stylish drawing room. Three prettily dressed harum-scarum girls dominated the action, hiding their sweethearts in and behind various pieces of furniture whilst their poor old father was trying to find out what was going on right under his nose — and failing. The story, while completely unbelievable, was very funny, and soon most of the audience was helpless with laughter. But the most amazing thing of all, as far as Rosina was concerned, was that the part of the old father was played by Tom Carey.

He was dressed like a doddery old man and dodder he did as his three daughters ran circles around him. He wore a wispy grey wig and Rosina guessed that he had used stage make-up to age his appearance, but it was the way he moved his limbs and the things that he did to his voice that revealed his acting skills. Rosina thought how wonderful it must be to have such power over so many people; to be able to take them into a land of make-believe and make them laugh and cry at will.

When the performance ended the applause was deafening and the folk up in the gods were stamping and shouting their approval. The actors on the stage took many bows, but at last Henry Greyling, the actor manager of the troupe, who had played the villain in the first play and one of the daughter's suitors in the second, stepped forward and raised his hands. He stood centre stage, gesturing for the audience to be quiet, and eventually they obeyed him and sat down again. With consummate skill he kept them waiting and Rosina began to feel the anticipation grow.

'And now,' Henry Greyling said, 'I think you know we have an honoured guest here in the theatre with us tonight.'

There was a collective indrawn breath of anticipation from all parts of the house.

'The celebrated lady is visiting her home town and decided to grace us with her presence.'

You could almost hear the silence. Everyone stared at the royal box but whoever was seated there remained in the shadows. All that could be seen was a white-gloved hand resting on the scarlet velvet padding at the front of the box. Rosina suddenly felt a little faint. She was flushed and she fanned herself gently with her programme.

The temperature in the theatre had grown warmer as the evening wore on and the air was filled with the cloying scents of the ladies' perfumes and the gentlemen's pomades. And there was something else, something baser: the unmistakable odour of sweat and unwashed bodies emanating from the cheaper seats.

Every actor on the stage was now also staring at the royal box. Henry Greyling turned to address the audience. 'How shall we tempt our guest to reveal herself? Can you tell me?'

There was a sudden burst of sound as members in the audience began to answer him but the actor manager held up his hands to silence them. 'Don't all speak at once,' he said. Then he smiled.

He's playing with them, Rosina thought admiringly. He's raising the pitch of the excitement. She watched as he cupped one ear and leaned forward.

'I think I heard you correctly,' he said, 'now tell me again.'

Rosina had no idea what was said in the babble of noise that followed but Henry Greyling laughed and held up his hands for silence once more. 'You're absolutely right,' he told the delighted crowd. 'We'll get the orchestra to play for her.

'Maestro?' Now the actor manager addressed the conductor of the orchestra. Rosina noticed that a spotlight had fallen on him, and very grand he looked in his evening clothes, his long wavy hair flopping down romantically.

'Yes, Mr Greyling?' the man said.

'Do you know a tune that might please our guest?'

'I certainly do.'

'Then please begin.'

The actor manager stepped back with a graceful gesture and the conductor of the orchestra tapped his baton on his music stand, raised it (a little overdramatically Rosina thought) and a beat later the orchestra began to play.

'Yes, yes!' Cries of approval came from the audience and Henry Greyling raised a finger to his lips and shushed them.

It was so unexpected that it took a while for Rosina to recognize the tune, but then she had the strangest feeling that she was being carried back in time to somewhere ... somewhere warm and wonderful where she had heard it before.

But almost immediately she realized that was impossible.

She had never heard this song played by an orchestra, for song it was. She rested her arms on the front of the box and leaned forward, staring down into the orchestra pit. She did not know it but her lips had started to move as she groped unsuccessfully for the words.

Had her mother sung this song to her? She searched her memory but all she could remember was the two of them singing nursery rhymes together. Her darling mother had never sung this song – so how was it that she, Rosina, knew it? And then another image came to her mind of herself tucked up in bed at Ravenshill, holding her old doll close to her body. She had cried over that doll. Why? But she had also sung to it – or rather hummed a tune that always brought a sad look to her mother's face. Another puzzle. If her mother did not like this song why did it evoke happy as well as sad memories?

She closed her eyes and in an almost trancelike state she became aware that the orchestra had stopped playing and that the audience were calling for an encore.

'Again! Again!' they shouted, and then they fell silent. A great sigh escaped them and Rosina heard Joanne whisper, 'Oh, my goodness, it's her!'

'Who?' Rosina asked, and Joanne nudged her.

'Open your eyes, you goose.'

Rosina did so and looked across towards the royal box just as the audience started clapping and cheering. A shining figure stood in a circle of light. At first Rosina was dazzled but as her eyes adjusted she saw that the object of the audience's adulation was a beautiful woman dressed in white with the sparkle of diamonds at her throat, her ears, and even scattered about her blonde hair. She was smiling and waving to the audience, raising her arm in a graceful gesture to circle the whole of the auditorium.

Suddenly, someone in the audience shouted out clearly above the noise of the crowd, 'Why don't you sing for us, Daisy?'

'Yes, sing, sing!' Others took up the plea.

The shining figure raised her arms and the audience fell silent immediately. 'What shall I sing?' she asked, and for some unfathomable reason Rosina thrilled to the sound of her voice.

'"The Doll Song"! "The Doll Song"!' the audience called with one voice, and their darling smiled and nodded.

'If you really want me to,' she said.

'We do! We do!'

'Very well. Be patient. I shall take my place on the stage.'

The level of excitement rose as the house lights dimmed again and the actors left the stage. The curtains closed and the sound of hurried clearing up could be heard. The orchestra played a selection of tunes and Joanne informed Rosina that they were all songs that Daisy Belle had made famous.

'Who is Daisy Belle and how do you know so much about her?' Rosina asked.

'Daisy Belle is one of the most famous entertainers in the country, the continent. She is wildly popular in Paris. And her career began right here in Newcastle. I told you about her once, remember? When she had just started out on her career she had rooms in a house in our street.'

Rosina did remember. She also remembered that something sad – not to say tragic – had happened. There had been a child . . . a little girl . . . the singer's niece . . . and the child had been killed in an accident. That had happened a long time ago . . .

If there was a signal Rosina missed it, but suddenly the orchestra stopped playing, the audience stopped chattering and everyone became still. A moment later the curtains rose to reveal the solitary figure of Daisy Belle standing centre stage. The set had vanished miraculously but the stage had been dressed with a single jardinière supporting a classical-looking pot containing a mass of white silk flowers and waxy-looking artificial trailing ivy.

Curiously Miss Belle, in her shimmering gown, was clutching an old doll, a broken doll with tangled ringlets and part of one arm missing. She was completely still for a moment and then she cradled the doll tenderly and looked down at it before raising her head, nodding to the conductor. There was a short musical introduction and then she began to sing.

' "I once had a sweet little doll, dears . . ." '

The words, so sweet, so sad, had a terrifying impact on Rosina. The dense shroud that guarded her innermost memories seemed to part instantly and before she knew what she was doing she had started to mouth the words silently as Miss Belle sang them. No, not *as* she sang them – Rosina realized that she was anticipating every word and her lips were forming it just a fraction before Daisy Belle actually sang it. This continued all through the song.

> 'Yet for old sakes' sake, she is still, dears,
> The prettiest doll in the world.'

The last lines floated sweetly out over the auditorium and her performance was greeted with thunderous applause.

'Encore! Encore!' came the cry from the stalls and the dress circle. And, 'Sing it again, bonny lass,' from the gods and the pit.

'I'll warrant you're not the only one crying,' Joanne said to Rosina. She had to lean as close as possible to make herself heard over the noise from the audience.

'Crying? Am I crying?'

'The tears are streaming down your face. Your handkerchief is a wet, crumpled wreck. Didn't you know?'

'No.'

'Here, take mine.'

Joanne handed Rosina a clean handkerchief. Rosina stared down at the flowers embroidered in the corners . . . edelweiss, she thought, how pretty, and she wondered why her mind was wandering like this when something so important had just happened. She knew the words to the song about the broken doll. And yet she still couldn't remember her mother singing it to her.

Other memories were heartbreakingly vivid – sitting by the fire in the nursery while her mother read stories, keeping herself from going to sleep for as long as possible while her mother sang lullabies – but not that song. She simply couldn't remember her mother singing that song. Or could she?

'What is it?' Joanne asked. 'Why are you frowning?'

'Oh, nothing . . . well, yes, it is something. I mean, I'm trying to remember that song. I seem to know the words and yet I can't remember why.'

'That's easy,' Joanne said.

Rosina was astonished. 'Easy? Why?'

'*The Water Babies*! It's the fairy's song from *The Water Babies*. Your mother must have read it to you.'

'No, I don't think she did.' Rosina tried to recall the books on the nursery shelves at Ravenshill, books she still had packed away in a little chest in her bedroom there. She knew about *The Water Babies*, of course, but she had never read it and she was sure her mother had not read it to her. Her mother had thought it might be too frightening.

They had not noticed that, as they were talking, the

audience had stopped shouting and there was once more an expectant hush in the auditorium. They heard the conductor tap his music stand rather more loudly than usual and they looked down to see him staring up at them and frowning.

'Oh, gosh, sorry!' Joanne blurted out, and they both withdrew into the shadows. 'She's going to sing it again,' Joanne whispered to Rosina behind her hand.

Daisy Belle began to sing again but she had not got far when she stopped and stepped forward. Holding the broken doll with one hand she made a wide gesture with the other arm as she invited the audience to join in.

'Don't be shy,' she said. 'I think you all know the words. Let's sing it together.'

The conductor turned to smile at the audience, raised his baton and brought them all in on time. Rosina listened with wonder as the sound swelled around her and then, she couldn't stop herself, she stood up and began to sing. Joanne tugged at her skirt but she was past noticing anything except the music and the song. She sang out so clearly that heads began to turn to look at her. Some members of the audience fell silent and then they shushed the others as everyone who could see her looked up in wonder.

By the time they had got to the line 'I found my poor little doll, dears ...' the only two people who were singing were Daisy Belle and Rosina.

The song came to an end and at first there was total silence. Then one or two people began to clap, more joined in and then everyone was clapping and cheering.

Joanne stared up at her friend. Rosina seemed bewildered. She stood there blinking in the glow of a spotlight that had been turned upon her. When had that happened? Joanne decided that it had been very soon after everyone else had stopped singing, preferring to listen to their darling Daisy and the young woman in the box.

And what an amazing voice Rosina had! Of course, Joanne had heard her friend sing before because they had both been in the school choir. But she had never sung like this, with so much passion and so much emotion, and all poured into a sweet little song from Mr Kingsley's tale of a poor young chimney sweep.

How well the voices had blended – that of the celebrated performer and that of the choir girl. Joanne was surprised to discover that she actually thought Rosina's voice to be the purer, the truer of the two. It was a sentimental little song that told of a child who had lost her doll while playing on the heath and then found it a week later rain-soaked and muddied, with her limbs broken, but as precious as ever to the child who loved her.

Daisy Belle had sung the song that had made her famous as sweetly as ever but to Joanne's theatregoing eye it was a performance – a magnificent performance but still a theatrical performance – whereas Rosina hadn't seemed to know exactly what she was doing and yet the sense of loss and love had rung out sincere and true. Joanne didn't know what to make of it.

'Miss Belle is behaving very graciously,' Joanne's father leaned forward and whispered.

Joanne looked down to the stage and saw that the famous star had raised one white-gloved arm graciously to direct the applause towards Rosina. By now most of the audience was standing and bellowing for more.

'Sing it again,' was the shout. 'The both of you!'

But after a while Miss Belle smiled and shook her head and swept off the stage. The curtains came down and stayed down. It was obvious, no matter how much noise the audience made, that there was not going to be a repeat performance.

'My dear, that was wonderful!' Joanne turned to find her mother, eyes shining, smiling widely as she complimented Rosina. 'Your voice is magnificent. If you were my daughter I would find you a singing teacher at once.'

Rosina hardly seemed to have heard her. She was still standing at the front of the box, gazing at the curtains, which were now firmly closed. The musicians had kept playing a selection of music associated with Daisy Belle but as soon as the last member of the audience was judged to have left the theatre they stopped playing and began to collect their music and instruments and leave the orchestra pit. One or two of them looked up curiously at Rosina then turned to talk to each other.

While Joanne's father collected the cloaks, Rosina remained staring down at the closed curtains. Then she looked out of the box at the rows of empty seats. As the last of the audience left, cleaning women entered and began tipping up the seats and gathering up discarded programmes and empty chocolate boxes.

Joanne took hold of Rosina's shoulder and turned her round. 'We must go,' she said.

As Mr Bartlett slipped the evening cloak around Rosina's shoulders, his wife asked, 'Did you enjoy yourself, my dear?'

'Very much.'

'We had no idea that you could sing like that,' Joanne's mother said.

'I don't think I did either,' Rosina responded, and tried to dredge up a smile for she still felt dazed by what had just happened.

Joanne, who had been talking to her father, stepped

forward, her eyes shining. 'I've persuaded Father to take us round to the stage door,' she said.

'Why?' Rosina was perplexed.

'We can wait for the performers to come out and perhaps ask for their autographs. We'll keep the programme handy.'

As they hurried out of the main entrance to the theatre, Mr Bartlett stopped them for a moment. 'I've agreed to this against my better judgement. There will be quite a throng there. You must promise not to stray from my side – nor swoon at that young actor's feet.' He smiled broadly. 'I won't be able to pick both of you up.'

'Are you coming, Mother, or will you wait in the cab?'

'I'm coming. Do you think I'd let your father go alone to see Daisy Belle? I'll have to make sure he doesn't declare his eternal devotion and make a complete fool of himself.'

The stage door of the theatre was down a narrow alley. The crowd waiting there was boisterous but good-natured; their excitement expressed in loud but respectful comments. The lamp above the door showed it to be firmly closed.

Mr Bartlett had used his broad shoulders to lead the way to the front of the crowd and his wife was hanging on to him, laughing but breathless. Once he had positioned himself he allowed the girls to slip round in front of him.

Rosina looked about her – first at the globe of the lamp, which, rather unnecessarily, she thought, had the words 'Stage Door' painted on its translucent surface. There were old playbills pasted to the brick walls advertising former theatrical events and entertainers. One such poster featured Dora Peabody and her Dainty Dancing Ducks.

'She puts them on a hotplate, you know,' Joanne said, leaning close and raising her voice to make herself heard.

'What are you talking about?' Rosina asked.

'Dora Peabody. The poor ducks jump up and down in

time to a jolly tune – or that's what it looks like. In reality the charming Miss Peabody has placed the poor creatures on a heated sheet of metal. No wonder they hop and quack.'

'But that's dreadful!' Rosina said. And would have said more but at that moment the crowd around her silenced dramatically.

All eyes focused on the stage door, which opened slowly and teasingly. The crowd seemed to let out its breath as one in a sigh of disappointment as the first people to appear were a group of cheerful young women.

'The lesser female members of the cast,' Joanne explained. 'They're not who the majority are waiting for but they'll have their admirers.'

Sure enough, several young men stepped forward and proffered programmes for the young women to sign or presented their favourites with bouquets of flowers.

'They're known as stage-door Johnnies,' Joanne told Rosina. 'They wait at the stage door for a particular young woman and in some cases it leads to romance. Sometimes even a chorus girl can make a grand marriage.'

The rest of the cast came out to be greeted with small bursts of applause or puzzled silence, and then the girls in the crowd gave audible sighs of pleasure when Tom Carey, the young actor emerged. He was an arresting figure in evening clothes with a slightly dated cloak hanging from his broad shoulders.

'Isn't he gorgeous and doesn't he just know how dashing that cloak makes him appear?' Joanne said laughingly, and then shrank back and tried to hide behind Rosina when his head turned and looked straight at her. 'Oh, no, he heard me,' she whispered.

'No,' Rosina tried to reassure her. 'I'm sure you must be mistaken.'

But then, to the girls' dismay, Tom Carey walked towards them. 'Good evening,' he said as he stopped right before them. 'Did you enjoy the show?'

Joanne, for once, was speechless, so it was up to Rosina to respond. 'Yes, thank you,' she said, fearing that she sounded like a polite schoolgirl. She stared down at the polished toes of her shoes.

'I'm glad that your friend likes my cloak,' he said. 'It was my father's and before that my grandfather's. A sort of theatrical heirloom.'

Rosina screwed up enough courage to look up into his face. The lamp above the door was behind him so his face was in shadow but she had heard the laughter in his voice and there was enough light for her to see his smile. It was obvious that he had not been at all offended by Joanne's remark. He was amused.

But his expression changed. He stared at Rosina and his eyes, dark brown, she thought, widened. 'You're the girl who sang, aren't you?'

'Sang?' The word came out like a croak.

'With Miss Belle. You sang "The Doll Song".'

Rosina, overcome with inexplicable nerves, could only stare up into his handsome face. Joanne came to her rescue. She stopped trying to hide behind her and addressed him boldly. 'Yes, it was my friend who sang. She was very good, don't you think?'

The young actor was just about to answer when a gloved hand was laid on his arm. The hand belonged to the actress who had played the parts of the heiress in the first play and the youngest sister in the second. Now, as herself, she was beautiful and sophisticated in a dark blue velvet two-piece. The jacket was nipped in at the waist and the skirt hugged her hips and then flowed out in a gentle flare. Her bright yellow hair shone through the delicate cloud of veiling attached to a tiny hat. She wasn't smiling.

'Tom, our table is booked at Alvini's.'

He answered without turning to look at her. 'All right, Sadie. I'm coming.'

'I thought you sang very well indeed, Miss ... er ... Miss?'

'Tom!'

Rosina was staring at him speechlessly so he shrugged and turned to go. 'All right, Sadie. I'm coming.'

'Oh, no!' Joanne exclaimed as the actor and actress walked away.

'What is it?' Rosina asked.

'We forgot to ask him to sign our programmes. Do you think I should ... ?' She made a move to follow them but Rosina grabbed her arm.

'No, look, it's Miss Belle!'

The crowd had fallen silent as the stage door opened once more and Daisy Belle appeared. Her white velvet cloak was trimmed with silvery fur that trembled in the night air as she breathed. Her angel-fair hair was piled high, and diamonds sparkled in the curls, hung from her ears and circled her throat.

'She's like a princess from a fairy tale,' Joanne breathed.

'Or the Snow Queen,' Rosina said. 'She looks like an ice maiden.'

'Mm.' Joanne nodded. 'But a beautiful ice maiden.'

Miss Belle paused in the doorway. She smiled as the crowd cheered. Then she raised an arm and the cheering stopped immediately.

'Thank you for your welcome,' she said.

'Lissen here, bonny lass,' someone shouted, 'why divven't you come home to live?'

'Aye,' another rang out. 'You've been away long enough.'

Daisy Belle raised her hand again and in the ensuing silence she said, 'I will come home to Newcastle as often as I can, I promise you. But now, forgive me, I must go.'

The crowd parted obediently to form a path, and Daisy Belle walked among them smiling and nodding her head. Some gave her flowers, which were taken by a young woman who must have been a maid. The other person with her was a tall well-set man in evening clothes. Rosina thought she had glimpsed him sitting next to Miss Belle in the box.

'Miss Belle!' Rosina was startled to hear Joanne's father call out from behind her.

Daisy Belle paused and smiled at him.

'I heard you sing many years ago and I have been an admirer ever since. Tonight you were magnificent!'

'Thank you.'

Maybe she would have said more but the man walking behind her put his hands on her shoulders and compelled her to walk forward. She looked back at Mr Bartlett and smiled her apology but then her glance fell upon Rosina.

'Oh,' she said, 'are you the young lady who—'

'Daisy, we haven't time to linger,' her companion said.

'Yes, I am,' Rosina said. But then Miss Belle's companion hurried her away down the alley towards the road where a cab was waiting.

After a moment of well-behaved silence the crowd came to life and swept after them. When the cab drew away they followed it, cheering as they went.

Mr Bartlett had put one arm around his wife and shouted to the girls to stay close but he need not have worried. By the time they were left alone in the alley Mrs Bartlett's hat had been knocked askew and the girls' programme was lying crumpled at their feet but they were quite unharmed. Rosina was standing quite still. She was frowning as she stared with an unfocused gaze after the retreating crowd.

'Are you all right?' Joanne asked her.

Rosina turned to look at her, frowned again, and then said, 'Yes, thank you.'

'You don't look all right.'

'No, really, it was just . . . just the excitement, I suppose.'

'Come along, you two,' Joanne's father said. 'Our cab is waiting.'

'If the cabbie hasn't given up in disgust and gone by now,' Mrs Bartlett said. 'Really, Augustus,' she added, 'you were like a callow youth just then. Making such a show of yourself before Miss Belle.'

'I am quite unrepentant and you are not really angry, are you, my dear?'

Mrs Bartlett smiled up at him and, linking arms, they led the way to the waiting cab.

Joanne looked down at her programme and then shrugged and decided to leave it there. She linked her arm through Rosina's and sighed. 'What a wonderful time we've had. We shall probably stay awake all night and talk about it.'

But Joanne was mistaken. They didn't talk for long because, once they were in bed, it was Rosina who, most unusually, fell asleep almost straight away. And began to dream . . .

She was a small child again and her mother was sitting on her bed in the darkened nursery and was singing to her. She was singing the doll song and her voice was pure and sweet. The light from the fire in the hearth shone on her golden hair. Rosina did not know it, but she frowned in her sleep for her mother's hair had not been golden and she had never sung that song to her. And then the strangest thing happened. In the dream her mother leaned over to kiss her.

'Go to sleep, my bonny bairn,' her mother said, and her voice had changed so much that the child in the dream opened her eyes wide and looked up into the face of Daisy Belle.

The dream, like most dreams, faded the moment she awoke. She tried very hard to remember but all she was left with was the delicate scent of roses.

Chapter Fourteen

It was time for Rosina to leave the Bartlett house and return to Ravenshill. Joanne travelled to the Central Station with her in a four-wheeler piled high with Rosina's luggage. They talked very little. After the excitement of their holiday together their mood had changed and they were both a little subdued.

Rosina felt awkward because she would have liked to invite her friend to come and stay with her. Joanne had never visited Ravenshill and Rosina believed that Mrs Bartlett must wonder why her daughter had never received an invitation. Rosina knew how much Joanne loved living in the city but she was sure that she would enjoy a taste of country life. Blanche Leighton had refused to allow it. There had always been some reason during their schooldays why it was not convenient.

But now that they were leaving school Rosina had asked again just a few weeks before. Her stepmother, adopting her sweet reasonable voice, had said, 'I know how fond you are of the girl and I suppose it was all right for you to socialize when you were at school. But now, perhaps, you ought to put a little distance between you. After all, her father is a shopkeeper.'

'Mr Bartlett has many shops, not just one. He is a

successful businessman.' Rosina rarely contradicted her stepmother — she had learned there was no point in doing so — but she had felt that her friend's family were somehow being belittled.

'Maybe so, but he is still in trade. He is not a gentleman.'

'But what about Amy's friend Beryl Earnshaw? I don't believe her father is a gentleman and yet you approve of that friendship.'

'Mr Earnshaw is a manufacturer. He is an important influence in the North of England and socializes with important people. That is quite different.'

'You mean he's very rich?'

Blanche's small mouth had tightened disagreeably. 'That will be quite enough, Rosina. I'm very surprised by your manner. Perhaps it's just as well that you are leaving school. Now please go to your room.'

'Go to my room? But why?'

'Because you have behaved in a disrespectful manner towards me.'

Rosina had felt herself flushing as much with distress as with anger. She had asked for very little in her life because she had been as happy as she could be in the circumstances. She had loved her time at school and had made friends, not just with Joanne, although Joanne had become her special friend and very dear to her.

She suspected that she had been allowed to visit the Bartletts only because it kept her away from Ravenshill. But now she was about to leave school and her stepmother had made it plain that she was to cut her ties with Joanne and her family. So, although visits to the Bartletts would mean her stepmother was free of her, Rosina supposed that even Blanche would feel embarrassed eventually if the hospitality was not returned. That and pure spite would be her motivation.

In a spirit of rebellion that she had never experienced before, Rosina had quietly resolved that she would disobey the order. She supposed that her stepmother would not object if she were to go into Newcastle now and then to visit the art gallery, the museums or do some shopping. She would arrange to meet Joanne for the day, although she would not tell her stepmother that that was her intention. She felt no guilt about this. Why should she?

Blanche Leighton was a snob, unlike her own mother, who had never seemed too much bothered by social distinctions and, if she had got to know Joanne as well as Rosina did, would surely not have objected even if Mr Bartlett was the owner of one small tobacco kiosk in the Grainger Market.

The station was busy and the train already waiting at the platform. Joanne summoned a porter and oversaw the stowing of Rosina's luggage into the guard's van. When Rosina boarded the train there was still time before it would depart so she stood in the corridor at one of the doors and opened the window so that she could talk to Joanne. 'I'll write,' she said.

'Me, too. I'll send you postcards from Honfleur.'

'Honfleur?'

'Didn't I tell you? My father intends to buy a home in Normandy. Honfleur is a pretty little harbour town and the coastline is said to be very beautiful. The Opal Coast, they call it. Apparently many artists make their homes there.'

'No, you didn't tell me. When are you going?'

'I'm not sure. My father has yet to decide who will be overall manager of the business — the sweets and the tobacco — while we are away.'

Suddenly there was a hiss and a shudder and the train began to move.

'Goodbye,' Rosina called.

'Not goodbye, we must say *au revoir*!' Joanne replied. And she stood on the platform and waved as the train moved with gathering speed out of the station. Joanne disappeared in a swirl of steam. Rosina took out her pocket handkerchief and wiped the soot from her eyes.

'There's no need for you to do anything, Miss Rosina. I can manage.'

Molly was unpacking Rosina's clothes and she looked surprised and flustered when Rosina began to help her.

'No, it's all right, Molly. I just want to sort out my books.' The parlour maid looked uncertain and Rosina asked, 'What is it?'

'It's just that Miss Fidler might scold me if she thinks I'm not doing my job properly.'

'Don't worry. I'll tell her that I don't trust you to handle my books carefully.'

'Miss Rosina!'

'I'm teasing. But, really, she will understand if I want to arrange them myself. And, in any case, there's no reason why she should come in here.'

'Oh, isn't there!' Molly pursed her lips.

'What do you mean?'

'Old Fiddlesticks pops up everywhere at any time. She says she's checking to see that we're doing our jobs properly but half the time there's no need for her to be such a busybody. No need at all.' Molly opened one of the drawers in the large chest and began to put Rosina's underwear away. 'She just wants to look busy, that's my opinion.'

Rosina had just taken an armful of books from one of the boxes and she placed them carefully on top of the bookcase before she asked, 'But why would Miss Fidler want to look busy?'

'Because the truth of it is she hasn't enough to do these days and she's worried that Mrs Leighton will dismiss her.'

'But as long as I can remember Miss Fidler has just about run this household. My mother was happy to leave many of the day-to-day arrangements to her.'

'But it's not your mother who is the mistress now, is it? Oh, I'm sorry! I shouldn't have said that.'

'It's all right, Molly, you haven't upset me, and I know what you mean. My stepmother has changed things, hasn't she? She has her own ideas.'

'High-falutin London ideas. That's why she's engaged a French maid all the way from Paris! Angelique! Huh! You'd think with a name like that she'd be sweetness and light.'

'And she isn't?'

'Don't get me started!'

Molly's indignant expression brought a smile to Rosina's face but she tried to hide it. 'Well, there's nothing wrong with my stepmother wanting a French maid. She has the right to arrange things as she pleases.'

Molly flushed. 'Of course she has. I'm sorry for speaking out of turn but you're so easy to get on with that sometimes I forget my place, don't I?'

Rosina didn't know what to say. She had never been comfortable with the way her stepmother treated the servants.

'Your place right now is to help me get this room in order,' she said with a smile. 'And when you've finished hanging those dresses in the wardrobe perhaps you would dust this bookshelf. I'm going to empty it and sort the books out properly.'

A little later, as Molly cleaned the shelves vigorously, no

doubt endeavouring to put herself back in her proper place, Rosina dusted each individual book with care. She had brought back those she had kept at Mrs Forsyth's boarding house. These were English and French dictionaries, a thesaurus, a world atlas and books of natural history, as well as the works of Jane Austen and Charles Dickens. Now Rosina intended to place these on her bookshelves along with the well-loved storybooks of her childhood.

Kneeling on the floor, she could not resist opening one or two of the latter and reading some of her favourite passages. She could almost hear her mother's voice and smell the delicate rose cologne she always wore. Rosina gave herself up to the happy memories of rainy days in the nursery, nestling on her mother's lap while the fire crackled and the windowpanes rattled, and the two of them escaped to the faraway magic lands conjured up by printed words on a page.

'Will that be all, Miss Rosina?'

'Mm?' Rosina looked up and saw the maid hovering uncertainly by the door. 'Oh, yes, thank you, Molly.'

'Would you like me to bring you a drink of something, miss? A glass of lemonade or a cup of tea? You've raised a fair amount of dust with those old books. Your throat must be dry. I know mine is.'

Rosina took the hint. 'Yes, that would be nice. Bring a jug of lemonade and two glasses – and some biscuits too. Tell Cook we haven't quite finished yet but we need a drink to keep us going.'

Molly smiled and hurried away.

The interruption had been enough to end her reverie and Rosina started to arrange her books on the shelves. She had pulled them out without looking closely at them; she realized now that she had been delaying this moment, but she could avoid it no longer. It wasn't long before she found the book that she seemed to have forgotten about, *The Water Babies*. So she did have a copy after all. But she was sure her mother had not read it to her. She closed her eyes and concentrated very hard. In her mind's eye she saw her mother leafing through a book that had just arrived in the regular parcel from the Army and Navy Stores. She saw her mother's face and heard her voice:

'Oh, I can't read this to you, my darling, it would make us both cry . . . drowned babies indeed . . .'

Rosina remembered that incident clearly now but she hadn't known which book it was at the time. It must have been this one.

But that still didn't explain how she had come to know the fairy's song – or 'The Doll Song', as it had become known by Daisy Belle's enthusiastic fans. Perhaps she had read the book herself ? Or skimmed through it until she had found the poem set out so prettily on the page. Perhaps that was the answer. But no . . . that couldn't be right because it didn't explain how she knew the tune; knew the tune better than she knew the words because she had sung it wordlessly so often to her own beloved doll.

She must have risen up too quickly, for Rosina suddenly found herself half falling on to the bookcase. She laid her hands flat on the top and steadied herself. Her heart was pounding. The doll. Her doll. Old and ragged and with half of one arm missing. Just like the doll Daisy Belle had held on stage when she sang that song . . .

Suddenly nothing seemed real and Rosina was overwhelmed with that old unnerving sensation – a feeling of not belonging. She hurried over to her old toy chest and raised the lid. There amongst the soft toys and the wooden building blocks lay the doll. The doll she had never named properly. She had simply called her Dolly. She picked her up and held her in her arms, then wandered over to the bed and sat down.

She had had this doll for as long as she could remember. There had never been a time when Dolly had not been part of her life. She had loved her as she had loved no other toy and yet . . . sometimes when she had held her and sung to her she had found herself crying. She remembered that her mother would become anxious when this happened and would try to distract her.

But there was no one to distract her now and no one to explain those unsettling feelings of not belonging here. But if she, Rosina, didn't belong, then neither did the doll, for it was so different from all her other toys. Perhaps it had belonged to her mother when she was a child? That would explain why Dolly was so old, older than Rosina herself. But there was no one to ask, no one to explain things. She held the doll more tightly and sought comfort in the knowledge that at least now she had remembered the words of the song. And yet, for some unexplained reason, that was no comfort at all.

When Molly returned with the lemonade and biscuits she found Rosina sitting on her bed cradling the old doll like a baby and sobbing her heart out.

'Honestly, Bridget, I just didn't know what to do.'

Bridget and Molly were working in Amy's room the next morning. Some of her boxes had been sent home from her finishing school and the clothes had to be sorted, washed and mended if necessary.

'Do about what?' Bridget asked.

'Miss Rosina. She was just sitting there crying and cuddling that raggy old doll. When I came in she dried her eyes quickly and tried to pretend there was nothing the matter.'

'Didn't you ask her what was troubling her?'

'Of course I did. But she said she was fine and that I was a dear for bringing the lemonade and biscuits. For goodness' sake! That's my job, isn't it? But Miss Rosina, bless her, always says thank you politely, not like some I could mention.'

The two girls stopped work for a moment and looked towards the door. It remained closed. But, even so, they lowered their voices when they renewed their conversation.

Bridget shook her head. 'Miss Fidler is getting worse by the day, isn't she? And it doesn't help that the mistress makes her dislike of her so plain to see. Sometimes I think this would be a happier house if only Miss Rosina was the mistress of Ravenshill, young as she is.'

'I'll never forget how kind she was to me when I first started work here,' said Molly, 'even though she was still a little girl.'

'She takes after her mother, that's why,' Bridget said. 'At least . . .'

'What is it?'

'Well, I should have said she takes after Mrs Leighton.'

'What are you talking about?'

'Nothing, I shouldn't have said anything. Forget it.'

Molly glared at Bridget. 'How do you expect me to forget it when you suddenly start acting all mysterious? What's wrong with calling Mrs Leighton Miss Rosina's mother?'

'Because she wasn't.'

'You've completely lost me.'

'Well, if I tell you what I mean you must never repeat it. Not if you love Miss Rosina as I do.'

'Of course I do. I would never do anything to harm her.'

'Look, I don't know what came over me. It's such an old

secret that I don't even think about it most of the time. But lately, when I've seen how Mrs Leighton is doing her best to put her own daughter forward, it worries me. I believe that sooner or later Miss Rosina may need friends here.'

'Well, you can count on me. So spit it out.'

'Miss Rosina was adopted.'

Molly sank down on to a chair her eyes widening. 'Adopted?'

'Yes. Anyone who was working here when she was first brought home knows the truth of it. But Mrs Leighton, the first Mrs Leighton, asked them never to reveal it. And everyone respected her so much that they never have. I suppose most people living nearby knew that Mrs Leighton had pregnancy after pregnancy so they just assumed that eventually she had been successful. Mr Leighton was happy to let folk believe that for the sake of his poor wife.'

'And Miss Rosina doesn't know she's adopted?'

'No. And Mrs Leighton couldn't have been a better mother if the child had been her own flesh and blood.'

'What about Mr Leighton? Did he mind her taking in a little waif from the Lord knows where?'

'He wasn't too happy, so they say, but he didn't object so long as Mrs Leighton didn't adopt a boy.'

'That's understandable. He'd want an heir for Ravenshill, an heir of his own blood. But I don't think this secrecy is right. Every child has a right to know who her own mother is – where she comes from.'

'Even if that place was a stinking rat-infested slum?'

Molly frowned and then nodded. 'Yes.'

'I've thought about that,' Bridget told her. 'I believe Mrs Leighton might have got around to telling her one day – when Rosina was older. But we'll never know so it's pointless discussing it. And let me tell you, if ever Miss Fidler hears you talking about it you won't last in this house another minute. She was the one who brought Rosina here and she has always been just as keen as Mrs Leighton was to hide the truth of the matter.'

Molly's eyes widened. 'Really? Old Fiddlesticks brought the baby here? But that means she might know who her—'

'Stop that!' Bridget said. 'We've already said too much. Now, let's see if we're finished here.' Bridget and Molly stood up and looked with satisfaction around the tidy nursery. 'That'll do,' Bridget said. 'Close the wardrobe door properly and stuff all those things I've left on the bed into a laundry bag. Molly! Did you hear me?'

'Yes, sorry, It's just I was thinking that explains a lot.'

'What do you mean?'

'Well, it's obvious that Mrs Leighton knows Rosina is adopted and she must hate the idea that Rosina is regarded as a Leighton while her own precious Amy isn't. And old Fiddlesticks is the one who brought Rosina into the house. I bet Mrs Leighton wishes she could get rid of both of them.'

'But now that Miss Rosina has left school perhaps it won't be too long before she leaves Ravenshill,' Bridget said. She had walked over to the window and looked out.

Molly joined her and peered down at the two figures below: Adam Loxley and Rosina.

'Just look at them,' Bridget said. 'Like children, they are.'

The two maids smiled as they watched the fun below. Rosina was racing along the drive on her new bicycle and Adam Loxley was trying to keep up with her. Then she turned round to smile over her shoulder at Adam and suddenly somehow she lost control. Bridget and Molly held their breath as they saw Rosina's bicycle wobble but the moment didn't last long and she fell sideways, fortunately, landing on the lawn.

'You wouldn't think she was eighteen years old, would you?' Bridget asked when Rosina sat up, recovered her breath, and began to laugh out loud.

Adam leaped off his own bicycle and sent it carelessly crashing down on to the gravel, then ran towards Rosina anxiously. Her shoulders were shaking. As soon as Adam saw that she was laughing and not crying, he flopped down beside her and joined in the laughter.

Bridget and Molly turned to smile at each other. 'You think she's keen on him, don't you?' Molly asked.

'I do and it's mutual, I'm sure of it. I've watched them grow up, remember, and they've always enjoyed each other's company.'

'I know,' Molly said. 'I hadn't been here long before I realized they were very close. But until recently I thought they were more like brother and sister.'

Bridget nodded. 'Perhaps they were at one time – before Master Adam was sent away to school. But things have changed and I wouldn't be at all surprised if they make a match of it. There'll be a lovely wedding and Miss Rosina will have a home of her own and all the happiness she deserves.'

Molly nodded approvingly. 'And Mrs Leighton and her precious daughter won't be able to make her life a misery ever again.'

A few days after Rosina had fallen from her bicycle, she and Adam were cycling slowly and carefully towards his grandparents' farm. It was very early, not yet breakfast time, and they wanted to take advantage of the beautiful light of the tranquil summer's morning.

'I'm sorry about what happened the other day,' Adam said, 'but I just didn't think that a girl would need a special outfit in order to ride a bicycle.'

'It was my own fault. The skirt I was wearing was too full. The hem caught on the pedal when I wasn't concentrating. This one is better.'

Adam glanced down at Rosina's blue skirt doubtfully. 'Even so, I'm not taking any risks. It would be mortifying if my present caused you to be hurt.'

Aunt Muriel was waiting for them with a solution to the problem. As soon as they arrived she hurried Rosina upstairs and showed her a plain grey serge skirt. But it was a skirt with a difference.

'Bifurcated,' Muriel Graham told Rosina.

Rosina was startled. 'I beg your pardon?' She knew Adam's aunt to be eccentric and she wondered if the older woman had just uttered something unladylike.

Muriel Graham saw Rosina's startled expression and laughed. 'Don't worry, dear, bifurcated simply means split into two parts. Look.' She shook the skirt gently and Rosina saw that it was more like trousers with flared legs, and it was constructed so skilfully that at first glance you couldn't tell that it wasn't an ordinary skirt.

'I made this for myself when I bought my first bicycle,' Adam's aunt told Rosina. 'Well, to start with I wore a pair of knickerbockers – baggy bloomers – but my dear old father said I was a disgrace and that folk had been laughing at me as I cycled through the countryside, so I came up with this.'

Rosina looked at the garment doubtfully. 'Don't worry, you'll look quite respectable,' Aunt Muriel said.

'I'm – er – sure I will.'

'What's the matter? Oh, I see. You're young and slender and I'm a stout old party. But I've taken it in. Did it as soon as Adam called by to tell me what had happened. I had to guess your measurements, of course, but I'm sure it will do. Here, try it on.'

Rosina was pleased to find that the strange split skirt fit her well and was comfortable to wear – although she'd had to abandon her petticoat. When they returned to the farmhouse kitchen she found that Aunt Muriel had made sandwiches for them. They were neatly wrapped in a clean cloth and were waiting on the table along with a stone jar of homemade ginger beer.

'You can borrow my cycle basket,' Aunt Muriel said. 'It will strap on to your handlebars – yours, I'm afraid, Rosina; it won't fit properly on to Adam's gentleman's bicycle.'

As well as the picnic Aunt Muriel put a tartan travelling rug into the basket. Adam put a map into a small canvas bag, which he slung over one shoulder and across his body.

'Goodness,' Rosina said, 'a map. I didn't realize this was going to be quite such an expedition.'

'We're not going far; it's just that I haven't been there for so long. It would be easy to miss the way.'

Rosina was intrigued but Adam refused to tell her more about their destination and there was nothing she could do except follow him along the winding country roads. The air was warm and sweet, but there was a cool breeze blowing in from the sea, which in Rosina's imagination got behind them and helped them on their way inland and uphill.

Soon she was lulled by the rhythmic swish of their wheels on the surface of the old roads. And was only when Adam had stopped and she pulled up alongside him that she realized where they were. He straddled the crossbar of his bicycle and turned to smile at her.

'I didn't need the map, after all,' he said. 'Do you know where we are?'

'The Roman settlement.'

They dismounted and pushed their bikes up the rutted cart track, and to Rosina it seemed only yesterday that they had come here as children and she had experienced one of the most perfect days since her mother had died. For a moment she gave herself up to blissful memories of that day and then wondered why Adam had brought her here. Did he have happy memories too?

For a while they walked among the ruins, neither speaking very much. Rosina glanced at Adam now and then, and thought that he seemed to be avoiding her gaze. She sensed there was a certain tension building up between them but did not know why.

'Let's eat,' he said suddenly, and he led the way back to the very same grassy bank where they had picnicked with Aunt Muriel. While they shared the sandwiches Rosina tried to keep a conversation going but Adam was only half listening. He had a distracted air as if he had something on his mind.

When the food was gone he stood up and shook the napkins vigorously, giving the crumbs to the birds.

'Are we going now?' Rosina asked.

'No, there's no hurry. Let's rest awhile.'

They lay back on the rug and closed their eyes. Rosina could feel the sun warming her skin and smell the sweet fresh air. An insect buzzed somewhere nearby, its insistent hum the only jarring note in this perfect day.

Rosina wondered if this was what her life was going to be like from now on; if she would spend many more days like this with Adam. And if she could look forward to being even closer to him than she was now. She turned her head and regarded him surreptitiously through half-closed eyelids. His eyes were closed and his breathing was even. She raised herself and rested on one arm while she looked at him – his strong profile, soft light brown curls falling over a wide, smooth brow.

He is handsome, she thought, in an open, robust way.

Not like Tom Carey, who is dark and clever and complicated. Rosina blinked. Where had that thought come from? She was surprised to find that the face of the young actor had suddenly appeared in her mind's eye. She squeezed her eyes tight shut as if doing so would banish the intruder. And it wasn't just the person she was banishing but the way of life he represented. The claustrophobic but deliciously exciting atmosphere of the theatre. She remembered she had been captivated by it – and wished that it had not been so.

She opened her eyes again and looked at her old friend. Adam and his like had populated the countryside for generations, she thought. Even before the Romans came to build their wall, she wouldn't be surprised if Adam's forebears had been living in these hills.

'Why are you smiling?' Adam had opened his eyes and was looking up at her curiously.

'Because what I was looking at pleased me.'

'You were looking at me.'

'No, I was looking at the hills – at the sky – at the clouds – at the skylarks.'

Adam shook his head and raised himself up on one elbow so that their faces were only inches apart. 'I was watching you. You were looking at me. Tell me why you were smiling.'

'It will only make you conceited, but I was thinking what a pleasant young man you are.'

'Pleasant? Is that all I am, pleasant?'

Before she could answer him he had leaned forward impulsively and placed his lips on hers. Startled, she fell back on to the rug but he moved with her and continued the kiss. For that's what it was. Her first kiss. She closed her eyes and gave herself up to entirely new sensations. The sweet scent of sun-warmed grass mingled with the citrus tang of his hair dressing. The ground beneath her was no longer solid, and clouds in the sky had descended to enfold them. The everyday world had vanished. Nothing was real any more except the two of them. She clung to Adam and returned his kiss with fervour. But all too soon he pulled away from her. The world stopped spinning and reality returned.

They looked at each other, not knowing what to say. They knew their old relationship had changed for ever. There would be no going back to the easy friendship that had meant so much to both of them. Adam took her hand. It was something he had done so many times in the past but now the gesture was charged with meaning and the feel of his skin on hers aroused a thousand pleasurable sensations. He looked as though he wanted to say something but then he dropped his gaze and let go of her hand again.

'I suppose we'd better be going home,' he said.

Rosina's spirits plunged into a cold pool of disappointment. Somehow she had been expecting him to say something significant – to at least acknowledge that the world was now a different place for them.

As Adam packed the rug and the picnic things back into the basket, Rosina stood and looked at the ruined settlement. She wondered what it must have been like for those long-ago people to live so far away from Rome and the civilized world they had been used to. She wondered if she could have been happy living here and decided she would have been if the person she loved was there beside her.

And that person was Adam, wasn't it? It seemed that all her life she had been waiting for this moment, the moment when he would take her in his arms. And it had been as wonderful as she had imagined. But strangely inconclusive. Adam hadn't said anything. Had not 'declared himself' as a hero in a romantic novel would have done.

On the way home they found themselves cycling into a

rising wind which made conversation, beyond a few shouted directions, impossible. Rosina was glad of it for she had much to think about. Joanne had assumed that she would leave school, go back to Ravenshill and marry Adam as soon as he asked her. And Rosina hadn't denied that that was what she was hoping for.

And yet . . .

She thought uneasily of the excitement of that night at the theatre. She had been taken over by more than enjoyment. It was as though she had been sleeping and had woken up in a totally different reality. For a moment she felt almost as if she belonged there. But that was crazy. This was where she belonged . . . in the country with Adam. She had known him all her life and in all those lonely years she had grown to love him; first as a friend and then something more. She knew that if Adam asked her to marry him and stay in the country she would give up all her dreams about the theatre.

Adam was glad of the wind. They couldn't talk and it gave him the chance to think. He had not intended to kiss Rosina – at least not in that way, with such passion. But she had looked so lovely, lying there with her dark hair disarranged by the breeze and spread out around her face. And she had smelled so fresh; of scented soap and clean linen and a delicate rose perfume; and her mouth had tasted so sweet. Adam was completely inexperienced as far as girls were concerned but there had been no mistaking the physical sensations that had been aroused. That was why he'd had to pull back, before he lost control and got carried away.

What could he do? The other lads at school, some of them more experienced than he was, had told him of encounters with the lower type of actress or prostitutes but he was afraid his inexperience would make a fool of him with such women and also there was the danger of contracting some disgusting disease.

No, there was no other solution he could think of. If life was to be bearable they would have to marry as quickly as it could be arranged. It was sooner than he had planned and he knew he was a little young. But if his father was keen to take him into the business he would surely prefer Adam to be settled with a wife and a home of his own to take care of and to work hard for.

Yes, he would speak to his father and then he would have to speak to Mr Leighton too. He couldn't see either of them objecting. Rosina was fun to be with and though she was obviously more intelligent than most girls he had met, she had always been happy to follow his lead. He had no doubt she would make an excellent wife.

Chapter Fifteen

Rosina was still out with Adam when Molly brought the post into the morning room where Mr and Mrs Leighton were sitting with coffee and the newspapers. Julian took the letters from the tray; all but one was for him. He scanned them quickly; they looked like business letters so he laid them aside to be dealt with later. He handed the other to Blanche with a smile.

'Addressed to you, my dear, postmark Harrogate. Must be from Amy.'

Blanche took the letter. 'No, this isn't Amy's handwriting; I believe the letter is from Mrs Earnshaw.' Blanche and Beryl Earnshaw's mother had exchanged letters while Amy's stay with the Earnshaws was being arranged so she recognized the spidery handwriting. 'But there may be a letter from Amy enclosed.'

'Well, why don't you open it and see?' Julian retreated behind his newspaper.

Blanche took up her ivory and silver letter opener from the small table beside her and smiled as she slit open the envelope. No doubt this would be something to do with Beryl Earnshaw's proposed visit. Originally, Amy had asked if she could stay with the Earnshaws until after her birthday, but Blanche had refused because she and Julian had already planned a celebration ball. The invitations had been sent and the guests had replied.

But Blanche had sweetened her refusal by saying that Amy was free to invite Beryl to come home with her and to stay as long as she pleased. Amy's response was a sulky silence. Blanche had been hurt that Amy could even think of being away from home on her birthday but had accepted that her head might have been turned by the opulence of Beryl's home and she could not find it in her heart to blame her. After all, this was an opportunity for her to meet the right sort of people. Beryl Earnshaw inhabited a far more elevated strata of society than Rosina's friend, the Bartlett girl.

There was only one sheet of notepaper inside the envelope and the handwriting was Mrs Earnshaw's. When Blanche saw what was written her eyes widened with shock. She read the brief letter and then read it again. Her hands began to shake. She glanced quickly at Julian and saw he was still immersed in his morning paper.

She folded the letter and put it back in the envelope. She was tempted to throw it straight on to the fire but Julian would only ask her why she had done that. Her husband must never know the contents of the letter. Blanche hoped to God that Mrs Earnshaw would be discreet. She imagined she would be for, after all, she had not proved to be a fit person to have an innocent young girl in her house. At least that's how Blanche saw the matter.

She slipped the letter into her pocket, gripped the arms of her chair and stared into the mid-distance, her mind working furiously.

Julian folded his paper and smiled at her enquiringly. 'Well, then,' he said, 'how is our darling daughter?'

Blanche managed a smile. 'Amy is fine,' she said. 'And I

know you'll be pleased to hear that she is on her way home.'

'On her way home? What . . . today?'

'Yes. And we must send a carriage to the station immediately. She may have arrived already.'

Julian looked concerned. 'She must have set off from Harrogate at the crack of dawn!'

'I believe she did.'

'But this is outrageous,' Julian said. 'What sort of people send a young girl off like a parcel to be collected from the station at will? I've a good mind to write and tell them what I think of them.'

'No!' Blanche felt panic rising like bile in her throat. 'Don't do that. It was Amy's fault.'

'Fault? What do you mean? What has she done?'

'Nothing! Amy has done nothing.' Oh dear God, Blanche thought. Let me get my wits together before I give the whole sorry game away. 'Apparently she was homesick. Yesterday she packed her bags and insisted that she would be leaving on the morning train. So all Mrs Earnshaw could do was to write a letter and send it posthaste.'

Julian looked doubtful. 'Amy homesick?' he said.

'Mrs Earnshaw said she was most insistent that she was missing us.'

'Really?'

Blanche nodded.

Julian smiled fondly. 'Poor little girl.' But then the smile vanished and he scowled. 'You don't think it's some sort of cover-up, do you?'

Blanche's heart thumped against her ribs. 'What do you mean?'

'Well, you don't think that they could have been beastly to her in some way? You can never tell with these *nouveau riche*

279

families. In the long run they simply don't know how to behave. Perhaps our girl found she couldn't stand them a moment longer.'

Blanche cocked her head to one side and put on a thoughtful expression. 'You may be right,' she said consideringly. 'We'll find out as soon as we see her.'

'Of course. And we've been wasting time. Amy might be waiting at the station already. I'll order the carriage and get straight down there.'

'No! I mean yes! Order the carriage but let me go to meet her. If she is upset she'll want to see her mother, won't she?'

'We'll go together.'

'That's thoughtful of you, Julian, but accept a mother's wisdom and allow me to meet her on my own.'

Julian's brow furrowed but he gave in gracefully. 'Very well.'

He walked over to the fireplace and pulled the bell rope. Both he and Blanche were surprised to see that it was Maud Fidler who answered the summons as if she were a parlour maid. Julian gave orders for the carriage to be brought round as quickly as possible as Mrs Leighton was going to the station to meet Amy.

As Blanche put on her coat and hat in her bedroom, she reflected sourly that Maud Fidler seemed to pop up everywhere these days. She had never really liked the woman and she suspected that Fidler in return did not like her. In fact, she didn't seem to like anybody and the only time she was remotely happy was when she was just about to set off for a visit to her brother's house in Newcastle. But that seemed to happen less often these days. Perhaps he was sick of her sour face too.

Blanche hadn't missed the way the woman's eyebrows rose when she was told Amy was coming home unexpectedly, and the sudden speculative gleam in her eyes. No doubt with not much of a life of her own she revelled in knowing everybody else's business. Halfway downstairs Blanche stopped as that thought penetrated the cloud of worries buzzing round inside her mind.

Maud Fidler was too clever by half. She had a nasty habit of gliding about the house so quietly that you didn't know she was there. Blanche was sure she heard things that she shouldn't have. The woman could be dangerous. Blanche thought she had delayed long enough getting rid of her, mainly because Maud Fidler had a knack of keeping the lower servants on their toes. But now Blanche thought it might be dangerous to let her stay.

When Blanche greeted Amy at the station, Angus, the Leightons' groom, would have had no reason to think that she was anything but overjoyed to see her daughter. He was too far away to hear the muttered, 'Smile for God's sake,' as Mrs Leighton enfolded Miss Amy in a motherly embrace. He might have been surprised at how quiet they were as he drove them home, but all he could report to an interested servants' hall was that Miss Amy looked a little peaky but that, no doubt, would be due to the fact that she had been overdoing it and having a whale of a good time with her rich friends in Harrogate.

Maud Fidler absorbed this information and didn't believe a word of it. She was pretty sure that Amy had been sent home in disgrace. There was no other way to explain Mrs Earnshaw's behaviour. Maud wasn't surprised. She had never liked the girl, who wasn't a patch on Miss Rosina. But then she found it very hard to like Rosina either – or rather she had never allowed herself to.

And she was honest enough to admit that guilt was the cause. Guilt at stealing a perfectly happy child away from its loving mother. That burden of guilt had been just about bearable when the first Mrs Leighton was alive. Mrs Leighton had been so grateful that, in her eyes, Maud could do no wrong. Though never exactly a friend, Mrs Leighton's companion had been so much more than a servant.

She ought to have left when Geraldine Leighton died. Then she would still have been young enough to find a good position and Mr Leighton would have written her an excellent reference because he was well aware that his late wife held her in high regard. But she couldn't in all conscience have left straight away. No one would think much of her if she had gone while there was a young motherless baby to cope with. But once Mr Leighton had married again it would have been more acceptable.

However, Jack, the brother she doted on, had persuaded her to stay. He had wanted her to 'keep an eye on things'. He had been worried that Julian Leighton, urged by his new wife, might tell Rosina she was adopted and maybe even ask her to leave. He couldn't have the girl wandering free like 'a loose cannon', as he put it, asking questions and trying to find out where she had come from. No, Maud must stay so that if anything untoward happened she could warn him and he would have a plan of action ready.

So she had stayed on, with her duties in the household becoming more and more ill defined. She had long ago accepted that helping Jack get rid of baby Rose had affected the rest of her own life – for the worse. And now that Jack was away so much travelling about England and Europe, she didn't even have the comfort of visiting him so often. And even when she did go it always seemed to her that he couldn't wait to get rid of her again.

So Maud was no stranger to misery – to desperation even. That was why it was so easy for her to recognize the same emotions in the pinched anxious faces of Blanche Leighton and her daughter Amy when they returned from the station.

As soon as Amy's boxes had been carried up to her bedroom, Blanche dismissed Molly. When the door closed after the maid Amy took off her coat and flung herself down on the bed.

'Get up,' Blanche said. Amy raised her head and looked sulkily at her mother but she didn't obey her. For the first time since Amy had been born, Blanche felt like smacking her. 'If you don't get off that bed immediately I shall tell your stepfather the contents of Mrs Earnshaw's letter.'

Of course she had no intention of doing that but the threat had the desired effect. Amy, surprised at her mother's tone, stood up. Blanche hurried towards her and, seizing her shoulders, she turned her round and propelled her towards one of the seats near the fireplace. She sat her down forcibly and drew up a chair to face her. She had never spoken to Amy in this fashion before but she was driven by anger. What Amy had done might have ruined everything – all her plans for a grand marriage for her. She had to find out the worst immediately. But to be fair she had decided to let Amy give her version of events first.

'Why did Mrs Earnshaw send you home, Amy?'

'Didn't she tell you in her letter?'

'I want you to tell me.'

Blanche watched her daughter's face. Amy was not good at dissembling and she was obviously trying to work out exactly what her friend's mother had said – and what her mother would believe.

'She was jealous,' Amy said at last.

Blanche was astounded. 'Jealous?'

Amy nodded.

'Jealous of whom?'

'Me, of course.'

'Amy, that's ridiculous.'

'No it isn't. Mrs Earnshaw thought that someone was paying me too much attention.'

'That someone being?'

'Her son — Beryl's brother, Maurice ...' Amy faltered.

'Go on.'

'Well, that's it, really. I mean, she dotes on him. Positively disgusting, it is.'

Blanche tried to hang on to her patience. 'But that still does not explain why you were suddenly sent home.'

Any squirmed uneasily. 'Beryl told me that the Earnshaws have hopes that Maurice will marry into some great family. That he will bring home the daughter of a duke. The Earnshaws have more money than they know what to do with but they are not really accepted into society. The sort of society that is on nodding terms with the royal family.'

'I see. And is there any chance of this?'

'Oh, yes.' Amy sounded bitter. 'Maurice has been to the right schools. He is good looking and charming. He has already made the acquaintance of the daughters of at least two titled families. And what's more, one of the young women has a brother who would do very nicely for Beryl.'

Blanche saw there were tears of frustration in her daughter's eyes. She wanted to stop the questioning then and there and comfort her. But she knew she must go on. 'Did you set your cap at him?'

Amy shifted in her seat and her gaze dropped. 'It was Maurice who sought me out. When he came to visit Beryl in Paris he particularly asked permission for me to join them.'

'So you already knew each other?'

Amy nodded.

'And was it Maurice's idea that you should come home with Beryl?'

'Yes — I mean no . . .' Amy's answer was barely audible. 'It was Beryl's idea.'

Blanche wondered at that. Perhaps it had been Beryl's suggestion but how much had she been prompted by Amy? 'And Maurice?' she asked. 'Had he . . . had he made you any promises?'

Her daughter shook her head and looked down at her clenched hands.

Blanche took the letter from her pocket and opened it. 'In that case,' she said, and she could hear her own voice shaking, 'why was he seen by one of the chambermaids coming out of your room in the early hours of the morning?'

Amy's complexion changed from curdled white to angry red. She stared at the single sheet of paper in her mother's hands. 'That's in the letter?'

Blanche nodded grim-faced. 'Do you deny it?'

'No I don't,' Amy said defiantly. 'But it wasn't one of the maids who saw him. It was Mrs Earnshaw herself. But no doubt she doesn't want to admit that she behaved so badly.'

'*Mrs Earnshaw* behaved badly?'

'Of course. Sneaking round at night, spying on her son and her daughter's best friend.'

Blanche knew it would be pointless to discuss Mrs Earnshaw's behaviour with Amy. Even if her daughter knew what had aroused her hostess's suspicions, she certainly wouldn't tell her; not while she was in this sulky defiant mood.

'However, you admit it's true? Maurice was in your room and not just on the one occasion?'

Amy swallowed a sob and lowered her head. Blanche stared at the golden crown of curls and felt like weeping.

Whatever had happened between Amy and Maurice Earnshaw it was obvious that he did not intend to do the honourable thing. She realised now that at least Mrs Earnshaw would keep the matter to herself because if she acknowledged openly what had happened then Maurice would have to marry Amy to save her reputation.

So the woman had packed her off home, saying that she no longer considered Amy a suitable friend for Beryl. She had instructed her daughter never to contact Amy again. Well, the loss of the friendship was neither here nor there. But now there was something Amy must tell her.

'Are you still . . . ? Did you let . . . ?' She faltered, then tried again. 'Did Maurice come into your bed?'

'Yes.'

Blanche almost gave way to black despair. 'And what took place between you?'

'What do you think took place? He . . . he forced me to submit to him. And now something that should happen every month has not happened.'

'How late are you?'

'Only a day or two. Oh, Mama, do you think that means that I am—'

'Hush! Don't say any more.' Blanche looked towards the door fearfully. You never knew if someone – Maud Fidler – might be listening.

'What am I going to do?' Amy wailed.

Blanche didn't answer her. She could hardly trust herself to speak. She suspected that Amy was lying when she claimed that Maurice had forced her. But whatever the truth of it, the predicament was the same. The Earnshaws were rich and powerful. Mrs Earnshaw was the only other person who knew what had happened and she would simply deny everything.

Amy had started crying and Blanche did not feel like comforting her. She could not even look at her. Her mind spinning with the possible consequences, she rose and walked over to the window. She gazed out at the well-ordered gardens and as she stood there she saw two figures walking up the drive; they were pushing bicycles. Rosina and Adam Loxley.

Blanche suddenly focused her gaze. There was something about the way Adam was looking at Rosina that disturbed her. This was no longer the look of a childhood friend. Something has happened between them, Blanche thought. Their relationship has changed.

The bottom half of the window was open and as they came nearer their voices became more distinct. They were talking about some ruins they had visited. Rosina mentioned the word 'fountain' and then went on to say, 'I'm sure that's what it was, Adam, and there may have been a stone figure of some kind. Maybe as tall as . . .' And here she gestured in the air, raising her hand several feet.

Adam, looking like a man who had suddenly made up his mind, reached for her hand, caught it and carried it to his lips. The gesture was so intimate that Blanche found herself holding her breath as she listened for his next words. 'Rosina, be quiet a moment, please,' he said.

Rosina stopped her prattle immediately. Blanche noticed that she did not take her hand away.

'You must know what I feel about you,' Adam said.

'I think I do.'

'And do you feel the same way?'

'Yes.' Her voice was hushed. Blanche almost felt the anticipation and knew that Rosina was holding her breath.

For goodness' sake, Blanche felt like saying to them. If this is a declaration of love then get on with it.

Adam smiled. 'My father is away at his Carlisle office for the rest of the week. When he returns I'm going to speak to him, and if he agrees then I shall speak to your father. You understand what I'm saying, don't you?'

Even from here Blanche could sense the uplifting of Rosina's spirits. 'Yes, I do,' she said.

'And are you happy?'

'Very much so.'

Blanche watched as Adam, still clutching the handlebars of his bicycle with one hand and holding Rosina's hand with the other, leaned forward and kissed Rosina on the lips. The gesture was clumsy but almost unbearably touching. She could see how pleased with each other the two of them were and, for a moment, allowed herself to imagine a wedding.

A wedding that she would have welcomed because it would mean the end of her responsibility for Julian's adopted daughter. But she repressed those imaginings quickly. The scene below had suggested a way out of her predicament. She hardened her heart and prepared herself to disobey Julian for the first time since she had married him.

'I do hope you don't mind my calling like this, uninvited and unexpected?'

Mrs Leighton sank gracefully on to a chair in the Loxleys' morning room. Sybil hastily tried to capture her stray wisps of hair and tuck them behind her ears. She observed her visitor almost with reverent admiration. Blanche's lilac dress was draped artfully at the front and the bodice gave the appearance of being sculpted to her body. The slight fullness at the top of the sleeves subtly softened the tailored look.

Her perky little hat was set forward on her carefully dressed hair. A little stuffed bird with dyed feathers was perched on the brim and in its cruel beak it held the beginnings of a veil, which cascaded on to the brim and then fell far enough to cover Blanche's eyes. Both the bird and the veil matched the purple trimmings on the dress.

'I don't mind at all,' Sybil said. 'I'm delighted to see you.'

Only half of that statement was true. Of course she was delighted to see the fashionable Mrs Leighton, but if she had had some warning she would have put on one of her new summer frocks and taken more care with her hair. However, she ordered the girl to bring coffee and ratafia biscuits and hastily pushed her copy of _One Life, One Love_ behind the cushion of the chair she was sitting on. She was not sure if the sophisticated Mrs Leighton would altogether approve of the sensational novels of Miss Braddon.

She watched as Blanche peeled off one of her gloves and sipped her coffee, and for a while they chatted about the weather, their neighbours and the latest fashions. Sybil began to relax. Perhaps Blanche Leighton really did enjoy her company and this visit was nothing more than a social call. And the more she relaxed the more indiscreet her visitor seemed to become. They giggled together like schoolgirls over the eccentric behaviour of the vicar's wife who had taken the new young curate under her wing to such a degree that the congregation suspected there was something more than thwarted mother love prompting her behaviour.

'Of course, I don't believe the poor woman has done anything scandalous,' Blanche asserted.

'Don't you?' Sybil was startled. A moment ago Blanche had told her the latest gossip was that the housemaid at the vicarage had caught her mistress tucking the young man up in bed when he had a slight fever.

'No, not at all. In fact I think the real story is rather sad.'

Infuriatingly Blanche said no more. She picked up Sybil's

latest copy of the *Ladies' Home Journal* and began to flick through it, pausing at an illustration of flower arrangements for the dining table.

'The real story?' Sybil ventured.

'Oh?' Blanche looked up. 'Oh, yes. I believe our vicar's wife loves the young man in a totally innocent fashion. Like a mother, in fact. I mean, it must be devastating to have had so many miscarriages when she was a young bride.'

'Oh, of course.' Sybil had had no idea that Mrs Benton had suffered miscarriages but she did not wish to appear ignorant.

'I'm told the last child she bore, a darling little boy, lived for a day and when he died the poor woman was demented.'

'How dreadful.'

'I'm surprised that Mr Benton, with his concern for the poor, did not consider adopting a child, aren't you?'

'Well, yes, I suppose so.'

Blanche sighed as if sympathizing with the vicar's problem. 'But as you know, adoption can be a risky undertaking.'

'Risky?'

'You don't know exactly what kind of creature you are taking into your home, do you?'

'I'm not sure what you mean.'

Blanche, looking earnest, explained, 'Well, supposing the Bentons had taken a poor little mite from the slums of Newcastle, or from one of the villages – there is much rural poverty, you know. Most of it caused by ne'er-do-wells, who won't work. Anyway, supposing the good vicar and his wife had taken a baby like that. No matter how much love and how much care they lavished on it, I believe that, in the long run, the family traits would become manifest.'

'I see what you mean. Just like bad stock, as my father would say.' Mrs Loxley paused and bit her lip. Usually she did not remind people that she was a farmer's daughter. But when she saw the expression in her visitor's face she was surprised and delighted. Blanche Leighton was looking at her as if she had just let pearls of wisdom drop from her lips.

'My dear, how wise you are. I mean, that's exactly what Julian told his first wife when she was so keen to adopt. I see you are surprised. Didn't you know that Rosina was adopted?'

'No, I don't think I did.'

After the slightest of pauses Blanche continued, 'Nevertheless, it is true.'

'I see.' Sybil fiddled with the wisps of her hair again. She sensed that some response was required of her but did not know what it was.

This time the silence was so long that Sybil began to get nervous. She knew that she was not as intelligent as her sister, Muriel, but neither was she completely muddleheaded as darling Hugh sometimes liked to pretend. She finally realized that Blanche Leighton had had a purpose in coming here today.

'I'm not sure why you are telling me this.'

Blanche's smile was sad and a little world-weary. 'Because, Sybil, my dear, I have reason to believe that your son is harbouring tender feelings for Rosina.'

'Harbouring tender feelings?' Sybil thought fleetingly that Blanche was talking like a character in one of Miss Braddon's novels. 'You mean he has fallen in love with her?'

Blanche nodded. 'Yes, I do.'

'But they are hardly more than children.'

'They are young adults. And Rosina, at least, is quite old enough to get married.'

'Married! You're not suggesting that Adam wants to marry Rosina, are you?'

'Indeed I am. In fact, I'm absolutely positive.'

'Has . . . has Adam already asked her? But surely he can't have done. I mean he wouldn't without talking with his father and me first.'

Blanche's thin lips tightened. 'Adam has not actually asked her to marry him. Although what he said to her made his intentions quite clear.'

'You overheard something?'

Blanche nodded. 'I was looking out into the garden when they returned from a bicycle ride. It was obvious something had happened when they were out together.'

'Something happened! Oh, no!'

'Don't worry, I don't mean that they had become intimate.'

Sybil felt the colour flood her face. 'Thank God,' she whispered.

'No, they were still behaving like innocents, but Adam took her hand and told her he was going to speak to his father and then he would speak to Julian.'

'Hugh is away from home.'

'For that you can be thankful. For now you can be prepared. You can forewarn your husband that his son and heir is going to ask his permission to propose to a young woman who was probably found in the slums of Newcastle; who for all we know may be carrying some inherited disease and who will bring nothing to the marriage except a modest inheritance left to her by Geraldine.'

'Inheritance . . .'

'A *modest* inheritance,' Blanche reiterated. 'I hope you understand that I could have said nothing. That I could have let the marriage go ahead simply to get the girl settled in life. But because you and I are friends I thought it my duty to tell you.'

Sybil coloured with pleasure. 'It's very kind of you,' she said.

'I felt it was my duty. After all, by encouraging the children's friendship I may have been at fault.'

'Oh, no, you couldn't have foreseen what would happen. And, as I said, they are so young.'

'Yes, it's surprising, isn't it? But I am sure that Adam is not to blame.'

'Adam . . . blame?' Her voice shook.

'Don't distress yourself, Sybil. You know I believe that Rosina may have encouraged him. After all, as I said, we have no idea what her true parentage is. Who knows what sort of woman her mother was — and what vicious traits she has passed on to her?'

'Oh, my goodness,' Sibyl gasped. 'Just imagine what could have happened!'

Blanche smiled reassuringly and sat back in her chair a little. 'Well, nothing has happened yet, has it? And forewarned is forearmed, isn't it?'

'Yes, indeed. I can't thank you enough, Mrs Leighton.'

'Blanche, please. But now let us talk about more pleasant matters. Did you know Amy has come home? She was staying with a school friend in Harrogate — a very grand family — but she suddenly decided that she was homesick, dear child. She wanted to be at home with her mother . . .'

Later that day Sybil discussed Blanche's visit with Muriel and was irritated to find that her elder sister was not at all understanding.

'I must say I'm disappointed in you,' Muriel Graham said. 'Rosina is a delightful young woman and would make a perfect wife for Adam.'

'But she's adopted.'

'So?'

'As Blanche Leighton pointed out, you never know what traits of character may be inherent in her.'

'Are you suggesting that Rosina may take to drink or become a vicious criminal?'

'No . . . well . . . I mean, you never know, do you?'

Muriel was outraged. 'I'm ashamed of you, Sybil. Geraldine Leighton was the forming influence on the child's life and the result is nothing but good.'

'Maybe so – but even supposing she has turned out well, she's not really from the right sort of family, is she?'

'To marry a Loxley, do you mean? It's a good job Hugh didn't think of that when he married you.'

'Muriel, how can you? Our family is perfectly respectable – and besides, Father was able to invest a substantial sum in Hugh's business.'

'I see. It's hopeless then.'

'Don't talk in riddles.'

'Blanche Leighton has obviously told you that Rosina will not bring a substantial sum of money to the marriage. If she had a tidy fortune I'm sure Hugh would not object to the fact that she is adopted.'

Sybil didn't answer. Neither could she meet her elder sister's piercing gaze. 'If Adam and Rosina are really in love then I can only hope that Adam will have more character than to listen to any of this,' Muriel said.

'He would never defy his father.'

'Filial duty aside, I hope that's not true. And, now, Sybil, I think I shall go home.'

If Sybil had been unsettled by the visit, Blanche was completely satisfied. The current gossip about the vicar's unfortunate wife had been a useful way of introducing the subject of adoption and finding out Sybil's views on the matter, or rather informing them. Sybil had risen to the bait nicely and Blanche had a pretty good idea that Hugh Loxley would be swayed by the financial aspect of it.

Julian had told her that Hugh had made some risky

investments of late. That was one of the reasons he had not encouraged Adam to go to university – he could barely have afforded it. No, he needed the young man to come straight into the business, and furthermore, although he might not have thought of it yet, he wouldn't object to Adam marrying someone who would bring a substantial sum of money with her. As Amy would. Of course, she would have to keep up the pretence of Amy's father being dead. It must never be revealed that she was illegitimate.

In a day or two's time they should know whether or not Amy was pregnant. If she was Blanche would have to find a suitable husband quickly. The only possible choice in the circumstances would be Adam Loxley.

On the evening of the birthday ball, the floor of the ballroom at Ravenshill was waxed to perfection and every column garlanded with dark green waxy leaves and delicately perfumed hothouse flowers. All white – Blanche had insisted on that. 'As a symbol of our darling girl's purity,' she told Julian, and the notion had tugged at his emotions.

He adored his daughter and he was gradually resigning himself to the idea that she was going to be his sole heir. And he loved Blanche as maybe he had never loved poor Geraldine. He made every effort to assure her that even if she did not manage to become pregnant again he would not reproach her.

After all, she was a good wife. She constantly tried to please him, putting him first in a way that Geraldine, with her casual attitude to housekeeping, had never done. They would be happy, he decided, and if the name Leighton would no longer be associated with Ravenshill in future years at least he would have the secret satisfaction of knowing that the heir was of his own bloodline.

It was nearly time for the ball to begin, and Julian watched his wife putting the finishing touches to her appearance with pleasure and even a stirring of desire.

'You look lovely, my dear.'

Blanche's ball gown of Parma-violet moiré, with its scooped neckline and large puffed sleeves, showed her magnificent shoulders and swan-like neck to advantage. Her hair was arranged in a soft pompadour and two diamond-encrusted combs held a few artificial ringlets in place. Her pendant earrings of diamonds and pearls matched her simple – but wildly expensive – single-strand necklace, and her full-length white gloves and large fan would have brought favourable comments in any London salon.

He knew that she got satisfaction from dazzling the bumpkins, as she unkindly called the country society in which they moved and, if he admitted it to himself, he got pleasure from the fact that not one of the local gentry had a wife as sophisticated as he had. Tonight there was a nervous intensity about her which, although he didn't quite understand it, excited him.

'And you look very handsome,' Blanche said as she turned from the cheval glass in their bedroom.

'Are you sure I don't look like the hired help in this jacket?' he asked.

'Of course not. The dinner jacket is very fashionable now.'

'Maybe so, but do our neighbours know that? I'm sure every one of them will turn up in the usual tail coat.'

'Then I shall make sure that by the end of the evening they all know that you are leading the way and they will all have to order dinner jackets from their tailors immediately.'

All the while she spoke Blanche had been fluttering her fan nervously and Julian reached for her hand. 'Everything will go well tonight, my dear. There's no need to be anxious.'

'Oh, I'm not anxious. But, naturally, I'm hoping that Amy will enjoy herself.'

'Of course she will. But . . .' he hesitated, 'I want you to remember that this is Rosina's celebration too.'

Blanche snapped her fan shut. 'There's no need to remind me and I can only hope that Rosina will appreciate all that I have done.'

Something about her tone alerted him. 'Is there any reason why she should not?'

'I'm not sure. She has been rather subdued these last few days. I wondered if there may be some jealousy at play here.'

'Jealousy?'

'Well, you know, I hardly like to say this but Amy is so pretty—'

'She's not just pretty. She's beautiful!'

'Exactly. And Rosina – well, Rosina is not.'

'Oh, I don't know. Some may find those dark curls attractive and she has a fine pair of eyes.' He saw the tiny cloud gathering on his wife's brow and added hurriedly, 'But I see your point. She's not in the same league as our darling Amy.' Blanche's smile returned. 'And now,' Julian said, 'we must go down and meet our guests.'

When Julian opened the door he was startled to find Maud Fidler standing outside with her hand raised as if she were about to knock.

'What is it, Fidler?' Blanche said as she came up behind Julian.

'I came to tell you that everything is ready, Mrs Leighton.'

'Thank you. You may go.' Blanche's tone was curt and Miss Fidler turned and walked away.

Blanche turned to Julian and muttered, 'She didn't come to tell us anything of the sort. She simply didn't get away quickly enough.'

'Whatever do you mean?'

They paused at the top of the stairs. They could hear the bustle below as the musicians began to tune their instruments in the ballroom and the servants hurried to and fro from the dining room with dishes for the buffet table. Blanche stopped with her hand on the banister.

'She listens. You must have noticed. She creeps about the house and listens at the doors.'

'But why should she do that?'

'Because she's a nosy busybody. And apart from that she is growing increasingly eccentric. Sometimes I think she's quite batty. The other servants have noticed it too. As far as I can make out, none of them likes her. I really think that she will have to go.'

'Geraldine thought much of her.' As soon as the words were out Julian realized what a mistake he had made. Blanche's stare became icy. But her next words were softly spoken.

'You've been very good to her, Julian. Keeping her on when there has been no need for some time now. But now I really think that the time has come to dismiss her.'

Julian was uneasy. He did not want to dismiss a long-serving member of the household, particularly one who had been instrumental in making Geraldine so happy. But he could see that Blanche was determined. And he knew he would give way as he did in most domestic matters.

'Perhaps you're right,' he said. 'But now let's go down and enjoy the birthday ball.'

Blanche smiled and took his arm. They walked down the grand staircase together. Just a little way along the landing Maud Fidler had heard every word. She was filled with rage and dismay. The hall below was filled with light but here, on the landing, darkness enclosed Maud. She gripped the banister rail to stop herself from falling. Her entire world was threatened and there was nothing she could do about it.

Behind one of the closed doors Rosina stood before the full-length looking-glass and inspected herself. Her new gown was made of pale blue bengaline covered with a layer of the finest white dotted net. An abundance of tiny dark blue velvet flowers trimmed the square-cut neckline and formed a deep hem on the flared skirt. The gown was the same style exactly as Amy's, except that Amy's was in pink. Blanche had chosen the gowns for them and the fussy style suited her own daughter perfectly. Rosina knew that she herself would have looked much better in something more understated.

She fingered the strand of pearls and diamonds at her neck. The pearls were shaped in the form of daisies with a sparkling diamond at the centre of each flower. Her father had given her her mother's jewellery when she had returned from the Bartletts' and this simple necklace at least gave her some comfort. If only her mother could have been here to see her wear it.

Rosina's thoughts about her mother were not the only cause of her despondency. She had not seen Adam since the day of their bicycle ride to the Roman fort two weeks ago, and she could not understand it. At first she had assumed that he was waiting to speak to Mr Loxley and then he would appear at Ravenshill ready to speak to her father. But his father must have been home for more than a week now and enough for that, and Adam had not called. He had not even written a letter.

Perhaps he was planning a happy surprise tonight. Perhaps he was going to claim every dance on her card and then, at some suitable moment, whisk her out on to the terrace and propose to her. But how could he do that when he had not been to talk to her father? Unless he had already been to see her father. He might have arrived secretly and, consent given, they were both in on the plan to surprise her. Rosina grasped at anything to appease her sense of hurt. But sheer pride made her smile as radiantly as she could when she made her way to the ballroom.

Neither Adam nor his parents were there. Rosina had to try very hard to keep some dances free on her card. She was prepared to give Adam a chance to explain himself and it reached the point where she had to hide behind a pillar to avoid an eager young gentleman farmer who was determined to claim more than his fair share of dances.

From where she was standing she could see without being seen, and she was puzzled to observe that Amy also was trying to avoid having her card filled. Perhaps she was just being perverse. Amy had been in a difficult mood ever since she returned from Beryl Earnshaw's.

The orchestra struck up and played the introduction to the first dance, a quadrille. Rosina heard a gentle cough behind her. She turned and tried to look pleased. Her gentleman farmer was ready to lead her on to the dance floor. It was while they were dancing that the Loxleys arrived.

Rosina, forgetting that she was cross with Adam, smiled brilliantly in his direction. He did not return the smile. He behaved as if he hadn't noticed and turned his head to talk to his mother. It was then Rosina knew that something was very wrong.

Adam felt his colour rise. He had seen Rosina's happy smile of welcome but he had not been able to return it. His parents should never have made him come here tonight but his mother had insisted. She would not have missed a ball at Ravenshill for the world, she said, and it would look very odd if his father and she had arrived without Adam. His father had added that he must be a man and face up to the situation. So here they were.

He had no idea what he was going to say to Rosina so he had decided to adopt the coward's way out and avoid her. He would wait until tomorrow – or maybe a few days' time – or maybe he should write to her. He had no idea what he would say. For in truth he didn't know if he could face her. In spite of what his mother had told him about her, he knew Rosina to be honest and true and he was ashamed of the way he was treating her.

His father whisked his daughter, Charlotte, on to the dance floor. Adam knew that he should have asked his mother to dance but he had decided the safest option was not to dance at all. He could pretend he had hurt his leg or some such excuse. He led his mother to one of the gilded chairs set down the side of the room and sat resolutely beside her. As the couples whirled by she got more and more cross with him. She began to prod him and whisper behind her fan that he was being boorish.

Adam stared down at his soft-soled dancing shoes. He could not bring himself to watch the dancers in case he met Rosina's eyes. He still loved her but he could not marry her. His parents had made it quite plain that Rosina would not be a suitable wife for him – not if he was going to join the family firm. And that was what he had wanted to do all his life.

When his father and his sister returned from the dance floor they brought someone with them. Adam stared at the froth of pink skirt covered in deep pink rosebuds around the hem and the pointed toes of the silver dancing shoes.

'Hello, Adam,' Amy said. 'I saved this dance for you.'

He rose quickly. 'Oh – er – I'd like to dance, really I would, but I think I've hurt my foot.'

'You only think so?' She laughed, and how could Adam not notice how beautiful she was?

'Well, yes, I have. My foot. Fell off my bicycle.'

'In that case I shall be very gentle with you but I really must insist that you dance with me. After all, this is my birthday ball.' She grasped his arm and led him on to the floor.

The orchestra were playing a waltz and they had already taken a turn or two around the floor when Amy asked, 'What are you looking at, Adam?' Her tone was flirtatious.

'I beg your pardon?'

'I ask because you are certainly not looking where you are going.'

'I'm sorry.'

'So you should be. For not only are you looking down but you are looking down at my . . .' she leaned forward and whispered, 'my *décolletage*.'

'Your what?'

'My neckline.'

'No! I mean, if I was, I didn't mean to.'

'Hush. It's all right. I'm teasing. But I beg you to concentrate on the dance steps from now on.'

Adam did as he was told and Amy kept up a constant flow of chatter. Most of it required just a nod or a smile, which was just as well for he could think of nothing amusing to say. Amy didn't seem to mind and he soon found that although not exactly enjoying himself in this awkward situation, he was at ease in her company. He couldn't help looking round anxiously now and then but whenever he caught sight of Rosina in her blue ball gown she was dancing in someone's arms. And then he lost track of her.

As the evening wore on he also danced with his mother and his sister, but more and more he found himself looking forward to the next dance with Amy. He was dancing with her when the guests were called to the dining room for refreshments. Instead of a sit-down supper there was a buffet, but the ladies sat on comfortable chairs while the men filled their plates and generally looked after them.

There was a very good selection of wines, including champagne, which Amy seemed to prefer. She kept sending Adam back for more. 'After all, it is my birthday,' she said, and very soon he began to feel less aggrieved with the world. But when he staggered and nearly spilt the contents of his glass on Amy's beautiful gown she rose quickly and stepped back.

'Don't be angry with me,' he pleaded.

Miraculously she was still smiling. 'I'm not angry but I think we should go somewhere where you can sit down for a while.'

'And where is that?' He had to concentrate on every word.

'The conservatory. We can be quiet there.'

Adam frowned. Amy's words seemed to be carrying some hidden meaning but he wasn't quite sure what it was.

'Right oh,' he said, and waited for her to make a move.

'You go first. It might be better if we weren't seen leaving the room together.'

'Why not?'

'Oh, Adam, just go.' Amy turned him round and pointed him in the direction of a door. 'Through that door, turn right in the passage and then right again through another door. I'll follow you in a moment.'

He did as he was told. At the door he glanced back and he thought he saw Amy talking to her mother; their heads close together. The only light in the conservatory came from the moon outside. It shone through the foliage, casting delicate shadows on the tiled floor. The atmosphere was warm and humid. Adam's head was spinning. He imagined he could hear his own breathing – or was it one of the plants over there by the door that led to the terrace? Don't be stupid, he thought, plants might very well breathe but you can't hear them. The thought made him smile but he also knew that this was not the place to come to clear his head.

He sat on one of the marble benches and waited patiently. When Amy came to him, he stood up and said, 'I think we should go out into the garden – get some air.'

'No, I think we should stay here.'

Amy put her hands up to his shoulders then pushed him back down on to the bench. He was expecting her to sit next to him and was taken completely by surprise when, instead, she sat on his knee. Immediately he was assailed by her perfume, heady and enticing. Amy took his hand and placed it on the smooth skin above the neckline of her dress. He could feel the rise of her breasts.

'Would you like to kiss me?' she whispered. And without waiting for his reply she placed her lips on his.

In the hushed warmth of the conservatory Adam felt his senses spinning. Amy's breath was sweet and the pressure of her body against his aroused him. In the moment before he responded to her kiss he thought he heard someone catch their breath, but it was only the leaves of a plant rustling in a draught from the door. Who had opened the door? Before he had time to wonder at it, desire had overwhelmed him. He did not hear the outer door close and the sound of swift footsteps running along the terrace.

Chapter Sixteen

Rosina couldn't sleep. Each time she closed her eyes she found herself reliving the scene in the conservatory. She could smell the warm muskiness of the vegetation; see the leafy plants in their brass pots and the pools of water on the tiled floor underneath the hanging baskets. The light from a bright moon cast mysterious shadows in the warm dimness.

Something – someone – moved the shadows. At first she had shrunk back, not wanting anyone to see her distress, but then she had realized the person who had just entered the conservatory was Adam. She remained where she was, hidden behind a tall plant. He did not see her.

Had he come looking for her? Had he come to apologize for ignoring her? To explain why he had not been near her for days? He sat down and she wondered whether she should approach him but before she made up her mind someone else entered the conservatory. Amy, moving through the pale light, looked like a fairytale princess in her pink ball gown. She was undeniably beautiful.

What happened next was shocking. Rosina tried to blank it out but every time she reached that point some perverse part of her will wanted to go on – to renew the torture – to experience the shock of seeing Amy sink on to Adam's knee; her blatant offering of herself and Adam's passionate response. The eager embraces that followed were nothing like the sweet kisses Adam and Rosina had exchanged on the fragrant summer hillside. Then she had sensed a restraint in him but now his increasing ardour met no resistance from Amy. Indeed, she seemed to be encouraging him.

Rosina clenched her hands as the seductive rustle of Amy's skirt and the soft sighs and gasps of pleasure whispered through the humid air. Icy cold in the sultry warmth of the conservatory, she opened the door and fled out on to the moonlit terrace, down the stone steps and across the grounds. She took shelter in the summerhouse in the wooded grove and, too shocked and miserable even to cry, she sat on the veranda and listened to the sounds of the night: the rustle of nocturnal animals moving through the woods, the hoot of an owl, the shriek of a vixen. Later she heard the carriages leaving Ravenshill when the ball was over. Laughter and sleepy voices calling goodbye.

Only when all sounds from the house had ceased did she move silently across the expanse of parkland towards the sleeping bulk of the house. The conservatory door was still open. No one had thought to check it. She hurried through, eyes straight ahead so she would not see the marble bench where Adam had betrayed her. She could hear the muted sounds of sleepy servants clearing up but saw no one as she ran upstairs and along the landing to her room.

Her satin dancing shoes and the hem of her ball gown were wet with dew. The stains would not come out. Rosina didn't care. She threw off her clothes and left them in a jumbled heap on the floor before flinging herself on the bed. Her head was aching with the effort of trying to understand why Adam had behaved like that. She had lain miserably awake until dawn.

Finally, when all hope of sleep had gone, she decided to

go out. She dressed hurriedly, not bothering to brush her hair but simply tying it back with an old ribbon. Normally only the most humble of the household staff would have been stirring at this time of the morning: the skivvies in the kitchen and the young maids whose job it was to make up the fires while the family were still sleeping. But today soft country voices drifted up from the dining room and the ball-room as the extra women brought in from the village started clearing up and cleaning after the celebrations that had taken place the night before.

Rosina walked swiftly and quietly towards the stairs. She paused when she reached her stepsister's room. The door was ajar and she could hear Amy and her mother talking. This surprised her. Neither Blanche nor Amy was an early riser. She was about to hurry on when she heard her own name mentioned. She shrank back against the wall and listened.

'Don't worry about Rosina,' she heard her stepmother say in answer to Amy's question. 'You have nothing to fear as far as she is concerned, but it is up to you to make sure he proposes.'

Amy laughed softly. 'Oh, he'll propose all right.' She paused. 'If I want him to. And at the moment I'm not sure if I do. There may be no need.'

'You'll know soon enough—' Blanche started to say, but she never finished the sentence because Rosina erupted into the room like a fury.

'Why?' Rosina said. 'Why are you doing this?'

Amy was sitting up in bed with a white silk shawl around her shoulders, her hair, last night's shining curls, now tangled like a witch's locks. Her eyes were puffy and her complexion pallid. She stared up at Rosina sullenly.

'Doing what?' she said.

'Why do you want to take Adam away from me?'

'Take him away? I don't know what you're talking about.'

'Don't pretend innocence. I saw you in the conservatory last night. You – you threw yourself at him!'

An ugly flush began to suffuse Amy's face. 'First of all, Adam doesn't belong to you. And secondly, to spy on people is despicable. So if you didn't like what you saw it serves you right.' She sounded like a petulant child.

'Amy, be quiet,' her mother said. 'Rosina, go to your room.'

'No, I won't, not until Amy tells me why she is talking of marrying Adam. He has always been my friend, not Amy's. And only two weeks ago he told me he wanted to marry me!'

'I don't think so,' Blanche said.

'He did!'

'He actually proposed to you? He asked you to marry him?'

Rosina faltered. 'Well, no, not in so many words but he told me how he felt about me. He said he would speak to his father.'

Blanche laughed. 'Young men can be fickle.'

'No! Not Adam!'

'Yes, Adam. And in any case, his parents would never have allowed him to marry a girl like you.'

'A girl like me? What do you mean? What's wrong with me?'

'You are simply not good enough for him. Considering what your background is, the Loxleys would never welcome you into their family.'

Rosina was completely mystified. 'My background? I'm a Leighton. The Leightons are an old and respected family.'

'So they are. But *you're* not one of them.'

Rosina heard Amy give a small gasp of astonishment.

'Not a Leighton?' Rosina said. 'You're talking nonsense.'

Blanche's gaze was cold and steely. 'No, Rosina, I'm not. You are not a Leighton. You are a nobody. Maud Fidler found you in the slums and brought you home because the woman you think of as your mother had miscarried so many times that she was fretting. Mr Leighton was not altogether pleased but he allowed it because he wanted to make his wife happy.'

Rosina felt as though she had been sucked up into a vortex. A whirling mass of air separated her from the world around her. Pinpoints of light danced before her eyes. 'I don't believe you,' she whispered. 'You're making this up.'

'Why would I do that?'

'Because you've never liked me. You've made that plain from the moment you walked into this house.'

'Even if that is true, it doesn't alter the fact that you don't belong here. And as soon as Adam knew the truth he obviously decided that he could never marry you.'

The world stopped spinning abruptly as Rosina realized the implications of what her stepmother had just said. 'You told them,' she accused. 'You told the Loxleys this pack of lies because you didn't want me to be happy.'

'It isn't lies, it's the truth, and of course I told them. I'm not going to apologize for that. I couldn't let my friends bring shame upon their family.'

'Shame?'

'Yes. Who knows where you really came from? What kind of mother you had. There is such a thing as bad blood, Rosina, and I thought it my duty to warn Mrs Loxley before Adam committed himself.'

Rosina felt sick. She could feel the gorge rising and the taste of bile at the back of her throat. She turned and fled from the room. She had suddenly realized that her stepmother could not have made such a story up, for both her father – or the man she had thought of as her father – and Maud Fidler could verify it if it were true.

Moments later, in the bathroom, she vomited until there was nothing left but a sour-tasting liquid that burned the back of her throat. She stood and clung to the wash basin until the shaking stopped. She washed her mouth out and made her way unsteadily to her room. She was icy cold. Since she had left just a few minutes before one of the maids had been in to make up the fire. Rosina sat by the hearth, pulled the collar of her coat up and then crossed her arms to push her hands into the opposite sleeves. She sat there shivering as she tried to absorb what her stepmother had just told her.

She puzzled over the fact that she was not as shocked as she should have been. Then she realized that in her heart she knew it must be true. If she was adopted it would explain the dreams that disturbed her sleep and yet vanished with the morning light, leaving only traces of themselves to worry and tantalize.

As long as she could remember there had been moments when she thought she didn't belong here. She had explained it to herself by reasoning that it was because the mother she loved had died and her father was a more distant figure. He had always been kind to her and yet she had never felt as though there was any deep love involved. Since he had married again she had sometimes thought that he even seemed to prefer his stepdaughter's company to her own.

Rosina glanced around the comfortable room and thought about her life here at Ravenshill. A counterfeit life based on a lie. She thought of Geraldine, a woman Rosina still loved and thought of almost daily. And yet she was not her mother. Did that matter? It seemed that Geraldine Leighton, longing for a child, had rescued Rosina from the slums, had loved her and provided for her as if she were her own daughter. How she would have wept to know of the way Rosina had been treated since she died.

For now Rosina acknowledged that Blanche Leighton was not just cold and selfish but was also capable of great cruelty. In a thousand subtle ways she had made it plain that she did not wish to accept Rosina's place in the household. And she could not have done this if Rosina had been Julian Leighton's real daughter. She must have known from the start that Rosina was adopted.

But why had her stepmother acted to stop Adam from marrying her? Despite Blanche's cruel words about her background and her assertion that it was her duty to inform the Loxleys, Rosina sensed that there was something more behind her spiteful behaviour. The only explanation that Rosina could think of was because she had known that Amy, her own daughter, was in love with Adam.

No, that couldn't be true! Why had Amy, who had never shown any interest in Adam in the past, suddenly decided to steal him away from Rosina? Amy was frivolous and shallow. She despised living in the country; she preferred city life. Whereas Adam was serious, not to say stolid, and would hate to live anywhere except in these northern hills. She could not think of any two people who were more unsuited to each other. And yet in the conservatory last night . . .

'No!'

She tried to banish from her mind the scene that had sent her hurrying across the parkland to seek refuge in the summerhouse.

But what was she to make of Adam's behaviour? If he truly loved her he would have come and told her what had happened instead of leaving her alone and anxious. He would have married her whatever the consequences and surely he would not have allowed himself to be seduced by Amy.

Rosina was not aware that she had been crying until she felt the tears trickling down her cheeks. All this had happened because Geraldine Leighton had longed for a baby of her own. Rosina could not condemn her. The woman she had thought of as her mother had surrounded her with love and made her childhood magical. But Geraldine was long dead and Ravenshill had become a sad and lonely place without her. Rosina rose to her feet. She knew what she must do.

As soon as Rosina left the room Amy asked her mother, 'Is it true? Is Rosina really adopted?'

'Yes.'

'You never told me.'

'No.' Blanche was distracted. She knew she must explain her actions to Julian. 'And you are never to talk about this matter,' she told her daughter. 'At least until I give you permission.'

Then, scarcely glancing at her daughter, Blanche hurried from the room. She would have to have her story ready and make sure she caught Julian before Rosina confronted him, as Blanche was sure she would. He had already left for his early morning ride. She would have to face him as soon as he came back.

She reflected bitterly that there was something else Amy didn't know. Something much more significant. Something she must never know, at least until she was mature enough to realize that she could never reveal to the world in general that she was Julian Leighton's daughter, not his stepdaughter. For Blanche was sure that the Loxleys – or any other respectable family – would be even more unwilling for their son to marry someone who was illegitimate.

Adam felt wretched. It did not stop him enjoying his breakfast but nevertheless he knew he had behaved badly and didn't much like what he had learned about himself. He had let Rosina down in the most ungallant manner. He supposed that anyone worth his salt, like a hero in one of the romantic novels beloved of his mother, would have stood firm and told his father that he loved Rosina and would marry her, whatever the consequences. He had been put to the test and he had failed. The biggest shock was the realization that perhaps he did not love Rosina enough to make a fight of it.

What was I supposed to do, he thought, disobey my father for the love of a girl I could not possibly hope to support without his help?

He tried to convince himself that Rosina would never have married him if his father had cut him off without a penny, as he had threatened to do if Adam did not come to his senses. What would they live on? He'd have had to find some clerking job in an office in Newcastle and, after the way Rosina had been brought up at Ravenshill, she would surely never consent to eking out his meagre wages in some tiny rented house in an unfashionable part of town. Adam knew that he could not live that way but he suspected that Rosina, honest and true as she was, would have accepted that fate gladly. So there was no comfort there.

He went to the sideboard and took a second helping of macaroni savoury, poured himself a large cup of coffee and returned to the table. For a moment or two he concentrated on the delightful hint of anchovy in the sauce but, try as he might, the troublesome thoughts would not go away.

Rosina had been his friend since they were small children. Their easy companionship had led him to believe that he loved her. When they had kissed on the hillside his senses had been roused. But now he reflected that his arousal had been nothing like that which had occurred in the conservatory at Ravenshill last night. He was still unsure why that had happened. He did not love Amy, he did not even like her very much, and yet he found her utterly desirable. He felt his loins quicken at the memory of what had taken place.

Adam stared down at his empty plate and then he got up and returned to the array of hotplates on the sideboard. The savoury fritters looked good. His father had already left the house and his mother was having breakfast in bed this morning. He might as well take all that was left . . .

Rosina paused outside the study and listened to Blanche Leighton talking to her husband. Blanche sounded anguished but Rosina, who had discovered a talent for acting in herself, detected the hints of a performance. Rosina could not hear the words but her father – or rather Julian Leighton – first of all sounded exasperated, then concerned and then consoling.

At this point Blanche began to sob; the door opened a little; there was a glimpse of maroon satin velvet and a waft of Blanche's heady gardenia perfume. Rosina heard her say, 'I hope you will forgive me, Julian, but I could not stand by and see Amy's heart broken.'

'Of course not, my dear. I quite understand. I suppose I should have told Rosina years ago but you know . . . Geraldine . . .'

'Yes, Julian. I know. You have been very loyal to her memory, my dear.' Blanche's voice had taken on a gently weary tone – weary but tender.

The door opened fully and Blanche swept out, holding a handkerchief to her eyes. She stopped when she saw Rosina and lowered the handkerchief. Rosina thought she had never in her life seen such a duplicitous expression. False tears sparkled in her cold blue eyes but her lips were twisted into a satisfied smirk as she looked at Rosina.

'Going out?' she asked.

'That's obvious. I don't usually wear my coat if I'm going to sit indoors.'

'You are insolent, Rosina, you always have been. But I suppose I shouldn't be surprised that you want to see Mr Leighton. I don't know what you are hoping for but you'd better go in. He is ready for you.'

Julian Leighton was sitting at his desk, looking troubled. He glanced up when Rosina entered. He frowned.

'Ah,' he said, 'Rosina. I'm very sorry to hear what has happened.'

Rosina was taken aback. Was he going to say that he was sorry that Blanche had been so cruel? But her hopes sank as he continued to stare at her. His gaze was wintry.

'You'd better sit down,' he said.

'I don't want to.' Hearing the tremor in her voice she knew she was behaving like a child but she was entirely in the grip of her emotions.

'Nevertheless you should.'

He pointed to a chair placed before the desk. Rosina sat down as she was told. He seemed to be waiting for her to speak.

'So it's true,' she said. 'I'm adopted?'

'Yes, you are but my wife — Geraldine — did not want you to know that. It comforted her to imagine that you were really her daughter. In fact, I think she came to believe it. The lines between her fantasy and reality became blurred.'

'I understand,' Rosina said softly. 'But I wish she had told me. I . . . I have a right to know.'

'I agree with you and, had she lived I might have persuaded her. Especially after George was born. Once she truly had a child of her own you might not have been so important to her.'

'No!' Rosina protested. 'She would have gone on loving me, I'm sure of it.'

Julian Leighton stared at her bleakly for a moment and then he shrugged. 'Maybe.' He paused. 'But she didn't live and neither did my son.'

Rosina felt the tears prick as she remembered her baby brother. His short lonely life in the nursery. Many a time she had wanted to hold him, to tell him stories, to sing to him. But she had not been allowed to. And Blanche Leighton had pretended to be so loving, so caring. Always visiting the nursery just as her husband came home but giving the impression to the Loxleys and other friends that she nursed the little boy constantly. But Rosina could never tell Julian Leighton this. His grief was too deep.

'I miss him too,' she said softly.

Julian Leighton looked uneasy. He had never been unkind to her but also he had never tried to become close. He had never engaged her in conversation nor sought her company as he did Amy's. That had puzzled her over the years but she had supposed it was because Amy was the daughter of the woman he loved whereas she, Rosina, might have reminded him of his first wife and his sorrow at losing her. But now she knew the reason. She was nobody's daughter. At least no one that she knew of.

He sighed. 'I should have told you you were adopted,' he said. 'I have been dilatory, but in fact for some time now I have been wondering how to approach the matter without — without upsetting you too much.'

'So you left it to her.'

'I beg your pardon?' He looked startled.

'Your wife. You left it to her to tell me.'

'First of all I had every intention of telling you myself, as was my duty, and secondly I forbid you to talk of your stepmother in such a rude and aggressive manner.'

Rosina felt her cheeks flaming. 'First of all, if you are not my father then she is not my stepmother,' she responded with spirit, 'and secondly, her behaviour is more than appalling.'

Julian Leighton rose from the table so abruptly that his chair fell over. He put both hands on his desk and leaned forward to stare angrily at her. 'No, Rosina. It was your behaviour that was appalling. You led Adam Loxley on in a most improper way. You encouraged him to . . . to be familiar with you.'

'Led him on? Familiar? What are you talking about?'

'My wife saw you. She was looking out of the window when you came home one day. She saw you kiss him in full view of the house, not caring who was watching.'

'But that's not true!'

'Isn't it?'

'Well . . . yes . . . he did kiss me, but I didn't invite it. He had just proposed to me,' she finished lamely.

'Had he? Had he really proposed to you?'

'Well, no, but he said he would speak to his father.'

'I have only your word for that, Rosina. When my wife went to visit Mrs Loxley—'

'To poison her mind!'

'Be quiet. When my wife did her duty and went to tell Mrs Loxley of your unknown parentage, the good woman assured her that if anything improper had happened between you and Adam then you must have led him on.'

'I don't believe you!'

'Are you accusing me of lying?'

'Yes – no – not you. *She* is lying, don't you see?'

'And why would my wife do that?'

'Because she knew Adam wanted to marry me and she had to stop that – because for some reason I don't understand Amy has suddenly decided that she wants Adam. And whatever Amy wants she always gets, doesn't she?'

'Enough!'

Rosina had never seen Julian Leighton so angry. For a moment she even thought that if the desk had not been between them he would have struck her. But after a moment of tense silence he sank back into his chair.

'I cannot have you behaving like this. It seems you do not appreciate all that has been done for you. Taking you from the slums and giving you a good and loving home—'

'You never loved me!'

'Perhaps not. But my wife did, and see how you have rewarded her love.'

'But I didn't know! How could I know I was supposed to be grateful when I didn't know I had been adopted? I thought . . . I thought I was your daughter.'

In spite of his anger Julian Leighton allowed himself a thin smile. '"How sharper than the serpent's tooth it is To have an thankless child",' he said, and he shook his head. 'And I cannot see how I can allow you to go on living here. I have agreed with my wife that it would be better for you to leave this house.'

'I have already decided to go.'

Irritation fleetingly marred his still handsome features. 'Don't interrupt me. Naturally I feel that I still have a duty of care for you so I will arrange respectable lodgings for you in Newcastle.'

'Thank you but there is no need. I wish to leave immediately and I'm sure my friend Joanne Bartlett will take me temporarily.'

'Very well.' His relief was palpable and his mood lightened immediately. He opened a drawer in the desk and took out some papers. 'I had better explain about your financial situation,' he said.

'I don't want anything from you.'

He looked exasperated. 'And how would you support yourself?'

'I'll find employment.'

'Don't be ridiculous. What are you fit for?' Without giving her time to form an answer he continued, 'I am not giving you anything, Rosina. Your mother ... Geraldine ... has left you well provided for. And before you protest let me remind you how fond she was of you. You would be insulting her memory if you refused to take it. Here.' He put the papers in a large envelope and passed it across the desk.

Rosina looked at the name and address clipped to the envelope. 'Mr Sinclair?'

'Your solicitor. Geraldine arranged it. His office is in Newcastle, in Dean Street. He will arrange for you to have a small allowance from the trust until you are twenty-one, when you may do as you please with it.'

They stared at each other awkwardly. 'I'm sorry it has ended like this,' he said.

'But you are pleased that I am leaving.'

'In the circumstances it's for the best.'

'You never wanted me here, did you?'

'That's not entirely true. Geraldine was a good woman. I wanted to make her happy.'

'And did you ... did you know my mother? The woman who gave birth to me?'

'Of course not. Maud Fidler found you. Or at least ...' he paused and frowned.

'At least?' Rosina prompted.

'A man she knew, a Mr Givens, I think. He worked in the slums – rescued children. He found you and handed you to Miss Fidler.'

'Like a parcel.'

'Don't be flippant. He probably saved your life. Just

319

imagine what would have happened to you if he had not found you.'

'And this Mr Givens – does he still work with children?'

'I can see where this is leading but I advise you to forget any idea of tracing your parents. There would be no point, as we were told your mother was dead – or dying. And after the kind of upbringing you have had you would not be able to cope with the horror of the slums. And in any case, if I remember correctly, Cedric Givens is now working in a children's home he founded in Australia. My wife and I contributed generously to the cause.'

'You bought me.'

'How dare you speak like that?' He stared at her with distaste. 'That is both rude and offensive. Please leave at once. I no longer wish to set eyes on you.'

The man she had thought of as her father for most of her life did not say goodbye. He did not rise from his seat to come and embrace her or simply to walk her to the door. He did not ask her to write to him or to keep in touch in any way. This would not have happened if it had not been for Amy, she thought, but now that I'm leaving I can sense his relief.

Then, when she had reached the door, he called out, 'Wait.'

'What is it?' she asked.

'If you need to know anything – if you need any sort of help you must go to Mr Sinclair. You are not to come back to Ravenshill. Take what you need today and then send for the rest.'

Rosina left the room. The first thing she saw was Maud Fidler hurrying away across the hall. She almost called her back but the woman had gone. Rosina knew she must seek her out before she left the house. She must talk to her. But

320

Rosina did not have to go looking for her. Maud Fidler was waiting for her outside her room. She looked distracted and her usually tidy hair was escaping confinement. Even as Rosina approached, one hairpin detached itself and fell on to the floor. Rosina thought of the times she'd had to chide Molly gently for giggling about Miss Fidler and hinting that the old thing was going mad. She certainly looked eccentric, Rosina thought. She was clutching a brown paper parcel.

'So now you know,' she said.

Rosina remembered the other things Molly had told her about Miss Fidler. 'You were listening at the door.'

Impatience crossed the older woman's face as if that were immaterial. 'You mustn't blame me.'

'For eavesdropping?'

'No, for bringing you here.'

'I don't. I'm sure you thought you were helping my— Mrs Leighton.'

'Yes, yes, of course, but I also wanted to please Jack.'

'Who is Jack?'

Miss Fidler looked shocked. 'Did I mention Jack?'

Even though Rosina had her own problems she began to feel concerned for the servant. 'Yes, you did,' she said gently. 'But that doesn't matter. Why do you want to see me?'

'I thought it was for the best. That you would be happy here.'

'And I was. At least until my . . . until she died.'

'Your mother loved you.'

'I know that.'

'No, no, you don't.'

Miss Fidler looked as if she were about to burst into tears but before Rosina could make any move to comfort her she thrust the brown paper parcel into her hands.

'What is this? A present?'

But Miss Fidler turned and fled.

'Wait,' Rosina called. 'I must talk to you.'

Maud Fidler glanced back over her shoulder. Rosina got the impression that she was frightened. 'Why?'

'I want to ask you where I came from – who my mother is.'

'I can't tell you that.'

'Why not?'

'Because I don't know. Jack – I mean, Cedric Givens, found you – in the slums – that's what he said. I knew him from childhood. He was a – a friend – I did him a favour. I don't know anything. I can't help you.'

'And Mr Givens? Where is he now?'

'No idea,' she said quickly. 'Lost touch. He went to Australia like Mr Leighton told you. I heard him.'

Rosina felt like screaming at her in frustration but it was plain to see that the poor old thing couldn't help her. And besides, it had been a good deed to bring her here. Why should Rosina torment her?

'Very well,' she said. 'But in any case I suppose I must thank you.'

Miss Fidler gave a sound halfway between a shriek and a sob, then she hurried away and vanished through one of the doors that led to the servants' quarters.

Dispirited, Rosina entered her room, threw the parcel on her bed and rang for Molly.

'I want you to help me pack some clothes,' she said. 'Just as much as I can carry with me in one suitcase. I will write to you and tell you where to send the rest.'

Molly looked bewildered. 'Are you going on holiday?'

'No.'

'Are you going to stay with your friend in Heaton for a while?'

'Yes, I'm going there, but not for just a while. I'm leaving, Molly. I'm leaving Ravenshill.'

The young maid stared at her, her fresh country face registering disbelief. 'Why are you leaving?' Molly mistook Rosina's suddenly grim expression. 'Sorry, I'm speaking out of turn.'

'No, that's all right, but I can't tell you — at least, I don't want to talk about it. Not now. Not yet. Maybe one day. And I will write to you — not just about my clothes. We'll keep in touch.'

Molly started to cry.

'Please don't,' Rosina said, 'or you'll set me off.'

But Molly sniffed and sobbed all the time she helped with the packing and eventually Rosina sent her off to make a pot of tea. 'Bring it back here with two cups,' she said. 'We'll sit together for a while before I go.'

When Molly returned there were three cups and saucers on the tray, the other one for Bridget, who followed her in.

'Mr Leighton has told Angus to bring the coach round,' Bridget said. 'We'll have this cup of tea together and then I'm coming to the station with you. Don't worry, Miss Fidler has given her permission.'

'Miss Fidler? That surprises me.'

'Why?'

'Well, she behaved very strangely just now.'

'Strange isn't the word for it,' Bridget said. 'After telling me I could come with you she dashed out of the house and said she was going for a walk and wouldn't be back until after you'd gone. Her coat was buttoned wrong and her hat was on sideways. She's as daft as a brush.'

The conversation was subdued as they drank their tea. 'I don't know why you're leaving,' Bridget said, 'but I'll warrant it has something to do with Miss Amy.' The sentence was formed like a question.

Rosina shook her head.

'All right, Molly said you wouldn't talk about it. But you've promised to write.'

'I have.'

'Well, if we've finished our tea Molly can take the tray back to the kitchen now. I'll help you if there's any more to pack.'

Molly did not trust herself to say goodbye. She looked at Rosina, her eyes brimming with tears, and then she picked up the tray and fled.

'This is a sad day,' Bridget said when the younger maid had gone. 'It would break your mother's heart. I remember when you arrived, a bewildered little bairn in raggy clothes. You brought nothing with you except that old broken doll.'

Rosina looked at her sharply. 'The doll came here with me?'

'Yes, pet. I reckoned your ma — your real ma — must have given it to you.'

'And you knew? You knew I was adopted?'

'Yes.'

'And you never said anything?'

'I promised Mrs Leighton that I would keep her secret. Everyone who worked here at the time did the same. Servants are not supposed to tell tales or carry gossip outside the house. They'd never find employment if their tongues were loose. And besides, they loved and respected her. They would never have done anything to upset her. And now that you're going, I've decided to leave Ravenshill myself. The second Mrs Leighton has made many changes; none of them for the better, in my view. And as for Maud Fidler, I think she's going batty. This is not a happy place to work.'

'Where will you go?'

'I don't know yet but it won't be difficult to find a

position, not with my experience. I may even go to America. Some of the richer families there like to boast that they have an English nanny or ladies' maid. And who knows? It's supposed to be a land of opportunity. Maybe I'll find a rich husband.' Bridget was trying to lighten the atmosphere but her laughter sounded suspiciously like a sob. 'I'll take your suitcase down to the coach now. Perhaps you'd like to have a last look around your bedroom on your own.'

When Bridget had gone Rosina opened the top drawer of her dressing table and took out the silk-lined leather jewellery rolls that contained Geraldine Leighton's jewellery. The woman she had loved as a mother had willed the jewellery to her and she felt no compunction about taking it from Ravenshill. She knew with certainty that Geraldine would have wanted her to do that.

Rosina put the jewellery in her travelling bag and looked around the room. She saw that the brown paper parcel Miss Fidler had given her was still on the bed. With the carriage waiting there was not time to open it so she put it into her travelling bag along with one or two of her favourite books. Then last of all she took her old doll from the chair beside her bed.

'Come along, Dolly,' she said. 'Apparently we arrived at this house together so now we'll leave together.' She placed the doll in the bag, buckled up the straps and left without looking back.

Dear Jack,

Rosina has gone. Mrs Leighton told her she was adopted and then persuaded Mr Leighton to send her away. I am worried that she knows too much. I know she cannot trace 'Mr Givens' but she was told that it was I who brought her here. She tried to question me but I told her nothing. You must believe me. I think I have convinced her it would be no use trying to find out where she came from.

And now I have been dismissed. I told one of the maids to accompany Rosina to the station and Mrs Leighton used this as an excuse for ending my employment here. She said I had no right to give such an order and that I had been getting above myself.

Don't be angry with me, Jack. There was nothing I could do to prevent this. And now Rosina is going to her friend's house in Heaton. It's just along the road from you know where. And she has that doll. That blessed doll.

I have been told to leave first thing in the morning. Where am I to go? By the time this letter reaches you in Vienna I shall be homeless. Why would you never let me have a key to your little mews house in Jesmond? You are hardly there and I could look after it for you.

Mrs Leighton says that in all honesty she cannot give me a reference. She is casting me out. I have some savings, thanks to you, but I do not know how long they will last. I hope you will still be sending the little cheques along, considering what I have done for you.

I have no friends here. I have no friends anywhere. I shall find lodgings in Newcastle but you must help me, Jack.

Your loving sister,
Maud

Chapter Seventeen

Rosina told the cab driver not to unload her bags. 'Please wait,' she said. She didn't want to turn up on Joanne's doorstep with her bags and baggage without first explaining why she was there.

Percy Willis, the cabman, looked at her doubtfully. Expensive clothes, educated accent and pleasant with it. But there had been an air of nervousness about her ever since she had hailed him at the Central Station. She had been carrying her suitcase and travelling bag herself. No sign of a maid or a companion of any sort. Was she a runaway?

The house he had brought her to on Heaton Road was the home of a respected Newcastle businessman. Now and then Percy had carried Mrs Bartlett or her daughter, or both of them, to the shops in the city centre and sometimes brought them back again laden with shopping. Percy supposed that the young woman must be a friend of Miss Bartlett's. But in that case why was she calling now? Percy could have told her what she would learn when the door was opened.

'Miss Leighton,' Mildred said. The Bartletts' parlour maid looked surprised. 'What are you doing here?'

Rosina was taken aback. 'I've come to see Joanne.'

'But she's not here. The family has gone to France –

Normandy, or some such place. Mr Bartlett has taken it into his head to keep a boat there and become a sailor.'

'Oh, of course, I remember.'

Rosina felt foolish. Joanne had told her that her father was buying a holiday home in Honfleur, but she hadn't realised they would be going so soon. No doubt Joanne would be sending her a postcard or two but she wouldn't be at Ravenshill to receive them.

'Would you like to step inside for a cup of tea?' Mildred asked.

'That's kind of you, but no thank you. I'm going into town to do some shopping – that's why I called – to ask Joanne to help me choose a new frock or two.' Rosina knew that she was blushing. She was too embarrassed to tell Mildred that she had been hoping to stay with the Bartletts for a while. She was glad that she had left her luggage in the cab, 'So – erm – I'd better be off.'

She turned and hurried down the path. The cab driver had been standing by, ready to unload the suitcase and the travelling bag. He looked at her questioningly and she shook her head. Aware that Mildred was watching she climbed back into the cab. The parlour maid shut the door. The cabman remained where he was on the pavement.

'Well, then, bonny lass, where to now?'

The man's attitude was inappropriate, Rosina thought, but his tone was kind and she was sure he meant no harm. To her dismay she felt tears welling in her eyes.

'I don't know,' she said truthfully.

'Running away from home, are you?'

'I've left home. There's a difference.'

'Hoity-toity,' he said, and grinned. 'There's no need to take that tone of voice with me. I only want to help you.'

'How can you help me?'

'By taking you back to the station and advising you to go home. You're too young to be out on your own.'

'I'm eighteen years old,' Rosina said. 'Many women of my age have been working since they were twelve.'

'Maybe so, but not you.'

Rosina looked down at his weather-beaten face. He looked genuinely concerned. 'I can't go home,' she said. 'I have no home.'

He stared at her for a moment and then looked as though he'd come to a decision. 'I'm not going to ask what drove you to this,' he said. 'That's your business. But you look like a respectable young lass and I can't leave you in this predicament. I could have told you that your friends were away. I was asked to bring the four-wheeler the other day and they all set off to catch the London train.' He began to climb back up to his seat.

'I'm not going home,' Rosina said sharply.

'Divven't fret. I'm taking you to me sister's.'

'But why? Where . . . ?'

Rosina's words were muffled by the clatter of a passing horse tram, and by the time the noise had receded into the distance they were on their way.

About ten minutes later the cab drew up outside a café on Shields Road.

'Here we are,' Rosina's new friend said. 'Come along, I'll help you down and bring your bags in.'

'Into the café?'

'Yes, I know it doesn't look like Tilley's or Alvini's, or even that fancy German coffee shop further down Shields Road. But it's clean and decent, and me sister owns the whole building. She'll find you a nice room upstairs – and the rent'll be reasonable. You can stay here until you sort yourself out.'

Then he looked at her doubtfully as if something had just occurred to him. 'You do hev some money, don't you?'

'Yes, I — I've been provided for.'

Percy Willis led the way and slid Rosina's suitcase and travelling bag under one of the vacant tables at the window. 'Sit here, pet,' he said. 'I'll just hev a word with me sister.'

Bemused, Rosina sat down and tried to take in her surroundings. The café was spotless, as the cabman had told her, but instead of fresh linen tablecloths the tables were covered with red gingham-patterned oilcloth. A cruet and a water jug were in the middle of each table with a menu propped up between the salt and the pepper. About half the tables were taken — some by clerks and shop girls, and some by rougher-looking workmen. But the latter were well behaved and obviously enjoying whatever they were eating. Enticing smells wafted out from the kitchen.

The large window looked out on to the busy road with trams and carts passing constantly. While Rosina waited, two smartly dressed young women entered the café and took seats at the next table. Rosina looked at them. Their clothes were fashionable but the cloth had a cheap unsubstantial look about it. However, they had obviously taken a great deal of care with their appearance. They were definitely not office workers or shop girls, Rosina thought, an impression that was confirmed when she heard them speak in exaggeratedly cultured tones.

'You go and order a pot of tea, Amelia,' one of them said. 'I think we can just about afford it.'

'Right oh, Dorabel.'

Both girls looked despondent. While they waited for their tea they sat and gazed at nothing in particular but when the waitress brought their tray each managed a smile.

'How did it go?' the waitress asked them.

'He said he'd let us know but we've heard that one before. We're not hoping for anything,' Dorabel said.

'I'm sorry.'

'In any case, they only wanted one girl, as it turned out, so it's just as well. Amelia and I don't like to be parted. We've got our nice little double act.'

'And something must turn up soon,' Amelia added. 'Talent like ours can't go unrecognized for ever.' She put on a brave smile.

Rosina was intrigued by the conversation and would have liked to learn more, but at that moment the cabman came over to the table with an older woman dressed in black bombazine.

'Meet my sister, Mrs Dickinson,' he said. 'She's a respectable widow woman and usually she wants references for young women lodgers but she's willing to bow to my judgement.'

Mrs Dickinson eyed Rosina sharply and said briskly, 'Another one of your waifs and strays, eh, Percy? All right, I'll take her on.' Then she said to Rosina, 'I'm busy right now but I'll send you over some sandwiches and tea. You can settle up later when we discuss terms.' She hurried away.

Her brother laughed. 'Don't be put off by her manner. Our Jane has a heart of gold. Now I must go. I've got a living to earn.'

'Thank you for being so kind,' Rosina said as she took out her purse and paid him, adding a large tip.

The cabman thanked her, and left.

The sandwiches – boiled ham and pease pudding – arrived soon after, along with a pot of strong tea. Rosina hadn't thought she would be able to eat anything but she found she was hungry. While she started on the sandwiches she wondered what she was going to do. She had learned she had money of her own so there would be no worry about paying for her board and lodging here while she made her mind up. She would have to go to the solicitor's office in Dean Street in the morning.

'Now then, young ladies.' A stern voice broke through her thoughts. 'You can't sit at one of my best tables all day with one pot of tea.'

Mrs Dickinson was standing over the two young women at the next table. They smiled up at the café owner graciously and slowly and deliberately lifted their cups daintily and drained the last dregs from them. Then they got up unhurriedly, adjusted the neat little eye veils on their hats and picked up their handbags. Dorabel opened hers and put a small coin under her saucer. Before closing it she took out a piece of paper, looked at it sadly, then scrunched it up and dropped it on the table. While this was going on Mrs Dickinson raised an imperious arm and summoned the waitress to clear away.

Once they were on their feet, Dorabel and Amelia seemed to notice Rosina for the first time. 'I hope you fare better than my sister and I,' Dorabel said.

Amelia smiled at her. 'It's Mrs Greyling you must impress, dearie,' she said. 'No matter how good you might be, old Henry wouldn't dare take on anyone his wife disapproved of.'

Then with a cheery wave they went out on to the street, leaving Rosina completely mystified.

Mrs Dickinson had taken up her position behind the till and the waitress started to wipe the table with a damp cloth. The cloth was hot and steaming and the girl's hands were red and sore-looking. When she'd finished she dumped the cloth on the tray along with the crockery and the paper that Dorabel had thrown on the table.

'Did you want something?' she asked when she saw Rosina looking at her.

'No . . . I mean yes.'

The waitress put the tray down on the table and, taking a notebook from the pocket in her pinafore and a pencil from behind her ear, she approached Rosina's table.

'What'll it be? Another round of sandwiches or one of Mrs Dickinson's famous rock buns?'

She nodded her head sideways towards the glass display case that formed part of the counter. There were two plates of rock buns piled high like currant-strewn Rocky Mountains.

'No thank you, I don't want to order anything,' Rosina said. 'I just want to ask you something.'

The waitress put her notebook back in her pocket and tucked the pencil into the hair above her right ear. 'Sorry, pet,' she said. 'I'm not allowed to chat to customers unless they're ordering something. The old termagant would tick me off for wasting time.'

Rosina began to wonder if Mrs Dickinson's heart was as golden as her brother believed it to be. 'All right,' she said, and picked up the menu. The waitress took out her notebook again.

'I wouldn't bother with any of them cakes,' she said quietly. 'The fruit loaf is dry as bones and there's barely any apple in the apple tart. But the rock buns really are good. Must be something to do with her stony heart.'

'Right, I'll have a rock bun – and you can bring me a fresh pot of tea.'

While the waitress was writing down the order Rosina asked her, 'Do you know what those two young women were talking about when they hoped I'd do better than they had?'

'They must have thought you were going to the audition. That's where they'd been.'

'What audition?'

'For the Greyling Players. They're on at the Raby. Look,' she nodded towards the window. 'It's over there and down a bit. We've had a string of hopeful young actresses in here over the last few days. Sitting with one cup of tea and getting their poor little hopes up. Dreaming of fame and fortune and a life like Daisy Belle's.'

'But why would Dorabel and Amelia think I was an actress?'

'Mebbes because you're young and you're bonny and there's a certain look about you. Why else would a girl like you be sitting in a café on Shields Road?'

'Annie, what's taking you so long?' Mrs Dickinson called.

'Just coming, Mrs Dickinson.' Annie picked up the tray she'd left on the next table. 'Here you are, that'll explain things.' She handed Rosina the piece of paper Dorabel had thrown away. 'Now I must go or the old harridan will dock my wages.'

Rosina opened the crumpled piece of paper and smoothed it out on the tabletop. It was a handbill, looking much like some of the advertising pamphlets handed out by nimble lads on street corners. But in this case no one was selling anything. This leaflet wasn't advertising a mammoth sale of oriental carpets or the latest miracle hair restorer. It was an announcement of auditions to be held at the Raby Theatre.

Celebrated Theatre Company Seeks Fresh Talent!

A rare opportunity presents itself for a young actress to join the Greyling Players, an old-established dramatic company with a distinguished history. With the prospect of being trained by Mr Henry Greyling himself it must be understood that the remuneration will be small while the fortunate young lady serves her apprenticeship.

However, board and lodging will be provided.
Only those who are prepared to meet the highest standards
of dramatic art need apply.
Auditions held daily in the Raby Theatre.
(A small private income would be helpful.)

Ah, so that's it, Rosina thought. Young women like Dorabel and Amelia would never have stood a chance of being taken on by Henry Greyling because he obviously was not going to pay enough to keep body and soul together. He required a young woman keen to join the acting profession and prepared to finance herself and perhaps contribute towards the cost of her training.

Annie came back with a fresh pot of tea and a rock bun. She looked embarrassed. 'If you don't mind, miss,' she said, 'Mrs Dickinson would like you to settle your bill for the food and drink now. She'll talk to you about the cost of the room as soon as she has a minute but she asked me to tell you that she expects a month's rent in advance as well as a deposit against any breakages.'

'Of course.' Rosina paid the bill, adding a generous tip. Then she rose and pulled her suitcase and bag out from under the table.

'Aren't you going to eat your rock bun?' Annie asked.

'I haven't time. It's been nice talking to you but I've got to go.'

'But I thought you were going to stay here. Take a room.'

'I've changed my mind.'

'She'll be ever so cross. She goes purple in the face when she gets annoyed.'

'Then I'm relieved I won't be here to witness it.'

'But where are you going?'

'To the theatre.'

'So you are an actress after all?'

'Maybe I am, maybe I'm not. But I think I'm about to find the answer to that question.'

A surge of enthusiasm carried Rosina across the road as far as the central island where the tall gaslamps stood. She paused, waiting for a gap in the traffic. It suddenly occurred to her that she might be mad. What on earth was she thinking of, setting off for an audition to join a theatre company? But whatever happened she knew she could not have stayed at Mrs Dickinson's establishment. The café, no matter how well run, had been depressing. And Rosina hadn't been there very long before she realised that her friendly cabman, no doubt influenced by family loyalty and his own good nature, had an entirely false conception of his sister.

'Watch out!'

'I'm sorry!'

Rosina had stepped off the kerb into the path of a grocer's lad, his bicycle basket full to the brim with provisions. She leaped back and watched with apprehension as the lad fought to keep control of his bicycle and smiled with relief when he remained upright and carried on down the road. Then he nearly overbalanced again when he took one hand off the handlebar to wave goodbye.

'No harm done, missus,' he shouted over his shoulder.

The suitcase was heavy, and what with that and her travelling bag, Rosina struggled to walk in a balanced manner. She put them down on the pavement gratefully when she reached the theatre, then stared in perplexity when she saw that the doors were locked. However, there was a notice in the playbill display case, which said: 'Auditions. Stage Door. Back Lane.'

Picking up her luggage again, Rosina made her way to the nearest corner. A little way down the street she found a lane that ran parallel to the main road and a short way up the lane she found the stage door.

There was no fancy globe above the door and the woodwork was in need of a coat of paint. But she had realized as soon as she had seen the entrance to the theatre that the Raby was not as grand as the Grand. She smiled at her own pun and pushed the door to see if it would open. It did.

She paused to let her eyes adjust to the dim, dusty light. There was a small room, more of a cubicle, to her right, which had no door. An elderly man sat on a high stool reading his newspaper. 'The auditions are over for the day,' he told her without glancing up.

The rush of adrenaline that had carried Rosina across the road from the café ebbed away. She felt flat and empty. But before she could turn and go a voice called out, 'That's all right, Charlie, let the young woman in. Mr Greyling can't make his mind up about one of the ladies who auditioned today. It might help him to see one more.'

A tall figure was walking along the corridor towards her. As he emerged from the darkness into the light from the open door behind her, Rosina was surprised to see that it was Tom Carey, the actor she had seen at the Grand.

'Why don't you put your bags and baggage in Charlie's little hideaway and come with me,' he said. 'Here, let me help you. Now, let me introduce myself. I'm Tom—'

'I know who you are. You're Tom Carey.'

'Have we met before, Miss . . . ?'

'Leighton. Rosina Leighton. And no, we haven't met before. At least, not exactly.'

Rosina remembered him emerging from the stage door at the Grand. He'd been a striking figure in his old-fashioned swirling cloak. A theatrical heirloom, he'd called it. She remembered how charming he'd been and how he had teased Joanne after he had heard her remark about his being aware of the effect he created. Rosina was embarrassed all over again.

'And how is it that we have not exactly met?'

She could hear the smile in his voice but she couldn't see his expression because she couldn't bring herself to look up into his face.

'I saw you on the stage,' she said. 'And afterwards my friend and I came round to the stage door and you – erm – you asked my friend and me if we had enjoyed the show.'

'And had you?'

'Yes, very much.'

'And where was that?'

'At the Grand.'

'Ah, yes, the Grand. Not so very long ago, then. I'm sad to say we've come down in the world since that engagement ended. But never fear, we shall rise like a phoenix from the ashes once we put our new programme together.'

Rosina had only a faint idea what he was talking about. She didn't know how to respond so she thought it best to remain silent. And she didn't realize that she had lifted her head to stare up at him directly until he said, 'I seem to remember you – and not just because of a hurried exchange at the stage door. There's something else . . . no, it's gone. Now we must get along before Priscilla carries Henry off for his afternoon nap.'

'Priscilla?'

'Priscilla Greyling. The redoubtable wife of our revered actor manager. There are some who say that it is really she who is in charge of our hopeful little band. But we have chatted long enough. Come along, Miss Leighton, your future is beckoning.'

Rosina stood alone on the stage. Tom Carey had left her there blinking in a light that seemed to be trained directly on her. She looked out at the auditorium. It was like a cave, she thought, but a cave lined with red velvet, warm and comforting.

Two people were sitting in the stalls. Tom had told her they were Henry Greyling, the actor manager, and his wife, Priscilla. He told her not to be nervous and advised her to give her best monologue so long as it wasn't too long. Then he told her he would watch from the wings, and he left her.

Soothed by his confident voice, she had nodded calmly but the moment he had gone, ice-cold panic gripped her. What did he mean 'give your best monologue'? She knew what a monologue was — it was a long speech in a play, spoken by one performer — but was she supposed to have prepared one for the audition?

She glanced down at the Greylings. They had their heads together as they consulted some notes. Rosina went racing after Tom. He was standing at the side of the stage in what he called the 'wings'. He looked at her in surprise.

'What is it?' he asked. 'Is it stage fright?'

'No, it's not stage fright. It's just that I didn't know I would have to have something prepared.'

'Haven't you been to an audition before?'

'No.'

He looked at her quizzically. 'Well, what did you think you would have to do?'

'Read something, I suppose. I thought you might give me a script — like they do when you're trying for a part in a school play.'

'Is that your only experience of acting? The school play?'

She couldn't lie to him. 'Apart from acting with my friend for fun, I'm afraid it is.'

Instead of telling her that she might as well give up and leave the theatre, Tom Carey's eyes lit up with amusement. 'Well, then, what are you going to do?' he asked. 'Do you remember any of the speeches you had to learn for these plays?'

'I do. But please take my word for it, they wouldn't be suitable for the grown-up theatre.'

'The grown-up theatre can be extremely childish as times, but I know what you mean. Well, how about a poem? A poem would be acceptable.'

'Well . . . I suppose . . .'

'What's happening, Tom?' a sonorous voice called from the stalls. 'Is Miss Leighton not ready to audition, for some reason?'

Tom Carey stepped out on to the stage and, shielding his eyes from the light, he looked down at Mr Greyling. 'She's quite ready, Henry,' he said. 'Miss Leighton is going to recite a poem.'

'Ah, a poem,' a female voice declared. 'I like a girl who chooses poetry. It shows a certain refinement of mind.'

Rosina remembered Amelia's advice and felt cheered. She had pleased Mrs Greying before she had even begun.

'Come along,' Tom said softly, and he took her hand and led her to the middle of the stage. Then left her there.

Rosina had been frantically considering every poem she had learned at school and dismissed most of them. By the time Henry Greyling called, 'Please begin, Miss Leighton,' she had decided on one of her favourites by Thomas Hood. She announced the title and began:

'I remember, I remember,
The house where I was born,
The little window where the sun
Came peeping in at morn . . .'

Very soon she had forgotten that she was standing on stage in a shabby old theatre. The words had taken her back not just to the classroom but to the evening her mother – Geraldine Leighton – had helped her to learn the poem.

'I remember, I remember,
The roses, red and white,
The vi'lets and the lily-cups,
Those flowers made of light . . .'

Geraldine's sweet voice echoed in Rosina's mind as she spoke the words. By the time the poem came to an end Rosina was lost in a vision of the golden past and when she heard voices saying, 'Bravo!' she had to close her eyes tightly and then opened them again to bring herself back to the present.

'That was very moving, my dear,' Mrs Greyling said. 'Don't you agree, Henry?'

'Oh, certainly.'

Rosina heard Tom's soft chuckle.

And then Mr Greyling said, 'You have a beautifully clear voice, good projection, a pleasing tone and you know how to inject emotion, Miss Leighton. But now we must see if you also have a gift for acting. Tom, are you ready?'

Tom came towards her holding some papers. She looked at him in surprise.

'That's why I'm here,' he told her. 'After the monologues I act in a short scene with each candidate.'

'But I don't know the lines.'

'You don't have to. You read from the script. But you can have a quick read-through first. Here, sit down.'

Tom pulled a couple of chairs forward. Rosina sat down, perching on the front of the chair nervously. But as soon as she started reading she relaxed a little. The scene was a piece of nonsense involving a lady and a highwayman. It reminded her of the plays Joanne used to write for them to perform together in the house on Heaton Road.

'Are you ready?' Tom asked.

She nodded.

'Then off we go.'

Rosina threw herself into the part of a quick-thinking young woman who outwitted a rather dim highwayman. They had hardly started when she heard laughter from the auditorium and when the scene came to an end both Henry and Priscilla Greyling were applauding enthusiastically. And Tom was smiling.

He walked downstage and said, 'What do you think, Henry?'

'Marvellous.'

'She's a natural,' Mrs Greyling added.

'Shall we try it the other way?' Tom asked.

'Yes, do,' the actor manager replied, 'but I don't think that will present her with a problem.'

'Right,' Tom said when he rejoined her. 'Now we change parts.'

'Why?'

'To see if you can play the highwayman while I play the lady.'

'No, you don't mean it!'

'Yes, I do. And remember, whatever happens, don't laugh unless it's in the script.'

Rosina knew why he had warned her the moment

he started playing the lady. Tall, dark and handsome as he was, she knew he would have the audience in hysterics as he flirted and minced without ever straying into overacting or vulgarity. No matter how much she wanted to give way to laughter it was vital that she stay in the role of the befuddled and bemused highwayman. It was hard but she managed it.

Only when the scene had come to an end with the 'lady' making off with all of the highwayman's booty, did she allow herself to collapse on to the nearest chair and laugh until the tears ran down her cheeks.

Tom sat beside her. 'Did you enjoy that?' he asked.

'Very much. What a wonderful sketch it is. Where did you find it?'

'Oh, I wrote it. It's one of the pieces we're going to introduce into the new programme, although, sadly, you won't be appearing in it.'

Rosina stopped laughing. 'Do you mean you're not going to take me on?'

'Well, that's up to Henry and Priscilla and, after that performance, I'm pretty sure that you will be joining the company. But I wrote that piece for Sadie.'

Rosina remembered the pretty young actress with the bright yellow hair who had been with Tom when they had emerged from the stage door of the Grand.

'Oh, of course,' she said, and she wondered at the dark emotion that suddenly took up residence in her heart. Could it possibly be jealousy? And if it was, was it because she would dearly love to act in the scene herself or because of the possessive way Sadie had placed her gloved hand on Tom's arm?

Henry and Priscilla Greyling had come up on to the stage. 'Just a question or two,' Mr Greyling said. 'Do your parents know that you have come here today? I only ask because you look so young.'

'I have no parents.'

'Is there a guardian? Someone whose permission you would need to seek?'

'There is no one. I am on my own.'

'An orphan!' Priscilla Greyling said dramatically. 'Never mind, my dear. If you join us I shall be like a mother to you.'

'And . . .' Henry Greyling paused as if considering how best to say something, 'and you do know that I cannot offer you a generous salary?'

'That doesn't matter.'

'Wrong thing to say,' Tom whispered in her ear.

'At first, I mean,' Rosina added. 'While I'm learning the craft – erm – from you and Mrs Greyling.'

'Just so, just so.' Henry Greyling looked pleased. 'You – ah – you have a private income?'

'Yes,' she replied, and Tom nudged her. 'A small one.'

'Ah, good. Then Mrs Greyling and I have no hesitation in offering you a place in our little troupe. I hope you will be happy. Now, Tom, do you think you could escort Miss Leighton to the lodging house? Mrs Greyling and I will repair to our modest hotel for a nap.'

'Oh – Mr Greyling,' Rosina called after him.

He turned and smiled at her. 'Yes, my dear?'

'Do you think I could be known as Rosina Lee? I've heard many actors have stage names.'

'Of course, my dear. Rosina Lee it shall be.'

The Greylings departed arm in arm and, somewhere in the theatre, someone dimmed most of the lights.

'Why the change of name?' Tom asked her. 'Leighton is a very nice name.'

'Maybe so but I don't want it any more.'

He looked at her quizzically but she remained silent.

'Very well, Rosina Lee. I shall escort you to the even more modest theatrical lodging house that the rest of us inhabit – oh, apart from Monica, who is the Greylings' daughter. But, tell me, where were you going to go if you hadn't been successful?'

'Why do you ask?'

'Because of your luggage. A suitcase and a travelling bag. It looks very much as if you did not intend to return to wherever you came from.'

'I didn't.'

'So, I repeat my question. Where would you have gone if you hadn't been invited to join the Greyling Players?'

She could have made a story up but there was something about Tom Carey that made her certain that he would not be fooled by a lie.

'I really don't know,' she said. 'But I would have thought of something.'

He looked at her seriously for a moment and then smiled that so engaging smile of his. 'I don't know what wind of fortune blew you into this theatre today, but I'm very pleased you have joined us, Rosina Lee.'

The tall old house where the rest of the cast was lodging was not far away, and when they got there it was deathly quiet. 'Everyone will be resting before they have tea and then go to the theatre for the first house,' Tom told her.

He introduced her to the landlady, Mrs Naylor, and then excused himself. 'I want to go over some new sketches I've written. We're going to start rehearsing them tomorrow morning.'

Rosina watched him walk away and suddenly felt bereft. She had entered a strange new world and until this moment Tom Carey had been her guide. Now she was on her own.

'You have come at a most fortunate time,' Mrs Naylor said. 'I have a very nice single room available.' The landlady looked at her shrewdly. 'No doubt you would prefer a room of your own?'

'I think so,' Rosina said. Until that moment she'd had no idea that she might have to share a room.

'Of course, it costs a little more . . .'

Rosina realized that the landlady was waiting for her to say something.

'Oh, that's all right,' she said.

'Good. Billy will take your bags up. It's right at the top of the house but I don't suppose the stairs will pose any problem to a healthy young person such as you.'

All this had been said in the most ladylike and refined manner. Suddenly Mrs Naylor turned towards a door at the back of a long passage and yelled, 'Billy!' in stentorian tones.

Rosina had to stop herself from jumping with fright. The landlady smiled at her. 'I used to be on the stage myself, you know.'

At that moment a tiny little scrap of a maid appeared. Her pinafore was too big for her and her mobcap covered her ears and most of her forehead.

'This is Wilhelmina,' Mrs Naylor said. 'But I thought the name a smidgeon too grand for a housemaid so we call her Billy.'

The broad smile on the girl's face indicated that she didn't mind this liberty.

'Billy, take Miss Lee's baggage up to the front attic.'

'Oh, no, I'll carry them,' Rosina said, but the scrap's grin widened.

'Divven't fret, miss,' she said. 'I'm stronger than I look. The missus, here, has been feeding me up.'

Without further ado she picked up Rosina's luggage and

set off up the stairs at a cracking pace. Rosina had to hurry to keep up with her.

'You'll hear the gong when it's time for tea,' Mrs Naylor called after her.

Tea was an ordeal. Rosina had hoped that Tom would be there to introduce her to the company but just before she entered the dining room Billy stopped her and said, 'Mr Carey asked me to give you this. It's for the first house because they sometimes get a handful of troublesome customers in the late show.' She handed Rosina a theatre ticket.

'But won't Mr Carey be having tea with the rest of us?' Rosina asked.

Billy grinned. 'Not likely. That Miss Sutton thinks she's too good to eat with the others so Mr Carey and her usually go and hev a pastry or the like in the German café just down from the theatre.'

'Sutton? Sadie Sutton?'

'That's the one.'

'And are they . . . friends? Miss Sutton and Mr Carey?' Rosina hadn't been able to stop herself from asking and she flushed when she saw the little maid's knowing grin.

'Well, Miss Sutton thinks they are,' Billy said. 'But gan on in and hev yer tea.'

All eyes turned towards her when Rosina entered the dining room. A young woman came up and introduced herself as Josephine Carlton and invited Rosina to sit beside her at the large table.

'You're Rosina Lee, aren't you?'

Rosina nodded.

'Tom asked me to welcome you and introduce you. This is Rosina, everybody. She's joining the company, starting with rehearsals tomorrow.'

That was news to Rosina – the bit about the rehearsals the next day – but while she was digesting this the men and the women around the table started calling out their names.

Rosina must have looked confused because Josephine said, 'Don't worry. We're very informal. And don't try to remember who everybody is right now. You'll get to know us as the days go on.'

Thankfully, after welcoming her, the talk turned to their work. They were worried and disappointed that they did not seem to be attracting big enough audiences and they had great hopes for the new material that Tom was working on. The plates on the table were piled high with bread and butter, slices of ham, scones and raisin cake. The assembled company, like a flock of hungry twittering birds, soon emptied the plates and hurried way in no particular order.

'Time for the curling tongs!' Josephine smiled as she rose to leave the table. 'You know where the theatre is? Of course you do. I hope you enjoy the show tonight and if you do you can tell me at breakfast in the morning. You'll probably be asleep before we come home from the second house.'

In no time at all it seemed Rosina found herself alone at the table. Billy entered with a tray. 'Is it all right if I clear up now?' she asked.

'Of course.'

'Yer divven't want owt else?'

'No thank you.'

Rosina watched as the diminutive maid began to pile the tray high with empty plates. She pictured the girl staggering back to the kitchen and she asked, 'Would you like me to help you?'

'Don't be daft. I can manage. Now gan on, get away upstairs and make yerself all bonny for the theatre.'

* * *

Later that evening Rosina returned from the show at the Raby, appalled at the step she had just taken. Would she really be capable of taking her place onstage with these joyful and talented creatures who made the world of make-believe come to life so vividly?

'What's the matter with you?' Billy asked when she opened the front door to let her in. 'You look as though you've lost a sixpence and found a ha'penny.'

'I'm fine,' Rosina assured her. 'Just tired and . . . well, I'm a little nervous about tomorrow.'

Rosina marvelled at herself. Why on earth was she confiding in this child who patently had a much harder life than she had?

'You'll do fine,' Billy said. 'They all get nerves. Every one of them.'

'Do they really?'

'Whey-aye. Well,' she grinned, 'mebbes not Miss Sadie. But come away in. Don't stand at the door looking as if you're going to run away. Mrs Naylor is round at her sister's so why don't you and me sit by the fire in the kitchen and hev a cup of cocoa together? And there might be some raisin cake left. The missus is very good to me with the leftovers and there's plenty of them in this house. Not like at home, where me poor ma never has anything left over after feeding fourteen of us.'

Rosina wasn't sure whether she ought to accept. She didn't want to get Billy into trouble but her need for company overcame any scruples. They sat cosily together like old friends. Billy looked so tired that Rosina wondered how on earth she was managing to stay awake.

'Where do you sleep, Billy?' she asked.

'Right here in the kitchen. Look — there,' she pointed. 'Under the table.'

'You sleep under the table?' Rosina was shocked.

'Don't be daft! There's a truckle bed there.' Billy leaned over and lifted the oiled tablecloth. 'See?' When all me work's done I pulls it out and puts it nice and near the range. Snug as a bug in a rug, I am. And I divven't hev to share a bed any more with four of me sisters like I did at home. Divven't worry about me.'

For the first time in her life Rosina found herself wondering what life was like for the servants at Ravenshill. She had made friends with Bridget and Molly, but she had never been behind the green baize doors that led to the servants' quarters. It shocked her to realize that she didn't even know how many people worked there. Did any of the young skivvies at Ravenshill have to sleep like Billy on truckle beds pulled out from under a table?

And then a more disturbing thought crept into her mind. Billy was no more than twelve or thirteen. She worked hard every day of her life. She had hinted how lucky she was to be here with Mrs Naylor. Her family was in all probability very poor. Rosina wondered what her own life would have been like if Geraldine Leighton had not adopted her. If Maud Fidler had not found her and taken her away from a life of poverty to one of luxury.

She supposed she should be grateful. If Geraldine had lived, her life would still be a happy one. She did not believe, as Julian Leighton apparently did, that Geraldine would have stopped loving her after the birth of her son. But would she ever have told her she was adopted? Rosina simply didn't know.

'Good night, Billy,' she said. 'I suppose you'll want to get to bed, now.'

'I might want to but I can't. Not yet. That lot'll be coming back from the theatre absolutely ravenous. They tell me that performing sharpens their appetite. Mrs Naylor will be back by then and I'll hev to help with the supper. You'll be in dreamland before I gets to tuck meself up in bed.'

Billy's cheerful acceptance of the way things were made Rosina feel ashamed. She knew she had been feeling sorry for herself but when she compared her life with Billy's – and others from the teeming slums just a short distance away – she realized she had very little to complain about.

But even so, she found it difficult to sleep. Bright moonlight filtered in through a gap in the curtains, illuminating the tiny room under the eaves. She had unpacked everything when she had arrived and put her clothes away in the wardrobe and the chest of drawers. There wasn't much room in either so she knew she would have to plan carefully what clothes to ask for when she wrote to Molly.

Julian Leighton had been adamant. She must not return to Ravenshill. Well, maybe she could do without some of her clothes but she was reluctant to abandon her books, especially as Geraldine had given them to her. As soon as Joanne came back from France she would go to see her and explain the situation. She was sure that, once her friend got over the surprise, she would agree to store things for her.

Still unable to settle, she began to distract herself by counting the flowers on the wallpaper. She had worked out how many blooms there were before the pattern was repeated when her eye fell on Dolly sitting in the cane chair at the side of the chest of drawers. She got out of bed, shivering as her feet touched the cold floor, and went to get her beloved doll. She would take her to bed with her just as she had done as a child.

But when she picked up the doll she saw something else. The parcel that Maud Fidler had thrust into her hands this morning. Was it only that morning? Her life had changed so much it seemed years ago. She took the doll and the parcel back to her bed.

Instead of lighting the bedside lamp, Rosina opened the curtains wider. Bright moonlight streamed in. She sat on the bed and undid the string. The parcel contained a bundle of neatly folded clothes so small that they must have belonged to a very young child. Rosina shook out an emerald-green coat with dark green trimmings. It was pretty but slightly old fashioned. There was also a bonnet, which although it was creased, looked brand-new. It was trimmed with green ribbons. A white dress, white underwear and white stockings were all of the best quality, just like the coat.

Were they Rosina's own clothes, she wondered. No, that couldn't be so. She had come from the slums and slum children did not possess clothes such as these. So why had Miss Fidler given them to her?

It was all too much for Rosina's tired brain. The only explanation she could think of was that the poor woman had lost her senses. Nevertheless, she decided to keep the clothes. She made up the parcel again and put it in the bottom drawer of the chest.

Not long afterwards sheer fatigue overcame her. Her limbs relaxed and her mind stopped worrying over all the questions she could find no answers for. Then, just before she drifted off to sleep, she realized with surprise that since she had left Ravenshill that morning she had not once thought of Adam Loxley.

Chapter Eighteen

When Rosina arrived at the theatre at ten o'clock the next morning a stagehand was arranging chairs in a semicircle on a bare stage. The rest of the cast was assembled and they took the chairs as they became available. The working lights were on, revealing a place from where the magic seemed to have fled. The people who were gathered there were workaday folk rather than the creatures of enchantment they had been in their costumes and make-up the evening before. At the moment they were ignoring her so she took the chance to observe them.

The robust young woman sitting next to Mrs Greyling was probably Monica, the Greylings' daughter. Rosina remembered that Monica had been in the plays she had seen at the Grand, and Mrs Greyling had delivered one of the more dramatic poems in the recitation interlude.

Tom and Mr Greyling were sitting together looking at a sheaf of papers. They must be the scripts, Rosina thought. Tom was so absorbed that he had not noticed her arrival. One or two of the others glanced at her coolly as she stood there uncertainly. They were taken up with their own affairs and their attitude towards her was entirely different from the way they had greeted her at teatime the day before. Josephine saw her and came hurrying over.

'Where have you been?' she asked.

'Am I late? Have I kept everyone waiting?'

'No, it's not quite ten. That's not it. We expected to see you at breakfast.'

'I had breakfast early. I had some business to do in town.' Josephine looked at her quizzically and Rosina felt she owed her some sort of explanation. 'I had to go and see a solicitor . . . about my allowance.'

'Ah, I see.'

'I didn't think it would take so long but—'

'Please, there's no need to explain.' The young actress smiled, her freckled face sunny again. 'We thought with you having a single room and all that you might think yourself too grand for the common herd and that you'd ordered breakfast in bed or even gone to the coffee shop with Sadie and Tom. Especially as Tom seems to have taken you under his wing.'

'Has he?'

'If you'd been here a little earlier you would have heard him enthusing to dear old Henry about you. He thinks you have a talent that's worth nurturing.'

Rosina couldn't have described the emotions that coursed through her veins.

Josephine laughed. 'But don't get your hopes up. It won't be Tom Carey who nurtures your talent. Sadie would soon put a stop to that. And, of course, if any of us had been thinking straight this morning we should have realized that you had not gone for breakfast with them. Sadie would never have allowed it. Now come along and sit with Gertrude and me.'

Gertrude Spode, one of the older members of the cast, was tall and thin. She sat hunched up and clutching a shawl around her shoulders.

'Poor Gertrude,' Josephine whispered. 'She feels the cold dreadfully and this old theatre isn't very well heated, I'm afraid. Still, it's much better than some of the ruins we've appeared in.'

The older woman looked up as they approached. 'I've asked Rosina to sit with us,' Josephine said. 'Come along, Rosina, sit here next to me.'

Gertrude did not smile a greeting. 'So you haven't deserted us,' she said. 'Josephine thought you might not have wanted to take breakfast with us, but I thought it more likely that you had taken one look at this sorry bunch of thespians and decided that a life in the theatre was not for you after all.'

'Rosina had some business to do in town,' Josephine explained.

Gertrude leaned across Josephine and lowered her voice conspiratorially. 'If your business is anything to do with money and, by the looks of you, you might have some, then don't let our dear leader learn anything about it, or before you know it he'll have you investing in the company. And I wouldn't advise anyone to do that until we see if Tom's new material can turn us around.'

'I'll take your advice,' Rosina said.

She sat between the two women and surreptitiously looked around at the others. She was aware that she was dressed, if not more fashionably than the other women, then at least in clothes of a much higher quality. Both Tom and Gertrude had warned her that she must be discreet about any money she had and she was suddenly filled with misgivings.

Had Henry Greyling taken her on simply because she was financially independent? Was he hoping that she would invest in the company, as Gertrude had suggested, or did he genuinely think she had talent? And what of Tom? He was trying to save the company by writing new plays and sketches. Did he also believe that she might be so eager to be an actress that she would buy her way in? But, no, he had hinted that she should play down the size of her income. Surely he was to be trusted?

Whatever the truth of the matter she would have to prove herself worthy of this chance she had been given to make a new and different life for herself.

Suddenly aware that both Tom and Mr Greyling were looking in her direction, Rosina smiled hesitantly. But almost immediately they turned to face each other again and continued their conversation. Eventually whatever they had been discussing seemed to have been settled for they broke apart and Mr Greyling raised his voice.

'All right then, Tom,' he said, 'let's give Miss Lee a shot at it. We'll begin as soon as Sadie arrives.'

'And who is taking Sadie Sutton's name in vain?' A melodious voice rang out theatrically across the stage as Sadie made her entrance. Rosina stared at her keenly. She was perhaps a little older than Rosina had first thought and her hair was an impossible yellow, but she was very pretty. There was an air of confidence about her as she walked towards the group already seated.

'Oh, do sit with me, Sadie, darling,' Monica Greyling called.

'So sorry I'm late, Mr Greyling,' Sadie said as she took her seat next to Monica. But her demeanour suggested that she was in no fear of being reprimanded.

'Dear Sadie always arrives after the rest of us,' Josephine whispered. 'She does like to make an entrance.'

Henry Greyling walked over and dragged a chair forward so that he could sit facing the semicircle of actors. But before he sat down he gestured towards Rosina. 'I think you've now all met Miss Lee,' he said.

356

'I haven't, although Tom has told me that you have taken on a new girl,' Sadie said. 'And I'd like to take this opportunity to welcome her.'

'Who does she think she is?' Gertrude muttered.

Josephine laughed softly. 'Sadie is Sadie, and in her eyes she's our brightest star.'

'And unfortunately for us, she is,' Gertrude rejoined.

'Quiet, please!' Mr Greyling called. 'We must begin.'

'Of course,' Sadie said. Quite unnecessarily, Rosina thought.

'And now I want you all to do a read-through of Tom's new musical play,' Henry Greyling continued. 'It's called—'

'*The Street Singer*,' Sadie finished his sentence. 'Dear Tom has written it especially for me.'

'That's right,' Tom said quickly. 'Sadie will take the lead as the street singer, and the comedy lead will be taken by Miss Lee.'

The expectant expressions of the cast changed to surprise. 'But, my dear,' Priscilla exclaimed to Henry, 'surely Miss Lee should begin with a small role, not a leading part.'

'I usually play the comedy lead,' Monica exclaimed indignantly. Shock and outrage opened her eyes wide.

'That's right,' her mother said. 'Dear Monica has a wonderful gift for timing.'

Rosina glanced at Mrs Greyling and her daughter, and her heart sank. Oh dear, she thought, this has caused trouble on my very first day. If she had pleased the actor manager's wife yesterday with her choice of a poem, and appealed to her motherly instincts because of her orphaned state, those feelings were swiftly draining away as the matron came to the defence of her own daughter.

Priscilla Greyling put her arm around Monica's shoulders and handed her a clean handkerchief, which she used to dab her eyes theatrically. Mrs Greyling's expression was one of wounded surprise.

'Mr Carey,' she said, 'Miss Lee has only just joined the company. I doubt if a newcomer to the stage, as Miss Lee is, could begin to tackle the part.'

Rosina saw several of the others nodding in agreement and she wished a hole would open in the stage and swallow her up.

Henry Greyling cleared his throat. 'My dear,' he said to his daughter, 'Tom thought you would be better in the romantic part. It calls for someone young and sweetly fetching. No one else would do.'

Monica stopped dabbing her eyes and looked at her father suspiciously. 'Really?'

'Er, yes, indeed.'

'Definitely,' Tom said. 'I had you in mind the moment I realized how romantic this part would be.'

'Hm,' said Monica, only half mollified. 'And how big is this part? How important is it?'

Tom stood up and faced them all. 'Every part is important in this play. As you know I like to think of the Greyling Players as a team. But why don't we study the scripts? We'll take a little time to read them quietly to ourselves.'

He made sure that everybody had a copy and then sat down next to Rosina. Her hands were shaking as she clutched her script.

'What is it?' he asked quietly. 'Are you nervous?'

'Yes, but not for the reason you may be thinking.'

'And what am I thinking?'

'That it's some sort of stage fright.'

'And it isn't?'

'No – or rather I haven't had time to suffer from that yet.

I'm anxious because I think you have caused trouble by giving me this part.'

'Oh, for goodness' sake . . .' he said.

Heads turned, causing Rosina more embarrassment.

'Please lower your voice, Mr Carey.'

'Sorry,' he said quietly. 'But you'll soon learn to ignore this sort of thing. It happens almost every time we cast a new piece. Everyone fights for the best part – or what they think is the best part. Often they have no real idea of what they are truly capable of – or what they shouldn't attempt.'

He sounded convincing and Rosina wanted to believe him. She glanced along the row at Monica and was relieved to see that the Greylings' daughter seemed happy enough as she read her script. But then she saw that Sadie had her head bent down towards her script but her glance slanting sideways towards Rosina and Tom. Her pretty blue eyes were sparkling with venom. There was no mistaking her anger. I have made an enemy on my very first day here, Rosina thought. This is not a good beginning.

She began to read her script. Henry Greyling had called it a musical play and it was a cheerful comedy with pauses every now and then for a song. The story was enacted in a city park where all sorts of characters met or took their ease. There were a few small parts such as a housemaid, who pushed an old invalid in a Bath chair, a crabby old park attendant, then a little more importantly a pair of star-crossed lovers, and a lonely old man and a lonely old woman who visited the park daily. These two started out by being grumpy but when they joined forces to help the young lovers they ended up falling in love themselves.

And while all this was going on there was a subplot concerning a pair of inept burglars who had hidden their booty in the park and were being frustrated in retrieving it.

Rosina had been given the part of the formidable young wife of one of the burglars and she would outwit the pursuing policeman at every turn. Rosina saw at once what a gift the part was and she hoped she had the skill to play it.

The different stories were threaded together with the songs of the beautiful street singer who wandered the park singing for money and who knew much more about what was going on than any other character in the play. Tom had not written any songs. He had scribbled notes on the script suggesting suitable popular songs of the moment, including 'The Doll Song'. Rosina wondered what it would be like to hear Sadie singing it.

'Are you to play the young lover?' she asked Tom.

'Why do you ask?'

'You look the part,' she said, and wished she hadn't.

He grinned. 'No, I like a part with a bit of character in it. I'm the policeman and not only do I get the burglars but I get the girl too!'

'The girl?'

'Sadie, of course, the street singer.'

'Oh, of course.'

Rosina was aware that her answer had been tart and was dismayed to discover that the jealousy that had taken up residence in her heart had suddenly grown stronger. However, Tom seemed not to have noticed.

'Right, you've had time to read it,' Henry Greyling said. 'Now let us begin.'

Tom leaned towards her and said, 'I should have asked. Can you do a local voice – you know – dialect?'

'I think so. I had to sometimes in the plays my friend wrote.'

'Good. That's what I want.'

Rosina hadn't been sure what would happen next and was

relieved to discover that at this stage they were going to stay in their seats and simply read their allotted part aloud. Even so, performers that they were, they started to dramatize their characters and soon the whole performance took flight and soared along, raising laughs from the stagehands and theatre cleaners. Encouraged by the enthusiasm of those around her, Rosina soon entered into the spirit of things and was acting away with the best of them.

As the choice of songs hadn't been finalized, Sadie sang only a few bars now and then. During one of them Josephine leaned towards Rosina and whispered, 'Much as I hate to admit it, Sadie has a beautiful voice, don't you agree?'

Rosina replied that she did but when Sadie sang 'The Doll Song' she could not help comparing the performance with that of Daisy Belle.

When the reading had finished everybody was in a better mood.

'Good stuff, Tom,' a man called Arthur Barnfather said. He was to play the part of the browbeaten burglar. 'And I've no qualms about the scenes with Rosina. She seems to be a quick study.'

By this Rosina thought that Arthur believed she was capable of learning quickly.

'Thank you, Tom, my scenes with Henry are very touching,' Mrs Greyling said. 'Of course, Henry and I will need our make-up skills to make us look old enough to play the parts of the old couple.'

'Of course,' Tom agreed. He turned and winked at Rosina.

Henry Greyling came over to tell Rosina that she would be on half-pay while she was rehearsing and go on to full pay when the play was performed. She wondered if this now made her a 'professional'.

'Tomorrow we'll walk through it,' Mr Greyling told them as he dismissed them for the day. 'And I expect you to know your lines.'

Some of those assembled groaned.

'It's all right for you,' Josephine whispered to Rosina. 'You have nothing else to do today but the rest of us have two performances to get through. Bang goes my visit to the hairdresser this afternoon.'

'I'll do your hair, Josephine dear,' Gertrude said.

'That's what I was afraid of,' Josephine whispered to Rosina and then, turning to the older actress she said. 'Oh, would you? What a darling you are. Come along, Rosina; let's walk back to the diggings for luncheon together. I'm starving.'

Josephine linked arms with her and swept her towards the wings.

'Wait a moment,' Tom called, and hurried after them. 'That was very good, Rosina. Just what I wanted.'

'Thank you.'

Sadie, trying not to give the impression that she was hurrying, caught up with Tom. 'Tom, I've booked a cab to take us into town. How about a spot of lunch at Alvini's?'

'I haven't really time for that, Sadie. I want to go over the other sketches.'

'Oh, bring your work with you, darling. You usually do. We'll ask for a private room.' Her smile was both proprietary and fond.

He sighed. 'Very well.'

As they were leaving Rosina heard Sadie say, 'I understand the new girl has a little money of her own. Is that why you've taken her on? Are you and Henry hoping she'll invest in the company?'

They were out of earshot so Rosina did not hear the reply

but embarrassment and fury surged through her.

'Don't take any notice of that cat,' Josephine said. 'They wouldn't have hired you if you couldn't act. And you can take my word for it, as I've been treading the boards since I was four years old in my darling departed parents' own troupe.'

'Does Tom take notice of her?'

'Tom Carey is single-minded as far as work is concerned. He's never been known to concede a point, not even to Henry. If you're worried that Sadie will interfere with your work you needn't be. Tom does his best to keep her sweet because she's the nearest thing the Greyling Players have to a big star. She can dance and sing and is a more than competent actress. Furthermore, she has what you call "stage presence". The audiences love her. So Tom doesn't want her to leave us.'

'Might she do that?'

'I think she's had an offer or two. And she's always hinting that she could go to a big London company if she had a mind to. The irony is she stays here because of Tom. She's sweet on him but she's clever enough to conceal that fact.'

'If she conceals it how do you know that's the case?'

'Tom is a mere man but Sadie is not clever enough to fool me — or Gertrude.' Suddenly Josephine looked at Rosina keenly. 'But something tells me Sadie will have to watch out from now on.'

'What do you mean?'

'I think in you we may have an even bigger star in the making.'

The days that followed were hectic as Tom took the cast through rehearsal after rehearsal of the new sketches. Rosina was surprised to discover how easily she fitted in to the hardworking and undoubtedly unconventional theatrical life. Everyone could be bosom friends one moment and then, as quickly as a flash of lightning, an argument could flare up about something completely trivial, such as a mislaid wig or a broken fan.

Rosina learned new terms: the obvious ones such as centre stage, stage right and stage left. She also learned that 'upstage' didn't just mean the area at the back of the stage but it could also be used as a verb when it meant that you forced another actor to turn his back to the audience and thus drew attention to yourself. Sadie was very good at this and the others would seethe with rage whenever she did it.

While the others were performing in the current show, Rosina stayed in her room at the lodging house and anxiously learned her part. She also made one or two trips to Mr Sinclair's office and he arranged a bank account for her. Geraldine Leighton had left her more than comfortably off, but Rosina decided at once that she was going to live modestly. Not because she didn't want Henry Greyling to ask her to invest in the company but because she didn't want the rest of the players to feel she was different. She would endeavour to live on her earnings as the others had to do.

The first night for the new programme drew near and Rosina began to wonder if she truly had been mad when she'd come along so hopefully to the theatre that day. But she needn't have worried. Once the curtains opened for her first performance on the professional stage, she was carried along by sheer enjoyment.

When the audience responded with laughter and applause, they lifted the cast on to another plane. Waiting in the wings for her entrance, Rosina had time to wonder if she was now one of those magical creatures who could transport people to another world where everyday cares and sorrows were forgotten.

When the show came to an end she was so exhilarated

that she thought she would never descend to earth again.

'Remember we have to do all this again for the second house,' Josephine told her. 'Now come along back to the dressing room. We'll brew up a pot of tea on the gas ring and I have a bag of currant buns to share.'

But when they returned to the dressing room Rosina shared with Josephine and Gertrude, they found Charlie, the stage doorkeeper, waiting.

'There's someone to see you, Miss Lee,'

'What, an admirer already!' Josephine shrieked. 'A stage-door Johnny? Does he bear flowers? Champagne? Or an interesting velvet case with the name of a jeweller on it?'

Charlie shook his head and smiled. 'Miss Lee's visitor is a young lady. Says they were at school together.'

'Joanne!' Rosina exclaimed. 'Oh, please, Charlie, can she come in?'

'If Miss Spode and Miss Carlton agree.'

'Is that all right?' she asked her two fellow performers.

'Of course it is,' Josephine said.

'You were wonderful!' Joanne said the minute she entered the dressing room. 'All of you were wonderful,' she said as her glance took in the other two, 'but Rosina is my oldest friend and I'm absolutely overjoyed for her.'

Joanne's face was wet with tears and Gertrude moved a pile of costumes from a small sofa on to the top of a chest and told her to sit down. 'Have a cup of tea, dear, and don't mind us. Just have a nice chat with your friend.'

Gertrude and Josephine sat at the dressing table and talked quietly over their tea and buns. Rosina sat with her friend, knowing she had much explaining to do.

But first she had a question. 'How did you know I was here?'

'How do you think? Your name is on the playbill.'

'No, it isn't. At least not Rosina Leighton.'

'I've written to you a few times since we got back from France and you didn't answer any of my letters. Then I met Amy in Bainbridge's and she told me you had left home. She didn't say why. Then walking down Shields Road one day I saw the playbill with a certain "New Talent, Miss Rosina Lee" advertised. It had to be you. So I bought a ticket — and it *was* you! Oh, Rosina, why didn't you let me know?'

'I'm sorry. I should have done. I'm ashamed I didn't. But life has been a little difficult.'

'Why did you leave home? Was it because of your stepmother?'

'Partly.'

'Only partly? Are you going to tell me about it?'

'I may do one day but not yet.'

Joanne's eyes widened. 'It's Adam, isn't it? He's let you down, hasn't he?'

'Please don't ask.'

'Oh, poor you.'

'Joanne, really, it's all right.'

And even as she said it Rosina knew that it *was* all right. Of course she had been hurt and she was still haunted by what she had seen in the conservatory, but the more she thought about it, the more she realized that a man who could behave like that would not have made her happy.

'Look, you mustn't blame Adam,' she said. 'There was something he didn't know. I'll tell you one day, I promise.'

'But how have you managed? Where are you living?'

'I'm in a theatrical boarding house with the rest of the cast.'

'You must come and live with me!'

'I came to your house the very day I left home but you were in France.' Rosina was aware that Josephine kept

366

glancing her way so she lowered her voice. 'It's a long story,' she said, 'and now is not the time to tell it.'

'But I want to help you.'

'Well, there is something you can do.'

'Anything!'

'I brought only the clothes I could carry. Molly is going to send them on when I write to her. Do you think you could find room for them – and some of my other belongings? You see, I won't ever be going back to Ravenshill.'

'Of course I'll keep your things. And whatever you say, I will keep a room permanently ready for you.'

'Thank you.'

'But now, tell me, why did you change your name?'

'I think it sounds well, don't you? And besides, I don't think the Leightons would relish seeing their name on a playbill.'

Joanne frowned, obviously puzzled by Rosina's formal way of referring to the couple she still believed to be her friend's father and stepmother. She looked as if she were about to burst with the effort of not asking any more questions, but seeing Rosina's resolute expression she shrugged and raised her teacup as if it were a glass of wine.

'Well, here's to your future success in the theatre. One day I know I'm going to be proud to say that the very first plays you ever appeared in were written by me!'

This lightened the mood and set them both giggling like the schoolgirls they had been not so very long ago. Before she left, Joanne made Rosina promise to keep in touch. Rosina agreed gladly.

Rosina soon got used to the punishing routine, the odd hours and the extra early morning rehearsals Henry called every time he wanted to introduce a new bit of 'business' to one of the sketches. Tom's play *The Street Singer* was the most important item in the programme and Rosina, along with all the other members of the cast, soon found herself humming and singing the songs that had been chosen in every spare moment.

One day when she was resting in her room at the top of the house after luncheon she couldn't sleep. The weather was foul and rain beat against the windows and drummed on the roof. It made Rosina restless. She found herself walking through Sadie's part and singing the songs softly to herself. There was a knock at the door and Josephine entered.

'You didn't tell anyone you could sing like that!' she said. 'And where did you get that doll?'

'Which doll?'

'The doll you've just placed on your bed. You haven't secretly been practising Sadie's part, have you?'

'No, of course not. I've had the doll all my life and if I was singing the song it's because it's so catchy.'

Josephine sat on the bed and picked Dolly up. 'This is much better than the prop Sadie uses,' she said.

'It's not a prop. I told you, it's a toy and I've had it all my life. Anyway, what do you want?'

'That's not very gracious – I don't want anything. Just to share a bit of gossip, that's all.'

Rosina smiled. 'What now? Has Gertrude run off with Charlie the stage doorkeeper? I know he's sweet on her.'

'Yes, he is, isn't he? You know, I wouldn't be surprised if Charlie proposes and Gertrude accepts. I know she's getting a little tired of the theatrical life and would like to retire.'

'Well, what is it?'

'What's what?'

Rosina threw a cushion at her. 'The gossip.'

'Oh, yes. It's not very exciting really. It's just that Sadie went into town after the show last night. She'd arranged with Tom to have supper at Alvini's. A lot of the theatre crowd go there. Well, Tom forgot and didn't go, and then it started raining and Sadie couldn't get a cab for ages and furthermore, one of those motorcar things drove by, right through a puddle, and soaked her from head to toe. Billy saw her coming in last night. She looked like the proverbial drowned rat. If you can imagine a rat with dripping yellow hair hanging down from under a ruined bonnet.'

Josephine stopped and they looked at each other. Each was holding her breath.

'Poor Sadie,' Josephine said.

'Indeed,' Rosina agreed. 'Poor Sadie.'

It was no use, neither of them could refrain any longer and they burst out laughing.

'We shouldn't,' Rosina said eventually.

'I know,' Josephine replied. 'But it's hard to be sympathetic, isn't it? I mean, she can be such a little madam.'

'She'll be furious with Tom.'

'She is. And it's not like him to forget an order from Sadie. But I think Henry has been having some trouble with the owner of the theatre. He came to see the show last night and Charlie heard raised voices. Tom had to stay with Henry and try and sort something out. Charlie told me this morning after rehearsal.'

The room darkened as the rain grew heavier and Josephine remarked gloomily that they would have a poor house tonight. 'They won't want to come out in the rain,' she said. 'And we don't want to end up looking like Sadie. We'd better put our mackintoshes and galoshes on.'

The news, when they got to the theatre, was bad. Henry held a conference on stage. Sadie had developed a feverish cold and was barely able to talk, let alone sing. The cast in the shorter sketches could be juggled around, with some people playing two parts, but Sadie was vital to the longer play, *The Street Singer*.

'I could take the part,' Monica said. 'I know all the songs.'

Sadie, wrapped in at least two shawls, and sitting shivering on a chair, shot her a scornful look. 'It isn't a matter of just knowing the words,' she croaked.

'That's true, my dear,' Priscilla Greyling said, and Rosina imagined that, fond mother as she was, she had no wish to see her daughter embarrassed as she surely would be if she attempted a singing role.

Henry looked grave. 'Gertrude, I want you to take the part of the housemaid; Charlie has offered to play the part of the invalid in the Bath chair so long as he doesn't have to say anything. Tom will rewrite it so that the maid has the lines.'

'Now, Sadie, my dear, I have called a cab for you and I want you to go back to the lodging house and go to bed. You must ask Mrs Naylor to send you up some hot milk with two tablespoons of whisky in it. And I pray you will get better as soon as you can. We need you.'

Sadie looked awful. Her face was pasty and her nose was red. She rose and adopted a brave long-suffering pose. 'Never fear,' she croaked. 'Sadie Sutton will not let you down.'

When she had gone Henry Greyling got back to the business in hand. 'None of the gentlemen's parts is affected,' he said. 'Our main problem is who is to play the street singer.' He looked around the company. 'Josephine, I think you will have to tackle it.'

'If you had asked me that yesterday I would have said, yes please. But that was before I heard Rosina singing when she thought she was alone in her room. You must give the part to her.'

'Rosina?' Henry Greyling said.

'Yes, Rosina. And I'll gladly take the part of the burglar's wife. You know me – I'm an all-round sort of performer. I can tackle anything.'

'Well – I don't know, I mean . . .'

'Please, Mr Greyling. Just ask her to sing.'

Tom had been standing a little apart. Now he came forward. 'Will you sing for us? "The Doll Song"?'

Rosina nodded.

'Mervyn,' Tom called for the pianist to take his place at the piano. 'You've got the music.'

'Wait a moment,' Josephine said. 'Shouldn't Rosina have the doll?'

The props mistress hurried forward with the doll that Sadic used in her performance. Rosina felt that what was about to happen was unreal. But a momentum had begun; an impelling force or strength that was carrying her forward to an unknown place. She only knew there was no going back. Everyone cleared the stage and she was left alone. Mervyn called up from the orchestra pit, asking if she was ready. She nodded and he began to play the introduction.

She was tense rather than nervous, but she soon responded to the dear, familiar music, which struck a deep chord within her. She began.

> 'I once had a sweet little doll, dears,
> The prettiest doll in the world . . .'

The song was simple, a song for the nursery, and the words and the music seemed to transport her to a time, deeply buried in her unconscious mind, when she had been supremely happy. She could not explain that feeling but she knew the simple little song was part of her and always would be.

'Yet for old sakes' sake, she is still, dears,
The prettiest doll in the world.'

When the last words were sung there was total silence. She peered out into the auditorium worriedly. She knew this was only a rehearsal but surely someone should have clapped or said, 'Well done.'

'Was I that bad?' she asked no one in particular.

She became aware of someone hurrying across the stage to join her.

'No, you weren't bad, you were wonderful,' Tom said. 'They are quiet because for once in their lives they don't know what to say. They have just witnessed true talent. Why didn't you tell us you could sing like that?'

'Like what?'

'No false modesty, please, Rosina. You must know how good you are.'

She shook her head. 'No, actually I don't.'

'Well I should have realized who you were the moment I saw you. You're the young woman who sang with Daisy Belle, aren't you? The young woman in the audience?'

While he was speaking the others had come back on to the stage. They crowded round her and every one of them congratulated her, even Monica.

'Rosina,' Josephine said, 'you actually made me cry.'

'Without a doubt you must take the part of the street singer,' Henry Greyling said. 'If I'd had the sense to ask you to sing at your audition you would have had the part in the first place. I didn't recognize you either, Rosina, but now I remember that night very well. The audience will love you!'

That night the audience was small, as Josephine had predicted. They came in out of the rain, dripping and subdued. The theatre was underheated as usual, and they sat there miserable and damp until the curtain went up and the entertainment began. The Greyling Players worked as hard as they ever had to dispel the apathy and eventually the audience began to respond to the jokes and join in with the regular banter. Rosina knew that the usual magic had begun to cast its spell.

And Henry was right. When *The Street Singer* came to an end the audience went wild. They called for Rosina time and again, and the rest of the cast were generous enough to enjoy her triumph.

'My dear, you are a star!' Josephine said.

'And we've found you in the nick of time,' Henry Greyling added.

Rosina wasn't quite sure what he meant by that and she would have liked to ask someone, but they were all too excited to talk sense. Henry decided to treat them to supper and sent Charlie to the fish-and-chip shop just a few streets away. The lad from the shop helped the stage doorkeeper to bring the order back and they all sat on the stage eating the battered cod and chips directly from the newspaper.

Mrs Greyling produced a bottle each of porter and stout and began to share them out. Tom had a bottle of champagne for Rosina.

'Where did you get it?' she asked him as he popped the cork.

He had taken her hands and drawn her to the side of the stage, away from the crowd. 'At the public house on the corner,' he said. 'I don't think it's a good champagne but it's all they had. And they lent me these two glasses.'

'But what about the others? Those bottles of Mrs Greyling's didn't go far.'

'I've asked for a crate of pale ale and half a dozen bottles of wine to be sent in – ah, here it comes. But the champagne is just for you and me.'

He had put his cloak on to go to the public house and there was a soft sheen of rain on the black material. Raindrops glistened in his dark hair. Rosina, still in the ragged dress that was her costume, could hardly speak. She was remembering the moment at the end of the play when Tom, as the clever young policeman, had taken her in his arms and they had sung a duet together, 'Love's old sweet song . . .'

They had not had a chance to rehearse and she had looked into his eyes throughout so that she could take the lead from him. And after they had sung the final words:

> Still to us at twilight comes love's old song
> Comes love's own sweet song

she had collapsed against him trembling, weak with relief, and he had held her close. 'Well, done,' he had murmured. 'Well done, Rosina, my darling.'

She had not attached any particular significance to his words. Everyone in the theatre called each other 'dearie' or 'darling'. And the embrace had been all too short, for the audience had erupted in thunderous applause and the exuberant cast had taken bow after bow.

But now, as he poured the champagne, he was looking into her eyes, not concentrating on what he was doing, until the glass frothed and overflowed. He laughed and handed it to her, then poured some for himself.

'What shall we drink to?' he said.

'To the Greyling Players?'

'Yes, of course, to dear old Henry who lets me write my plays and choose my parts, and to all our friends gathered here tonight who put up with me.' He turned and raised his glass in the direction of the others. 'But most of all we should drink to us. To you and me, Rosina.'

He smiled at her as they clinked glasses and when she raised her glass to her lips and drank, she did not know which was the most exhilarating – the sparkling wine or the look in his eyes.

The next day was Sunday, and Rosina rose early to find a sleepy Billy setting the table in the dining room.

'Nothing's ready yet,' she said when she saw Rosina. 'Old Ma Naylor's still stirring the porridge. But I could make you some toast if you're in a hurry.'

'Toast would be lovely,' Rosina said. 'But I'm not in any particular hurry. So you can finish what you're doing first.'

'You off to church?' Billy asked when she brought Rosina her toast and a pot of coffee.

'No, I should go, I suppose, but I just thought I'd go for a walk.'

'Not much to see round here,' Billy said. 'Unless you gan along to the park.'

Rosina was too unsettled to do much more than nibble at her toast and Billy kept shooting her disapproving looks. Finally she spoke. 'Lissen, if you're not going to make a proper meal of that, can I hev it?'

'Of course.'

Billy sat next to her, perching on the edge of the chair like a bird ready to take flight. She ladled honey on to the toast and spread it thick.

'Do you want some coffee?' Rosina asked. 'You can use my cup – turn it round and sip from the other side.'

'Mm,' Billy nodded, and Rosina poured a fresh cup of coffee for her.

'Doesn't Mrs Naylor feed you properly?' she asked.

'Whey-aye, I've telt yer. She's feeding me up but I didn't hev breakfast this morning.'

'Why not?'

The girl looked at her over the rim of the cup. 'Promise you won't tell.'

'I promise.'

'I gets up long before Mrs Naylor in the mornings and gets the range going, start boiling the water and the like. She leaves bread and dripping out for me so's I can make me own breakfast . . .' She paused.

'And this morning?' Rosina prompted. 'Did she forget?'

'Nah, it's not that. It's just that I never eats it because I give it to me little sister.'

'Your sister? Does she work here too?'

'Nah. She's only five years old. But she comes to the back door each morning and I gives her whatever I can to take home for her and the other bairns. I telt yer, Mrs Naylor is very good about the leftovers and I send them home too, as much as I can.'

'So that's why you never put any weight on?'

'Mebbes.'

'Couldn't you just ask Mrs Naylor for more – for bigger helpings?'

'Me mam says I mustn't appear greedy or I might lose me position and I like it here.'

Rosina was perplexed. She didn't know what to say.

'Now divven't worry about me, Miss Rosina. I gets plenty dinner and I eats it in the kitchen with Mrs Naylor watching to see every scrap goes down. She's real kind. And the lodgers are good to me too. Like you now, letting me hev your toast. And as for Mr Carey –' the girl's eyes suddenly shone – 'Mr Carey brings me pastries from the coffee shop and even Miss Sadie lets me hev the bonbons she doesn't care for before she throws the box away. Now I must get on. That lot'll be down for breakfast soon and they'll be ravenous as usual.'

Rosina could hear sounds from above as the rest of the Greyling Players came to life and began to get dressed. She wondered if the mood of enthusiasm would have lasted and whether there would be a few sore heads after the beer and the wine they had downed so cheerfully. But she didn't intend to stay and find out.

I should go to church, she thought, as Billy had suggested. It would be a short walk to the church on Heaton Road where she could join the Bartlett family in prayer. She wondered if Joanne would expect her too, but nothing had been said when she visited the theatre.

She felt slightly guilty as she set off instead in the opposite direction. At first she walked down Shields Road towards Byker Bridge, but then turned left into one of the steep cobbled roads that led down to the river. The cobbles and the pavement were still wet from the rains of the day before. Usually the hammering from the shipyards could be heard even on Shields Road, but today was Sabbath quiet. However, the wind was blowing up from the river and these respectable working men's homes could not escape the smell from the bone yard.

Here and there a window or a door was open and the smells of breakfast frying or the Sunday roast beginning to cook wafted out to mingle with the odour of the boiled carcasses. Rosina had to force herself to go on. She had been told that some of the most wretched slums in the city were down by the Ouseburn, a small river that ran into the Tyne, and that area was only a short walk away. Could it be that that was where she had lived as a child? She knew that she had been far too young for any memory to linger but she felt she had to go there.

The further down the long, steeply slanting street Rosina went, the less well cared for were the houses. The doorsteps were unscrubbed, the door knobs unpolished, and at some of the windows old sacks hung instead of curtains. And then, with the river in sight, she became aware of footsteps behind her. Not the footsteps of an adult but the small pattering sounds that children make. But many children. She turned to look and saw a silent host, boys and girls, some carrying even smaller children, emerging from houses and alleyways and all making towards a dirty stretch of sludgy, rubbish-strewn water that must be the Ouseburn.

Most of them were ragged. At least half of them had no shoes. They had a pleased excited look about them but they hardly spoke. They were all intent on getting somewhere but, for the life of her, Rosina could not make out where. She stood still and let the tide of children flow round and past her. And, curiously she began to follow them.

At the bottom of the street they turned and made towards a large unattractive red-brick building that looked like a factory of some sort. A man and a woman, respectably clothed, stood at each side of a large open door and directed the children inside. 'That's right,' she heard the woman say, 'down the stairs to the basement but mind you don't push and shove. We don't want any accidents.'

All kinds of horrors went through Rosina's mind. Why were these children being ushered into this grim-looking building? What was going to happen to them? Concern drew her on and eventually, the woman noticed her. She looked Rosina up and down and smiled briefly.

'Have you come to help?' she asked.

Rosina stared blankly.

'There's no need to be nervous.' The woman's features softened. 'They won't bite you, you know. They are just children, no matter how poor and brutal some of their lives are.'

'I'm afraid I don't know what you're talking about. But tell me, please, what are you going to do to the children?'

'Feed them, of course. I can see that you don't live around here and I thought you must have answered the call for volunteers to help at the breakfast.'

'No, I'm sorry, I know nothing about it.'

'We advertised in the *Daily Chronicle*. Do you know we had as many as one hundred and fifty children here last week and there's only half a dozen of us to make sure they each get a full bowl of porridge and a glass of milk. And then there's the washing up.'

'I'll help,' Rosina said. 'I may not be able to come every week but I'll get here whenever I can.'

'Good. What's your name?'

'Rosina.'

'I'm Mrs Bain. Come along then, I'll find you a pinafore.'

Over the next two hours Rosina learned that the breakfasts were funded by local businessmen, societies, and private individuals. The owner of the factory allowed his basement to be used on Sunday mornings and had the churns of milk delivered. A group of bakers provided the bread, and sometimes a few crates of fresh oranges were sent along by some greengrocers in the Grainger Market.

She saw how grateful the children were for the simple meal and raged inwardly that it should be so.

Mrs Bain must have read her mind. 'No bairn should have to live like this,' she said as she sent her to the table with a large jug of milk. 'When I think of my own children in our warm, clean house with good clothes and shoes and a full larder, it fair breaks my heart.'

'What will happen to these children?' Rosina asked when she watched them scraping the last drop of porridge from their bowls.

'They'll come along next week for another breakfast, and people like me and the good folk you met in the kitchen will do whatever we can.'

'But that won't be enough, will it?'

'No, my dear. It will never be enough.'

Rosina looked at the children, pale-faced and hollow-eyed, and tried to imagine that she was one of them. She thought with horror of what her life might have been like if Maud Fidler had not found her and taken her to Ravenshill.

How fortunate I have been, she thought. No matter what has happened since, I have been spared a life like this.

Dear Jack,

Why don't you answer my letters? Where are you now? In France with Daisy? I've tried everywhere I know of, including the theatres where Daisy has been performing. I follow her progress in the newspapers. You have made her a great star. Have you forgotten how much you owe to me? I think you have because otherwise you would not treat me like this.

I hate living in this poky little house after what I have been used to at Ravenshill. I have to share a bathroom and a kitchen, and the other tenants are not the sort of people I have ever had to mix with before. Now you have stopped sending me money I don't know how long my savings will last.

You know I have always loved you and looked out for you ever since our dear mother died. Now you are rich is it too much to ask that you look after me?

I'm frightened, Jack. I don't want to live alone.

Sometimes I think I'm being punished. You know what for. I pray the Lord will forgive me.

Your loving sister,
Maud

Chapter Nineteen

On Monday morning Rosina, Josephine and Gertrude were hurrying to the theatre for an early rehearsal when a ragged urchin thrust leaflets into their hands. Gertrude didn't even look at hers. She crumpled it up and threw it after him.

'Whatever they're selling I don't want one,' she said. 'That same cheeky little beggar gave me a brochure for Madame Eglantine's Beauty Masks last week and when I asked him if he thought I needed one he said, "Not half, missus."'

'No, it's nothing like that.' Josephine had stopped where she was to read it. She sounded excited. 'Look – it's for the Greyling Players – us!'

Rosina looked at the leaflet and felt faint.

'What's the matter?' Gertrude asked. 'You've gone pale.' She came and looked over Rosina's shoulder. 'My, my,' she said, 'the old devil has been quick off the mark. He must have got the printer to open up on Sunday.'

'But it's wonderful,' Josephine said. 'And so clever of him. This should bring the audiences in.'

Rosina stared at the leaflet wordlessly.

'Say something!' Josephine said at last. 'Aren't you pleased?'

'I don't know.'

'Well, you jolly well ought to be.' Josephine began to

read the words out loud as Rosina stared down at the bold letters:

ROSINA LEE, the girl who sang with DAISY BELLE,
will be appearing twice nightly at THE RABY in
TOM CAREY'S sparkling new play,
THE STREET SINGER.
Come along and bring all the family to see
a GRAND show!

Rosina folded the leaflet and put it in her pocket. She would think about this later.

She was about to turn and go towards the back lane but Josephine pulled her further up the street.

'Where are we going?' Rosina asked.

'Look!' They had reached the front doors of the theatre.

Everything seemed as before. The well-trodden steps that dipped in the centre, the double half-glassed doors that lacked varnish.

'Look at what?' Rosina asked.

Josephine pointed to the glass cases at each side of the doors, which held the playbills. 'I thought so,' she said. 'Dear old Henry has had new posters done.'

The posters were pretty much like the leaflets, but they also had a sketch of a sweetly pretty ragged girl holding her hands out as if she were singing a song. Notes of music with wings flew around her head and a little bird trilled in the top corner.

'If the audience expect me to look like that, they'll be disappointed,' Rosina said.

Josephine studied the drawing, looked at Rosina and then back at the poster. 'Yes, I suppose they will, but they'll have to make do with you as you are,' she said, and then burst into laughter at Rosina's expression. 'I'm joking!' she said.

The three of them hurried around to the stage door and arrived on stage to find everyone in the highest spirits.

'Thank you for coming in early,' Henry said. 'You all did very well when we had to change parts around, but now I'd like to go over the finer points. Oh, and Tom has written a new scene for *The Street Singer*. Don't worry, Rosina, there aren't many more words to learn, just two new songs, and Mervyn will go over them with you in the rehearsal room after we've had a quick walk-through.'

The first scene had barely started when a hoarse voice rang out. 'I see you are doing very well without me.' It was Sadie.

Ill though she undoubtedly was, she made a dramatic entrance.

'Ah — er — Sadie,' Henry said. 'We weren't expecting you.'

'That's obvious.' She began to cough pathetically. Monica Greyling rushed towards her.

'Sadie, dear,' Henry's daughter said. 'You're not well. You shouldn't be here.'

'I couldn't let you down, could I?'

'Yes, and it's brave of you to come.' Priscilla Greyling hurried over to comfort her. 'But it's too soon. You will damage your vocal cords. You should be tucked up in bed with a warm drink.'

'That's what you all want, isn't it?' Sadie retorted.

'I don't understand.'

'You want me to stay away from the theatre so that you can steal my part and give it to this — this interloping greenhorn.'

'Sadie, dear, it isn't like that at all,' Priscilla said. 'You were ill, someone had to take your place — you know the show must always go on – and Rosina was the best person to stand in for you.'

'Is that what she's doing?'

'I don't understand.'

'Is Rosina merely standing in for me?'

'Well . . .' Priscilla Greyling glanced uneasily at her husband.

'Because if that's so, what is the meaning of this?' Sadie thrust one of the pamphlets into Mrs Greyling's hands. 'Why has Mr Greyling gone to the trouble and the expense of having all these leaflets printed – and the posters too – if Rosina is merely standing in until I am better?'

Henry Greyling stepped forward. 'Sadie, I'm sorry you are upset but we couldn't know how long you were going to be ill. You know very well that we have not been doing well lately – nobody's fault I hasten to add! The owner of the theatre has been getting restless. We are not making much profit for him. He is even contemplating closing the theatre. So when we heard Rosina sing and realized who she was—'

'Oh, yes, the little nobody who pushed herself forward that night and had the audacity to sing with Daisy Belle!'

Henry ignored her remark and continued, 'Whatever you think, we knew we must make the most of the opportunity to bring the audiences in again.'

'And Rosina will "stand in", as you put it, while I am ill and cannot sing?'

'Er . . . yes. That's it.'

'I see.' Sadie was dangerously calm. 'And then will I get my leading role back?'

Henry was acutely uncomfortable. 'Well, I'm – er – not sure. I mean, Rosina is very good and—'

'No, Sadie, you won't be playing the part of the street

singer again. At least not while Rosina is part of this company.' Tom's voice carried clearly across the stage and everyone turned to see him walking into the circle of players.

Sadie stared at him, white-faced and furious. 'You wrote the play for *me*!' she said.

'I wrote the part for the best singer in the company.'

'And that's me!'

Tom remained silent and he looked at her gravely as if he were considering what to say. 'You must admit that is not so at the moment.'

'But when I have recovered?' she challenged.

'The play's the thing,' Tom said. 'You are a true performer. You know that.'

'So Rosina is to keep this part?'

'Henry and I think it would be for the best.'

'And what do you plan that I should do?'

'Play the burglar's wife, of course. It's a marvellous part for an actress as accomplished as you are.'

'But it's not the leading role.'

Nobody spoke and Sadie drew herself up and then turned and left the stage. Rosina was torn between feeling pleased that she was being given a chance to sing, and feeling sorry for Sadie. She acknowledged that she would have felt sorrier for her if she hadn't been so antagonistic right from the start.

Everyone was subdued for a while after that but soon the usual camaraderie took hold of them and they worked long and hard until they got things right.

That evening the audience was bigger. Just before curtain-up, Josephine went on stage and, parting the curtains a fraction, she peered out into the auditorium. When she came back to join the others waiting in the wings her eyes were shining.

'Word has got around already,' she said. 'It's very nearly a full house.'

A queue began to form outside the theatre even before the first house was over. Every seat was taken for the second house.

The cast went home in a state of high exhilaration but it was not the shared excitement that kept Rosina awake for most of the night. It was the memory of being held in Tom's arms at the end of the play. She wondered if he had felt her trembling and if his senses had been as stirred as hers were. Then she remembered what he had said when he had poured the champagne.

'. . . *most of all we should drink to us. To you and me, Rosina . . .*'

Since then he had said nothing remotely personal to her and she was beginning to believe that his words had been prompted by his pleasure in finding someone whom he believed could do justice to his play. It was their theatrical future that he was drinking to, nothing more.

Rosina decided she must concentrate on her new career and not be distracted by personal feelings.

For a short while the players enjoyed a degree of success. Sitting in the stalls one day while they watched Mrs Greyling rehearse a new dramatic monologue, Josephine whispered to Rosina that she thought the whole cast was performing better. 'And that's because of you,' she added.

'How can it be? I'm still learning the craft.'

'Of course you are. And that's part of it. Most of us enjoy helping you – not that you need much help, but it's your success that lifts everyone's spirits. You are a generous performer, Rosina. You don't play all those little tricks to upstage people and get attention like Sadie does.'

As she said this they heard a rustle behind them. They turned and saw a shadowy figure a few rows back. The figure rose and made towards the exit at the back of the stalls. When the light above the door shone down on impossibly yellow hair they realized it was Sadie.

'Oh dear, do you think she heard?' Josephine asked.

Rosina's answer was subdued. 'I'm afraid she probably did.'

The Greyling Players had barely got used to their renewed success when their engagement at the Raby came to an abrupt end. They arrived at the theatre one morning to see the stagehands tearing down the sets and tossing props into open chests.

'A department store!' Henry Greyling explained in despair. 'The theatre is to become an extension of the department store next door.' He explained that the owner of the theatre had been threatening to close it for some time because of falling attendances and by the time the company had begun to revive it was too late; he had made arrangements to sell the building and couldn't withdraw from the contract.

'I am afraid he wants us out as soon as possible,' Henry said. 'You must clear your dressing rooms of personal possessions. Then, if you wait in the theatre, I will give you any wages that are owing to you. I am afraid I just don't know what is going to happen to us all. This ...' he paused and looked genuinely heartbroken, '... this may be goodbye!'

Everyone gathered his or her belongings together and waited despondently on the stage. Rosina wondered if her career in the theatre was over already. If so, it had been a spectacularly short one. As they sat there without talking she looked around and realized that she had not seen Tom that morning. Had he left the company already?

No doubt he was one of the performers who would not find it difficult to join another company. Not only because he was a good actor but also because of his playwriting skills. Even though she had not known him long she knew how ambitious he was. Did he care what happened to the rest of them?

But when Henry Greyling returned Tom was with him and they both looked pleased and relieved.

'Tom has saved our bacon,' Henry declared. 'He has been out and about and discovered a new opening for us.' Immediately the air of dejection lifted a little. 'The leading lady of the Sunny Seasiders has run off with a brawny stagehand, her husband, the comedy lead, has taken off after her and the company has collapsed. They want us down at Whitley-by-the-Sea immediately,' he told them.

In the joyous commotion that followed Mr Greyling's announcement, Tom explained to the cast that they would be taking over for the rest of the summer season.

'But there's very little of the season left,' someone called out.

'I know,' Tom replied. 'So Henry thinks it better to stay in our present lodging house and get the train down to the coast each day – don't worry, Henry will pay the fares. Meanwhile this will give us time to find some new engagement.'

There was only one dissenting voice. Rosina overheard Sadie complaining to Monica that she never would have thought she would be one of those end-of-the-pier performers. 'Nevertheless, we shall all do our best, I'm sure,' she said when she saw Tom was looking at her and she gave him a brilliant smile.

Henry looked troubled as he called for quiet. 'There's only one fly in the ointment,' he said. 'The manager expects three performances every day. A matinée, and then the first and second houses. For the holiday-makers, you know. Our present programme is too long. I'll have to cut it.'

The cast exchanged worried looks.

'But don't worry, Tom has agreed to take on the task. He'll make sure that every one of you is treated fairly. However, the dramatic recitations will have to go, my dear.' He couldn't quite bring himself to meet his wife's eyes. 'Tom thinks they're not quite the thing for the seaside holiday crowd.'

Tom rescued him. 'You will all have less to do but you will all be featured. That means performing two, possibly three, of our sketches and we'll end the programme with *The Street Singer*. I'm sorry, Rosina, that will be your only part.'

Rosina didn't mind at all. How could she? The part of the street singer had already developed into something much greater than it had been. She was just grateful that her days as a member of the acting profession were not yet numbered.

The theatre wasn't at the end of the pier, as Sadie had suggested, for the simple reason that Whitley-by-the-Sea didn't have a pier. Instead it was on the lower promenade under the shelter of the cliffs, and yet exposed to the winds from the sea.

But in the days that followed, Rosina enjoyed herself so much that she forgot that it was only a short engagement. Then all too soon the weather broke, the beaches were left deserted and Rosina began to appreciate how precarious the life of an entertainer could be.

Henry became gloomy again. 'There goes our audience,' he said when the boarding houses began to empty and holiday-makers made their way to the station in droves.

But to everyone's surprise and delight, another sort of audience began to fill the seats. Word had got round that it was a good show and people began to come down from Newcastle and all the stations on the way. Rosina often found herself travelling to the coast on the same train as excited theatregoers, determined to get there early and queue for a good seat.

One day she had been to the Bartletts' for lunch with Joanne. It had rained all morning and Rosina lingered, hoping the rain would stop. When it became clear that it wouldn't, Joanne lent her an umbrella and she ran to the station, only to find that the train was packed. The guard refused to allow any more standing passengers so she had to wait for the next one.

As she ran along the promenade at Whitley, a gust of wind tore the umbrella from her hands and sent it whirling out across the sea. By the time she entered the dressing room she was already damp with the rain. Only Sadie was in there. The other women were on stage in one of the sketches.

Sadie was in costume as the burglar's wife and applying her make-up. She looked up when the door opened and scowled at Rosina's reflection.

'Think you can turn up late, now, do you? Just because they like the little songs you sing?'

Sadie herself was the worst timekeeper in the troupe, but Rosina didn't want to get into an argument, not with so little time to get ready. Her costume was simple: a ragged dress – which still managed to look fetching – and a shawl. Rosina went behind the screen, divested herself of her coat and dress and dabbed at her face and hair with a towel. Then, without looking, stretched a hand out behind her to take her costume from the rail. Her hand met the cold wall. The rail wasn't there.

'Where on earth . . . ?' Rosina began.

'Looking for the dress rail? I pushed it along a bit to give more room,' Sadie said.

Rosina looked out from behind the screen and saw that Sadie must have been waiting for this moment. She was staring into the mirror and could see everything that happened in the room behind her. Rosina was not surprised. Sadie had found many little ways to make her life difficult, such as 'accidentally' knocking her make-up off the dressing table so that the powder scattered all over the floor and 'mislaying' the pages of a new bit of dialogue Tom wanted to introduce, then swearing that she had handed them to Rosina as requested.

Moving the clothes was nothing compared to Sadie's previous tricks. So, irritated but determined not to show it, Rosina pushed the screen aside and found the rail just a little further along. It was under the open window. The window was high in the wall and it was small but quite big enough to let in the rain. Rosina's costume was soaking wet.

'Oh dear,' Sadie said. 'You look like a drowned rat already, and you'll catch your death if you put those clothes on. You might even lose your voice.'

'I imagine that was your intention,' Rosina said coolly. 'You must have stood on a chair to reach the window.'

'How could you think such a thing?' Sadie feigned wounded feelings. 'But then I'm not surprised. You take every opportunity to hurt me, don't you?'

Rosina was rendered speechless by this blatant reversal of their roles.

'But you'll have to get a move on,' Sadie said. 'You don't want to miss your entrance, do you?'

Rosina did not want an argument just before she went on stage. She decided to let the matter drop and began to pull on the dress. She wore the wet clothes; it was all she could do. But she soon discovered that Sadie hadn't finished with her. During one of the pieces of knockabout comedy when the street singer was singing to the young lovers and the burglar's wife was dodging the policeman, Sadie deliberately bumped into her and when Rosina backed away she realized too late that Sadie had planted a foot deliberately on a trailing piece of ragged hem.

Rosina began to fall, but if Sadie had intended to hurt her or make her look foolish, the plan went wrong. Tom, seeing what had happened, sidestepped quickly and caught Rosina in his arms. He did it with such a flourish that the audience thought it was deliberate, and cheered and applauded as the policeman took the opportunity to hold her a little longer than was necessary and gaze into her eyes.

His quick thinking made it look as though it was part of the play and Rosina soon realized what he was doing and reacted accordingly. But even so, she found it difficult to remember she was acting. She had schooled herself to control her emotions when he held her in his arms at the end of the play. But this wasn't part of the plot, this hadn't been rehearsed, and looking into his eyes she imagined that she saw shock there. It was as if he had suddenly become aware of the electricity that flowed between them.

After the final curtain, Henry praised Tom for his quick action in catching Rosina. Sadie swore that it had been an accident and apologized sweetly. 'Poor Rosina,' she said, 'you were still in a tizzy after arriving late, no doubt, and you just didn't move as quickly as you usually do. Then of course you've had to wear that wet dress. I wish I'd realized that you'd left it so carelessly under the open window. I would have moved it for you.'

Rosina bit her lip and kept her own counsel. She didn't want to argue in front of the cast. But she was amazed that some of them, particularly Sadie's old friend Monica, seemed to believe every word Sadie uttered. Sadie was as good an actress offstage as on.

In the intervals between the performances there was no

time for Rosina to get her costume dry, and even if there had been there was no means to do it. It was a chilly, draughty little theatre, even at the height of summer. Some days the wind blew in across the sea straight from the Russian Steppes. And now, at the cold, dismal end of the season, the conditions were worse than ever.

Josephine insisted that Rosina take the costume off between shows and she even hunted through the wardrobe – a large old wicker basket – for some other dress that would do.

'I could have sworn we had a beggar girl's dress,' she said, 'but it's not here and the only spare frock is far too glamorous. Priscilla would have a fit if I dirtied it up.'

'It doesn't matter,' Rosina told her. 'I'll manage. And I'll take the dress back with me tonight and get Billy to dry it on the pulley in the kitchen.'

Sadie, who had been listening, wrinkled her nose. 'Oh, dear,' she said, 'tomorrow you'll smell of boiled beef and fried haddock, no doubt. But I suppose we'll all have to put up with that.'

Rosina thought of telling Josephine what had really happened – that Sadie had undoubtedly opened the window and placed the costume rail underneath it so that the dress would get wet – but she decided not to. It would only cause trouble and she didn't want to give any of the others cause to think she was difficult, that she was becoming a prima donna.

At the end of the evening Henry asked them all to come back on stage. He struck a dramatic pose. 'I have something to tell you. Some good news. Our fame has spread. A famous theatrical impresario has heard of our little show and is planning a visit. I received a letter from him this morning.'

'Why didn't you tell us before curtain up?' Arthur Barnfather asked.

'I wanted to discuss the plans with Tom first.'

'The plans?'

'Just a few adjustments to the programme. We'll have an extra rehearsal in the morning, then I'll be depending on you to give the best performances of your lives.'

Back in the lodging house the atmosphere was fizzing with excitement. Rosina's head was whirling as she listened to the conversation.

'I wonder who it can be?' Gertrude said.

'Someone from London?'

'Paris?'

'New York?'

Everyone laughed at the very idea and Arthur Barnfather suggested more practically, 'More likely someone from the Northern Circuit. With any luck we'll be setting off on a tour of Barnsley, Birkenhead, Barrow, Birmingham . . .'

'Oh, do be quiet, Arthur!'

'Well, wherever it is, I wish you all luck, because I'm not coming,' Gertrude said. 'I think it's time I retired.'

'To a nice little house with Charlie!'

They all laughed and to Rosina it seemed that their voices were coming and going as if caught on a breeze and blown back again. But then the laughter started whirling round the room and her head began to pound.

'Rosina . . . Rosina, can you hear me?' Someone had taken hold of her shoulders and was peering into her face. Josephine. 'You're shivering,' she said. 'I think you've caught a chill. Come along, I'll help you up to your room.'

Rosina allowed Josephine to take her upstairs and help her into bed.

'Now go to sleep. I'll come in to see how you are in the morning.' Josephine sounded worried.

'It's only a headache,' Rosina told her.

'I hope so, I really hope so.' Her friend went out and shut the door.

But it wasn't only a headache. Her breathing became ragged and her throat felt as though it was closing up. She had caught a cold and it was probably because she had spent all that time wearing those wet clothes. But she couldn't afford to have a cold. She had to be fit to sing in the show tomorrow. The impresario was coming to see the show and Henry was depending on everyone to do his or her best.

The worry of it made her feel even worse. She knew she must do something to help herself. Then, out of nowhere, a memory came to her of her comfortable room at Ravenshill and her mother comforting her one night when she had had a feverish cold. Geraldine ... my mother ... not my mother ... but I loved her and she loved me.

Scalding hot tears began to course down her cheeks as memories of her former life came flooding back. Her carefree childhood in a comfortable home so different from the decaying dwellings just a few streets away from where she was lying now. Had she really come from that poverty-racked world where even at midday the alleys were dark and where half-starved children survived as best they could? And had that been sufficient reason to make Adam abandon her?

But that didn't matter now, did it? Her old friend, the boy she thought she had loved, had proved inconstant and shallow. She was glad he had done what he had done even though it rankled that it was Amy he had deserted her for.

She knew now that she would never have been truly happy living the comfortable predictable life that Adam had planned for them. She realized that, apart from her childhood days with Geraldine, she had never been so happy and so alive as she was now with the Greyling Players; 'this sorry bunch of thespians', as Gertrude had laughingly referred to them.

Apart from Sadie, and Monica, whose loyalty lay with her friend, they had welcomed her and made her feel part of the troupe. The Greyling Players were like a family. And now when there was a chance that they could prosper and Henry had urged them to do their best for him, she was going to let them down. She mustn't do that. She had to be well enough to sing tomorrow.

The house was quiet when she pulled her robe on and crept down to the kitchen. Billy was asleep on her truckle bed by the fire but she awoke immediately.

'Whey's that?' she hissed. She sounded scared out of her wits.

'I'm sorry,' Rosina croaked. 'I didn't mean to wake you.'

She felt guilty. Poor Billy was up at five every morning to light the fires and couldn't go to bed until she had scrubbed the kitchen floor last thing at night when everyone else was asleep.

Billy had scrambled up from her bed. She slept in her petticoats and Rosina gazed at the pitiful stick-like limbs, and began to cry anew.

'What on earth's the matter with you?'

'I didn't mean to bother you. I've got a cold ... my throat ... I was going to warm myself some milk. I didn't think Mrs Naylor would mind.'

Billy took charge. 'Of course she won't mind. Sit in this chair by the fire – there's still some warmth in it. I'll warm the milk for you and put a dollop of honey in it, an' all. Unless you'd rather hev whisky? I know where she keeps a bottle – for medicinal purposes, she says. She swears a couple of teaspoons of the stuff in her tea every morning keeps her right as rain.'

Rosina allowed the girl to guide her to the chair by the range. Billy warmed some milk and said, 'Well? Whisky or honey?'

Rosina's head was swimming. 'I don't know.'

Billy poured the milk into a large cup, spooned some honey in and reached for a bottle on a shelf of the dresser. 'Belts and braces, as me da says.' And she measured two spoons of whisky into the milk as well.

Billy stoked up the fire as Rosina sipped the milk. 'You shouldn't hev come down the stairs like that, with no slippers on. You'll catch your death of cold.'

'I think I've already caught it,' Rosina said.

'Aye, I think you hev. Now drink up like a good lass.' When the cup was empty Billy helped her up from the chair. 'I'm going to see you back to bed and tuck you in like a bairn while you can still feel that milk doing you good.'

'I'm so sorry,' Rosina croaked as Billy led her upstairs.

'What are you sorry for?'

'For disturbing your sleep. You get little enough.' She began to sob.

'Whisht, now. You'll wake the house up.'

'I'm sorry.'

'Now divven't start that again. I'll come up and see how you are in the morning as soon as I get up.'

The warm milk and honey was soothing, and the whisky seemed to relax her. Soon it seemed as if her headache was loosening its grip on her temples. As she drifted off to sleep she felt both happier and hopeful. But as soon as she woke in the morning to find Billy standing over anxiously, her hopes were dashed.

'How are you?' the young maid asked.

Rosina opened her mouth but could only produce a croak.

'I'll fetch your pal,' Billy said.

A short while later she was back with Josephine, who had pulled on her robe and still had curling rags in her hair. Josephine was worried. She sat on the bed and held Rosina's hand.

Rosina opened her mouth and patted her own throat, gesturing with her hand that she couldn't get a word out.

'You've lost your voice,' Josephine said unnecessarily. She placed a hand on Rosina's temple. 'But you don't feel particularly feverish. I'll run out and buy some linctus for your throat.'

Rosina shook her head despairingly. She knew that however much linctus she took she would not get her voice back before the matinée.

'Oh dear,' someone said, and they both looked towards the door. Sadie stood there. She was also in her robe and looked unattractively pasty in the morning light.

'What do you want?' Josephine asked.

'I came to see how Rosina is.'

'Why?'

Sadie pretended hurt surprise. 'Don't take that tone of voice with me, Josephine. It should be obvious why I came. I was worried about Rosina.'

'Worried that she might be well enough to sing today?'

'I don't know what on earth you mean by that!'

'I think you do. It wasn't Rosina who left her costume under the window. I believe it was you, and you did it deliberately in an attempt to make her ill.'

'Why would I do such a wicked thing?'

'Partly because you've never forgiven her for taking over your part and partly because you knew there was an impresario coming to see the show.'

'How could I know that?'

'Your little friend Monica told you. And now please go away. Your nasty little plan has succeeded and you will probably have to sing today.'

Sadie didn't deny any of it. She simply smiled and said. 'Then it's a good job that I found the beggar girl costume in the wardrobe, isn't it? I shouldn't have to wear a dress that smelled of fried bacon and haddock. Do look after yourself, Rosina, dear. Now I must go and make sure I sing my best for Mr Hart.'

'Who is Mr Hart?' Josephine asked.

'Why Warren Hart, the impresario, of course,' Sadie said grandly.

'So Monica told you his name then?'

Sadie, realizing that she had given herself away, departed quickly.

Josephine got up, slammed the door shut behind her and said despairingly, 'Oh, Rosina, what are we going to do? You must get better quickly, not just for yourself but for all of us. You're the best thing that has happened to the Greyling Players for a long time and even with Tom to drive us on, I don't believe we can succeed without you. And as for tonight and Mr Hart . . .'

Rosina looked anguished.

'I'm sorry, that was selfish. Just concentrate on getting better.'

Rosina stayed in her room and tried to rest. Normally in good health, she had been able to fight the infection. Her fever had subsided but her throat was sore. She knew her only hope of getting back her voice was to rest it. Billy looked after her well, bringing her variously milk and honey, beef tea and a packet of lozenges that Mrs Naylor had in her medicine chest. As the hours passed she experimented hesitantly with her voice and as the silence turned into a croak and the croak into a passable imitation of normal speech she began to hope that her indisposition would be short-lived.

But if her physical condition was improving her mind was in torment. She couldn't stop thinking about what was happening at the theatre. The players were all capable of making the best of any circumstance and they would adapt easily to any new part required of them. And Sadie? Sadie would give her very best performance, delighted to have her old part back again. After all, Tom had written the part for her originally, and even though there was no love lost between them Rosina could understand Sadie's feelings of anger and jealousy.

In fact, she had never understood them so well than at this moment when exactly the same emotions were raging through her even more heatedly than her recent fever. She felt ashamed of herself and yet she accepted that it was all part and parcel of a career on the stage. No matter that Tom kept insisting that they were a team, they were all driven by ambition.

They all wanted good parts. They each wanted the limelight. As the shadows lengthened into evening, Rosina grew more and more restless and at last she could bear it no longer. She could not wait until Josephine came home to discover whether the Greyling Players had been tried and judged by Mr Warren Hart. She had to find out for herself what was happening at the theatre.

By the time the train drew up at the platform in Whitley-by-the Sea the station was already filling with theatregoers returning from their night's entertainment. They were a jolly crowd and as Rosina hurried towards the exit, she scanned their faces anxiously. What was she hoping to see, she wondered. Did she want them to be disappointed? Did she want to hear complaints about the fact that she had not been singing that night?

But everyone was cheerful and although half of her was glad for the Greyling Players, the other half of her, the prima donna half that she was chagrined to admit existed, couldn't help feeling aggrieved that she hadn't been missed.

The wind was cool as she hurried through the streets of the seaside town and she was glad that she had had the sense to wrap up warm. It was Billy, outraged that she was going out at all, who had stopped her in the hallway of the lodging house and implored her to wrap a shawl around herself on top of her coat.

'I don't even own a shawl,' she'd said, her voice almost back to normal.

'No problem,' the endearing child had replied. 'One of our old guests left a bonny fine one here. We had no address to forward it to. Mrs Naylor has kept it in case the lady ever returns for it.'

Billy had opened the seat lid of the hallstand and took out the shawl. It was good quality, probably cashmere, and Rosina had allowed Billy to wrap it round her and fasten it with the clasp that was still pinned to its folds. Now Rosina was glad of it; she eased it up to cover her head.

The moon shone intermittently through the wind-blown clouds, and gaslamps lit the promenade where there were still a few people walking – courting couples and lively young men. No one took any notice of Rosina. The caretaker was just about to lock the entrance doors of the theatre when Rosina slipped inside. He was about to stop her when she pushed her shawl back a little and he recognized her. He looked surprised but stood back to let her enter.

The ticket office was closed and the foyer was quiet but she could hear a murmur of voices coming from inside the auditorium. Usually the players hurried straight back to the lodgings for supper and the sleep they needed. But tonight they were still here. Rosina felt nervous tension coil inside her. She hesitated for a few seconds before entering the auditorium and then, just as she pushed the door open, she heard cheering.

Everyone was on stage, gathered around a small dark-haired man. Rosina kept to the shadows as she tried to make sense of the babble of voices. Only the working lights had been left on so she could not see all the faces, could not tell who was talking and who was quiet. But then, like an actor, the small man held up a hand and the others were all silent.

'So, Henry, I like this young feller's musical play very much and that must be part of your new programme.'

'It shall be,' Henry assured him.

'And Tom, the girl is a true star. Just made for the part of the street singer. There'll be no problems there?'

'No problem whatsoever,' Tom replied. 'And I wouldn't have it any other way.'

Rosina had to stop herself from crying out. She turned and fled through the foyer and rattled at the brass railings on the doors until the startled caretaker hurried forward and opened them for her.

The wind from the sea caught at her skirts and hurried her away from the theatre, up through the quiet streets towards the station. As she ran she remembered the night Tom had poured the champagne.

'. . . we should drink to us. To you and me, Rosina . . .'

But now she knew that she wasn't important to him at all. It was only the play – his play – and the success of the troupe that meant anything to him.

'I wouldn't have it any other way,' he'd said. Sadie had taken Mr Hart's fancy, and no matter what Tom might think he was not going to spoil the Players' chances of a profitable tour.

How foolish she had been to think that she might mean something to him. To have believed that he was as moved as she was when he held her in his arms. She should have realized what he was like when he dropped Sadie so readily. Sadie had been the best singer when he wrote the play but as he became convinced that Rosina was better he gave her the part without considering Sadie's feelings. So what could Rosina expect now? That he would tell her that the part of the burglar's wife was made for her?

The station was crowded and when the train drew up there was a crush of people making for every door. Rosina felt herself being pushed and shoved. Someone stood on her foot. Then just as she was about to climb up into a carriage she was grabbed from behind and pulled back on to the platform. She saw the door close with a slam and heard the guard shouting, 'Stand clear!' before he blew his whistle. There was a hiss of steam as the train started and Rosina began to cough and choke.

In a fury of frustration she turned to berate the person who had prevented her from boarding the train and found herself face to face with Tom.

'You . . .' she began but her voice failed her and she began to beat his chest with her balled fists.

Too easily he captured her hands, released them swiftly and pulled her into his arms.

A wag leaned out of a carriage window of the departing train and yelled, 'Nice work, bonny lad,' and there was a burst of laughter from his companions.

Tom smiled briefly in their direction and turned his head to look down at Rosina.

'Let me go,' she croaked.

'Not until you tell me what you're playing at. I was told

you were ill – too ill to go on stage tonight. I was frantic with worry.'

'Because of your precious play!'

'No, I was worried about you. I admit that I wanted Mr Hart to hear you sing but that was nothing compared to the fact that you might be really ill. If you had been I might have been obliged to throttle Sadie with my bare hands.'

'You knew what she did?' Rosina whispered.

'Josephine told me.'

The steam swirled and cleared and she looked up into his eyes. She saw nothing but concern. However, a voice inside her head reminded her that he was an actor. A vision of the first time she had seen him emerge from the stage door at the Grand invaded the already jumbled images in her head. 'You're wearing your cloak,' she whispered inconsequentially.

'My grandfather's cloak. It was the only thing he saved when the Lyceum burned down. He passed it to my father, who gave it to me when I joined my first company. It has always brought me luck. But you are ill and we mustn't stand here on this draughty platform.'

He took hold of a fold of his cloak and raised it to wrap around Rosina's shoulders. With his arm around her shoulders, and keeping her close inside the cloak, he led her to the waiting room where a cheerful fire burned in the hearth.

'And now let us sit and sort out this muddle.'

'Are we in a muddle?'

His smile was tender. 'I believe we are, my darling.'

Tom sat next to her and held her hand as he explained that he had been surprised to see her at the back of the auditorium earlier and then puzzled and alarmed when he saw her turn and run.

'I think the trouble is that you heard only half of it,' he said.

'But that was enough.'

'No it wasn't.'

'Mr Hart wants Sadie to play the part of the street singer.'

'No he doesn't.'

'But I heard him. He said that Sadie is a true star.'

Tom shook his head. 'I think Mr Hart's words were "the girl is a true star".'

'Well?'

'That girl is you.'

'But how can it be?'

'Mr Hart came to see the show last night.'

'But the letter . . .'

'His letter to Henry did not tell the complete truth. He likes to see a company or a person that he's interested in without giving them time to prepare for his first visit. Then to be fair he will go along again. He had already decided that you were true star material and that's why he asked me if there was a problem.'

'Because I wasn't there tonight,' she whispered.

'That's right. Rosina, my love, we are on course for success and stardom. And the most wonderful part of all this is that you and I will be together.'

'Is that important to you, Tom?'

'How can you doubt it? I love you. Haven't you realized that?'

'No . . . yes . . . I mean, I hoped you did.'

Tom reached for her hands. 'Because?' he asked softly.

'Because I love you.'

She could hear the fire crackling in the hearth, the tick of the clock on the wall, and the sound of footsteps on the platform outside as other travellers arrived to wait for the next train. Then everything diminished and vanished altogether as, despite her protestations that he would catch her cold, he drew her close and kissed her.

Jack,
Here I am in this wind-blown little town by the sea. The weather is bad for my bones. Don't you care?

I hope this letter reaches you. I never know whether you've received my letters or not because you never answer them. You made a big mistake. You shouldn't have got rid of baby Rose. Did you know she is now an actress? Not just an actress but a singer, and she has a fine voice, even better than her mother's. You could have had two great stars in your grasp and now you have only one who will grow old as we all do, and whose fame will be outmatched by her very own daughter.

Oh, I know you will tell me that Daisy is still young, still in her thirties, and there will be many years ahead for you to grow even richer. But what if a new star should rise higher in the firmament? The theatregoing public is fickle. You used to tell me that. What if people forget about Daisy Belle and transfer their affections to a younger, fresher singer?

I have seen her. I saw the posters outside the shabby little theatre on the lower promenade. Her name is Rosina Lee, and I knew it must be Rosina Leighton. I went to see the show. She is magnificent.

I even thought of waiting at the stage door and telling her the truth of who her mother is but I dared not do it for I am as guilty as you are. Kidnapping, child stealing, deceiving a loving mother – whatever it was we did, it would mean prison and I am too old to go to prison. I would not survive. Unless Rosina took pity on me. She might even reward me. As you should do.

Your sister,
Maud

Jack Fidler sat by the fire in the comfortable surroundings of his London club and stared at his sister's letter with a mixture of irritation and alarm. Was Maud losing her mind? Probably. But, more important, was she telling the truth? Was Rosina Lee really baby Rose? He would make it his business to find out more about the girl and keep a close eye on developments.

Of one thing he was sure: no one was a patch on Daisy. What did Maud know about the theatre? She was probably just trying to frighten him. Blackmail him. That was it. But whatever the truth of the matter, Daisy must never find out about this. Jack supposed he must answer this letter and start sending Maud a modest allowance again. Just enough to keep her sweet.

Angrily he crumpled up her letter and threw it into the fire.

Chapter Twenty

September 1900

September sunlight glistened on the rain-streaked windows of the railway carriage. Rosina leaned back and closed her eyes. The seats were padded and, although there were no armrests as in the first-class carriages, they were comfortable enough for her to be able to relax and sleep for a while if she wanted to.

The Greyling family — Henry, his wife, Priscilla and their daughter, Monica — were travelling first class. Mr Greyling had offered Rosina a first-class seat, saying that as the star of their little troupe it was only fitting. She had declined, saying that she would rather be with the rest of the company in second class. She was still uneasy with her position of the leading lady, and besides, she would not have liked to travel separately from Tom, who was sitting next to her. They were going back to Newcastle.

The last three years had been both exhilarating and exhausting with never a moment to relax between engagements. Every member of the players had profited financially. The only player to have left the cast was Gertrude, who after she had saved enough money to 'set us up', as she called it, had gone with everyone's good wishes to marry Charlie.

The programme they offered was varied as they tried out different dramatic and comic sketches and also individual acts. Rosina had become a versatile performer. But the one piece they performed most often was Tom's play *The Street Singer*. Sometimes they were booked on the strength of this act alone, Rosina's growing reputation as the street singer having preceded them.

Henry Greyling was grateful to Rosina for pulling in the audiences, as were most of the cast. Tom was delighted for her and pleased that his instinct about her had been proved right. Only Sadie Sutton remained antagonistic, although she had learned to conceal her hostility.

Now Sadie was sitting opposite Rosina and her *chypre* perfume, lavishly applied, was beginning to invade the whole carriage. Rosina would have liked to get up and open the small section of window that slid back, but she realized that the speed and direction of the train would ensure that the rain would slant in and land on those sitting on Sadie's side of the carriage.

If Sadie had been sitting there alone, Rosina thought mischievously, she might have opened the window anyway and felt no compunction if sooty rain had besmirched Sadie's artificially enhanced peaches-and-cream complexion. That would be no more than she deserved.

The repetitive rhythm of the wheels on the tracks, combined with the warmth emanating from the heaters under the seats, was soporific, and Rosina was soon lulled into a state of half-sleep. A state where she began to go over the events of the past three years. What a wonderful time she had had. She didn't think she would ever become blasé about the sheer excitement of opening a new show, facing a new audience and waiting for their response. Then the marvellous feelings of triumph and exhilaration if all went well.

Tom had been at her side throughout all of it. From the moment he had told her that he loved her they had become inseparable; their shared love of the theatre binding them together. But at first there had been doubts. One day after a long difficult rehearsal that went on until after midnight, Tom and Rosina had walked back to yet another lodging house together and he had suggested that instead of suffering the usual breakfast fare of porridge and kippers they should go out in the morning and find a little coffee shop.

'That's what you used to do with Sadie!' she said, shocking herself with her outburst.

They stopped in the quiet street, the lamplight above them shining through the leaves of a large tree and casting mysterious fluttering shadows on the pavement. Tom took hold of her shoulders and his eyes widened as he took in her mutinous expression.

'I beg your pardon?' he said.

'You used to take Sadie to a coffee shop for breakfast, didn't you?'

'Yes and no.'

She removed his hands from her shoulders one at a time and glared at him.

'I love it when you're angry,' he said.

'Don't be so bloody flippant. I'm serious.'

Rosina turned to walk away but he reached for her and pulled her back. 'I'm sorry. Yes, Sadie used to come with me to the coffee shop on Shields Road but I didn't take her. It was her idea, not mine. As you know, I never have enough time to work on my sketches and I started going along to the coffee shop with my pencil and my notebooks. I don't know why but I seemed to find inspiration there. Watching the passing scene through the windows, the other customers; they all gave me ideas. Then one day, Sadie followed me there. I could hardly send her packing so we had coffee and rolls together. And then . . . well, it became a sort of habit.'

'Poor you.'

'What do you mean, poor me?'

'What a trial it must have been having breakfast with an adoring Sadie.'

'Don't be sarcastic, Rosina. It doesn't suit you. And no, it wasn't a trial. Slightly irritating, yes, because the whole point of going there was to have some time to myself to get on with some writing. But Sadie soon caught on. She learned not to interrupt me. She would sit there and drink her coffee and behave herself, bless her.'

'Oh, bless her indeed!'

'Rosina, darling, please don't be jealous.'

'I'm not jealous.'

'I think you are. Indeed, I hope you are. But there's no need. Sadie was and still is a true professional. Her heart is in the theatre just as ours are. Furthermore, she could be good company and I used to like her a lot. And probably I would still like her if she hadn't revealed such a spiteful streak when she tried to hurt you.'

And there in the shadows, he had pulled her into his arms and kissed her and her doubts had melted away.

'Wake up, Rosina,' Tom said softly now. 'We're nearly there and your public awaits you.'

Rosina opened her eyes to see Tom smiling at her. 'What nonsense you talk,' she murmured softly as she responded to his smile.

'No, I'm being serious. I believe there's quite a crowd waiting in the Central Station.'

'But how is that possible?' She was aware that Sadie,

although pretending to gather her hand luggage together, as were the other members of the cast who shared their compartment, was listening to their conversation. 'Don't tease,' Rosina said.

'I'm not teasing. Henry sent an announcement ahead to the local newspapers. "Miss Rosina Lee returns to her native city in triumph!" I believe that's how it begins.'

'Well, they won't have printed that rubbish.'

'I'm pretty sure they will have done. You're a local girl who has made good. It's a gift for the newspapers — especially if it's already written out for them in decent, grammatical English.'

While he spoke the train was slowing down as it crossed the River Tyne by way of the High Level Bridge. A couple of minutes later it pulled in to the station and, with a great hiss of steam, came to a stop. When the steam cleared Rosina saw the crowds of people waiting on the platform. Their faces were eager as they peered through the windows of the train. Tom pulled the blind down quickly.

'Wait a moment.' He waited until everyone else had left the carriage and then he said, 'Keep them waiting a little longer. Then make an entrance.'

'Tom, I'll be leaving the train, not getting into it!'

'You know what I mean. Appear in the doorway — pause — look surprised — delighted — overwhelmed. Wave one gloved hand gracefully like Princess Alexandra does — remember, hold your head slightly to one side—'

'Stop! I'll never remember all this.'

'Yes, you will. Your dramatic instinct will take over. And only when they are shouting themselves hoarse are you to step down.'

Rosina suddenly felt apprehensive. 'I'll be crushed to death!'

'No you won't. Henry and I will be waiting directly in front of the door. We'll help you down and if necessary we'll carry you shoulder high through the crowds.'

'You've had this planned.'

'Of course. We couldn't be sure how many would turn out – but just listen to them.'

They both stood still and silent as they listened to the growing excitement on the station platform. Then Tom took her in his arms, brought her close and kissed her. The moment of togetherness was all too brief.

'I'm going now,' he said. 'Count to twenty, then follow me.'

Jack Fidler stood at the back of the crowd in the station and watched the excited crowd morosely. Daisy was back in Newcastle on one of her regular visits to keep faith with her fans, so the arrival of Rosina Lee could not have been more ill timed. The night before, Jack had sat in his room in one of the best hotels in Newcastle and read the local papers.

He had sensed the hand of the actor-manager in the announcement, a clever enough piece of publicity, and he had wondered gloomily how much of a reception there would be for the girl. Now he knew, and the omens were not good. Not only did Daisy now have a powerful rival but that rival was her daughter – the child that she had thought dead for all these years.

Even the most devoted followers could be fickle. They would attach themselves to someone new if that person took their fancy. Jack had to see for himself if Daisy was in any danger of losing her place in the people's hearts.

He stepped forward to mingle with the crowd. He kept his head down and listened to what people were saying.

'She was discovered when she sang with Daisy Belle, wasn't she?'

'Aye, that was a grand night – I was there!'

'A grand night at the Grand!'

This drew forth laughter.

'A grand night at the Grand. That's a good 'un. You should be on the stage yersel'!'

'Whisht, man, here comes the train.'

Jack could feel the shiver of expectation that ran through the crowd. At first there was silence and then as the train steamed into the station the murmurs grew into a roar of welcome. Some foolhardy folk started to run up and down the platform, peering in the windows, but when the blinds on one of the windows was quickly pulled down they knew where their quarry was.

Clever, Jack thought, when the carriages gradually emptied and still Rosina Lee did not appear. She was keeping them waiting. Still, I would have advised her to do the same. Then when Rosina did show herself in the carriage doorway and stood there looking so innocently surprised, Jack knew that this young woman was a serious rival.

Two men stepped forward to help her down. The older one would be the actor manager, Henry Greyling, and the younger man the actor and budding playwright, Tom Carey, Jack surmised. They took up positions at each side of the girl, who waved and smiled as they began their slow progress. The good-natured crowd parted to let her through.

The other members of the Greyling Players had already left the station and were now waiting outside along with a mound of luggage, which the porters had just deposited by the cab stand. But Jack noticed that one of them had lingered. A pretty, but overdressed young woman, who had left the train with the other members of the troupe, was standing still and watching Rosina Lee's progress with undisguised resentment.

Jack edged nearer to her. At that moment Rosina and her two escorts passed by quite closely and the folk standing nearby raised a little cheer. The young woman looked more put out than ever. He positioned herself a little behind her.

'Why do you dislike her?'

The young woman turned round, startled. Then she scowled. 'I've no idea what you mean,' she said, and started to move away.

Jack put a hand on her arm and stopped her. 'I saw you leave the train with the others. I guessed you're one of Henry Greyling's troupe and there was no doubting the look in your eyes.'

She edged away. 'Let go of me. It's nothing to do with you.'

'Wait, I'm not going to harm you. I'm curious, that's all. What's your name?'

'Sadie. Sadie Sutton.' She spoke her name as if she hoped he had heard of her.

'That's a good name for someone in the theatrical profession.'

'What do you know about it?'

'Quite a lot. It's my profession, too. And I'm a much bigger fish than Henry Greyling.' He gave her his card.

She read it and her eyes widened. 'But you're the manager of D—'

'Hush!' he breathed. 'No need to let folks know I'm here.'

'So why *are* you here?'

'I'd heard about Rosina Lee. I'm curious, that's all.'

'Are you going to offer to take her on?'

'Maybe. Maybe not. Perhaps she isn't the type I'm looking for.' With his smile he tried to convey that Sadie herself was more to his liking.

Her eyes widened hopefully. 'I'm a better actress than she is!'

'So why are you jealous of her?'

'Because it's so unfair!'

'How is it unfair? Does she get the best parts?'

'Time and again she does. And I know I'm just as good as she is!'

'Then why do you think Henry favours her? Is she . . . is she special to him?'

'Lord, no. Not if you're suggesting what I think you're suggesting. Mrs Greyling would kill him if anything like that were going on. No, it's Tom Carey – that dashing young man at her side – who is in love with her. Everyone knows, and he is becoming more and more important in the company as Mr Greyling gets older.'

'So he gives her the best parts because of their special relationship?'

'Not really.' Sadie looked uncomfortable. 'I mean, Tom Carey wouldn't do that sort of thing – favour an actress because he's sweet on her. No,' she said reluctantly, 'it's because of her voice.'

'Her voice?'

'Don't pretend to be surprised, Mr Fidler. You must have heard her yourself that time she sang with Daisy Belle. They sang "The Doll Song", didn't they? Daisy Belle's trademark?' She looked at him slyly. 'Well, Rosina sings it again and again. She makes folk forget their sad little lives. She lifts them up to someplace else, somewhere wonderful, for a while. There, I've said it even though I sometimes hate her for it.

'And, furthermore, I don't believe you're the slightest bit interested in offering anyone a job. You just wanted to know something – anything that might be used to her discredit.

And whatever my feelings about her, she's one of the Greyling Players and so am I, so you won't hear anything from me.'

Jack let her go. He felt even gloomier than before. Sadie's grudging description of Rosina Lee's talents revealed that the girl had the ability to be a truly great singing star.

In the cab on the way back to the hotel Jack thought about what his sister had written in one of her increasingly eccentric letters. She'd told him that he should never have got rid of baby Rose. It was nonsense, of course. The child was preventing Daisy from concentrating on her career. Also, the image of Daisy he wanted to present as a virginal innocent would have been ruined if it was discovered that her 'niece' was in fact her illegitimate child.

Maud was crazy even to think that he should have let Daisy keep her daughter just because the child might prove to have a great voice one day. They could never have suspected that. But now Rosina, because of her voice and her identity, was a double threat. He would have to think of some way of nipping her career in the bud or at the very least get rid of her while Daisy was in Newcastle.

Jack paid off the cabman and was just about to enter the hotel when he heard cheering. He turned to see what it was about and blanched when he saw the carriage coming towards him with the cheerful crowd following happily in its wake. Don't say the wretched girl is planning to stay here, he thought, in the same hotel as Daisy and me.

But the carriage went by and the crowd with it. One or two of the rougher elements in the crowd were becoming unruly; some were obviously drunk and had no idea what they were doing or who they were following. As well as the drunks there were always some empty-headed folk who would attach themselves to any bit of excitement just for the hell of it and people like that would be open to persuasion — of a monetary kind. An idea began to form in Jack's mind.

Rosina was to stay in the Bartlett house on Heaton Road. The crowd that had followed her through the town, waving and cheering, thinned out as they went. But even so, many of them stayed outside the house until Rosina made an appearance on the doorstep and asked them politely to go home as she needed to rest before her performance the following evening. They left with much good-natured banter, and Rosina went in to impart all the news and gossip to her dear friend Joanne.

Tom, who was staying in the same comfortable hotel as the rest of the cast, was invited to dine with the Bartletts that evening. He was his usual charming self at the table, but Rosina thought he looked tired. For some months now he had taken over more of the responsibility for the Players. Henry had been happy to leave much of the stage management and even the rehearsals in each new theatre to Tom.

One evening, just a week or so ago, they were relaxing in the lounge of a grand hotel in a smoky industrial city when she'd asked him what the matter was.

'Nothing's the matter. I'm just a little tired.'

'I think it's more than that,' she'd said. 'And I wish you'd tell me.'

He shook his head and smiled. 'There's nothing to tell.'

'Don't lie to me, Tom.' Her tone was sharp.

He sighed. 'All right. This isn't what I wanted.'

Everything had been going well and Rosina was puzzled. 'I don't know what you mean. Is the new play not working?'

'No it's exactly as I planned it. It's my life that isn't going to the original plan.'

'And what was that?'

'My father and mother were both in the theatre. We never settled anywhere for long and, although that is exactly the way they themselves had been brought up I think they felt guilty. As soon as I was old enough I was sent away to school. A good school. I think my mother hoped I would become a doctor or a lawyer or some such respectable person.'

'But you wanted to be an actor?'

'By the time they sent me to school it was already too late. I had tasted success in a nativity play that was part of a Christmas entertainment. It was written for the children of the other actors in the troupe and I was a star – I mean that literally – I was a star in the sky over Bethlehem.'

'How on earth did they manage that? Did they suspend you on a wire?'

Tom grinned. 'No need. They had a piece of scenery at the back of the stage shaped like a hill and above the hill there was a cloud. I was behind the cloud standing on a box and all I had to do was wave a wand with a silver star above my head every time the star had to speak.'

'And what did the star say?' Rosina asked.

'Not much. "Follow the star, follow the star." That was to the Wise Men, you see, and I think to a bunch of shepherds too. I kept on at them until they arrived safely at the stable.

'Insignificant as that part was, there was enough magic in the experience to make me realise that's what I wanted to do for the rest of my life. To be part of that wonderful world where twinkling stars could speak and the audience suspend their belief for an hour or two and go home feeling better for it.'

'And your parents?'

'They gave in gracefully. They just made me promise to finish my education. They're retired now and I think that secretly they're pleased that I'm carrying on the family tradition.'

'So what did you mean when you said your life isn't going to plan?'

'Ah, clever Rosina. I thought I'd distracted you.'

She looked at him sternly and he shrugged and continued, 'The truth is I intended to gain some experience in a group such as Henry's and then go on to a more serious acting career — and perhaps write plays too. I never intended to be the actor manager of a jolly little troupe such as the Greyling Players.'

'Well, why don't you go?' Rosina asked. 'I'm sure that companies much more illustrious than this would be glad to have you.'

'Henry is becoming more and more dependent on me. I feel I would be letting him down. I think I'll have to wait until he and Priscilla are ready to retire. And I just don't know when that will be. And another thing: there's your future too. You're too good for this little troupe now, Rosina. Maybe we're holding you back.'

Rosina didn't know what to say. Now was not the time to tell him that she had already begun to feel restless. But not because she thought she was too big a star to stay with the Greyling Players. There was another reason entirely.

Tom had taken her hand and looked into her eyes questioningly. 'Rosina, my darling, what are we going to do?'

She had searched her soul and found no answer to give him.

But life with the Greyling Players had gone on as usual and neither she nor Tom had referred to that evening again. And now, here they were back in Newcastle where her theatrical career had begun.

After they had finished their meal with Joanne and her

parents, Tom excused himself. He had to go along to the theatre to see if all the instructions he had sent in advance had been carried out. The theatre, the New Tyne, had a complex system of machinery under the stage and Tom had written new sketches to make use of the trapdoors and flies but he had never actually tested them. Not wishing to have characters appearing and disappearing at the wrong time, he had called a late-night rehearsal for those involved.

After he had gone, Joanne and Rosina sat by the fire in the first-floor drawing room and reminisced about their childhood and the fun they'd had acting in Joanne's plays.

'By the way,' her friend said, 'your young man is gorgeous.'

'My young man?'

'Oh, please don't pretend. Not with me. It's obvious that you are in love with Tom Carey and he with you.'

Rosina smiled. It was pointless to protest. And in any case why should she?

'Are you going to get married?'

'One day.'

'Why not now? What's stopping you? You are your own woman, quite independent of the Leightons. Oh, I'm sorry!'

'Why are you sorry?'

'I shouldn't have said that. About the Leightons, I mean. I know you wrote to me and told me why you had left home so suddenly but you asked me never to mention it.'

'It's all right, Joanne. The hurt is fading.'

Rosina said that in order to make her friend feel comfortable but when she examined the statement in her mind she realized it was true. Her life had been so interesting and exciting over the last few years that she had not had time to brood. She could have put the past behind her entirely if it had not been for her desire to find out where she had come from.

'Well . . .' Joanne said tentatively, 'what about Tom?'

'You're like a dog with a bone, aren't you? You just won't give up.' Rosina smiled at her friend to show that she wasn't angry. 'And yes, Tom has asked me to marry him. We simply have not had time. I mean to say, I should have to meet his parents – they have retired to the south coast – I should have to buy a trousseau; we must decide whether we should buy a house to come back to in between engagements. You know the sort of thing.'

'It all sounds very much to me as though you are procrastinating. You are certainly not behaving like a couple madly in love. What's the problem?'

'There's no real problem. It's just that . . . oh, it's difficult to explain, but I am not the sort of woman who would be content to simply be a wife. I love Tom very much but whatever happens I should want to carry on with my career. I don't think I could ever give up the stage.'

'Would he expect you to?'

'No, of course not. He is as ambitious for me as I am for myself. It's just that he has ambitions, too, and I don't think either of us is quite certain yet what paths we will follow. But I'm sure we will find a way, one day.'

'Well, don't wait too long. I don't want to be an elderly bridesmaid.'

They looked at each other and laughed and then Rosina asked, 'But what about you? Is there anyone in your life?'

'A man, you mean?'

Rosina nodded.

'Well, yes, I think there is,' Joanne said. Her smile was radiant.

'Tell me.'

'He's called James and he's a representative of one of the confectionery firms my father deals with. You know I've started working for my father? Well, whenever James calls at the office we always seem to find something to talk about – other than business, that is.'

'And what do your parents think?'

'Well, it's early days but my father thinks James has a good head for business and my mother is prepared to like him because I told her he shares our love of opera.'

Rosina was surprised. 'I didn't know you liked opera.'

'Neither did I until recently. But you know how my father has become quite boring about sailing? Well, now, whenever we go to the house in Normandy, my mother and I settle him in, leave instructions for the staff not to let him drown himself or become shipwrecked, and then we go on our travels.

'When we were in Milan everybody was talking about a singer called Enrico Caruso. Curiosity took us to La Scala – that's the opera house – and we saw him sing the part of Marcello in *La Bohème*. If I wasn't such a sensible girl I might have made a fool of myself and become one of Caruso's devoted followers!'

Joanne's enthusiasm made her lean forward in her chair, she was so eager to share her passion. 'And do you know,' she said, 'my hero is not altogether free from scandal. It is said that he has formed a close attachment to a married lady, the beautiful dark-eyed soprano Ada Giachetti. She reminds me a little of you. I can just imagine you singing the roles she performs. Oh, Rosina, you would just love that music and those songs.'

'Yes, I'm sure I would.'

Then Joanne said, 'But I have been remiss. I was so greedy for your company and a chance to gossip that I have withheld your letters. I'll get them for you now.'

The two friends had decided from the start that the

Bartletts' house would be a kind of poste restante for Rosina, and Joanne would bundle the letters together and send them on as soon as she knew where the company were playing. This time, knowing Rosina was returning to Newcastle, she had kept them.

When Joanne returned with the letters she asked Rosina if she wanted to be left alone to read them. 'No, please stay,' Rosina said.

'I'll read my novel, *The Forest Lovers*. It's a wonderful tale of damsels in distress, knights in shining armour and wicked mistresses, set in the depths of a mysterious forest.'

There were only two letters. Rosina recognized the handwriting on the envelopes. She knew which one she would open first and which to put aside and maybe not open at all because she knew only too well what it would say.

The first letter Rosina opened was from Molly, the maid she had befriended when she was a child.

Ever since Rosina had left home, Molly had been writing to her care of Joanne. But after Molly's first letter Rosina had told her that she had no desire to know anything about the Leightons. The letters were to be personal. Rosina had burned that letter but she could still remember the news it had brought her.

Adam Loxley and Amy were to be married and both sets of parents were arranging things so that the marriage could take place as soon as possible.

'And we all can guess what that means!' Molly had written.

Rosina had replied curtly, 'I really don't want to know about the doings of Amy and Adam, nor, for that matter, about the Loxleys or the Leightons. Their lives simply don't concern me.'

Since then her old friend had respected her wishes and, apart from telling her that 'old Fiddlesticks' had left

Ravenshill, she had written only of her own life and of Bridget, who had gone to America as she'd said she might, and was working as a nanny in the household of a widowed gentleman who had one little boy. Rosina settled back in the comfortable armchair to read Molly's latest missive.

Dear Miss Rosina,

What do you think? Bridget's gentleman, Mr Kowalski, has asked her to marry him. He says he is so grateful for the way she has looked after young Anton and that she has brought happiness back into their home. He is a writer and Bridget says that writers talk like that. But she is very happy.

And I have some special news, too. I have become engaged to a young man who came to Ravenshill to install a telephone. The company he works for is in Newcastle and when we get married I will be moving to the city! I will miss the countryside but I would live anywhere with Colin.

I am going to meet his parents soon and I think I will be in town when you are there. Colin says we must all come to the theatre to see you. He says he is proud that his future wife can claim a friendship with such a great star.

I hope I will hear from you soon.

All good wishes from your old friend,

Molly

P.S. You can telephone and leave a message at Colin's house.

Molly gave her fiancé's telephone number and Rosina could imagine the pride with which she'd written that. She smiled as she folded the letter and put it back in its envelope. She resolved to find out exactly when Molly would be in town and leave a message that four tickets would be left at the ticket box office in the foyer. She smiled to herself when she decided that she would reserve a box for them and see to it that refreshments were served in both intervals.

She glanced across at Joanne, who was absorbed in her novel. Still smiling, Rosina folded Molly's letter and put it back in the envelope. The mood here in the Bartletts' comfortable home was so relaxed, so reassuring, that she felt strong enough to open her second letter, although she did so with misgivings.

The scrawled handwriting on the envelope was a forewarning of the undisciplined statements she would find inside. These letters were always addressed to 'Miss Rosina Lee', but never started with 'Dear Rosina' or even 'Dear Miss Lee' and they were never signed. They weren't so much letters as wild disjointed phrases and there was always the hint that the writer would have liked to say more.

The first such letter, if she could call it that, had consisted of three words: 'She loved you.' The next had declared: 'I really believed that it was for the best.'

Other letters had been on a similar theme and then the writer had started begging for forgiveness.

Remembering the strange way Maud Fidler had behaved the day she had left Ravenshill, Rosina had guessed almost from the start who the letters were from and she had decided that the poor woman was mad. But some of the things she had written made Rosina believe that the woman who had given birth to her might not be dead after all. That she might not have been orphaned, as Blanche Leighton had believed. If that was the case where was her mother now? Did she know that her daughter had become a famous stage star? Did she care?

And also what was the meaning of the parcel of children's clothes she had given her: the beautiful emerald-green coat, the pretty little bonnet and the white dress? Not the clothes of a slum child. She didn't know what had compelled her to do it but Rosina had kept the parcel of clothes close to her ever since. She felt those clothes were important – and in a strange way they brought her luck. She even took them to the theatre with her and kept them in her dressing room.

Rosina had almost decided to go back to Ravenshill, no matter what she might face there, and confront Miss Fidler; ask her to explain the clothes and demand to know where she had come from. But the poor woman had left shortly after Rosina herself had, and nobody knew where she had gone.

So all she had were these unsigned letters. Each one brought more frustration. Rosina steeled herself to face the latest revelation and opened the envelope and took out the letter. The handwriting had deteriorated further. It was barely legible.

'You owe your great gift to your mother. May God forgive me for my part in separating you.'

When Henry Greyling went along to the Palace Theatre after a good dinner at his hotel he found Tom was still going over the practical details with the stage manager. Henry realized how much he depended on Tom these days and he felt guilty. But then he had a plan that might just put things right. Priscilla was tired of the endless traipsing round the country. The mood of the audiences was changing and she said that she felt like a dinosaur, an extinct creature still trying to live by the old ways in a world that had moved on.

Priscilla's sister lived in Harrogate, a handsome town where cultured folk lived, Priscilla said, and the Greylings almost had enough money put by to be able to buy a nice little house there and enjoy a happy retirement.

The only problem was that Monica did not want to give up the stage. So Henry had decided to ask Tom to take over, although the troupe would keep its name and Monica would be the figurehead. Monica had already decided that the company should be called from then on the Monica Greyling Players.

Henry was not sure if Tom would agree, and even if he did, he might be tempted to change the nature of the troupe, indulge in a bit of classical drama now and then. Henry would not object to that so long as the company that bore his name continued into this new century and did not become a bit of theatrical history. He would wait until the time was propitious and see how Tom felt about the plan.

Tom looked up and smiled as Henry joined him on the stage. 'It's all done, Henry,' he said. 'We can start rehearsals first thing in the morning.'

'And is Rosina quite happy about the new sketch?'

'Not entirely.'

'Ah. Just that one song, I presume?'

'Yes, "The Doll Song".'

'But haven't you told her that I believe that we can't do a tribute to three great ladies of the music hall without including Daisy Belle?'

'I have, and I've also told her that I agree with you.'

'Good man. She respects your judgement, I know she does. So what's the problem?'

'Rosina believes that although Maud Santley and the ghost of poor Nelly Power might be flattered to be given a tribute, Daisy Belle will not like Rosina to sing a song she has so much made her own.'

'She's never made that objection before.'

'We've never appeared in the same town as Miss Belle before. You know she's here, of course.'

'I do.'

'Well, Rosina suggested that we choose another song from Miss Belle's repertoire rather than the song that has become her trademark.'

'That just wouldn't do and you know it.'

Tom sighed. 'I do.'

'So have you got the props?'

'We don't need one for Nelly Power's "The Boy I Love". Rosina must be dressed as prettily as possible and direct her song to the gallery. She can wear the same dress and put on a policeman's helmet, a whistle round her neck and carry a truncheon for Maud Santley's, "The Bobbies of the Queen", and then for the last song all she needs is the broken doll.'

Dear Miss Belle,

Do you know that Miss Rosina Lee is in town? This is quite a coincidence. I've heard that she once sang with you. Although you may not remember that night at the Grand, folk here still talk about it. I think you should go to the theatre and hear her sing the song that made you famous. I believe you would discern at once the reason why she is so talented.

I pray that you and the Lord will forgive me.

Chapter Twenty-One

The next morning Jack Fidler rose early and was just about to leave the hotel when someone called his name.

'Mr Carver, could I have a word?'

He turned to see the desk clerk smiling at him.

'What is it?' Jack said somewhat testily.

He had urgent business to conduct and he wanted to get back to the hotel before Daisy was up and about. At his suggestion she had decided to sleep late and have breakfast in bed. He'd told her to have a rest today and not to go anywhere until he came back and was able to escort her. If she wanted anything she could send out for it.

The desk clerk was holding an envelope and looking at it doubtfully. 'This letter came for Miss Belle. I was going to send it up when she orders breakfast but,' he frowned, 'I'm a little concerned about it.'

'Why is that?'

'Well, it was delivered by hand late last night by an – I'm not sure how to put this – an odd-looking woman. She seemed to be very intense – perhaps a little off balance, if you know what I mean.'

'I think I do.' Jack began to feel uneasy.

'We've had many theatrical people staying here,' the clerk continued, 'and I know they attract eccentrics and sometimes quite dangerous people. Well, the long and the short of it is, we don't want Miss Belle upset while she's a guest here. I thought as her manager you ought—'

'Quite right, give it to me,' Jack said.

One look at the scrawled handwriting on the envelope and his heart sank.

'Did I do right?' the desk clerk asked.

'Mm?' Jack looked up distractedly. The man was looking at him questioningly. 'Oh, yes, quite right,' Jack said, and he handed him a florin. 'And if there are any more letters please give them to me.'

The desk clerk smiled and pocketed the coin with alacrity. 'Thank you, sir. Anything to oblige such honoured guests.'

'I'm going out for an hour or two. I don't want Miss Belle disturbed for anything or anyone. Do you understand?' As he spoke he took another coin from his pocket, a sovereign, and pushed it across the highly polished surface of the desk.

The clerk bowed his head deferentially before reaching for the coin. 'Perfectly, sir. No one will get past this desk. You can rely on me.'

Jack waited until he was in the cab before he opened the letter and when he read it his face purpled with anger. What on earth was wrong with the woman? He had started to send her an allowance again; she had been able to move to a decent enough set of rooms at the coast, so why had she decided to betray him by writing this letter to Daisy?

Thank goodness the desk clerk had had the sense to hang on to it. But that was no guarantee that Maud would not find some way of reaching Daisy. He would have to go and see her and prevent her from even trying. But first he had other business to see to.

* * *

Long after the others had finished their morning rehearsal and gone to have lunch at Alvini's, Rosina and Tom stayed in the theatre to rehearse her new act. Rosina sang as well as she ever did but Tom could tell her heart wasn't in it. Eventually he told Mervyn, the troupe's pianist, to have a break, and took Rosina aside.

'What is it?' he asked.

'What do you mean?'

'There's something the matter.'

'No, of course there isn't. I'm just a little weary, that's all.'

He didn't believe her and he controlled a spurt of irritation. This wasn't the Rosina he knew and loved; the girl who threw herself into rehearsals wholeheartedly, no matter how many miles they had travelled or how hard she had been working.

'Don't prevaricate,' he said. 'If there's something wrong please tell me.'

'That would be pointless.' She sighed and looked unhappy. Then just as quickly her expression changed. She sounded contrite when she said, 'Oh, Tom, I'm sorry. I'm behaving like a spoiled child or, worse, a temperamental, conceited prima donna. Forgive me?'

'Of course I do. And I think I know what's troubling you. You don't like the new act, do you?'

'To be honest, no.'

'Tell me why.'

'It's not the act itself – I think it's a marvellous idea to pay tribute to three of great stars of the music hall. But well, it's the songs you've chosen.'

'Those are the songs they sing – the songs they are known for. They make a perfect tribute.'

'I know. It's me who isn't right. I don't do the songs justice.'

'You have a wonderful voice.'

'You know that's not what I mean.'

Reluctantly Tom admitted to himself that he knew very well what she meant and he stared at her bleakly. 'Tell me,' he said.

She breathed in and then, as if she had suddenly made up her mind, she said in a rush, 'Well, if you really want to know I'm not jolly enough to sing "The Bobbies of the Queen", "The Boy I Love" is too sickly sweet for words and, as for "The Doll Song", it's just ... just ...'

Rosina turned and walked away from him but not before he had seen the tears in her eyes. He caught up with her in the wings and took hold of her arm.

'Rosina – I'm sorry.'

She turned on him in fury. 'Why are *you* apologizing?' she demanded. 'It's me who's behaving badly!'

'Rosina, please ...' Tom was disconcerted to see the tears flowing freely.

He tried to pull her towards him; she resisted for a moment and then almost fell into his arms completely, overtaken by a storm of weeping. He stood there holding her gently until the tears subsided, then he led her back on to the stage and sat her down beside the piano where there were several chairs and also a small table covered with sheet music.

The pianist reappeared. He was carrying enamel mugs of tea.

'I got the doorkeeper to make these for you,' he said. 'Sorry about the mugs but it's all he had. I've put plenty of sugar in; I think Miss Lee has been working too hard.'

'Thank you, Mervyn,' Tom said. 'I think maybe you should go home now.'

Mervyn moved some of the sheet music aside so that he could place the mugs on the table. 'I'll leave these here for you to look at again, Miss Lee,' he said. 'I can get them tomorrow.'

'Thank you,' Rosina said as she wiped her eyes. 'You've been very helpful.'

Tom was surprised by her words but he supposed that Mervyn, a kindly older man, had been doing some extra rehearsals with Rosina and probably, judging by the friendly familiarity, for some time.

When Mervyn had gone, they drank their tea in silence for a while.

It was Rosina who spoke first. 'I shouldn't have behaved like that.'

'I suppose you're entitled to a tantrum or two.'

'We all know what to think of people who have tantrums,' she replied. They both smiled.

'Well, you've got that out of your system. But I didn't realize you were quite so unhappy with the tribute act.'

'I really don't think that the songs are right for me.'

'You can sing anything and make it sound good, Rosina.'

'You keep saying that, but have you considered that I might not be right for the songs? Mervyn knows what I mean.'

For a moment Tom suffered a spasm of jealousy as he contemplated the fact that Rosina had been confiding in Mervyn, but he quickly realized that that might be his own fault. Goodness knows, she had been trying to tell him for some time that she was not entirely happy and he just hadn't listened.

Rosina placed her mug on the table and picked up some of the sheet music Mervyn had left there. 'Mervyn has been taking me through some of these songs. He said my voice was wonderfully suited to them.'

Controlling his impulse to say something sarcastic about her growing regard for Mervyn, Tom took the sheets of music from her. He looked through them and tried to hide his dismay. They were songs from works by Verdi, Rossini and Puccini. Opera. If this is what Rosina wanted to sing then no wonder she was unhappy with the Greyling Players.

He didn't know what to say and he looked at her anxiously but her thoughts seemed to have moved on already.

'And, Tom, there's something else.'

For a moment she looked so sombre that cold fear gripped his heart. Was she going to tell him that she was mortally ill? But she went on in the manner of someone who has made her mind up to reveal some truth.

'Have you ever wondered why I left home and, completely inexperienced as I was, decided to audition for the Greyling Players?' she asked.

'Of course I have.'

'Why have you never asked me about it?'

'I thought you would tell me if you wanted to.'

'Wise Tom. And patient.'

'Are you going to tell me now?'

'I'll try to. But shall we sit down? I really am tired. It wasn't just an act before.'

Tom pulled a couple of seats forward and they sat on the stage with a painted backdrop behind them and the plush cavern of the auditorium in front of them. But Tom knew very well that they were not characters in a play. The story Rosina was about to tell him was very real.

'My mother, Geraldine Leighton, died and my father married again. And now I suppose you're going to say that I'm going to tell you a typical wicked stepmother story. The sort of story invented by a spoiled unhappy child.' She sounded defiant.

'I wouldn't dream of suggesting that. You are far too good a person to behave in such a way.'

'My stepmother was cold, but not exactly cruel. It's understandable that she doted on her own daughter but she was never able to conceal the fact that she didn't want me there. But I loved Ravenshill because I had been so happy there in the past when my . . . my mother was alive.

'But when I discovered in the cruellest fashion that Geraldine Leighton was not my mother at all – that I had no blood ties to the place – I knew I could stay there no longer.'

'No blood ties? You were adopted?'

'Yes. An orphan from the slums. Or so I was told. But now I have come to believe that Geraldine Leighton may have been lied to.'

'What makes you think that?'

'I have received letters. None of them signed. But I believe them to be from the person who took me to Ravenshill, and if I could find her I would learn the truth about why my real mother gave me up. I may even discover that she is still alive.'

Tom reached for her hands and clasped them. He felt utterly inadequate. For all he spent his days putting words in characters' mouths he could not find the right words now to comfort the woman he loved. 'That may be too much to hope, my darling. I shouldn't like to see you hurt. But whatever you decide to do, you know I will help you, don't you?'

'Dear Tom, of course I do. And now do you want to take me through those songs again?'

Tom knew that no further rehearsal would be possible now. Trouper though she was, Rosina was in a dangerously emotional state. And besides, he had sent Mervyn away and he was in no mood to accompany Rosina himself. He would just have to rely on her talent and experience to see them through tonight's performance.

'Do you want to go home now to rest?' he asked. 'Back to the comfort of the Bartletts' house?'

She looked at him gratefully. 'I do. But don't worry, Tom, I'm not going to let you or Henry down. I'll do my very best, I promise you.'

Tom hailed a cab for her and sent her on her way. He still had arrangements to make with the stage manager. He'd believed her when she'd said she would do her best tonight, but he knew in his heart that Rosina's talent had grown and developed in a way he should have foreseen. Her days with the Greyling Players were surely numbered. But the world he was sure would welcome her with open arms would have no place for him.

'Are you sure this is where you want to be dropped off?'

The cab had clattered to a stop on the quayside. Jack descended and paid his fare without looking up into the face of the cabman. 'Yes, I'm sure.'

'Watch yersel', then. There's folk at this end of the quay who wouldn't think twice about slitting yer throat for that diamond tiepin or those ivory buttons on yer waistcoat, or that fancy gold-headed walking cane.'

As the cab pulled away Jack cursed himself for not adopting some sort of disguise. He was pretty sure the obliging desk clerk would have found him a shabby old coat to cover his fine clothes and kept quiet about it if he had tipped him generously enough. He had got used to wearing the very best tailor-made suits, and fancy furbelows such as the diamond pin the cabman had mentioned. Not to mention his gold pocket watch and chain. Hastily he removed the tiepin and his gold signet ring and slipped them in a pocket along with his watch chain.

Then he began to walk downriver along the quayside, away from the noise of loading and unloading the many ships that sailed into the Tyne daily, and away from the incessant bustle of all those the river gave employment to. It didn't take long to reach the narrow street that cut up the bank side to Carver's Song and Supper Rooms.

He paused outside. The place was shabbier than ever but the saloon bar was open for business and there was the usual collection of regular drinkers coming and going in various stages of inebriation. Jack glanced inside and saw that a large, formidable woman was in charge of the bar. Another step or two brought him to the door he knew led to Harry Carver's private quarters. There was no bell so, looking over his shoulder to make sure there was no one watching him, he knocked as vigorously as he could.

Footsteps echoed along the hollow passage. The door was opened by a slatternly girl. She was tall and large-boned, but her face was that of a child of about eleven or twelve. Her dress was of good quality but in need of a wash, and her hair hung in greasy rat's-tails to her shoulders. She gave off the unmistakable smell of an unwashed child. She stared at him with a certain degree of insolence.

'What do you want?' The tone was challenging.

'That's none of your business.'

The child began to close the door. Jack put a hand out to stop it. 'Wait, I want to see Mr Carver.'

'Well, I don't suppose me da wants to see you. Not if you don't hev a name, that is.'

Jack couldn't help admiring the girl's cheek. 'Tell him it's an old friend.'

She looked him up and down. 'Go on. Me da never had friends like you.'

'Look, you're wasting my time and I'm wasting yours. Especially when you could be spending this in the sweet shop.'

Jack took a shilling from his pocket and held it in front

of the girl's eyes. The sullen young face was transformed by a knowing grin. She reached out to snatch the coin but Jack flicked it over his shoulder and sent it bowling down the cobbled street. She made to follow it but he caught her shoulder. 'Don't come back for at least half an hour,' he said.

Desperate to retrieve the coin before it rolled into the river, she nodded agreement and then took off after it. Jack walked into the house and closed the door behind him.

Memories flooded back. This passage had once been an outdoor alleyway between two tottering old buildings. At some stage it had been roofed over and Harry Carver, who owned both properties, used most of one half for his business and the other half for his living quarters, and also to provide a basic dressing room for the performers who sang there nightly.

Jack could hardly credit now that this was where Daisy had begun her career. Daisy Belle, one of the greatest stars that music hall had ever known and it was all thanks to him. He had found her in the streets, clutching her brat, and he had trained her and transformed her into the successful woman she was now. But now that very same brat, the child he thought he'd got rid of, was threatening to knock Daisy off her throne. Well, not if he could help it.

As Jack made his way along the stinking passage he gagged at the sour smell. He hadn't known Harry Carver was married but if that woman she had seen in the bar was his wife then she wasn't much of a housekeeper. There was no need for them to live like this. After all, Harry couldn't be poverty stricken. Not with the amount of money he took every night from the fools who knew no better than to drink their lives away.

The door of a room at the back of the building was open. Jack walked in and regarded the huge form of the man he had come to see sleeping in an armchair by the fire. The curtains at the only window were closed and the light was dim. He looked around for a lamp and saw that there was a candelabrum on the wooden tabletop. It held three half-burned candles. There was a box of matches on the table. He walked over, lit the candles and sat down. Harry Carver went on sleeping. He was breathing heavily and his rubbery lips trembled at every outgoing breath.

Jack took his silver cigar case from an inner pocket and removed one of the fine Havana cigars. When he was ready he leaned across and lit it from one of the candles, then he sat back and waited. Carver was a powerful man. He had seen him deal with unruly customers. Once he had lifted a man at least as big as himself and hurled him out into the street. And although Jack could look after himself there was no point in startling the man into an act of violence.

He drew on his cigar, a hand-rolled corona, and sat back. He half closed his eyes and gazed through the smoke, all the time watching Harry Carver. And then he saw that the man's eyes were open, pinpointed by the firelight. He was staring at Jack as if he wasn't sure whether he was awake or dreaming. His breathing became laboured as he pulled himself upright in his chair. Jack gripped his walking cane, the shaft was pure ebony; he might need its strength.

'Who the hell are you?' Harry asked at last.

'An old friend.'

'Oh, aye, and what do you want?'

'I want you to do me a favour.'

Harry Carver heaved himself up and walked towards Jack. He placed both of his powerful hands on the table and leaned forward. 'Your voice is familiar.' He peered through the cigar smoke suspiciously. 'Jack, is it? Jack Fidler?'

'Whisht, man. The name doesn't matter.'

'Then, why should I do you a favour?'

'This is why.'

Jack took a money pouch from his pocket. Aware of the avaricious gleam in the innkeeper's eyes, he took his time untying the drawstring, then eased the pouch open and emptied its contents on the table.

Harry Carver stared down at the pile of sovereigns glinting in the candlelight. 'You know how to persuade a man.'

'Listen carefully to what I want you to arrange, and if you do it well there'll be the same amount again.'

Harry pulled a chair up to the table and sat down. He listened attentively while Jack lowered his voice and told him what he wanted him to do. After a while Jack asked, 'Can you get the right people?'

'Of course I can.'

'They'll be discreet?'

Harry laughed. 'The fellows I have in mind are too stupid to wonder what it's all about. I'll tank them up just a little before they go and after they've done what's required of them I'll give them enough money to drink themselves stupid.'

'And they'll buy their drinks here, of course.'

'Of course,' Harry laughed.

'So you'll end up with all the money.'

'Or most of it. But that's not the only reason. If any one of them looks like he's going to blab or cause any kind of trouble, the river's just a step away.'

When Rosina returned to the house in Heaton, instead of resting, as Tom had urged her to do, she poured her heart out to Joanne. She told her friend not only of her strange dissatisfaction with the way her career was developing but also of her desire to find out who her mother had been.

442

Joanne reminded her that at least she'd had an adoptive mother who loved her.

But now what was Rosina going to do about her career? She loved the theatre. She couldn't imagine not being part of the magic, the excitement, the make-believe. But she was beginning to feel that she needed more of a challenge than the cheerful song-and-dance routines of the music hall. But how could she leave Tom?

When Daisy woke up she tried to be enthusiastic about being here in Newcastle. Jack insisted that she should return every now and then to please the fans who had set her on the road to stardom. In truth she hated coming here. In the years since Rose had died she had never forgiven herself for not going to the park herself and for trusting her precious daughter to her maid, Edna.

She was not here to perform. No show had been arranged. She was here this time simply to make a gracious appearance at a civic reception to be given in her honour. When she was there they would ask her to sing, she would appear reluctant and then give in graciously – as they all knew she would.

Jack had told her to relax today. Indeed, he had been most insistent. This had puzzled her because he usually told her to go out and about, and show herself. He would always accompany her on these outings, of course, and no doubt the reason why he had told her to stay in the luxurious confines of the hotel today was because he had some business of his own to conduct.

Daisy never questioned Jack's business dealings. She was happy to let him guide her career because he at least seemed to care what happened to her. She was not so naïve that she did not know that he was doing very well for himself by being her manager, but why not? He took away the cares and worries of day to day existence and left her free to sing.

She sang because that was all she knew how to do and she, as much as the audiences who adored her, could for an all too brief hour or two lose herself in a different world and forget the pain that would haunt her for the rest of her life.

Today she had decided that she would be perfectly happy to stay in the hotel and take up Jack's suggestion to have Bainbridge's and Fenwick's send along a selection of the latest fashions for her to choose from. She could have anything she wanted. But instead of this thought making her happy, she found that tears were streaming down her cheeks as the wraiths of a ragged girl and her baby appeared and refused to be banished from her consciousness.

Daisy dried her eyes when there was a respectful knock at the door. Her maid, Janet, entered and opened the curtains. Daisy told her to order breakfast to be brought to her room and then gave her a list of the sort of clothes and accessories she wanted sent along from the department stores. Janet was to take the list to the shops herself.

When her breakfast tray arrived, Daisy sat propped amongst a mound of pillows and picked at scrambled eggs and toast and marmalade. While she drank her tea she read the newspaper that had been brought up with her tray.

Janet returned from her trip to the department stores to find Daisy reading the paper intently. She barely glanced up as her maid removed the tray.

'Do you want me to help you dress now, madam?' the maid asked.

Daisy looked up from the paper. 'No, not yet, but you can draw a bath for me and while I soak for a while I want you to run along to this theatre – look – the New Tyne. Get me a box for tonight.'

'Which house?'

'There's only one performance tonight. A grand opening show, it says here. They claim that this girl Rosina Lee once sang with me.'

'And did she?'

'Yes . . . I remember. It was at the Grand. She was in the audience.'

'And now she's a star.'

'So they say.'

While she lay in the rose-scented water of her bath, Daisy closed her eyes and tried to understand why it was so important for her to go to the theatre and hear this girl, this potential rival, sing. She was confident enough in her own talent not to feel unduly challenged. So why did she feel uneasy? As the water cooled and she reached for the towel, she decided it was something to do with the song they had sung together. 'The Doll Song'.

The more he thought about it, the angrier he got. How could Maud be stupid enough to urge Daisy to go to the theatre to see Rosina Lee? Jack had seen the girl at the station. She did not have the angel-fair colouring of Daisy, but that was not the point. The young woman she had grown into was as dark and as bonny as she had been as a child. Surely a mother would see the resemblance. Perhaps not. But he could not take the risk.

And not only must he make sure Daisy did not go to the theatre to hear the girl sing, but he must find a way of destroying Rosina Lee's career. He had no intention of allowing a rival to challenge the woman he had made into a star. The instructions he had given Harry Carver for tonight were only a diversion. Once the girl came out of the theatre there might be an opportunity to effect a more final solution.

In the crush he was hoping to orchestrate it would be easy enough for her to be knocked down, or even end up trampled by a horse as she was supposed to have done all those years ago. The trouble was, it would be too dangerous to reveal that part of the plan to anyone else. He would have to be there himself.

But now he must seek out Maud and put a stop to her meddling, once and for all. Bearing in mind the cab driver's remarks, he walked up the steep streets that led away from the river and as he went he glanced along every side street and alleyway. At last he found what he was looking for. A second-hand clothes shop.

Jack knew he was paying over the odds but no questions were asked and he emerged from the shop wearing a shabby black overcoat, a muffler and a cloth cap. The odour of old sweat and hair oil was disgusting, but it was the price he had to pay for anonymity. He made sure he kept the head of his walking cane covered and, not wanting to take a cab – cabmen were too perspicacious by far – he walked to the Central Station and took the train to the coast.

At Whitley-by-the-Sea he was faced with the problem of finding where Maud lived. He knew the address from her letters but he did not know this town and he had no idea where he was going. He did not want to stop anyone and ask the way. Maud's constant complaints about her rooms made him aware that the house couldn't be too grand so it made sense to turn away from the better part of town.

It had started to rain, which had the advantage of driving people from the streets but the disadvantage of releasing further foul odours from the old clothes he was wearing. He felt his rage at his sister growing. Why couldn't she have left things alone? She was a liability, and no longer useful to him. Eventually, after seeming to trudge round in circles, he found the house in a square not far from the church. The house had once been grand but was now divided into tenements. The wide front door, which gave on to a stone passage, was open.

There was no one about. He slipped inside. He found Maud's door; luckily for him it was on the ground floor. He knocked softly. There was no reply. Why had it not occurred to him that she might not be in? That she might already be in Newcastle, ready to waylay Daisy and cause trouble? His fury mounted.

He heard shuffling footsteps and the tapping of a stick. He withdrew into the shadows under the stairs. An old woman came along the corridor from the back of the house. She paused right beside him and frowned, then she turned to look at him. He gripped his cane but then realized that her gaze was sightless. She stayed for a moment longer and then carried on towards the entrance, tapping with her white cane. She left the house.

Jack emerged from his hiding place and risked knocking a little louder. This time he heard footsteps within the room and a moment later the door opened. His sister stared up at him. She frowned at first, perhaps not recognizing him in the second-hand clothes, then after a moment of puzzlement, her eyes widened with joy.

'Jack!' she said. 'You've come at last. I should have known you would not forsake me.'

He pushed her back into her room and closed the door and then he turned on her in fury. Maud didn't even have time to cry out before he brought his cane down hard across her head. His sister's expression changed to unbelief and then grief before her eyes glazed over and she fell to the floor.

'Why?' she sobbed.

But his only answer was to strike her again and again until she stopped moving.

* * *

Tom was ready to go to find a sandwich when Henry arrived at the theatre and told him that the time was now right to have a talk about the future. He put forward his plan that Tom should take over when he and Priscilla retired and keep the troupe going for Monica.

The silence between them lengthened and Henry's face fell. 'You don't want to do it?' he said.

Tom didn't answer directly. 'Have you considered anyone else?'

'Who else is there? I don't want to bring in an outsider.'

'How about Arthur Barnfather?'

'Arthur? He . . . well, he lacks style. I mean, you are a gentleman.'

Tom smiled. 'Because I speak more like a classical actor, I suppose you mean? More like you, in fact.'

'Yes. And you have education. Whereas I don't think Arthur ever went to school of any kind. He's been in show business since his mother gave birth to him in the dressing room at the Alhambra.'

'Exactly.'

'What do you mean?'

'Arthur Barnfather knows this business inside out. He'd make a marvellous manager.'

'But what about the plays? The sketches?'

'Arthur is more than capable of developing new sketches and, as for the longer plays, well, I promise I would still go on writing them for the Greyling Players whenever I could and, furthermore, I'll stay on until Arthur is established. I'm sorry, Henry, but that's my best offer.'

'Then I suppose I shall have to accept it. But where will you go? What will you do?'

'I'm not sure yet.'

Henry shook his head. 'I never thought you would leave the Players, Tom. Especially now that we have Rosina.'

Tom knew that this was not the time to tell Henry Greyling that they might not have Rosina much longer.

Backstage there was the usual excitement and anticipation before the opening of a new show. But Rosina was subdued, thinking about her unknown past and her uncertain future. However, she had promised Tom that she would do her best, so she sat in front of the mirror and got on with the job of getting ready to go on stage.

Most of the programme was made up of tried and tested acts and sketches. Rosina's tribute to three great ladies of music hall was going to be the very last item. Henry hoped it would prove to be a sensation. He knew Daisy Belle was in town and he'd asked the theatre manager to keep a box free. Henry would pay for it himself. Then he had taken an invitation to her hotel. He had hoped to see her but the desk clerk said he'd had instructions that the great star was not to be disturbed and had taken the invitation from Henry and put it in a cubby hole behind the desk.

Henry could only hope that Miss Belle would get the invitation in time and would come to the show. He had visions of her and Rosina singing together again. 'The Doll Song', of course. But this time Rosina would be on the stage and Miss Belle would be in the audience. It would be a sensation.

He had told the conductor of the orchestra that after Rosina had sung it once he was to stop the music, turn to the box where Daisy would be sitting and make a graceful gesture inviting her to sing. Henry was sure that the great star would not be able to resist the invitation. Rosina was to let Daisy Belle sing alone for a while and then join in. The crowd would go wild. But so far there had been no response from

Miss Belle. Henry could only hope that she would decide to come but as curtain-up approached he was beginning to think that she had ignored his invitation.

Jack kept his second-hand clothes on for the journey back to Newcastle. He was conscious of the spattered stains which showed as darker marks on the faded black cloth of his rain-soaked coat. But he knew that if he tried to wipe them off his hands would be smeared with blood. He hoped no one would notice the dirty pink puddles forming at his feet on the carriage floor.

As soon as he left the Central Station he turned right and hurried along to an arch that went under the track and led to an area where some of the most squalid houses in the city tumbled down the hill towards the river. There was the usual collection of homeless souls taking shelter in the tunnel. Some of them sleeping, some of them drunk.

Quickly he took off his coat, cap and muffler and, bundling them up, he placed them beside a sleeping vagrant. It amused him to think that when the fellow awoke he would find the clothes and probably think some sort of miracle had occurred. That is, if he had not been dispatched to heaven in his sleep by another of his ilk who spied the clothes before he woke.

He hurried back to the hotel and went straight to his room. He would have to bathe before he saw Daisy. When he took off his shirt he saw the spatter of blood on his cuffs and blanched. Maud's blood. Had he walked through the town with the evidence of what he had done so openly on show? But he persuaded himself that no one could have noticed. The rain had brought black clouds and the streets were already dark, lit only by the gaslights. No one could possibly have noticed the state of his shirt.

He bundled the shirt up and pushed it under the mattress in the bedroom. He would dispose of it later. Once he had shaved and dressed himself in clean clothes, he applied a bay rum dressing to his hair and soothed his face with his favourite cologne. But the spicy smell of the hair dressing mingling with the lavender and citron of the cologne did not seem strong enough to dispel that other smell — the smell of the clothes he had worn when he had murdered his sister.

Ready at last, he went along to Daisy's room and knocked at the door. He had ordered a table for two in the hotel dining room, and over dinner he had decided to inform her of his plans to take her to America. There was no reason why she could not be as great a star across the Atlantic as she was in Europe.

But when Janet opened the door there was no sign of Daisy. He had just missed her, Janet said, but her mistress had left a message. If Jack got back in time he was to join her in her box at the theatre. She had gone to see Rosina Lee.

Chapter Twenty-Two

The orchestra had nearly finished playing the usual jolly light music to get everyone in the mood. Soon the curtain would rise and the show would begin. The cast was ready for the opening chorus. Then the theatre manager came backstage to find Henry. He looked worried.

'What is it?' Henry asked. 'Empty seats?'

'No, not at all, we've had to turn people away.'

'Good, they'll be first in the queue tomorrow.'

'Mr Greyling . . .' The man looked uneasy.

'Spit it out, man.'

'Two things. Miss Belle has not yet arrived.'

'Don't you think she's coming?'

'She might not want to. After all, Miss Lee is singing one of her songs, isn't she? She might think it a liberty.'

Henry was dismayed. He'd set so much store by the finale he had imagined. 'Do you think we should delay curtain-up?'

'Definitely not. That's the other thing. They're in a funny mood tonight . . . The audience. I mean.'

Henry frowned. 'What sort of mood?'

'I'm not sure. Restless. There's something else odd about it. A lot of people who look as though they shouldn't be able to afford it are in the best seats in the stalls and in the dress circle.'

'They've been saving up for their tickets. That happens sometimes.'

'Yes, I know, a poor family or two who want a treat, perhaps,' the manager said. 'But these aren't family parties. They're ... I don't know ...'

Henry lost patience with him. 'What are they, for goodness' sake?'

'They're ruffians. They're beginning to annoy the decent folk around them. Evicting them might prove ... difficult.'

Henry frowned. He felt uneasy. Theatre managers had a very good idea of the sort of people who should or shouldn't be there. What was happening here, he wondered. But he didn't have time to question the man further because the overture was coming to an end. He made his mind up quickly.

'No, don't even try to throw them out. They could cause trouble in the streets. Word will get round and it will be bad for us. We'll get on with it. We'll start as planned. Once they begin to enjoy themselves they'll settle down.'

'I hope so.'

'Don't worry. My little troupe is used to dealing with troublesome audiences. And as for Miss Belle, she's a great star and a great lady. She'll slip into her box unobtrusively as she has done before. In fact, that's probably why she has decided to be late — so that she won't take the audience's attention.'

The orchestra began to play the music for the opening chorus; the cast was waiting in the wings, ready to respond to Henry's signal.

'Don't worry,' Henry told the theatre manager, 'all will be well, you'll see. Let the show begin.'

The old woman returned to the house in the square carrying her evening treat: a gill of ale in a jug. She paused in the doorway and sniffed the air. All was safe, the man had gone. When she had left the house earlier she had not needed eyes to know that someone had been hiding under the stairs no more than a foot away from her. A man.

She had smelled the hair oil and the rancid smell of the old coat. And that was a puzzle. Because the hair oil had been expensive, good bay rum, yet the smell emanating from the clothes was that of a poor man. A man who could not afford to wash very often, and who could certainly not have afforded that hair dressing.

Menace had been in the air. She had sensed danger and yet, whoever it had been, after a swift intake of air he had held his breath as if he had not wanted her to see or hear him. And that was why she had turned her face in his direction — so that he could see that she was blind and posed no threat to him. And thus she had left the house safely.

Those same senses now told her that he was gone. It was pointless to speculate on his identity. Whoever it was he had come to find, it was not her. She tapped her way along the passage and would have carried on to her own quarters if she had not heard a faint moan. She paused and listened intently. From the number of steps she had taken she knew she was outside Maud Fidler's door.

There it was again, the same moaning, interspersed with sobs.

'Maud?' the old woman called querulously. 'Is that you?'

This time the moan was louder and the old woman knew there was something very wrong. She put her jug down carefully next to the wall and pushed at Maud's door. It opened. Whoever had gone out last had left in some haste without securing it. The old woman felt her way forward with her cane and very soon the cane encountered something soft. A body. Maud was on the floor.

'What is it?' the old woman cried fearfully. 'What has happened here?'

She heard a whisper and she stooped to listen more carefully.

'My brother . . .' Maud said.

'Are you ill? Have you fallen? Do you want me to fetch your brother? Is that it? You'll have to tell me where he lives.'

'No! Don't fetch my brother!' Fear gave Maud's voice strength.

And the old woman understood. 'It was your brother who did this to you?'

'Yes.'

'God help you, Maud. I'll go and get the polis.'

Despite the theatre manager's worries, all did go well at first although the audience was certainly a little boisterous. They laughed at the jokes, clapped heartily when Sadie sang her comic songs and even rose to their feet and cheered at Mrs Greyling's portrayal of Britannia. Priscilla was ecstatic, although the other members of the cast guessed uneasily that the overenthusiastic response was false and that they were making fun of her.

Henry kept glancing at the box he had reserved for Daisy Belle but it remained empty. But then he caught a glimpse of an elegant figure in white in another box and knew that it was her. She must have slipped in unobtrusively not long after curtain-up, just as he had hoped she would. She sat back in the shadows and nobody would have known she was there, save for the glimpse of white gloves holding a fan.

When Jack joined Daisy in her box the show was well underway, and try as he might he could think of no reason or excuse to get Daisy to leave. She turned and smiled at him distractedly and then continued to watch the stage, giving the proceedings her complete attention. During the interval she was subdued and Jack took the opportunity to ask if she was tired.

'Not particularly,' she replied.

'Well, you look tired,' Jack said. 'And I'm sure you want to look your best for the civic reception tomorrow. Perhaps we should go back to the hotel now.'

Daisy frowned. 'Is something the matter, Jack?'

'No, why should there be?'

'You look agitated.'

'No – I'm not. I'm just concerned about you.'

'There's no need to be. And I'm not leaving until the show is over.'

And Jack, worried that he would only make her suspicious if he continued, decided that would be safer not to argue with her. From the look of her she was already puzzling over something and he did not want to rouse her suspicions further.

The curtains opened for the final part of the programme and all that was on stage was a theatrical hamper. Henry Greyling, dressed in an evening suit, carried a chair on and, placing it stage right, he sat down. The orchestra began to play and Rosina strolled on dressed as a country girl in a pretty floral dress and an old-fashioned bonnet trimmed with artificial flowers. She carried a posy of matching flowers. She stood centre stage while Henry rose and announced:

'And now Miss Rosina Lee will pay a tribute to Miss Nelly Power!'

Rosina began to sing 'The Boy In The Gallery', the innocently charming lyric that Nelly Power had made famous and that Marie Lloyd had 'borrowed' from her. Her manner was so unaffected and her voice so true that, at first, the audience was spellbound. But gradually the unruly members of the audience began to get restive.

> 'The boy I love is up in the gallery.
> The boy I love is looking down at me ...'

She went into the chorus for the second time and a few catcalls rang around the theatre.

'What a soppy song!' someone called.

'Give us something with a bit of life in it!' called another.

This brought forth angry shushing noises and there was quiet for a while. But when Rosina reached the final verse, the words 'we'll live on love and kisses' brought forth raucous laughter and the comment, 'Forget that useless laddo! I'd give you a lot more than kisses, darling!'

There was more angry shushing and raised voices from both the unruly and the outraged. Rosina bowed to the applause and walked over to stand behind the hamper. Henry sprang forward to lift the lid, which was high enough to conceal what Rosina was doing. When he closed the lid again Rosina was revealed in a change of costume – or rather a half-change – for she had pulled on a policeman's blue, silver-buttoned jacket, fastened a belt around her slender waist and replaced the bonnet with a policeman's helmet.

'And now, Rosina Lee will sing "The Bobbies of the Queen", as rendered by Miss Maud Santley!' Henry proclaimed before going back to his seat. The orchestra began to play and Rosina launched into the cheerful and rousing song.

'You've sung about the navy and our brave and
bold Jack Tars,
You've sung of Tommy Atkins and our gallant
song of Mars
But what about the boys in blue who promenade
the street . . .'

She wasn't allowed to sing much more before the heckling
began.

'Hey, that's all wrong!' bellowed someone from the gallery.
'Maud Santley wears tights. Where are yer tights, Rosina?'

'She probably hasn't got the legs for them,' someone yelled
back, and laughter broke out.

Rosina carried on singing as if none of this had
happened.

The next one to interrupt shouted, 'Where's yer whistle?
Bobbies hev whistles.'

'And yer truncheon. No bobby would go out without his
truncheon!'

Rosina ignored them and went on singing. The orchestra
increased the volume.

'I'll lend you my truncheon if you like, hinny,' a ruffian
cried. 'Do you want to come and see me truncheon?'

At this there was an outbreak of lewd laughter but Rosina
still went on singing. The rest of the troupe had gathered in
the wings and were peeping out at what they could see of the
audience.

'What's going on?' Priscilla Greyling hissed loudly
enough for her husband to hear from his seat on the stage.
He turned and gave a small helpless shrug. She turned to
Tom, who was standing behind her, his jaw clenched and his
hands balled into fists. 'Do you understand this?' she
whispered. 'The Greyling Players have never attracted this

sort of audience before.' She said it as if she thought it was somehow Rosina's fault and Tom's anger increased.

'I don't know why this had happened,' he told her. 'It's almost as though someone has sent a claque along. But instead of paying them to applaud they've been paid to jeer at Rosina and damage her reputation.'

'But who would do that?'

'I don't know.'

In her box, Daisy's attention was focused on the girl on the stage as she carried on valiantly throughout the noisy interruptions. Jack stared at her beautiful profile and wondered what was going on in her head.

By the time the song came to an end with the rousing line, 'Not the soldiers, nor the sailors but the Bobbies of the Queen!' many in the audience were stamping their feet supposedly in time to the music but in reality creating an unholy din. The conductor in the orchestra pit signalled for his musicians to wait a moment, hoping that the din would subside and, in fact, it did die down a little as Rosina walked over to the hamper again.

Henry lifted the lid so that she was hidden from view and whispered to her, 'Are you all right, my dear? Do you want me to have a word with the audience? Beg them to give you a chance?'

Her reply was tight-lipped. 'Certainly not. I don't want to appear as if I need help to manage an audience — even an awkward one.'

Henry knew that this was much more than an awkward audience. Like Tom, he suspected that something underhand was going on. And he had no idea who would do such a thing.

When Rosina was ready he lowered the lid and stepped

forward to address the audience once more. 'And now a tribute to Tyneside's own great star, Miss Daisy Belle!'

The orchestra struck up the opening chords of 'The Doll Song'. Rosina had taken off the policeman's jacket and helmet. She had pulled out the pins from her dark hair so that it fell loosely to her shoulders. There was no doubting how pretty she looked in the simple floral dress, and the better behaved members of the audience sighed with approval. Her only prop was a broken doll, which at the moment was held in one hand and hanging down by her side.

The music began; she raised the doll, looked at it tenderly, and began to sing, "I once had a sweet little doll, dears ..." '

This time the jeers began straight away.

'The cheek of it!' A voice echoed down from the gallery. 'Singing her song. You're not a patch on Daisy Belle!'

The clamour grew.

'That's Daisy's song!'

'How dare you!'

'Gerroff!'

'Yes, gerroff!'

And then they began to throw things. Rotten apples, oranges, fruit of all kinds and even a lump of mud. The mud caught Rosina on the cheek and then fell, smearing her face and her dress on the way down. She went on singing.

Jack glanced at Daisy anxiously. He had not meant her to see this and he had no idea how she would react. He did not have to wait long to find out.

Daisy rose to her feet. He saw that she was shaking. She put both hands on the front of the box to steady herself and leaned forward. He saw her mouth form a word but it came out as a groan. Alarmed, he moved to her side and saw that tears were streaming down her face. Before he could say anything she tried to speak again and this time succeeded.

'Stop this!' she commanded with all the power that all those years on the stage had taught her.

Not only did the shouting stop but so did the orchestra. All faces turned to Daisy. After a moment's shocked silence someone called out, 'It's Daisy!'

Others took up the cry and they began to chant her name. Some applauded; some cheered and stamped their feet. Daisy stood upright and raised her hands commandingly. The racket stopped and everyone waited to hear what she would say.

'Let the girl sing!' Daisy commanded. 'Let her sing my song. She meant no harm. She meant it as a tribute and I accept it as such.'

She gestured with one graceful arm towards the orchestra pit. The conductor tapped his music stand with his baton and they began to play. This time when Rosina began to sing there was total silence and as she reached the end, Daisy, who had remained standing, gave a signal to the conductor and the musicians began to play it again.

'This time we'll sing it together,' Daisy said. 'That is, if Miss Lee agrees.'

Rosina, who was staring at Daisy intently, nodded and they began to sing.

Neither of them made the slightest attempt to face the audience. They were looking at each other as they sang. There was a catch in Daisy's voice giving it a husky quality that contrasted with the girl's crystal-clear tone. There was no doubt about it, the little song that Jack had always privately believed to be trite and sentimental had never been sung to such effect. Watching the tears that were still streaming down Daisy's face he grew more and more uneasy.

It surely couldn't be because of the words of the song.

Not after all the time she had sung it over the years. She barely got to the end of it before her voice broke entirely.

'Encore! Encore!' The cry was taken up throughout the theatre.

But Daisy shook her head. 'Another time,' she managed to say, 'we'll sing together again, I promise you. But now please allow the cast to perform their finale.'

And as the curtains came down on Rosina's act, Daisy turned to Jack and stared at him with loathing and contempt. 'How could you?' she said.

'What do you mean?'

'It's Rose, isn't it? That girl is my daughter, Rose.'

'That's impossible. Rose is dead. You know that. You buried her yourself.'

'Did I?'

'You were at the funeral. I can show you the grave.'

'Yes, there's a grave, but who is in that grave, Jack?'

'Rose, of course.' He began to sweat.

'You never let me see her in her coffin, did you?'

'It would have been much too distressing – the accident – it was horrifying – her poor little body—'

'Stop that! Whoever or whatever was in that coffin it was not my daughter!'

Daisy's voice had risen and the people in the stalls who had settled in their seats while the orchestra had begun to play the final medley, looked up curiously.

'Hush, Daisy,' Jack began, 'you don't want people to hear this.'

'Why ever not? It was not my idea to pretend that Rose was not my daughter. I was never ashamed of her. Never! So why did you take her away from me? And how did you do it? Did you bribe Edna to help you? Was she part of the wickedness?'

'I didn't do anything. Rose is dead. I've already told you—'

'You told me a pack of lies! And furthermore I believe you organized this disgraceful behaviour tonight. Those hooligans in the audience. How much did you pay them? And why? Do you want to bring the girl's career to an end? Is that your plan?'

'Daisy, this is madness – you're tired – you've been working too hard – you're imagining things.'

'Am I?'

'Yes – somehow you've persuaded yourself that this girl is your daughter – perhaps you imagine there's some likeness to Rose—'

Daisy suddenly grew less agitated and she was deadly calm when she said, 'And am I imagining the doll? The doll you told me you had placed in Rose's coffin?'

'I did. It was buried with her.'

'Then how is it that Rosina Lee had it in her arms when she sang just now?'

'That could be any doll.'

'But it isn't any doll, Jack. It's Rose's doll. How could I forget it?'

The curtain rose and the cast began a final song-and-dance routine. Rosina was not part of it.

'But if you still persist in your lies, Jack, why don't you come backstage with me? Come and face the girl you betrayed all those years ago.'

'No, Daisy – don't—'

Jack caught at her arm to try to prevent her but she pushed past him with almost inhuman strength and opened the door of the box. She fled along the corridor with Jack following and then, suddenly, their way was blocked by three men. Two of them were in uniform. Policemen.

'Mr Fidler?' the gentleman in plain clothes said.

Daisy, momentarily halted in her flight, stood to the side while the two uniformed policemen took hold of Jack's arms.

He looked astounded. 'Did you send for the police, Daisy?'

'I have no idea what this is about,' she told him.

'Inspector Cullen, sir. We've come about your sister.'

'My sister?'

'Yes, sir. Maud Fidler. She's in hospital.'

Daisy thought that Jack suddenly looked frightened.

'In hospital? Has she had an accident?'

'Oh, I think you already know what happened, Mr Fidler. You see, she might have been left for dead but she didn't die. And she's told us what happened. Her chances of recovering are very poor and if I were you I'd start praying for a miracle. That will be the only way you will escape the hangman.'

Daisy watched bemused as Jack was led away but she did not have time to wonder what had happened. As soon as they had gone she continued her flight, found the narrow stairway that led down to the backstage area and seized the arm of the first stagehand she came across.

'Miss Lee's dressing room,' she said. 'Show me where it is.'

Rosina was sitting before the mirror and Tom Carey was leaning against the dressing table, half sitting on it. They both glanced up as Daisy entered the room. They showed no surprise. It was as if they had been expecting her.

'Where is it?' Daisy said. 'The doll?'

And then she saw that the broken doll was lying in Rosina's lap. Daisy started forward at the same time as Rosina rose from her chair. She was clutching the doll with both hands. She lifted it up.

'May I?' Daisy asked, and Rosina gave it to her.

Daisy stared down at the doll. 'Dolly . . .' she breathed.

The blonde ringlets were tangled and there was a jagged scratch across one of the rosy cheeks. The blue eyes were fringed with dark lashes, but one eye was wide open and the lid of the other was half closed, giving it a dozy, drunken appearance. The dress and petticoats had been washed and mended but Daisy remembered how ragged and dusty they had been when she had first found the doll in the empty house. The poor thing had only one arm. Or rather one and a half. One arm ended in a neat little hand, the other was broken off at the elbow. It was the doll that Rose had loved.

Daisy raised her head and looked at Rosina. 'Where did you get this?' she asked.

Rosina shook her head. 'I don't know. It's been mine as long as I can remember.'

Daisy took a step towards her. 'Rose . . . ?' she said.

Rosina's eyes widened, expressing bewildered surprise and then dawning comprehension.

'They told me you had died,' Daisy said. 'An accident. But it was all lies.'

'Am I . . . am I your sister's child?'

'No, I have no sister. That was another one of Jack Fidler's inventions.'

'Jack Fidler? It was a Maud Fidler who took me to Ravenshill — to the woman who adopted me,' Rosina said. 'Look, she kept these clothes.'

Rosina picked up the parcel that she always kept by her and opened it to show Daisy Belle the child's emerald-green coat and the white dress.

Daisy's face was ashen. 'That was what you were wearing when Edna took you to the park. I watched you go downstairs and when you reached the bottom you stood in a pool of sunshine and looked up at me. I thought how beautiful you were. That memory was all I had of you in all the years to come. I never saw you again.'

'Then you are my mother?' Rosina could barely speak.

'Yes,' Daisy whispered, 'and you are my beloved child.'

They stared at each other in wonder.

'You were so young. Did . . . did you remember me at all?' Daisy asked.

'Not consciously.. But your perfume . . . rose . . . you're wearing it now.'

'I always do.'

'Geraldine Leighton wore that scent. That is probably why I accepted her — came to believe she was my mother. But the song — "The Doll Song" — it puzzled me that I seemed to know it.'

'I used to sing it to you.'

'And the sound of it lived on in my memory.'

'Was she kind to you?' Daisy asked. 'I couldn't bear it if she wasn't kind to you.'

'Yes, and she was not at fault. They told her I was an orphan. If she had not died I might still be living there and we would not have met.'

Daisy shook her head slowly. 'So much,' she said. 'We have so much to tell each other.' She had been grasping the doll throughout the conversation. Now she laid it down gently on the dressing table and took hold of Rosina's hands. 'But we have the rest of our lives to do it in.'

Tom knew then that he was intruding. He moved towards the door and went out quietly, leaving mother and daughter alone together. Neither of them noticed his departure. They were weeping in each other's arms.

Daisy insisted on taking Rosina and Tom off to Alvini's for supper. She ordered the best of everything, including champagne, but Daisy and Rosina only picked at the food, for they hardly stopped talking. Neither could Tom do the food justice; he felt far too gloomy. He was thrilled that Rosina had found her mother; she deserved to be happy. But the more the two women talked, he sensed her growing further and further away from him.

His attention was caught when he heard Daisy say, 'Your voice is far better than mine. Much too good for what you are doing. You ought to be an opera singer.'

'Do you really think so?' Rosina's eyes were shining.

'Certainly. You should start training at once.'

'Well, I have a little money, thanks to Geraldine Leighton, but I don't think I could afford to go to Paris or Rome.'

'But I can afford to send you there – to whichever teacher you prefer – and nothing you could say will prevent me from helping you. I have not been able to care for you for all these years so now you must allow me to make up for what was taken from both of us.'

She is leaving me, Tom thought. Her talent is too great. And love her as I do, I must not stand in her way.

Eventually Daisy said, 'Whatever has happened tonight, if you are a daughter of mine you still have a show to do tomorrow. You must go home to bed. Tomorrow I shall come and meet the Bartletts and thank them for being such good friends to you. And then I shall carry you away with me. I don't intend that we should ever be parted again.'

Tom saw Rosina back to Heaton in a cab. They didn't speak. Eventually she turned to him and asked what the matter was.

'Nothing. I'm very happy for you.'

'Then why do you look so sad?'

'Because I love you and I'm afraid I've lost you.'

'No, my darling,' she said. 'You haven't lost me. I've been

found. And for the first time in my life I feel truly complete. I love you, Tom, and I always will.'

And as he enfolded her in his arms he knew that whatever happened, whatever paths they followed, they would find a way to be together.

Epilogue

Some Years Later

Miss Lee has studied under some of the best teachers on the continent and she has been able to combine her studies and burgeoning career with the most happy of domestic situations. While studying in Italy she was visited by an old friend, the successful actor playwright Tom Carey, and with the blessing of her mother, they married there. They love Italy so much that they have bought a house in Florence to which they return as often as their separate work commitments allow.

Miss Lee told this reporter that she inherits her talent from her mother, the great music-hall star Daisy Belle. And, who knows, we may be witnessing the foundation of a theatrical dynasty; for according to her fond father, the couple's enchanting four-year-old daughter, Mae, can already sing and recite many nursery rhymes from memory.

Joanne loved London, the streets, the atmosphere, the bustle of a great city, and she insisted that she and James walk from their hotel in the Strand to Covent Garden. She'd had her hair dressed at an expensive salon and she was wearing a new leaf-green satin gown and evening cape. She knew that with her sandy hair and freckled face she was not conventionally beautiful, but she was tall and slim and she had 'good bones'. People spoke of her as elegant.

And as for James ... Not only was he clever but he was tremendously good looking. Joanne tucked her hand into the crook of his arm and glanced surreptitiously at their reflections in a shop window. He saw her glance and he smiled.

'What a handsome couple we are!' he said. 'Are you happy, Mrs Norton?'

'Blissfully.'

'We're nearly there,' James told her. 'Excited?'

'Very,' Joanne said. 'This is not only the first time we've heard Rosina sing in opera but to hear her in *Madama Butterfly!*'

'And to be singing with Mario Zenatello!' James said. 'Rosina as Cio-Cio-San and Zenatello as the handsome cad Pinkerton. Marvellous.'

When they reached the theatre they left their outdoor clothes in the cloakrooms and met up again in the foyer. Joanne suddenly gripped her husband's arm.

'What is it?'

'Have you got a handkerchief ?'

'Goodness, Joanne, what a question for a grown man.'

'No, I'm serious. You know how affected I become. What with Rosina and Puccini, and that sad, sad story, I shall weep buckets at the end, and this little embroidered thing of mine simply won't do.'

'Don't worry, sweetheart.' Her husband smiled at her. 'I know very well what you're like and I've come prepared with two large handkerchiefs. We can have one each!'

'Joanne? Is that you?'

Joanne and James looked up to see a tall, handsome man crossing the foyer towards them.

'Tom!' Joanne exclaimed. 'I hoped we'd see you before the show starts. James and I are not sure where to go for the party afterwards.'

'Don't worry, get your things from the cloakroom and slip back into the auditorium. Sit at the back of the stalls. I'll find you there. But now, excuse me, I must dash.'

Tom hurried away towards the curving marble staircase. Heads turned as the tall, distinguished playwright eased his way through the first-night crowd. There were murmurs of excited recognition.

The musicians were beginning to enter the orchestra pit. It would not be long before curtain-up. Daisy sat in one of the boxes with her small granddaughter. Mae was excited to be allowed up so late and she asked her grandmother question after question. Daisy answered patiently and allowed the little girl to play with her fan made of white lacquer sticks decorated with sparkling sequins and a cloud of blue-grey swan's-down.

Mae wore an exquisite party dress of white silk taffeta with tiny pink satin rosebuds scattered over the bodice and the puff sleeves. Her sash and the ribbons in her dark hair were the same pink. Daisy could not resist buying clothes for her granddaughter, and every time she did she remembered the all-too-brief days she had been able to buy pretty clothes for Rose.

When her son-in-law entered Daisy looked up and said, 'Tom, I think I've got stage fright!'

Tom smiled. 'You, Daisy? As far as I know you've never had stage fright in your life, and in any case, you're not performing tonight.'

'But I'm anxious for Rose.' Daisy had never been able to

call her daughter Rosina. Even though they had been parted for years she still thought of her as Rose.

'There's no need to worry, I've just come from her dressing room. She's calm and completely prepared.'

'You're sure?' Daisy asked.

'I'm sure.'

Tom could see how tense Daisy was. She looked magnificent in ice-blue satin. A treble row of sapphires and diamonds sparkled at her throat and the same stones dripped from her ears and sparkled in her piled-up hair. She looked every inch the grand lady of the theatre that she had become, and yet Tom suspected that Daisy's greatest pleasure in life was not the riches her talent had brought her but her family, especially her little granddaughter, Mae.

Mae, who looked so like her mother with her dark curls, and who both Rosina and he thought of as their most precious gift. He sat down and lifted his daughter on to his knee. He prised the fan from her small fingers and returned it to Daisy.

'I think some of the sequins have fallen off,' he said.

Daisy shrugged and smiled as if to say that didn't matter at all.

Tom did his best to conceal the fact that he also was feeling nervous. He looked around the crowded auditorium and realized that some of the leading members of society were here tonight. But opera did not only appeal to the rich. Music lovers from all walks of life had come to hear Rosina, and he knew that they would not be disappointed.

The musicians were beginning to tune their instruments and in every part of the theatre the audience was settling down and preparing themselves for the evening's entertainment. The excitement and anticipation were almost tangible.

Rosina was alone in her dressing room waiting for her

call. She was ready in costume and make-up and she liked to sit quietly for a few minutes, gathering her strength before a performance. She glanced in the mirror and hardly recognized the delicate oriental face that looked back at her. She had not needed a wig; the company's hairdresser had been able to arrange her own abundant dark hair in the correct style. For that she was profoundly grateful. The wigs were hot and heavy and would probably have given her a headache.

She glanced at the photographs displayed round the mirror on her dressing table: Daisy, Tom, Mae, and then a family group that included herself. She thought of Mae, allowed to stay up late for this special occasion and now no doubt being spoiled disgracefully by her doting grand-mother.

She remembered the stories Daisy had told her of her own childhood, sleeping in her pram in dingy dressing rooms. She understood completely why her mother had done that; she was young and poor and had no one else in the world to call her own. Thank God, my circumstances are so different, Rosina thought. I have my mother and my beloved Tom to help me look after my own darling daughter, Mae.

But it was time to put all thoughts of her own life behind her. It was time to think of that tragic girl who was so sadly betrayed by the man she loved. Rosina stood up and gazed at the girl in the mirror. The girl wore a lilac oriental robe delicately traced with flowers. She willed herself to become that girl, that beautiful and fragile fifteen year old. Puccini's glorious music would evoke love and yearning and pain. It would be up to Rosina to make the audience experience the loss and hope and despair that tormented poor Butterfly.

The call came. Rosina left the dressing room and made her way to the stage.

Just
for You

BENITA
BROWN

Just
for You

Learn...
All about the real music hall legends

Picture...
Benita Brown's Kind of Day

Revealed...
Benita's favourite classic novels

Don't miss...
These top writing tips

[© Norman Brown]

Just for You

The real music hall legends...

The idea for FORTUNE'S DAUGHTER first came to me after a conversation with my mother-in-law. She asked me how I came to be called Benita. I told her I was named after a 1930s movie star called Benita Hume and then I asked why she had been called Florrie. She answered that she had been named after the music hall star Florrie Forde, who was at the peak of her fame during the First World War with songs such as 'Pack Up Your Troubles In Your Old Kit Bag' and 'It's A Long Way To Tipperary'.

These songs, and those sung by the other music hall stars, have lived on, even if we have forgotten who first sang them. Popular songs were 'Daddy wouldn't buy me a bow wow', 'Oh, Mr Porter', 'Sweet Rosie O'Grady', 'She's a lassie from Lancashire', 'I do like to be beside the seaside', 'Show me the way to go home', 'She was one of the early birds', 'Dear old pals, jolly old pals', 'The boy I love is up in the gallery', 'All the nice girls love a sailor', and many, many more.

Some of the music hall entertainers did not really have very good voices but they made up for that with their energy and personality. Like the pop stars of today the great stars could make huge fortunes, but life was not easy. A life on stage may have looked glamorous but there was a punishing schedule, with performers expected to work six days of the week and then travel on the seventh. It was no wonder that many of them succumbed to the lure of alcohol, late nights and fast living. Many of them were dead by their mid-forties.

George Leybourne, for example, who was born in my native Newcastle and became famous for the song 'Champagne Charlie', went from being a factory worker to a successful songwriter for other performers, as well as a star himself, but died at the age of forty-two.

No matter how short or long their lives, however, performers such as Marie Lloyd, Vesta Tilley, Little Titch, George Robey, Florrie Forde, Hetty King and Vesta Victoria had huge followings of devoted fans during their lifetimes and are remembered even now. Others, such as Daisy Dormer, a pretty waif-like woman, may have been forgotten, even though we remember the song that she made famous, 'After the ball is over'.

As a little girl my mother-in-law sang the old music hall songs and when she left school at fourteen she joined a theatre troupe as a singer and dancer, calling herself 'Little Florrie'. It was a hard life touring all over the British Isles, doing several shows a day, staying in poor theatrical digs and, after sending money home, being left with barely enough to live on. She also told me there were some unscrupulous managers and agents who exploited the girls for profit and who cared little for their welfare.

When the idea for FORTUNE'S DAUGHTER came to me, I borrowed the name 'Daisy Belle' from another of Florrie Forde's songs and began to weave a story about a girl who started by singing in the streets, graduated to being a singer in a rough and ready Song and Supper Room where the audience ate and drank at long tables during the performances, and eventually became a world-famous singing star. And, unlike some of the real music hall stars, my Daisy would have the voice of an angel. And what if Daisy had a daughter from whom she became separated? And what if this daughter became equally famous, so much so that she became her own mother's greatest rival? Once these ideas were in place, my novel FORTUNE'S DAUGHTER was born.

Sadly, my mother-in-law died before the book was finished but she certainly would have recognized Daisy Belle, her daughter Rosina, and their struggles to succeed in the theatre.

Just for You

My Kind of Day...

When my four children were small I had to write when they were in bed, sometimes working until long after midnight, although I did snatch an hour or two during the day once the youngest started nursery school. Now they are all married with homes of their own and instead of hectic breakfasts and the school run I have time for a second cup of coffee and the crossword in the newspaper. I love crosswords but Su Doku remains a mystery to me!

Another luxury now is a room of my own – my study – and a proper desk instead of having to work on the dining table amidst the bustle of family life. I usually start my writing day by reading though everything from the previous day. I like to edit and make notes as I go, rather than hurrying through to the end of the book before editing, as some writers do.

If I'm lucky I'll get through this before lunch. I like to leave things in the middle of something interesting so that I'll be keen to get back to work. Often I get carried away by the story I'm telling and forget to stop every now and then and walk about as you're supposed to do when you're working at a computer. I'm often completely astonished when my husband announces that it's teatime!

After tea, I'll take a break before getting back to work for an hour or two. Old habits die hard and I believe I still get my best work done in the evening – the time I used to have to work when the children were in bed.

Not every day is like this. If I need to do some research it could mean a visit to an old house, a museum or the library to look at old photographs and newspapers. Sometimes I just walk around Newcastle, where a lot of my books are set, and try to imagine how it was a hundred years or more ago. I love the sights and sounds and smells of the old Grainger Market and often take my characters there when I'm telling their stories. I also go to the quayside, magnificent now with the redevelopment and the new Millennium Bridge, but where it's not difficult to imagine how it was in the old days when both steam and sailing ships thronged the River Tyne.

When I finish work for the day I like to watch a little television and while I'm doing so I knit socks. I love knitting socks; it's so satisfying turning the heel! But I've reached the stage when everyone's sock drawers are overflowing and my family are begging me to stop!

Also, not a day goes by when I don't have a book on the go. I read both fiction and non-fiction. Often the non-fiction books are to do with the background material I need for my novels. My mother, a dedicated reader herself, taught me to read before I went to school – and I've been reading ever since.

Just
for You

My favourite classic novels . . .

It's very hard to make a list of favourite novels; I have so many. I like crime novels and novels of suspense, historical novels, and thumping big generational sagas. But as some of these books are written by people I know (and I don't want to offend any friends by leaving them out!) I've decided to restrict my list of favourites to ten novels written in the nineteenth century.

I believe the nineteenth century was the golden age of the novel, with compelling stories and unforgettable characters. It would be impossible for me to choose an absolute favourite, so the following books are in no particular order.

LITTLE WOMEN by Louisa May Alcott

Meg, Amy, Beth and Jo. I've met many grown women who read this book as girls and can still tell me which sister they identified with. For me, it's Jo.

LORNA DOONE by R. D. Blackmore
First published in 1869, this novel has never been out of print. The heroine of one of my books is called Lorna — and John Ridd gets a mention, too.

VANITY FAIR by William Makepeace Thackeray
Beautiful, ruthless and self-centred Becky Sharp is surely one of the great anti-heroines, and so much more interesting than industrious, sweet, obedient Amelia Sedley.

A TALE OF TWO CITIES by Charles Dickens
Both the novel's opening, 'It was the best of times, it was the worst of times', and its closing, 'It is a far, far better thing that I do ...', are among the most famous lines in English literature. Dickens said it was the best novel he had ever written.

THE COUNT OF MONTE CRISTO by Alexandre Dumas
This tale of justice, vengeance, mercy and forgiveness is often included on lists of the best novels of all time.

MADAME BOVARY by Gustave Flaubert
Flaubert was tried on charges of immorality when this novel was published but he successfully defended himself by arguing that the novel illustrates the consequences of sin. Poor Emma.

ANNA KARENINA by Leo Tolstoy
Another famous opening line: 'Happy families are all alike; every unhappy family is unhappy in its own way'. A wonderfully doomed love story — but, perversely, I always feel sorry for her husband, poor old Karenin.

THE TENANT OF WILDFELL HALL by Anne Brontë

Anne Brontë's novels are less well known than those of her two sisters and maybe not as well written, but this is my favourite Brontë novel. A critic pronounced it 'utterly unfit to be put into the hands of girls'. And all because a wife slammed the door in the face of her abusive husband! This could even be considered to be one of the first feminist novels.

TESS OF THE D'URBERVILLES by Thomas Hardy

This novel shocked critics of the time for its sympathetic portrayal of a 'fallen woman'. But who could not sympathise with poor Tess — and fail to be exasperated by Angel Clare?

GREAT EXPECTATIONS by Charles Dickens

There are some truly memorable characters in this book: Magwitch, Miss Haversham, the beautiful cold-hearted Estella and, of course, Pip himself who must learn that possessions and wealth do not change who the person is inside. The original ending of this novel was deemed by the publisher to be too unhappy for the readers so Dickens rewrote it with Pip and Estella leaving the garden hand in hand and 'no shadow of another parting from her'.

[I make no apology for Dickens appearing twice on my list. I could add more of his novels: DAVID COPPERFIELD, BLEAK HOUSE, A CHRISTMAS CAROL . . . but I've already used up my ten places!]

Just
for You

If you want to be a writer . . .

If you want to be a writer, don't just think about it, start writing.

Set aside a corner in your home where you can work and, if necessary, tell your family this is your place and your time. Get into the habit of writing something every day. Set yourself a target of so many hours or so many words, whatever suits you best. Keep a good dictionary and thesaurus on your desk. If you think your grammar is shaky, there are grammar guides and books of usage, too. Sign up for an evening class if that would give you confidence. Treat yourself to some 'How-To' books. I love 'How-to' books! I find it interesting to learn what other writers do, even if I don't always agree with them. And nowadays you can find plenty of advice on the Internet, even how to lay out your manuscript.

It will help to have some sort of filing system because, if you're like me, you'll be cutting things out of newspapers and magazines, anything and everything that you might be able to use.

And read, read, read! Not only the sort of books you'd like to write but other genres, too. We learn from the way other writers write. Observe the world around you; people are fascinating. Don't be a snoop but casually listen to them talking. Sometimes a snatch of conversation will get your imagination going. Keep a notebook handy and jot down ideas.

Maybe you have a story to tell but don't know where to begin. In ALICE IN WONDERLAND the King told the White Rabbit, 'Begin at the beginning and go on till you come to the end: then stop'.

But where exactly is the beginning? Every good story begins just as something important, some change, is about to happen. Don't waste time describing the previous lives of the characters or the scenery; once the story is going along nicely you can fill in the details. Give the readers a character they can care about and make a start. Then keep going no matter what.

Never give up, even on the sort of day when inspiration has fled. Don't sit staring at a blank screen. Write anything, even if you think it's rubbish. You can always change it the next day. If you want to be a writer, write.

A Safe Harbour

Benita Brown

'Breathe in deeply and you could almost be there'
Northern Echo

Cullercoats Bay, 1895. Titian-haired Kate Lawson is
eighteen when the sea claims her beloved and leaves
her with a broken heart – and a shameful secret.
Banished from home by her violent father, Kate relies
on the kindness of her aunt, until she too is cruelly
taken from her.

When Kate meets Richard Adamson, the owner of a
fleet of steam trawlers, she knows she should despise
the man who's stealing the livelihood of hardworking
fisherfolk – yet she can't stop herself falling in love
with him. Has Kate found her safe harbour at last, or
will the sins of the past destroy her chance for
happiness?

Praise for Benita Brown's captivating sagas:

'A delightfully interwoven story of passion, love, loss
and the power of friendship' *Sunderland Echo*

'*The Captain's Daughters* has a wonderfully Dickensian
flavour . . . Everyone in the book is alive and believable'
Historical Novels Review

'A must for Catherine Cookson fans' *Wiltshire Times*

0 7553 2326 2

headline

The Captain's Daughter

Benita Brown

When his beautiful young wife dies in childbirth, Captain Samuel Walton is grief-stricken. He had idolised Effie, despite her spoilt and headstrong ways, and he now faces the task of raising their two daughters alone. Fifteen years later, and the baby girl who brought such tragedy is the mirror image of her mother. But flaxen-haired Flora is also showing signs of Effie's tempestuous temperament. Sensible Josie worries her younger sister may be led astray. But even she could not predict how a chance meeting between Flora and a seductive stranger would plunge the whole family into danger . . .

Lose yourself in the lives of the unforgettable Walton girls – as different as day is to night, but bound by an unbreakable cord: the love shared by sisters.

Praise for Benita Brown's popular sagas:

'A splendidly powerful and touching saga of love, passion and lust' *Newcastle Evening Chronicle*

'Breathe in deeply and you could almost be there' *Northern Echo*

0 7553 0167 6

headline

In Love And Friendship

Benita Brown

Newcastle, 1890. A school outing to Cullercoats Bay almost ends in tragedy when two girls are cut off by the incoming tide. But from the panic and confusion something wonderful emerges – a lifelong friendship between three girls: Ruth, Lucy and Esther. Each is a world apart from the other two, but together they form a strong and unbreakable bond that will see them through the years ahead, when the happy, carefree days of childhood are nothing but a distant memory.

In Love And Friendship follows the twists and turns of the girls' changing fortunes, from the uncertainties and disappointments of youth, to the heartbreak and responsibilities of courtship and marriage. Through it all, one thing is constant and true . . .

Don't miss Benita Brown's previous novels, also available from Headline

'A splendidly powerful and touching saga of love, passion and lust' *Newcastle Evening Chronicle*

'Romance, heartache and local history make a magical mixture . . . passion on every page' *Northern Echo*

0 7553 0165 X

headline

Now you can buy any of these other bestselling books by **Benita Brown** from your bookshop or *direct from her publisher*.

FREE P&P AND UK DELIVERY
(Overseas and Ireland £3.50 per book)

A Dream of Her Own	£6.99
All Our Tomorrows	£6.99
Her Rightful Inheritance	£6.99
In Love and Friendship	£6.99
The Captain's Daughters	£5.99
A Safe Harbour	£5.99

TO ORDER SIMPLY CALL THIS NUMBER

01235 400 414

or visit our website: www.madaboutbooks.com

Prices and availability subject to change without notice.